Patience, patience, patience, is what the sea teaches.

—Anne Morrow Lindbergh

REELING

Also by Sarah Stonich
Published by the University of Minnesota Press

Fishing!

Vacationland

Laurentian Divide

These Granite Islands

Shelter: Off the Grid in the Mostly Magnetic North

REELING

A NOVEL

SARAH STONICH

University of Minnesota Press
Minneapolis • London

Published by the University of Minnesota Press
111 Third Avenue South, Suite 290
Minneapolis, MN 55401-2520
http://www.upress.umn.edu

ISBN 978-1-5179-0899-7 (pb)
Library of Congress record available at https://lccn.loc.gov/2021022932.

Printed in the United States of America on acid-free paper

28 27 26 25 24 23 22 21 10 9 8 7 6 5 4 3 2 1

For the nurses

CONTENTS

1. DENIAL

"I've run over Dot again. This time in the grocery store parking lot."

RayAnne had tried out the line in the mirror that morning while rinsing and spitting. Realizing how crazy it sounded, she's decided not to tell Hal about her disturbing visitations. In the months since Dot's passing, RayAnne has backed over Dot in her own driveway; in the WYOY employee parking ramp; and once exiting the lot at the train museum with her six-year-old twin nephews in the car. She could tell her boyfriend of two months that the dashcam on her car is haunted with her grandmother's specter and see how long it takes him to gather his own toothbrush and spare boxers and back slowly out the door.

Actually, she doesn't run over Gran so much as *through* her. She appears onscreen just within the yellow safe lines, lounging on the pavement as though on a comfortable chaise, sometimes with a highball in hand, ice clinking. And each time, Gran is about to say something critically important just as RayAnne sees her and hits the brake, when her image pixilates and dissolves.

Dead again.

She's thought of disabling the dashcam but it's connected

to the navigation system, which she needs, being directionally challenged—the reason for buying the car in the first place, which Gran called "newfangled" with its warning blips and icons that flash when lanes are strayed. It doesn't help that the car's digital voice, the ultimate backseat driver, is so unrelentingly calm and unflappable that RayAnne cannot help feel uncalm and flappable in comparison.

They are in Hal's freezing-cold Jeep. RayAnne is trying to lighten the mood, rapidly batting her lashes at him, which is a schtick that usually gets a chuckle but is falling flat. She hates these goodbyes, and this morning neither of them is in top form. She's still travel weary from the last trip, barely home from filming several episodes of *Fishing!* in the lovely but exceedingly windy Chiloé Island off the Patagonian coast, where they'd seen a penguin get blown off its rock. Her producer Cassi had observed the place wasn't so much windswept as *windplowed,* which rendered fishing conditions less than ideal. The trawler constantly rocked and pitched; the camera crew were often seasick, and wind made their eyes stream like faucets, which at least allowed RayAnne the odd bawl with no one the wiser (except Cassi, of course—no one pulls the wool over her laser-blue stare).

When ocean fishing grew too fraught, they decided to fish for chinook in inland streams, recruiting the island's only lady ghillie, a flame-haired sixtysomething unpronounceably named Blodeuwedd. Who knew there were Welsh settlements on the coast of South America? Blodeuwedd cheerfully guided them to and from the best fishing streams, speaking with such a thick accent her words registered mostly as good-natured gargles and burrs. Watching the playback each night at the villa, Cassi had had to solicit the help of the innkeeper to transcribe Blodeuwedd's words into a script to send along with the dailies so the video editor could add subtitles. Their adventure in Patagonia had been at turns exhilarating and exhausting, with occasional fuzzy interludes in tiny cantinas, where the locals plied them with *pisco,* keen to talk American politics—as if either Cassi or RayAnne could explain the current stew that is Washington, D.C., even when sober.

RayAnne has only been home for a week and is now heading to another Location, this time across so many time zones that where she's going it's already tomorrow. She reminds herself to ask who came up with New Zealand as a destination. Surely there are closer places with interesting women who can fish?

All during the drive to the airport Hal has been quiet—bleary from lack of sleep, he'd put up with her restless leg syndrome all night. The nocturnal high-kicking had him tossing until the wee hours when he mumbled something about the Rockettes and rolled from the futon to sleep on her carpet. When he woke, tufts of Rory's fur were stuck to his stubble and his face was embossed with the rug pattern.

When she traced the dents on his temple, he explained, "Dermographia."

One of the many things she loves about this man is that he uses words she has to look up, yet he never makes her feel stupid.

Poor guy looks completely worn out—but in a sexy-drowsy way.

RayAnne hadn't slept well herself, bicycling through dreams of being late for her plane. Really, she should give in to her mother's hounding and try some of the Ayurvedic this-and-that she's always peddling. Just the week before, Bernadette had tried slipping some homeo-mickey into RayAnne's bubble tea.

Hal's approach is more pragmatic. "My mother swears by eating more bananas, but maybe a real bed with a real mattress might help?"

The moment they stop at the passenger drop-off, the windows begin to frost up. He gives her a half-smile. "We'll see you when, again?" *We*—the man and dog duo—have grown quite tight during her absences.

"Three weeks? Maybe four." Her voice sounds as drawn and unconvincing as she feels. Meeting his eye, she says hopefully, "Maybe less?" Cars and vans are banked three-deep at the curb—no time or place for a lingering farewell. Outside, people wearing fat down jackets bump together in quick hugs to kiss numb faces with pinched lips before scurrying for various doors.

Just ahead of them, a hotel van is disgorging luggage. A cab has wedged in behind the Wagoneer, inching up nearly to Hal's tailpipe, trapping them. When a honk blasts from a few vehicles behind, Rory leaps from the back seat directly into Hal's lap and snuffles into his open parka to his favorite spot in all the universe, her boyfriend's armpit.

"It's okay, pal." Hal gently extracts Rory, glances in the rearview, rubbing the dog's ears. "Just some dickhead in a Humvee."

RayAnne frowns. She shouldn't care that Rory went for Hal's armpit and not hers. When he says, "Just you and me again, Dogface," she wonders if his *again* qualifies as passive aggressive. But it is Rory and Hal thrown together again, because she keeps flying off, and even though he could as easily go to DogGone Inn or BoneVoyage, Rory's not crazy about other dogs, perhaps not realizing he is one. Like RayAnne, he can be awkward around his own species.

Besides dog minding, in the short span of their newish relationship Hal has performed other such boyfriendly tasks as thawing the pipes in her old brownstone; unclogging her drains; and recently, installing the set of shelves she'd abandoned after a cutting blade mishap left her with several stitches and reverse enthusiasm for DIY. Now that she has an actual salary, she could afford hiring out such things as tuck-pointing or radiator bleeding, but Hal is that guy always on the prowl for things that need fixing. Not one to stand around with his hands in his pockets, possibly because growing up in Pelican Point, Ontario, the only places to loiter were his father's lumberyard, the canoe outfitters, his uncle's float plane docks, or his mother's shop—places where an extra pair of hands was always welcomed. And Hal is very good with his. Even his bad hand is handy.

Very.

As if reading her mind, he does that thing, slowly pulling her close, fingertips gently plowing from the nape of her neck high into her scalp.

Gran's face pops up in the rearview mirror, crow's-feet crinkling as she winks. *Enjoy that while you can.* Dorthea Dahl's voice is as clarion-clear as if a tiny version of her has taken up residence in the cove of RayAnne's ear.

Her grandmother can be just as annoying dead as alive. RayAnne closes her eyes in an effort to banish Gran, leaning in for the kiss.

A pretty great kisser, Hal also has a very broad shoulder to cry on. If RayAnne were honest, this is something she's taken for granted too often over the past months. Their kiss is rushed, Rory wriggling underneath to lick both their chins, which while darling does not imbue any romance to the moment but does suddenly remind her of what she meant to tell Hal. She breaks away. "Give him dental chews when his breath gets like this? And a raw egg on his kibble in the evening?"

"Uh-huh."

"And his blue squirrel?"

Hal nods. "I sewed its tail back on with eighty-pound test. We won't have the same drama again."

"Really? You can sew, too?" Even while speaking, she can hear Dot. *Oh, for godsakes, just kiss the man.*

She considers the human/canine pairing next to her—just the handsomest creatures on the planet, and both with eyes to drown in, should one want to drown in either Windex or a nut-brown ale. Her own eyes threaten to well up, but before she can tilt her face to Hal's for a second kiss, a taxi lays on its horn. Rory yelps. The moment tilts.

RayAnne sighs. "I'm gonna miss you."

"It's the plane you're gonna miss. Go, girl." Hal manages a crooked grin and nods at the terminal doors yawning, the warm indoor air turning to vapor as if the building is breathing. He starts to unsnap his seat belt. "I'll grab your bag."

"Nah. I got it." After a decade on the pro sport-fishing circuit, RayAnne may never get used to chivalry.

She aims a kiss-face *muah* at Hal, mashes her forehead to Rory's, and crushes her lips to his furry snout. Then she's out on the pavement, pulling her bag from the back seat and slamming the door quickly. What people from normal climates cannot grasp until they experience it firsthand is that pure Minnesota cold *hurts.*

She fights the urge to climb back in the Jeep, hug her dog, and plant such a kiss on her boyfriend that his enamel will remember.

But she won't, because while going away is the last thing she wants to do, she'd promised Gran that she'd do her damnedest to make the show work. It has become a mission. Thanks to Cassi's vision, they seem to be succeeding. Who'd have dreamt the show would generate the buzz it has: not just fluke-buzz, but real, actual interest. Also, it is attracting the sort of high-profile sponsors commercial network shows would kill for. After the first season's ratings shot through the roof, *Fishing!* was assigned a bigger crew and budget; production values were ramped up. All of which means there's more riding on the show, not just for RayAnne and Cassi but for a whole bunch of people.

As Gran would say, "You take on a thing, you *do* it." And so RayAnne has, even when it means traveling halfway across the world on perhaps the coldest morning of the year, when any sane woman with a boyfriend like Hal would be burrowed into bed with him.

At least the job is keeping her too busy to dwell on Gran, which is good.

Right?

Like the song, you don't know what you've got 'til it's gone. Only in Gran's absence does RayAnne realize the scope of all she's lost: aside from the unconditional love of a grandmother, Dot Dahl was the only human RayAnne has ever trusted completely to be utterly, painfully honest with. Gran was, to a degree, RayAnne's conscience. The person she aspired to live up to. Her bar.

The question now is, how to navigate once that's gone?

The weepy, surreal weeks after Dot's exit stage left had been made even more surreal by Hal's sudden presence in the thick of her loss. RayAnne cannot count the times in the past months she's found herself simultaneously laugh-sobbing while folded into Hal's embrace—the times he's palmed away tears and snot . . .

Suicide. Her father and brother won't even say the word, let alone talk about it. Big Rick has joined a nearly cultlike AA group, while Kyle has taken a more pragmatic approach, reading up on the stages of grief, because stages have some form and progression while sadness is simply too shapeless to make sense of. Weeks ago, Ky informed her they should both be entering the second quarter of the first phase of grief, joking they were sharing the same boat. "Heading down da Nile, right?"

"I don't think it works like that, Ky." Like any good statistician, Kyle thinks in columns. After his latest text informing RayAnne that he's left his current stage to sail headlong into Anger, she's taking him at his word, letting his calls roll over to voice mail.

She has no idea what stage she's in. Her mother encourages her to "feel her feelings" and to "practice self-care." RayAnne went to a single suicide survivors' support group and left feeling like a fraud after sitting across from a set of parents who'd lost a twelve-year-old son, bullied into such despair he hung himself. Or the new father of an infant daughter, whose postpartum wife jumped into the Mississippi from the Stone Arch Bridge weeks after giving birth. Those losses are in a different class of misery altogether, so when it came time in group to "share," RayAnne hung her head and mumbled Dot's story: eighty years old, riddled by pancreatic cancer with only a few months to live, had injected herself with an overdose of insulin. And, as if sparing her loved ones a gruesome death watch wasn't enough, Dot had cooked a freezer full of family favorites, assuring nobody would go hungry in the aftermath.

Still. RayAnne is making the effort: she practices the breathing thing, walks mile after city mile with Rory and Hal. She's tried the Japanese practice of Shinrin-yoku, but icy trails are difficult and forest bathing in five-degree temps isn't all that. Spending so much time outdoors in winter drives home just how stark it is—everything buried, frozen, inhospitable. There are squirrels and raptors, one out to get the other. She downloads the droning, binaural vibes on Spotify and doses up with feel-good CBD gummies and teas Bernadette digs from her bottomless Guatemalan duffle.

RayAnne has tried joking about suicide and has tried laughing about it. None of it changes the fact that Gran is gone.

Just as she reaches the automatic door of the terminal, Rory's muffled yelp tugs her around. Both paws are on the glass. Out of her mouth comes the first thing—just what she shouts to Rory a dozen times a day—"I love you!" A man walking past hitches sideways in alarm. RayAnne locks onto Hal's face as he cocks his head in the same posture as Rory's, as if waiting for the "You too!" sure to follow. But somehow RayAnne falters and frowns, her mouth stuck shut a nano too long. Hal's smile slowly pulls level and the dimples sidling his mouth smooth to flatness. She'd hesitated too long, it's too late.

She had come so close to saying it lately. Because she does love Hal, more every day, but the right opportunity hasn't presented itself. And because this is the big, real deal, she needs to proceed cautiously. This moment certainly isn't perfect—at an airport curb with the automatic doors about to slide another layer of glass between them?

He loves *her.* She feels it. Plus, he's said as much, albeit in such a comical circumstance it's impossible to know if he'd been sincere in the moment. They'd been binge-watching *Fleabag,* and she'd gone to the kitchen to get more salsa. Coming back she set the bowl on the coffee table and backed up to launch into a sort of belly flop to land across Hal's knees in spank position—a little aerial feat she'd performed a few times in the past to their mutual amusement. Except this time when she landed, a loud clown fart escaped her.

Her very essence compressed like some zip file of yellow humiliation. Hal laughed uproariously.

Hiding her face in her hands she'd groaned, "Oh no. We're not *there* yet."

One minute they were in the prefart stage of their relationship, the wonder-of-me phase with all its "You complete me" and "I don't where you begin and I end" blather, and the next minute she was outed as human, with human plumbing.

"Girl! That'll take the paint off!" Hal grabbed a pillow and fanned the air. As if the sound wasn't enough, it was a perfect reeker, inciting Rory to leap to the couch as if RayAnne was a great burrito splayed across the big man's lap.

"Sorry! Sorryyyy!" Finally admitting to herself she may actually be lactose intolerant as her mother insists. Of all the unfairness in the world, why did ice cream have to process within her like rounds of ammo?

Hal had pointed to the paused television screen where the actor's face was caught in mid-grimace, as if even she could smell it. RayAnne laughed for real then. Hal smacked her bottom with the pillow. Still laughing, he pulled her to sitting, then kissed her forehead, saying, "Don't worry, Dahl, I'll still love you."

I'll still love you.

Had that counted? The suggestion being he already loves her and might continue to in spite of her gaseous self?

She does love him. And will soon tell him.

Lately their lovemaking has been literally just that—all breath and wonder, their bodies feeling somehow secondary. Lying in the dark afterward, a little dumbstruck, she'd had the thought, *If this isn't it, I don't know what is.* She should have said it ten times by now. But she hasn't, and now he's steering away into bumper-car traffic in a cloud of frigid exhaust.

Damn. She's just shouted "I love you" to the dog she loves, but not the man she loves. And now she won't see him for weeks. She pivots to slouch into the terminal.

After checking her suitcase, she sees Cassi down the line, unloading the cart with the overweight baggage—equipment cases stenciled *Fishing!,* ticking them off her iPad and barely glancing up as RayAnne approaches. "About time. I was afraid you'd miss the flight. Hand me that tag."

A season ago Cassi was a mere production assistant, but in her new role as Location producer she seems tense as a spring. To the surprise of everyone but RayAnne, Cassi has turned out to be a powerhouse. RayAnne sees the wheels constantly turning behind the pale forehead, knows how hard Cassi works pulling the show together every week.

She barely glances at RayAnne, saying, "Hold this. See those small cases? Gimme the long one."

RayAnne juggles her own bags and hands things over. "Since when are you so bossy?"

"Since I'm your boss." Cassi scrutinizes her, a pierced eyebrow snailing with concern. "Since when are you so pink? You're flushed."

"Since my awful, sucky goodbye to Hal."

"Oh." Cassi lowers the iPad long enough to pat RayAnne's hand—her version of a hug. "Sorry, Ray. I'm slammed here. We'll talk on the flight?"

She'll call Hal after they land in LA. He'll be back from the dog park by then and hanging at his place with Rory. Hal is the only homebody RayAnne's ever dated. His loft, part of an old factory, is almost cozy with thick rugs laid over everywhere and Hudson Bay blankets on the walls to quell drafts and echoes. The place is so sunny it's hard to imagine caskets were ever built there. The giant kitchen range that was salvaged from a convent always has something bubbling on it because he cooks. It rankles RayAnne that Gran ducked out without meeting Hal—she'd have appreciated his style in the kitchen, nearly every meal an experiment.

Last week she'd walked in to find him holding a glinting cleaver, two clear plastic bags full of bloody bones on the counter. Freezing in her tracks, RayAnne fluttered her hands heart-ward. *I knew it,* she thought, *I knew this was too good to be true.* Some of the bones were long as tibiae, others slender as fibulae. She squeezed her eyes shut and waited for her life to flash before her, wondering where the cleaver might strike. When it did not, her eyes opened to slowly scale Hal, from his shoes up the front of his bloody apron to the cleaver, certain he'd be grinning maniacally. But he was only smiling his usual smile, steam from a stockpot rising behind him.

He'd looked from her face to the bones and back before busting out laughing. "The look on your face!"

"What look?" Her nervous laughter gave her away.

"That one." When he indicated with his cleaver, she jumped back, making him laugh so hard he almost dropped it. "You. Thought . . . *What*? That these lamb bones were . . . ?"

Lamb bones? "Human? Or that you'd kill and dismember me?

No. I wasn't thinking that! You're making bone b-broth. I know that."

Admittedly, she has an overactive imagination.

She could just accept Hal for what he is: a bone-boiling, dog-loving hottie that she'd hate to lose—or become too attached to—because being with him feels too good to be actually real. They board their plane and buckle up.

After landing in Los Angeles, there's no time for phone calls. Besides, it's Sunday so there's the chance Hal will have unplugged his phone. She follows Cassi, who is heading for the luggage carousel with the stride of a longshoreman. Elbowing through a jostle of passengers, Cassi heaves all seven cases from the carousel onto the two trollies, counting them off in grunts.

They scramble to get to the luggage recheck area and load the cases onto the X-ray conveyor. The bored-looking TSA guy watches half the cases go through, then backs up the belt to reexamine the long tubular case holding fishing rods. He frowns and pulls the case from the belt, saying, "Follow me." He nods to the carts. "Bring the rest."

They follow, carrying on a silent conversation with their eyebrows. *What the? You pack anything weird? No, you?*

He opens the door to a windowless room, presses a mic button on his shoulder, and says, "Assist in 4B." A stony-faced officer arrives and stands at the door with her arms crossed, openly staring at Cassi's hair, then her neck. RayAnne sometimes wishes Cassi would wear a scarf or turtleneck, just for staff meetings and maybe such instances as this, because neck tattoos aren't all that tempered by press credentials—even from public television.

Another agent strides in and kicks the door closed. "You're going where, ladies?"

"Um, New . . ."

"Zealand."

When the agent snaps on a pair of purple latex gloves,

RayAnne and Cassi silently yelp at one another. She pries items daintily from the packing cases before smashing them back in. When she gets to the case with fishing rods and tackle, she calls in another agent obviously more senior given the deference he is shown. He's not wearing a uniform.

Cassi blinks.

To his questions, they rush to explain, rather awkwardly, that they are going to New Zealand for work, to fish.

"Which is it, to work or to fish?" He looks from one to the other.

"Both. To film segments," RayAnne offers.

"For the show," Cassi says.

"We have a fishing show?" Why do they both suddenly sound guilty of something?

"A fishing show?"

"Actually, a fishing talk show. Called *Fishing!*"

"*Fishing* what?"

"Just *Fishing!*" Cassi makes to pull her iPad from her backpack. "Here, I can show you . . ."

"Drop it!" The officer at the door reaches for her holster. Cassi drops her pack to the table and raises both hands. The male agent pulls out his own iPad and starts tapping. The others lean in.

"Spelled like it sounds?"

"Yes. *F-i-s—*"

"I didn't ask how to spell it. I asked if it was spelled like it sounds."

"Right." RayAnne is not about to argue with armed, overworked Homeland bots who spend eight hours a day in the airless bowels of an airport looking through the belongings of people who get to fly away from the hell they are trapped in.

"Hang tight," the iPad agent says.

Hang tight? When a result for the show comes up on the iPad screen, the three file out into the next room, leaving the door open a crack. RayAnne and Cassi look at each other when the tinny soundtrack of the credits for *Fishing!* come up. Soon enough all three are laughing, and the woman says, "Oh, *that* show."

The guy asks, "You watch it?"

"*I* don't. But my sister does." The woman is no longer laughing. "She dropped our Sunday bowling league to stay home and watch it."

Cassi mouths, *Oh shit.*

Then they are back in the room and the agent pins Cassi's open passport to the table with an index finger and slides it toward her.

"And you're the producer?"

Cassi sighs. "Imagine that."

RayAnne steps firmly on Cassi's foot and leans toward the agent in the alpha posture Gran always used around bossy men, adopting her mother's voice of authority. She plants her knuckles on the table like an orangutan protecting its young. "If we are keeping you from your jobs with our stupid amounts of luggage and gear, I sincerely apologize for that." She manages a tone of disdain. "Travelers like us taking up even a minute of time you could be spending rooting out human traffickers or terrorists? That must be maddening for you."

Cassi stares.

RayAnne checks her Fitbit as if it is a watch, saying, "I imagine our flight crew will be wondering where we are if we detain you any longer." There is dead silence as eyes dart around; then, as if the room is being monitored, a husky male voice emits from the shoulder mic on the guy. "It's okay, Nelson, pass 'em through."

Nelson blinks up to a corner at a tiny camera, presses his mic button, and says, "Copy that, Captain."

The voice bellows. "A *women's* fishing show! Can you beat that?"

After being escorted down the hall and set free, they go

through the recheck and walk to their concourse with purpose, not looking back. Once out of earshot, Cassi grabs her arm and pulls her close, "What the? Who *were* you back there?"

RayAnne shrugs. "My mother says that when you feel cornered, get into the heads of the cornerers and turn what they are doing right back on them."

"And?"

"It works, apparently."

They walk along to their gate. RayAnne feels slightly lightheaded. Sticking her elbows out to circulate air to her clammy armpits, something makes her turn so that she's faced with an arrivals screen, where, wedged between flight arrivals from Raleigh and Rochester is the message: RAYANNE DAHL, WAY TO GO!

She detects a sudden waft of vanilla extract *eau de* Gran, who often smelled like a cooling rack of snickerdoodles. Fellow travelers do not stop and sniff, and those watching the same arrivals screen don't even blink. RayAnne stops in midstream and passengers flow around her like water around a boulder. From several paces ahead, Cassi turns back with a questioning look. RayAnne mouths, *Go ahead.*

She glances casually back at the screen, but of course the message is gone.

The back of her throat tingles like it does when tears threaten. This is how it happens—out of nowhere grief will stop her in inappropriate places at inopportune times. Veering into one of the concourse shops, she takes cover at the wall of magazines. Her eyes swim across glossy, blurred covers where jumbled titles and faces shift and clunk together as if in a kaleidoscope.

After a minute she regains focus. An elderly man stands a few feet away with arms akimbo, wearing a confused look. He scans the rack as if he means to buy a magazine but is overwhelmed by the variety. RayAnne gets the sense he's wondering how he got where he is. Gran called it *destinesia*—finding yourself somewhere with no recall of why you are there or how you even got there. She knuckles away a tear. The old man turns a full circle, looking over the candy rack toward the door as if searching out someone, then looks down at his feet.

She takes a step, asking, "Can I help you with something? Are you looking for someone?"

He peers up, hopefully searching her face. "Judy?"

Oh dear. She pats his arm. "I'm not Judy. But I imagine she'll be by any minute."

"She was just here." He looks around.

"Well . . . I'm sure she'll be back." She's not. "Um. My name is RayAnne. What's yours?"

Just as she asks, an old woman wheels around the corner in a walker, and when she sees the man her furrowed brow goes soft with relief. "Ronald! There you are!"

A look passes between RayAnne and the woman.

Now that he's been found, some inner switch flips Ronald's expression and he resumes looking at magazines, this time with purpose, drawn to the how-to and gardening section, back from the trenches of whatever memory war had engaged him.

The woman's voice lowers. "That's right, Ronald. You pick out a nice magazine." She turns to RayAnne.

"Thank you, dear."

"I. I didn't do anything."

The woman is reaching to touch her; she *is* going to touch her. And it's too late. It happens, a warm hand laid on her bare arm, an old woman's soft touch, making RayAnne's eyes fill and blur again.

The hand pats with each word. "Yes. You did, dear."

RayAnne buys some five-dollar gum for takeoff and makes her way to the gate. Passengers are already boarding, Cassi at the front of the line, unmistakable with her multicolored dye job approximating a propane flame: white-hot roots transitioning from blue to smoldering orange to the yellow ends licking her shoulders like flame tips.

Judy and Ronald had been in their eighties—maybe nineties. What must it be like to grow that old together? All the excitement and romance passed, all the milestones of living behind you, time doing a number on your knees, your sight, *your mind.* To be gray and shuffling and keeping an eye on each other, doling out pills instead of kisses, going to the clinic instead of on dates. Would any sweetness survive that?

Hanging back, she pulls out her phone and ducks behind a pillar to speed-dial Hal's number. When he doesn't answer she leaves a message.

"Sooreeee, that was sort of a dumb goodbye, I mean, it's just . . . I'm not always the most articulate—this message being a prime example. Anyway, TSA just pulled us in and grilled us over our equipment and trip. So that was fun." She looks up at the ceiling of LAX, a terrible airport by any standard, and breathes out the next sentence. "And then I saw this old couple in the shop and they were . . . Oh well, I'll tell you when we talk. So, we'll talk, really talk soon? Like on Skype?"

She toes the pillar, then softly smacks it with her temple. "Anyway, thanks for taking Rory, again. And, by the way, I *do.*" She nods as though he can see her. "I mean, you, too . . . and I *do,* you know."

Hanging up, she glares at her phone as if blaming it for her idiocy and half-considers tossing it into the bin. *What did I even just say?*

By the time they are buckled in their seats, the crew are already shutting the doors and announcing the prohibition of electronic devices.

"Once we get to the outback, will we even have cell reception?" RayAnne asks.

"Not the outback." Cassi shakes her head. "You're thinking

of Australia. Once we get to New Zealand, don't even mention Australia, Crocodile Dundee, Men At Work, or Russell Crowe."

"Right. I know that."

"You do?"

"Sure. New Zealand is to Australia what Canada is to the U.S., right? Like the buddy in a buddy film. The little brother, the sort of pretty friend."

"It is?"

"Hal's Canadian," RayAnne adds, as if this makes her some expert. "I hear the Kiwis are just as laid back."

"I wouldn't count on it. I just hope nobody wants to talk politics. You s'pose we'll be expected to explain again what's going wrong in the U.S.? Like we did in Patagonia?"

"At least there we had the excuse of the language barrier. Besides, *is* it even explainable?"

"Explicable," Cassi corrects. "And, no."

Truth be told, RayAnne feels sheepish for ignoring politics for as long as she has. Among her peers she's not alone. How many millennials can identify every Kardashian versus how many can name their own state senators? Maybe they all feel like she so often does, jaded and wondering what the point is. Because most days just reading the news makes the whole mess seem insurmountable.

Her mother rails at that attitude, having come of age in the late '60s. Bernadette spent her eighteenth birthday at Woodstock chanting and topless in a fug of hash fumes. She cannot *not* be politically involved. While RayAnne would never chain herself to a bulldozer or shout at a police officer, let alone call one a pig, she does admire her mother's commitment. Her mother is the roots in grass roots, having evolved by necessity of her times into a megaphone-mouthed protester ready to debate any figure of authority standing in the path of what is right and just. It helps she has the smarts to back it up, the glare of a trial attorney, and the tenacity of a wolverine.

Since Gran's death, RayAnne and Bernadette have grown closer in grief, spending the week after Dot's suicide together, blubbering in tandem and sleeping fitfully in their Florida motel room, waking damp-eyed, arms tangled like puzzle monkeys. These days RayAnne sees too little of her mother—their overlapping travel schedules often mean she's just arriving home as Bernadette is flying off to some far-flung ritual hot spot to guide her mavens along on their Blood-Tide Quests.

RayAnne misses her mother's fusty kitchen with its smells of weed and withered herbs hung from the beams. She's even found herself craving Bernadette's ginger-kale mocktails. The needlepoint pillows on Bernadette's window seat have campy adages like "A woman's place is in the House—and Senate"; another is embroidered with a circle/slash over a wire hanger; another sports the Eleanor Roosevelt quote, "Well-behaved women seldom make history." The stacks of protest-ready illustrated placards printed with "Elephant in the Womb" and "Black Lives Matter" are at the ready, should a last-minute rally pop up at the state capitol.

While Gran's suicide had been a major gut punch for both, Bernadette—pro-choice in every sense—has been more accepting of her mode of departure. Dot had been more like a mother than mother-in-law to her, and after the divorce the two stuck together, often as a united front in the face of Big Rick.

"For whom allowances are made . . . ," Bernadette would begin.

"Entirely too often," Dot would sigh. He'd been a remarkably beautiful little boy, a face one could hardly slap, despite his frequently slappable behavior. RayAnne has seen pictures, unfair but true: beautiful people do get away with more.

Dot usually found some forgiveness for Big Rick's antics, but when it came to his collection of wives, she'd quip, "Don't get me started on the understudies," meaning the pageant of five wives who tripped down the aisle post-Bernadette, none making it to the second act. Dot had refused to meet any of the wives after the third, a dismissal that rankled Big Rick to no end. When just weeks after Big Rick's fifth divorce was final, he announced he was engaged again, to Number Six (no one bothers much with their names anymore). Dot snapped, "Jesus wept. Can you not try living on your own for a single season?"

Bernadette, the wife all subsequent wives paled in comparison to, has never come close to remarrying and avoids commitment as one would land mines, remaining happily, promiscuously trisexual, and polyamorous, no matter whom she is currently "shagging." RayAnne worries over what she considers her mother's recklessness (what Gran shrugged off as "Bernie's antics") and is able to tally her intimate partners on her own fingers, whereas Bernadette would require an abacus.

"Show me a man who can settle with a truly independent woman. Scant few have any clue how to be alone."

Hal is apparently one of the scants, because while RayAnne's travels have meant they've spent more time apart than together, he seems fine with it. He's told RayAnne that solitude is fuel for him; she clearly remembers how he'd startled her as if he had some great confession to make, preemptively apologetic.

"I should tell you . . . ," he began.

Oh my God, she'd thought. Scenarios whirled. *He's married. He's not married but widowed, or divorced with small children.*

Hal's actual confession was simple: "I'm kind of a loner."

She misunderstood. Having expected the worst, she heard *loaner,* as if suggesting he was only a temporary boyfriend on loan from some other woman, who now wanted him back. Upon realizing he only meant *loner,* she laughed too loudly, for a beat too long.

Well, he might have just said! She understands the need to keep one's own company, take time to step back from the noise. Those who fish tend to know this, especially fly fishers.

She used to just take off, whenever her favorite crime writer came out with a new book in her series. RayAnne would nab a copy and drive off to some river. And those weekends did feel slightly illicit and delicious. One boyfriend, Paul (ripped but not particularly bright), broke it off with her after one of these weekends, refusing to believe she'd been reading and fishing and not cheating on him. Paul had stomped around her apartment gathering his guitar picks, protein powder, and the barbells he so annoyingly, gruntingly curled when watching television. She laid his shirts on the pile in his arms at the door, where he gave her a last chance to come clean.

"Just . . . tell me his *name*."

"His name is Jackson," RayAnne giggled, trying and failing at a Scottish accent. "Jackson Brodie."

She likes to think Paul had Googled the name.

Hal, despite having rafts of friends, gets the solitude thing. He's that guy always starting conversations with the Lyft driver or the waiter at the sushi bar, the aunt at a wedding, but is just as happy on his own. Since RayAnne has known him, Hal has ventured off alone three times to hike sections of the Pacific Crest Trail. He frequently makes the rounds to visit his stores in western states before crossing up to the provinces, finishing up in Ontario where he can work remotely, just over the border where he has a nearly finished timber-frame cabin on Lake Superior. He teases her with the progress regarding the bathroom, which will soon have an operable toilet, employing a seductive growl to describe the item on order. "Mansfield model six-seven-eight-three-three ivory vitreous china one-point-two-gallon flush. It's coming, baby."

What can she say about a man who can make her spine feel liquid while reciting plumbing specs?

When not working on the cabin, Hal designs and carves prototypes of new fishing lures and devises other new products for Lefty's—most recently a fishing glove called Thriller, with a rough palm for gripping slimy fish and LED fingertips that shed light on chores like removing a hook or weaving a leech.

He named his piney shoreline Nysa, which he explained was a valley of nymphs from Norse mythology. The one and only time RayAnne had been to Nysa, she looked around at poplar stumps and propane tanks. "I don't see any nymphs."

Hal scanned her slowly, from snow boots up to her folded arms and parka-hooded face before giving her his single-dimple half-grin, purring, "Well, I do. This guy, *moi,* does." He can be as hokey as he is funny.

Also, Hal is the only man who has ever complained about her *losing* weight. So, yes, she intends to keep this guy.

While at Nysa, they discovered Rory is less enthusiastic about woods and nature than your average dog. The cawing of ravens and swooping of whiskey jacks set off barking jags; the sight of a moose crashing through the brush incited him to cork himself into a hollow stump, from which he could not be coaxed until he had to poop. While Nysa is lovely, the price for the solitude-with-a-view is sketchy cell reception and a long driveway of rutted ice dubbed The Road Less Graveled. Venturing there in late February seems like asking for it, but Nysa is where Hal will take Rory during the weeks RayAnne is in New Zealand.

An hour out of LA, dinner is served. Before RayAnne can finish her rubbery cheesecake, the cabin lights are dimmed and most passengers settle in to sleep. RayAnne watches two forgettable movies she would never watch while on Earth. Cassi snores along next to her. After the movies, she tries to read a paperback but the print grows smaller with every line. Unable to concentrate, she tries very hard to fall asleep. After an hour she gives up and attempts reading again. The book is boring enough that she finally does nod off, just as the captain announces the beginning of their descent.

She blinks blearily over the coast of New Zealand. Far below are beaches, headlands, and hillsides splotched with flock upon flock of sheep, which from a few thousand feet look like clusters of maggots. New Zealand is green enough to appear fake, like some virtual reality or video game.

Once they land and are taxiing to the terminal RayAnne's phone dings out a dozen notifications. Most are from her father, one very long message broken up into eight texts with subtexts. Big Rick has been sober for over ninety days—his longest run so far—and since his last stint in rehab, last *ever* stint, he claims he is done, fini, caput, will never, ever take another drink. These days he texts his every move, as if RayAnne is interested to know he's just back from Costco (where he didn't drink) or is headed out to shovel his walk (not drinking!) or is at the indoor driving range trying out a new iron (definitely not drinking).

He had tearfully promised to give it up over Gran's ashes (though at the time he did not know the urn actually held two pounds of McCann's steel-cut oats scented with cigar and cigarette ash harvested from saucers and ashtrays after Dot's farewell banquet). Gran's body had been donated for research and was only recently returned to RayAnne in ashen form, science having finally finished with her. RayAnne tried hard to not imagine what might have happened to Dot's body during that time, hoping the medical students and instructors at least gave her a fitting nickname and were respectful enough to not take any selfies while holding her liver or an eyeball. She's now safely stowed in the urn, etched:

Dorthea Elizabeth Aronson Dahl
Born October 1931. Adored.

It's a comfort for RayAnne to see the urn on her bedroom mantel, despite the fact that in certain light only the capital letters reflect her initials, D E A D, which is tragic-funny. There is no date of death: Bernadette had lobbied to leave it off, insisting that closure on a life cannot be determined by a mere date, since there is no one day, month, or year a person stops living in our hearts.

"Or in our dashcams," RayAnne mutters.

"Nhuh?" Cassi is groggy after her nine-hour nap.

RayAnne has smuggled a few ounces of Gran into her backpack, stirred into an old Mary Kay powder compact. The long-term plan is to sprinkle a little of Dot here and there—places she knew and loved, or had dreamed of visiting. RayAnne has vowed to take some of Gran back to Italy where she attended cooking school after the war; maybe to powder the noses of ancient Roman statues; toss a few grains between the ribs of a gondola so that she might again travel the canals of Venice. RayAnne hopes to travel to Malmö, Sweden, where Dot's parents had lived before emigrating, find the old house where Dot had been conceived and add a teaspoon of her to the garden. Some of these missions have been dreamed up by her, some with Dot's input during one of their "conversations," though these days RayAnne can't trust where her own whack notions end and Gran's begin. Which of them, for instance, thought smuggling human cremains across the equator was a good idea? RayAnne double-checks her bag, where Dot shifts like sand in her plastic compact. They land in Auckland.

She follows Cassi down the narrow aisle, both laden like Sherpas with their backpacks and carry-ons. After their experience in LA, they are skittish in the customs line, but the avuncular agent with bushy eyebrows only smiles when asking what places they will visit. When they mention the name of one town, he suggests they get cake and tea at "a place called Mellie's, or Millie's. You can't miss it—the takeaway window is made from the jaws of a sperm whale."

"Oh?" Cassi brightens, no doubt framing a shot in her head. When their passports are stamped, they look warily at the customs agent. That can't possibly be all.

"Go *on*." The agent shoos them good-naturedly. When they are halfway to the exit, he shouts, "Girls. Girls!" They both freeze.

"The café! It's called Melville's!"

They grin like idiots and wave. Spilling from the terminal, they push their carts out into the glare of a summer morning. Stumbling with exhaustion, RayAnne follows to a bench to wait for their crew. After Cassi converts Celsius to Fahrenheit on her phone, she elbows RayAnne. "It's exactly one hundred degrees warmer here than in Minneapolis."

"Which is?"

"Minus twenty-three."

"Jiminy." Sometimes it feels as if she is channeling Dot, right down to her nasally voice. In the humid warmth she feels the tight muscles in her neck yield as ocean-scented air fills her lungs, her dry winter shell reconstituting itself. She slumps Gumby-like across the bench and watches vans and cabs pull up to disgorge travelers—a sporty, tanned crowd mostly, many with backpacks and serious hiking boots.

Cassi nudges and hands over the largest tube of sunscreen in the world, warning, "The ozone layer here is nil." She's donned a pith helmet with a neck flap and a mirrored visor. RayAnne blinks at this headgear mashup of Lawrence of Arabia and RoboCop.

The crew should already be there to meet them but aren't. Several vans drive by, none slowing. According to Cassi's notes, three guys, named Rangi, Rongo, and Chad comprise Tripod, the digital production crew that came so highly recommended by a producer from NZP TV.

"So where in tarnation are they?"

In answer, a large, green-eyed man walks toward them holding a hand-scrawled sign that reads *Fishing!* He's a "big 'un," as Gran would say. He stops in front of them, casting a shadow like a minor volcano.

"Sorree? But you walked right past my sign inside. You are RayAnne Dahl—star of *Fishing!*?"

"Star?" RayAnne nearly looks behind her.

Her role on *Fishing!* is a fluke: her position feels transient despite the signed contracts. Most days she feels almost comically miscast in her role of interviewer/fishing guide. The TSA agent in LA had mocked it as had so many others, laughing. "A fishing show for women?"

"Star?"

"Host." Cassi is on her feet, pumping the man's baseball mitt of a hand. "I'm Cassi. The producer."

The man steps closer but instead of shaking his hand, RayAnne touches the lettering on the sign he holds—*Fishing!*—and reads, moving her lips as she closes her eyes.

Fishing is only what she's done since, well, always. As a child, fishing was a thing you did, like walking or eating or going to school. Tagging along in the boat with her father garnered points; *catching* a fish was given the sort of attention and praise other fathers reserved for nailing a recital or clever science project. Encouragement or compliments weren't blithely tossed around by Big Rick, but fishing was an exception. She'd been Daddy's girl then. After her brother was so annoyingly born prematurely, RayAnne was dropped into Big Rick's lap by Bernadette, who effectively disappeared for the next three years to tend tiny Kyle, who would grow from a three-pound-one-ounce shrimp-colored shrimp into a broad, two-hundred-fifty-pound star forward recruited by the Chicago Blackhawks for one shining season (before permanently blowing out his shoulder).

In the meantime, while her mother attended puny Kyle, RayAnne wandered among the legs of fishermen as if roaming a stand of khaki trees, beer bottles dangling like fruit from the plaid branches of sleeves. She often rode on the shoulders of these men, and from that canopy-view grew to recognize "Uncle" Bob or "Uncle" Chip by the diameters of their bald spots or patterns of wrinkles on the backs of their necks. When set down into the grove of trousers, she was level with belt buckles, outlines of wallets, and the jangle of keys. This world smelled of cigarettes and Old Spice, engine oil and minnows. Since she laughed easily and was not inclined to whine, cry, or vomit, she was accepted into their club. She was given her own small tacklebox and rod and was doted on by the softies. Off they would go, someone nearly always remembering to buckle her into a life vest.

Every lake they visited was the territory of some clan of fish; every river or brook was a road fish traveled on their way to other fish places. RayAnne was ferried along excellent waterways to some beautiful habitat, from mountain lakes in the Rockies to golden ponds in Maine and the inland seas of Superior and Michigan.

If Big Rick taught her anything of value, it was to afford every lake and stream the same respect you would visiting a family home. She learned to treat the water as the gracious host it is, leave nothing behind, take nothing (save the occasional life of a fish, because while most of their catches were released, not all made it, and of course some got eaten). While Big Rick hasn't always been the model father, he is an exemplary steward of fresh water. He would never drop his motor into a lake unless his prop was immaculate. He uttered *milfoil* and *invasive carp* in the same tone he and his cronies saved for *liberal*. Conversely, RayAnne has caught her father tossing candy wrappers out of car windows and grinding cigarette butts into flower beds. It is not lost on her that the word *conversely* is one often connected with her father, whose own fishing show *Big Rick's Bass Bonanza* was carried on several hundred network affiliates. Even back when producing his show or touring the pro circuit, he always took time to lobby for the Sierra Club or Clean Water Action. With RayAnne in tow he would ring doorbells, smooth his hair, and charm the ladies into writing checks.

Young RayAnne believed fish were mysterious, fascinating creatures. She named each one caught, sometimes making up stories about the fish's family to tell her mother, who for some reason did not like to fish and so missed out on all the fun. Distracted, Bernadette patiently listened to these little adventures and dramas and often muttered the same mysterious line: "Ants throw up more pies." Only much later did RayAnne learn the word *anthropomorphize.*

By simple immersion, RayAnne developed a keen eye to species' behaviors and habitats, discovering what sort of pondweed drapes rainbow trout preferred; what underwater structures best suit the brown trout; what depth of lair walleye will seek but pike avoid. A sucker smells nothing like a sunnie; bass will not bite in choppy water. When her fingers were too cold to hook a worm (a ritual that always included a silent apology), it only reasoned that the worm would be too sluggish to tease a pike. After nearly thirty years of fishing every condition in every imaginable body of water, RayAnne can intuit not only when a fish might strike but what it might be hungry for and where it would prefer to dine.

Later, working college summers on the pro circuit, RayAnne began to win tournaments and took enough prizes that she could finally stop waitressing. By her fifth year she routinely took top trophies and was making a decent if erratic living tooling around the circuit. With her second big endorsement, she was able to buy and restore her sixteen-foot runabout, *Penelope.*

RayAnne's face appeared in fishing magazines, in cable ads, on blogs. Sponsors made it all possible: she wore their clothing and fished from their boats with their gear and tackle. She was a girl in a man's–man's world, a minefield of egos to be navigated gingerly and warily. She was tolerated, if only for being Big Rick's daughter. Because she was female and not ugly, RayAnne got pestered and pursued in all the ways one would expect, accruing enough #MeToo encounters to stock a 3.2 tavern with unrequited boners. She perfected a steely "In your dreams" glare. And since certain men were a workplace hazard, she'd had to act as her own OSHA—carrying mace and learning secondary self-defense (Bernadette insisted) while managing to keep clear of situations that might call for either. Until she quit the circuit,

RayAnne hadn't realized how much energy it took just to stay safe. She resents it now, having to be so buttoned up and mindful of her dress and behavior, having to be so careful.

The circuit would have been an even more isolating place if not for the stacks of dog-eared books Bernadette and Dot plied her with. RayAnne traveled in the company of dead women: Edna Ferber, Patricia Highsmith, Katherine Anne Porter, and dozens of dames like Jane Elizabeth Howard or Barbara Pym, one always tucked in her Filson pack. Books did double duty: when shielded behind one, wearing chunky reading glasses, unwanted attention was more easily deflected; it was preferable to be perceived as bookish rather than aloof. Better to be the "dork" or "nerd" than the "stuck-up bitch" or worse.

RayAnne did not fish out of any competitive streak. Far from it, she was in it to be outdoors, on the water, where by some fluke she also managed to earn a living catching fish, of all things. A decent career right up to the autumn of the election that had so many people on edge. She took stock of her priorities and knew she could not spend another season among so many men eager to vote for a man who'd throw half the population under the *Access Hollywood* bus—never mind the things they said about Hillary.

She told only some of the stories to Gran, who shook her head. "No man wants to be shown up by a menopausal woman with bigger balls." One could always count on Dot, her girlish-sounding delivery always making her zingers that much funnier.

Compelled to do something worthwhile, but with no solid plan other than to nest somewhere after a decade of motels and motor homes, RayAnne slapped down earnest money on a Near North Minneapolis brownstone that was affordable for its state of decrepitude. Alas, RayAnne's savings were not limitless. When after three months no aha moment occurred and her roof turned out to be a leaker, she took a temporary gig on a fledgling public television show as its fishing consultant. *Fishin' Chicks* was hosted by former reality show sensation Mandy Cox, from *Tomboy Trucker Wives,* bearing an uncanny resemblance to Stormy Daniels. In any case, with the show's corny name and format of B celebs aboard to "fish and dish," RayAnne could see the writing on the wall before it could spell *canceled.*

No one was shocked when difficult, moody Mandy walked off the set. What surprised many was RayAnne's being shunted into the host's seat, even temporarily, until another celebrity could be found.

Gran encouraged, "Pish. Can of corn. Interviewing ladies? How hard can *that* be?"

"Women, Gran. Professional women."

"Really? That's a career nowadays?"

RayAnne opened her mouth. "Gra—"

"It's simply a matter of faith, sweetie. You need only convince yourself you can do a thing, and eventually you'll be able to."

Logic aside, if ratings were to be believed, she has nailed it, though not in the way the producers had expected. RayAnne met Cassi, the ghostlike production assistant who popped up everywhere, somehow able to answer any question and solve any problem while possessing the uncanny ability to convince producers and crew that all her best ideas were theirs. Cassi saved the show from itself. Fringy, more oddly accomplished women were slipped into guest slots. Impressed, RayAnne began to collude—not like they had anything to lose.

Producers changed a few small things, then a few not-so-small things, including the name of the show, believing their own genius was responsible for the uptick in ratings for this new incarnation, called *Fishing!* RayAnne's girl-next-door demeanor was relatable and nonthreatening. The audience didn't mind the gap-toothed grin and her sometimes squeaky voice. With her scrubbed looks she was the opposite of sensuous Mandy, who sort of . . . oozed. Unlike Mandy, RayAnne cannot flirt with the camera, is known to miss cues, and forgets the mic is hot, which has made for some hilarious outtakes. Perhaps the occasional fumbles and self-effacing humor put viewers at ease. When wholly absorbed in an interview, she can forget the cameras altogether. It's all easier when the guests are interesting. Who wouldn't want to talk to a racehorse masseuse or the scrappy bounty hunter of deadbeat dads?

RayAnne was—astonishingly—offered a two-season contract, which she would have signed the instant it was proffered if Hal, who up to that point was just "that hot sponsor" hanging around set, hadn't pulled her aside and pointed out her unique bargaining position. That he showed up at that moment seemed a coincidence at the time. They put their heads together and came up with a rider of conditions: one being that she be able to fish from her own boat, thus *Penelope* floated into frame and soon had her own Instagram account; a second condition was that Cassi be promoted from production assistant to Location producer. They thought there would be resistance, but it seemed some force behind the scenes had their eye on Cassi as well, noting her contributions in molding the show into something sustainable.

And now *Fishing!* has found its niche, as has RayAnne. Her aha moment had simply been drawn out—the *ha* taking many months to back up to the *ah*. The idea to take the show abroad had been Cassi's. After ten years living on the road, RayAnne wasn't initially keen, but far-flung travel was exactly the sort of thing Dot was always encouraging RayAnne to do, so she relented. *Have yourself an adventure, RayBean.* She gave in to the ghost. If she has taken anything away from Gran's suicide, it is to live life all the way, out to its edges.

RayAnne snaps back to attention, letting her hand fall from the *Fishing!* sign as the shadow of the big man shifts sideways and a burst of New Zealand sun blinds her. She stands, wobbles, and is able to remember the names of the crew while shaking the man's hand. "Of course. You must be either Rongo, Rangi, or . . . Chad?"

"Rongo." He frowns. "Oy. Do I *look* like a Chad?"

Now that he mentions it, no. He grins and thumbs in the direction of a slight, reddish-blond guy coming up the rear. "Do I look like a ginger twit?"

"Ahh? I . . ."

Just as she realizes he's joking, Cassi says, "RayAnne didn't get any sleep on the plane."

"Sorry. Taking the piss." He holds out his big hand. "Rongo. Rongo Enoka."

He pumps RayAnne's hand as she ponders "taking the piss."

"Having you on. Sorry. I'm the gnarly one, in general."

The other fellow is pale and lanky, obviously a ginger but less obviously a twit. As he approaches with a cart, Cassi nearly claps. "And you must be . . . ?"

"Chad." He parks the cart with a bang. "Damnit, Rongo. Just once I'd like to meet the talent *before* you plant that meme in their heads."

Cassi and RayAnne look at each other, fighting little grins. Talent?

Under his breath Rongo coughs out a good-natured something that sounds a lot like "Suck it." Watching the exchange, RayAnne is perking up.

Chad turns to Cassi and RayAnne with a formal little bow. "Chadwick Hall, at your service. Pleasure to meet you."

"RayAnne."

"I'm Cassi."

Chad runs a hand through his rather lustrous ginger mop and turns to Rongo. "Where's Rangi?"

"Where'd ja think?"

"Not again." Chad politely explains, "IBS."

"BS is more like," Rongo offers.

Cassi asks, "What's IBS?"

"Irritable bowel syndrome," RayAnne says, seeing double as Rongo steps out from behind himself. Great. More hallucinations. After shaking her head, the visage is still there, reaching out his hand. Not Rongo but his double, in the exact dimensions, with identical features, wearing a different shirt and sporting a soul patch.

"Right. I'm Rangi . . ."

"Let me guess, Enoka as well?"

"Nothing gets past you, does it?" His smile is disarming. "Good to know." Turning serious, he says, "I see you're down with the gastrointestinal terminology." Shooting Rongo a look, he continues, "So with that detail out of the way . . . how do you do?"

She pumps his hand and states the obvious. "Twins."

"Nah," Rangi laughs, "he's just had heaps of plastic surgery, desperate to look like me."

Rongo rolls his eyes and faces RayAnne. "Never tires of that one. I'm older, obviously."

"By twenty minutes," Rangi says.

"Yeah? My nephews are twins."

Chad and Rangi start transferring cases from the airport cart to their own, and Rongo turns to pitch in.

Cassi and RayAnne follow to the parking lot where the doors of a van are flung open and the guys load in the cases, shaking their heads at any attempts to help. "Oh, no. Neither of you is to lift a finger," Chad admonishes. "That comes from the very top, by the way."

Several seats have been removed to accommodate gear.

"There are only three seats," Cassi announces, as if it might be news to them.

"Uh, yuh." Chad slaps the hood of the next vehicle, a shiny red Range Rover. Their rental. "Here's your chariot."

"I get to drive!?" Cassi springs to attention.

"Well," Chad hems, "we assumed one of us would, for starters . . . I mean, aren't you knackered?"

"I slept nine hours on the plane. No problem. I got this."

Of course she does. Cassi can drive anything from a jet ski to the thirty-foot RV they stay in at Location, where she tears around on the four-wheeler that transports guests to and from the lodge and expertly pilots the unwieldy pontoon boats, ferrying camera crews. Cassi reckons navigating and piloting are in her blood, between her great-great-grandfather, who'd been an astronomer, and her great-grandmother, who'd flown a cargo plane between airbases during World War II, drove an open-pit mine truck with story-high tires, and in semiretirement had a beer route, often taking along young Cassi, who against all rules ever made learned to drive a double-axle, five-ton Budweiser truck.

RayAnne would not be surprised if Cassi showed up at the reins of a stagecoach.

"You're gonna drive? Fantastic," Rangi says. "Saves us the bother. I'll just ride along and navigate."

"Yesss!" Cassi is chomping at the bit.

"To the motel, right?" RayAnne asks. "We're going to our motel first?"

"Well . . . ," Chad begins gently, as if to break the news, but Rongo butts in.

"Nah. Too early to check in yet. Besides, it's downcoast a good way. This morning we'll show you 'round a bit—lay of the land, right? And keep you both awake until dark."

"Dark, but that's . . . tonight?!"

"Yeah . . . ," Rangi says. "That's typically when dark happens here." He nods apologetically. "No worries, though, you'll get a second wind."

Rongo laughs. "She sits behind *you,* she will. Just follow us. We'll swing by Tough Beans, get you both some caffeine."

"Oh, yes, please."

Cassi spins. "Will we get to see the ocean?"

RayAnne braces against the van, wondering if she could sleep standing up.

"Ocean's pretty much what you get 'round here."

A back door is opened and RayAnne is pressed headfirst into the back seat as if into a squad car, Cassi making sure she's belted in and propped upright. Once settled behind the wheel, Cassi rubs her hands together as if to produce sparks, as energized as RayAnne is exhausted.

And they're off. Rangi is as good as his word, acting as tour guide while keeping an eye on Cassi's driving, explaining the traffic laws, giving directions, not that many are needed with the van speeding just ahead of them. Cassi keeps the Rover uncomfortably close to the van's bumper, as if in a NASCAR heat.

Rangi regales them with New Zealand facts: the country is a hundred-thousand square miles, most of them stunners, with a human population of just under five million. "Fewer stunners there." There are seven sheep for every person. "*And* we rank ninth in the world for cannabis consumption."

"Hmm. Similar to Minnesota, really." Cassi is all about facts.

"Similar how?" In the back seat RayAnne is slow to catch up, asking sleepily, "Square miles, population, or weed consumption?"

"All the above."

"Hmm."

In the rearview Cassi glimpses RayAnne drooping and lowers all the windows so a cyclone of wind turns her hair into whips, lashing her awake.

West of the city they travel a winding two-lane road that narrows and becomes hilly, taking them through a canopy of trees along banks shagged with massive silver ferns—the national symbol, they are informed. The terrain is very steep; occasional rock outcroppings seem to lunge at the vehicle. On the opposite side the road falls off into a bottomless green trench. RayAnne slides to the middle to avoid looking out either side and concentrates on the road ahead. Mercifully, the van has slowed considerably. After miles of curving road with RayAnne trying to stay upright, things straighten some near sea level, and soon they arrive at an outdoor café near the black sand beach of Piha.

After they order lunch, Rangi and Rongo keep up a running dialogue that is both entertaining and exhausting. RayAnne is served a second dose of caffeine. When the topic turns to America, she slumps.

"We used to love making fun of Americans," Chad says. "Now it's too easy, so thanks for ruining that for us."

"Hang on," Cassi says. "*We* certainly didn't vote for—."

"No. No, don't say his name and spoil our time together." Rangi presses his hands in pleading fashion.

Cassi laughs, which is enough for RayAnne. They will be spending weeks on the road with this trio. It could be worse.

Rongo teaches them how to pronounce the Māori name for New Zealand, *Aotearoa*.

"Ow-tay-ah-row-ah." Cassi nails it on the first try. RayAnne mumbles something that sounds like "ah-tear-uh-oh" and shakes her head. "Try me again tomorrow?"

Rangi explains: "Means 'land of the long white cloud.'" He nods Chad's way. "It's the bloody colonists named it New Zealand."

"Deal the white-guilt card." Chad rolls his eyes. "I might mention I'm not directly responsible for my great-great-grandparents' actions. But since you mention *bloody,* I reckon you wouldn't want to claim all your ancestors' doings either."

"Fair enough."

"What's he mean?" Cassi turns to Rongo. "What'd your ancestors do?"

"Ate a few enemies." Rongo shrugs. "So what?"

"It was only sometimes," Rangi adds, "and only for revenge." He points to the sandwich Cassi has abandoned, asking, "Gonna finish that?"

As they walk toward the beach, RayAnne is informed that it's one of the wildest and most dangerous in the country, making it the place to surf. They are in a huge, nearly empty horseshoe bay with rollers crashing, low clouds piling in from offshore like great billows of plowed snow. They watch the rescue boats and a camera crew, all wearing bright swim shirts that say *Surviving Piha.*

"Reality show," Chad explains. "They film the rescues."

"And sometimes recovery missions."

"Of bodies?" RayAnne blanches.

"Yeah, sometimes."

"That's a show?" Cassi blinks.

"Welcome to New Zealand."

Chad catches Cassi's eye. "Don't go too far out?"

"Out? Don't worry, I'm not going in that water."

"Trails too. You don't have to be in the water to disappear 'round here."

"What do you mean?"

Chad doesn't answer them but turns to Rangi. "We could stop at Mercer Bay and show them the *pou* on the way out."

"*Pou?*"

"*Pou whenua.* It's a wooden marker, carving really."

"Marks a local legend."

From Chad's look, RayAnne surmises it's not a happy legend.

Feeling a bit loopy, she gives up on keeping anything straight and heeds her mother's usually annoying advice, deciding for the moment to trust the universe—or if not the universe, at least the small pod of humans she currently moves among. She wanders the beach, walking the black sand toward the water, stopping to shuck her shoes and peel off the socks that have been adhered to her hot feet for thirty-six hours. Her bare heels look like cantaloupe rinds. Pressing them into the wet sand feels better than sex. At the surf, she eases her winter-white feet into cool, ankle-deep salt water and nearly weeps.

Looking around, she endeavors to take in the details of her surroundings, commit them to memory. She scans the horizon, turning a slow three-sixty to take in the far headlands, the distant beach houses, paths marked by pauses in the seagrass. Facing the ocean, she tips her face skyward and digs toes in to stay upright against the push and pull of the sea. There is the crash and boom of the rollers, distant laughter and squeals of kids playing at water's edge. Surf breaks across her shins and recedes, pulling the rug of sand out from beneath. Feeling the salt crystallize on her skin and the thrill of sand shifting underfoot, she gives in to the rhythm of the surf. The sea sloshes; wind rearranges her clothing. Of course she's off-kilter, having traversed half the globe in the space of a day. How will the rest of her ever catch up?

The others have wandered off. Few other people are on the wide beach, looking idly for shells, dragging sticks, watching the rollers, the occasional surfer. Cassi is far down the beach, executing an awkward cartwheel. Rangi and Rongo are talking with the rescue boat crew. Chad is picking up litter blown from a bin, watching kids in the water like a deputy lifeguard.

RayAnne fishes out her phone to take a video to send to Hal, lingering on her submerged feet, the glints of red nail polish reminding her of colorful lures. Panning from her toes, she aims the lens upward to the headland called Lion Rock because it vaguely resembles one. The clouds have now broken to allow great columns of sun to move across the sand in slow ballets. "Just look at this beach." The frame catches Cassi doing a second cartwheel, this time falling and laughing. Turning the phone around she looks at the lens. "Here I am. *Arrived.*" Was it only just yesterday they'd said farewell in a cloud of cold breath, kissing with chapped lips?

They spend a dreamlike hour on the beach before setting off again. Next stop, just down the coast is Mercer Bay. Rangi and Chad hang at the parking area while Rongo leads them down a path to Te Ahua Point to show them the *pou whenua* that marks a legend. It's a stylized carving of a female figure in wood, fierce looking with circular tattoo-like markings on her shoulders and arms; her fingers meet in what looks like an eloquent gang sign.

"She's badass, huh?"

"Well, stubborn for sure. She was an Â Ngaoho named Hinerangi after some Tūrehu ancestress. Her husband was a chief, and they lived near here at Karekare. Story is he went fishing one day and never came back, lost off the rocks at Te Kawa. So she packs a sad and parks on the cliff to wait for him, refusing to believe he won't come back. A likeness of her is supposed to be visible in the tall cliffs at the south end of this bay. At least that's what they say. Some people swear they see her face in the stone in certain light."

Cassi looks around. "Chad implied people have gone missing here? Recently?"

"Three women in the past ten years. So, yeah, it's a pretty bizarre coincidence. Some say the place is cursed now."

"What do you believe?" RayAnne asks.

"Being Māori doesn't mean I believe in curses."

"Well, no, I . . ."

"'S aight. Some women disappeared around here, and no one wants to really think about what sorts of bad ends they came to, so would rather trot out some legend." Rongo shrugs. "People prefer that sort of thing when the truth isn't nice, right?"

RayAnne examines the carving, blinking until Rongo nudges her from her reverie.

"Yeah? Should we go now?"

They drive another hour before stopping to hike a steep, rutted track to an overlook with a view that is so perfect it looks utterly fake. "Where's the volcano, exactly?" Cassi asks.

Chad grins. "You're standing on it."

"Ah."

They are being kept awake with gently torturous sightseeing, when sleep so tantalizingly beckons. After another half-hour they stop for ice cream at a little oceanside stand. RayAnne demurs, staying in the car. "None for me," she says, hoping she might sneak in a catnap while they're busy.

Besides, she's still wrestling the final five of the fifteen pounds gained after Gran died. Even posthumously, Gran managed to reign as the relentless feeding machine she'd been in life, having prepared and frozen all the Dahl family favorites in advance of her suicide—all the comfort foods her family could stuff themselves with against the grief of her exit. Knowing her loved ones were stress eaters, she'd provided accordingly.

No sooner are Cassi and the others out of the vehicle than she closes her eyes. Within a minute or two a muffled static disturbs her. *C'mon,* she thinks, *lemme sleep.* The static comes from the dashcam and she opens one eye to peer between seats to see the screen flicker to life like an old television, and there is Dot on her lawn chair placed between the green lines, feet up on the Rover's bumper, the newspaper folded open to the crossword puzzle in her lap, pen in hand.

"Gran?"

"Go on, RayBean. Go have some ice cream." There are sponge rollers in Gran's white hair, a coffee cup balanced on the chair arm. She's wearing the tattered bathrobe everyone made such fun of. RayAnne is surprised, not so much at Gran's specter, but that she's been followed halfway around the planet.

"You haunt across international date lines?" She checks out the rear window—not that she expects to see Gran—then turns back to the dashcam to hiss-whisper, "What are you doing here?"

Gran shrugs. "You brought me."

"Brought?" RayAnne asks.

"Fresh Petal Beige?"

"That?" RayAnne reaches for her backpack and feels the front pocket for the outline of the Mary Kay powder compact. "So, if I hadn't brought . . ."

"If you hadn't brought a handful of my ashes, would I be here?" Gran laughs. "Even I can't know that, goose."

"But Gran, you're . . ."

"Dead?" Gran sighs. "Don't I know it! Listen, I won't keep you—just popping in to say go have some ice cream. It's very good here."

"What? No!"

Gran sounds wistful. "I wish I'd eaten more ice cream." She picks up the crossword and looks straight at RayAnne, asking, "What's a six-letter word for *disavowal*? Starts with a D."

"How would I know?"

Gran sighs.

"Gran, you've come here, to tell me to have ice—" Abruptly, the screen sputters to blackness. ". . . cream? Come *on*, Gran!"

RayAnne bolts upright, having been slumped against the window. She palms away the drool on her cheek. She has barely been asleep long enough to have a dream.

Rongo suggests Hokey Pokey, a flavor RayAnne has never heard of. Chad, who does not seem apt to agree with Rongo about very much, does.

"You gotta have Hokey Pokey. It's essential."

They sit on a beached log under a pōhutukawa tree, shaped like an oak but with crazy red flowers and pine-green foliage. Chad nods. "Not called the New Zealand Christmas tree for nothing." In the shade of the blooming pōhutukawa, eating ice cream between Rangi and Rongo, RayAnne feels quite petite. "Five pounds, five schmounds," Gran would say. The sun commences setting at the same pace as RayAnne's ice cream disappears. Hokey Pokey, as it turns out, tastes like it comes from a magic cow—creamy vanilla mined with crunchy bits of honeycomb toffee. It is hands down the best ice cream RayAnne has ever eaten. As if childhood is among the ingredients, Hokey Pokey is somehow cartoon flavored, each lick conjuring up Disney versions of gamboling cows and dwarfish milkmaids, animated bees, fairies churning ice cream with their wands.

Jet lag, she reckons, isn't so different from coming down from mushrooms.

On the horizon the sun is a red ball like some great clown nose about to sink into the ocean.

When Gran pops up, it often seems she's voicing old regrets—a roster of shouldas and couldas. Lessons to spare RayAnne from making the same mistakes? Or just reminding her, "Life is short! Enjoy the 'smalls' like ice cream, and live large the 'biggies' such as this trip to New Zealand."

Chomping the waffle cone down to its tip, RayAnne watches as the clown-nose sun sinks into the Tasman Sea. As it begins to disappear, the entire sky glows with pink and crimson streaks that slowly deepen to neon brilliance. The boys (as she is beginning to think of them) seem to barely register the phenomenon. Cassi has been moved to stand, staring skyward, openmouthed. RayAnne is reminded of a night when she'd been a teen, out on a guiding trip with her father. They'd taken a group of fishermen from Georgia to a fly-in camp on the Canadian border. They watched the men's reactions to seeing the Northern Lights pulsing in the sky for the first time.

"Lord God," said one of the men.

"Amen," said another.

"Miraculous."

RayAnne, having recently finished a paper for her astronomy section in school, piped up. "Not a miracle at all. Storms on the sun hurl gusts of charged solar particles across space, and when the Earth is in the path of the particle stream, our magnetic fields and atmospheres react; molecules get rattled and they light up. It's all about electrons and photons."

The men blinked at her, silent for a beat before chuckling as if she'd told a silly story. Her father dismissed her with a joke. "Photons? Looks more like a neon shower curtain."

Her father relied heavily on his guided fishing clients. After *Big Rick's Bass Bonanza* had been canceled, such trips comprised the bulk of his income. Once they were alone, he had lectured her. "No need to be a know-it-all."

"I wasn't being."

"You could be less opinionated, is all I'm saying."

"Science isn't an opinion." RayAnne crossed her arms.

"Well, it is to some, and nobody appreciates a smart attitude—"

"Right." RayAnne finished the sentence before he could: ". . . especially from a girl."

They leave the pōhutukawa tree and walk back to the vehicles. Their motel is another hour away, meaning bed is within sweet reach. Wouldn't you know it? RayAnne's just getting it—that second wind.

Rangi takes over driving. Cassi switches to the back seat and RayAnne to the front, where she can better watch what is still visible of the scenery. Soon the ocean grays into the gloaming. With her window open, she takes in the scented, darkening world as it whizzes by against the soundtrack of Slayer and Metallica that Rangi plays at volume to keep Cassi from dozing in the back seat. No problem for RayAnne, now wide awake.

By the time they've had a dinner of fish and chips (delicious—why has RayAnne never thought to put vinegar on fries?), it's after 11 p.m., but she has ceased trying to translate real time into body time.

They arrive at their motel to find their late arrival has meant that two of their five rooms have been forfeited and that they will have to share: no problem for Cassi and RayAnne, who shared a crummy trailer on Location for an entire season. They are given rooms with game-show numbers of 1, 2, and 3. She and Cassi are given the largest of the two-bed rooms. Chad wins the coin toss and gets number 1 to himself, and Rongo and Rangi grumble a little about theirs having "beds the size of boogie boards."

Once their luggage is hauled in and their door is shut, the sight of beds acts like a horse tranquilizer on Cassi, who stumbles through the motions of climbing into pajamas and is still holding her toothbrush when she sits down on her bed and begins to tip. RayAnne is just able to snatch the foil-wrapped candy from the pillow before Cassi's temple smashes it. Finding an extra blanket, she lays it over Cassi. Marveling at the apparent depth of the girl's slumber, RayAnne mindlessly unwraps and bites into the fern-shaped chocolate.

She stops, discovering the chocolate is not solid but filled with something thickly gelatinous, and spits it into her palm, crimson and sticky. It had tasted perfumey like something dug from the bottom of an old woman's purse, though it would look more at home in a stainless steel kidney dish. Any guilt at eating Cassi's candy is assuaged by having spared her the shock of it. The wrapper reads Turkish Delight.

The aftertaste lingers in a not entirely unpleasant way. She plucks the second sweet from her own pillow and repeats the gumming. Gran always said, "Never say never" until you've given something a second chance—men only sometimes, but food always, because while a thing might not grab you on the first bite or not look good, one should withhold quick judgments, because whatever it is might be ambrosia the second time around. Oysters, for instance. Who likes those on the first go?

The gummy candy tastes vaguely of flowers. She could get used to it.

After turning the lights out, RayAnne lies prone, staring at the shadows on the ceiling, listening to the unfamiliar night sounds and Cassi's asthmatic exhalations. She thinks of Hal, counts hours on her fingers and determines it would be morning back home. He'd be up by now, making breakfast.

She texts. HELLO YESTERDAY, WHAT'S COOKIN'?

Hal cooks—not as much as Gran of course, but ten times

more than any other guy RayAnne has been with. Over the past few months he's been experimenting with Gran's recipes.

In the days after the funeral, the family robotically cleared out the condo at Dune Cottage Village. Going through her material life was awful, but at least Dot had labeled everything she'd wanted people to have, so that's one check in the Pro's column under Suicide. But after the furniture and belongings had been allotted, disposed of, or dealt with, the family sat in the living room and stared at two shallow crates containing nothing useful or of value, and everything of Dot. Inside were several tin recipe boxes with alphabetical dividers fuzzed with age; a half-dozen spiral notebooks filled with more recipes, scribbled notes, observations, diagrams, and drawings that attested to the fact that while Dot was terrible at writing things down, she could draw, sometimes hilariously, as evidenced in sets of instructions for how to "truss a goose" and "weave lattice piecrust."

RayAnne thumbed through a recipe box marked "A to D." The first was Abalone Fritters: "Beat abalone steaks heartily with a mallet; tenderize multiple steaks with a cricket bat." The last recipe in the box was for Durian Mooncake: ingredients included "one pair nose plugs." Many of the handwritten recipes had Italian or French footnotes. Cards were bent, scorched, edited, folded, torn, and mended with brittle yellowed tape. Between recipe cards a hodgepodge of ephemera was tucked here and there: butcher's receipts, Italian labels peeled from anchovy tins, grocer's orders.

Wedged under the recipe boxes was a framed canceled check—final payment on the mortgage of the last Dorthea's supper club. An envelope of black-and-white snapshots from Dot's time in culinary school in postwar Naples. There was only one of The Italian, Gran's first husband who was only ever whisper-mentioned, and then always as "The Italian." A dashing blur with a five o'clock shadow. There were Polaroids of Gran's kitchens, as well as the exteriors of Dorthea's in three iterations. All had a similar dinner-jacket style of ivory stucco facades with black trim and shutters; doors flanked by neat boxwood hedges or spears of arborvitae. And always the long black awnings over the doors. "So that you felt you were arriving somewhere," Gran explained. Above each elegant entrance was the neon flourish in fiery cursive, *Dorthea's*. In RayAnne's imagination, the name was followed by an exclamation point.

There were autographed eight-by-ten glossies of long-dead starlets, crooners, shovel-jawed actors, and sundry public figures: Walter Cronkite, Bella Abzug, Buzz Aldrin, Ed McMahon, Walter Mondale, Shirley Chisholm, and several Democratic governors. These headshots once graced the walls of the bars, now removed from their frames into a stack, with endearments and wishes for Dot scribbled with fat felt pens. One features Gran posed with Julia Child, whose chin easily cleared Dot's chef hat. The autograph was prim, like some auntie's, but the scrawled message looped broadly: "Femme adorables!"

RayAnne had reached for it, thinking of the perfect place to hang it in her kitchen. The chef's hat was also in the crate. RayAnne had extracted it from its nest of tissue and held it in her lap, laying claim. The French linen toque had always perched so neatly on Gran's head, like a pleated soufflé. "My crown," she'd say when donning it. Dot's kingdom was steaming pots and flaming pans; her kitchens were not huge but seemed so to young RayAnne, who had only ever been allowed as far as the pastry stations. In the forbidden center was the excitement, the flash of knives chopping, food somersaulting from pans, flames from the big stoves, and coarse language more often in French than not. In the corner—absolutely verboten—was the deep fryer for *pommes frites*.

When wearing her neat white hat, Gran was not quite Gran: in this realm she belonged to others, rather a shock to RayAnne, who assumed Gran existed for her and her alone. While the rest of her family rummaged and pawed photos, RayAnne took the chef's toque to the bathroom, sat on the edge of the tub, and sniffed the linen folds for traces of Dot. There she was, ever so faintly. RayAnne snuffled into the hat, dampening its pleats.

Back in the living room the family had moved on to the more fascinating contents of the second crate. All Dorthea's restaurants had been located near horse tracks. Gran had alluded that she might have been a rather wealthy widow, had it not been for Dead Ted's sole shortcoming: a gambling habit she generously called "Teddy's weakness."

Jockeys and backstretch boys often moonlighted for Dot at the front of the house, waiting tables or bartending. Over the years, quite a few retired or injured jockeys shifted from track to table full time. In fact, so many diminutive former jockeys worked at Dorthea's that the floors behind the bars were built up by several inches. A few of her "boys" had gone on to success and had gifted Dot precious memorabilia like silks from winning races, even trophies. Photos of the jockeys were peppered in among the celebrities. Foil matchbooks from the restaurants were printed: *DORTHEA'S* SHORT ON SERVICE, LONG ON TRADITION.

Ky spoke up. "I'd take some of this racing stuff."

Hal, having only just met the family, had been quietly backing in and out of the room, first with a tray of sandwiches, again with a fresh box of tissue, fresh coffee, and cookies pulled from Dot's freezer, the soft molasses kind mined with blasts of candied ginger.

Most every paper item in the boxes was marked or ringed with a dribble of this or that, and in a few cases, a smear of blood. *A cook with no scars is no cook.* Gran's hands were pearl-pocked with grease spatters; the heels of both palms had been shiny from flame, fingerprints rerouted by old scars. The tip of her left pinky and nail were misshapen, the result of a greasy cleaver wielded too near the end of a Saturday seating.

No one knew quite what to do with the recipes: Gran left no instructions, which seemed odd considering she'd planned her own funeral dinner down to the lime garnish on the gin fizzes. Perhaps she hadn't thought her history would interest anyone. No one in the family had ever learned to cook—why would they, with Gran piloting the stove?

Hal up to that point was regarded as another in RayAnne's erratic parade of boyfriends. He'd known the Dahl family for a grand total of three days when he cleared his throat and suggested that he could digitize the recipes and photographs into a book and print copies for everyone. He assured them it would be a piece of cake. Everyone, including RayAnne, looked at him anew. Hal had their attention, explaining how he used to cobble together his own Lefty's Bait and Tackle catalogs, how easy it would be to photograph Dot's memorabilia and scan recipes and photos into a book.

"Really. I'd be happy to do it."

RayAnne blinked at him. They hadn't even slept together yet—at least not properly or for an entire night in a bed—and he was taking on this? The moment he made the offer, RayAnne knew the bitter sadness would not pull her entirely under.

Indeed, as he loaded his duffel and the recipes into his Jeep, she also understood that the vulnerable situation she was in didn't exactly make for ideal timing to start a relationship. They climbed in the back seat because there was nowhere else private.

She blurted the question, "Are you taking advantage of a damsel in distress?"

"Um. No."

"I'm not a pity poke?"

"A what!?"

"I don't know." Then, with a journalistic tone, she asked, "Are tears a sexual turn-on?"

"Noooo. Although a single, well-timed tear wouldn't turn me off. Or are we talking blubbering and/or snot-sobbing?"

She snorted, holding out her imaginary microphone. "Do you or have you ever stalked women at funerals?"

He played along. "I do not. To the best of my recollection, I have not."

"Do you understand the girl you're . . . interested in . . . isn't currently firing on all cylinders? And feel free to fill in some equally inane analogy here—you know what I mean."

He looked squarely at her. "You mean, do I understand that she is grieving and distraught, and pissed off at her grandmother but unable to say so, even to herself?"

She could only nod.

He considered her a long moment before sliding over and pretending to take the microphone from her hand, pulling her onto his lap, then saying nothing, which was exactly the right thing to say.

In the months after, as if making a cookbook wasn't enough, Hal actually tested Dot's recipes. Tripping into his kitchen to smells of Gran's cooking could be simultaneously discombobulating and comforting to RayAnne. He'd set up a tripod aimed at the counter in order to take shots of his finished, garnished creations. He was spending an awful lot of time on the Dot book.

He hasn't texted back. It's been ten minutes, but time warps. It's less than forty hours since she stood on the curb in frigid Minneapolis and failed to say, "I love you." Being blasted from the depths of winter to wind up at the height of summer feels like a very complicated amusement park ride. It's almost too lovely to sleep with the night air slicing in the louvered windows, deliciously humid and droning with the sounds of crickets.

But sleep she does, falling into a formless dream in which she dreams she is watching herself sleep.

Tuesday—or is it Wednesday?—dawns. All RayAnne knows is that a full day was ditched crossing the international date line. The morning is warm and harshly bright. She and Cassi are up well before the others. They close their door quietly and once outside pause at the next window to giggle at Rangi and Rongo, snoring in tandem like a skit of men snoring. They meander past the picnic tables on a singular mission. Coffee.

Down the road is a cluster of shops where the only open establishment has a sign that has the identical font as the show, except the O is a pastry run through with a broadsword, oozing raspberry jam: they'd have found Game of Scones in any case by following the smells. Inside, they are confronted with a chalkboard menu of unfamiliar coffee terminology: *long black, flat white*. The woman at the counter answers their questions and settles into the process of grinding their coffee with a hand crank, frowning as if each bean had been a personal friend. They wait three minutes, then five. RayAnne is almost overcome with jonesing, but watching the coffee brew only makes it come more slowly. They look out the windows at foreign trees, different birds, at the languorousness of summer, and wonder aloud what the guys, what Tripod has in store for them this morning.

RayAnne tells Cassi about her dream of watching herself sleep.

The woman making their long whites pauses in her task (no!) to ask where they are from.

When they answer Minneapolis, she nearly claps. "Did you know Prince?"

"Well, no . . ." RayAnne is watching the woman's hands, wondering when they will move again to finally pour the now-brewed coffee into the cups. *Multitask!* she chants inwardly. "I mean, did anyone really know him?"

"*We* did," Cassi says.

RayAnne pivots. "We?"

"My family," Cassi shrugs. "He was one of my dad's pals."

"Pal?" Prince was someone's *pal*. "Really?"

"He was godfather to my sisters, the twins."

"But . . ."

"He just was." Cassi sees both the woman and RayAnne want more, so adds, "He taught me how to do the jump splits."

"No!"

Outside, RayAnne looks at Cassi anew. "You never mentioned knowing Prince."

"Why would I?"

"But in there . . ."

"The lady asked."

"Right."

"I felt sorry for him." Cassi extracts raisins from her scone and lines them up on the railing for the birds. "I mean, not being able to do what we just did—walk into a bakery and order coffee without it becoming some spectacle."

"I suppose." RayAnne gulps coffee. "Fame isn't all that."

They sit a moment. "People die," Cassi says, "in stupid ways."

"Such stupid ways," RayAnne agrees.

Walking back to the motel they pass a cash machine. Giving it a wide berth, RayAnne is wary, not putting it past Gran to fizzle to life on an ATM.

She turns to Cassi, musing, "What if the dead . . . say, some dead, such as my Gran, or Prince . . . what if they're not entirely gone?"

"Whaddya mean?"

"I mean . . . not gone-gone. More like . . . part of them is still here."

"Here?" Cassi cocks her head.

"Well, obviously not alive-alive like we are, but some form of energy that lingers, like particulates or something?"

Cassi looks thoughtful as if trying on the idea. "What does anybody know? I mean, not like anyone's ever really come back to report anything. Still, I'd put money on it that your grandmother and Prince are gone-gone. Like, pretty much entirely."

RayAnne shrugs. Sometimes Cassi can come off as rather smug—so sure about being sure.

Back at the motel everyone is up and outside seated at a table by the pool, planning the day.

"You're awake!" Rongo says. "Thought you'd still be down for the count."

Over breakfast he and Chad prep them for what essentially looks like a three-week road rally, maps spread on the table with their routes marked in red. Blue lines denote flights, for times they'll travel back and forth to the South Island. If Rongo is the dad in the crew, Chad is definitely the mum, always checking that everyone understands what's expected of them and has what they need; he makes a production of doling out forks and napkins and shows them backup plans in the event any of their guests have to cancel. While eating, they go over the schedule and logistics. Their first taping will take place the following day aboard a commercial fishing trawler.

Rangi appears to be the geeky gadget wiz. His realm is equipment, devices, cases, wires, mics, and drones. He explains that when weather allows, they will fly drones in addition to various mounted GoPros. They'll also employ a steady-cam, which is strictly Rongo's territory.

"Aight." Chad claps his hands and casts an eye over the messy table. The coffee is gone, all the fruit and pastries have been devoured, a fly is buzzing on its back in RayAnne's drained juice glass. "Remember to assign a room number to all your charges for any room service."

"Or minibar?" Cassi jokes.

"Yeah, nah, we don't have those." Chad shrugs. "Bit of a weird concept, innit? Who but the Yanks would provide a chillybox of baby whiskeys in a motel room, then toss in a bible?"

RayAnne had not thought that odd until now.

After breakfast they walk to a nearby soccer field and Rangi sends his drones up. He sets them with data and images of RayAnne so it knows to follow her and her alone. Smart-Stalk is a feature that memorizes her face, shape, average speed, even her gait. Rangi asks RayAnne to run, walk, turn, crouch, and stagger.

"Actually," he admits, "you don't need to stagger. Just having you on."

"So Big Brother," marvels Cassi.

"It is creepy." The drone camera lens not only resembles an eye, it moves like one. RayAnne makes a face, half-daring it to respond.

Artificial Intelligence.

What if—in some alternate reality—one could program their DNA into some digital version of themselves, able to live on afterward?

Nah. Not even with her circadian rhythms whacked by jet lag would RayAnne buy into such scenarios.

"Dismount! That's us, done for the day."

"What?" RayAnne's watch reads all of 10 a.m.

Rangi shrugs. "Tomorrow's a long one, so today you can take it easy."

Cassi, hoping for a dose of local culture, opts for a trip to a surf shop up the coast with Rongo and Rangi. Chad claims to have work, quipping, "At least some of us do."

"I'll stay here," RayAnne says. Chad eyes her, as if wondering if she'll need babysitting.

"I'm gonna walk, hang by the pool maybe. I've got reading to do. I'm fine doing nothing."

"Right on." Cassi nods. "Find everything in nothing!"

It's an inside joke. A few months back, they had interviewed a downsizing guru RayAnne hadn't particularly liked (for good reason): they later learned her coaching service had defrauded clients of "extraneous material anchors," that is, valuable art, jewelry, and furnishings. Her appearance on the show had tipped off authorities. The so-called guru, whose motto had been Find

Everything in Nothing, is currently living a minimalist's dream in a minimum security correctional facility.

RayAnne does walk, then reads by the pool. Like Chad, she does have actual work to do: reading up on the guest bios, news articles, and profiles on the women they will be interviewing in New Zealand.

She retreats to their room, opens her laptop, and starts reading the bio of their first guest, Ellie Mann, a tuna trawler captain they will fish with the following morning. There's nothing particularly enlightening or revealing in her bio—just the facts, along with a picture of a sun-browned woman in mirrored glasses, her golf visor corralling spiky blond hair, looking like she means business.

RayAnne skims other bios: an author of historical fiction; a dog trainer known for her controversial methods; a master flytier who makes lures for heads of state and dignitaries; and an antifashion clothing designer. RayAnne reads until one bio bleeds into the others and her eyelids begin to itch. She is suddenly, utterly exhausted, limbs leaden. It's all caught up with her. Even when her phone dings to notify Hal has texted, she cannot find the energy to swipe a fingertip to open the message.

Crawling on hands and knees across the sand-colored carpet she pauses at the base of the high twin bed, remembering that Sir Edmund Hillary was from New Zealand. He probably was never as tired dragging himself up the side of Everest as she is at this moment. RayAnne scales the bedspread to collapse at the summit of snowy pillows.

"An adventure," Gran had said.

As her eyelids flutter shut, RayAnne mumbles, "Adventure indeed."

2. ANGER

In the low-lying fog of predawn, their two-vehicle caravan has the bum luck of being behind a dairy tanker that takes a curve too fast. When Rongo sees it begin to careen, he yelps and takes his foot from the gas. "Ah, jays-*us*!"

RayAnne reaches for the dash to brace herself. "Ohhh, crap."

Rongo hits the brakes and protectively flings a big arm across RayAnne, nearly knocking the air out of her. They watch in awe as the gleaming tanker lifts from its double set of wheels like a dog fixing to pee.

"Oi, oi, oi!" Chad chants from the back seat, as if the power of *oi* might set the tanker's wheels back to the pavement. With each *oi,* his voice raises an octave as if his pants are growing tighter.

The truck tips to the point of no return. Coming up fast from behind are Cassi and Rangi. RayAnne pivots in her seat to see Cassi's face just as she hits the brakes and the Rover squeals to a stop inches from the van's bumper.

"Crikey." They watch helplessly as the dairy tanker topples, hitting the road with the most horrendous metallic din, sparks shooting from underneath the tank like a hundred bottle rockets in the still-dark sky. RayAnne covers her ears as the wreck skids another forty feet to make a second, sparkful arc before screeching to a halt.

For a suspended moment everyone sits agape, unmoving. The tanker's engine rattles to stillness. Once the driver sticks his head out of the sky-facing cab window, everyone breaks into action—seat belts unbuckle, doors fling open, and they all head for the wreck, RayAnne sprinting ahead.

The driver looks dazed but uninjured save a smudge of blood on his lower lip. As RayAnne reaches him, the truck tires are still rotating.

"Hey! Hey, there! You okay?"

He blinks. "Bit my lip." He shakes himself, looks behind her, and then at her. "Are you guys in a band?"

"What?"

It takes a nano, but when RayAnne looks over her shoulder she sees the staggered entourage as the driver must—an indie-album cover photo: two big Māori men who wouldn't be out of place on lead guitar and drums coming out from the darkness; Cassi, with her multihued, propane-burner hair would be on keyboard, surely; skinny Chad in his skinny jeans and cooler-than-thou black wraparound sunglasses is slicing through the ground fog with sharp knees, the picture of a lead vocalist. RayAnne knows exactly who and where she'd be in this band: stage-right backup singer on bass. Maybe tambourine. She hates to disappoint the poor driver, tempted to make up something on the spot, if only to distract him. *Yeah, opening for Brandi Carlile. Tour's a bitch but we're killing it.*

"We're not quite a band. Listen, we should get you down from this cab." When she reaches up, he just looks at her hand. He's sitting on the door now, heels against the cab roof.

"Du-uude." Rangi calls from mid-jog. He stops and quickly scans the ground, sniffing. RayAnne realizes he's checking for leaked fuel. "C'mon, mate, let's get you down." He reaches up to lift the driver by the waist, like a figure skater. "You aight?" He sets him down.

The driver nods.

Chad ambles up to state the obvious. "Bad luck."

Rongo is pacing, poking his cell phone, dialing 111. Cassi at his sleeve, prompting, "We're going to need a tow truck—a big one."

Rongo gives the operator their location.

"With a crane," Cassi pipes up.

"With a crane," Rongo repeats. "Yes, a milk tanker."

Rangi and Chad lead the driver to the verge, where Chad presses him to sitting on the guardrail and looks into his eyes. "Did you hit your head?"

"Dunno. Don't think so."

"Feel all right?" Chad asks cheerfully.

The driver stands, turns to the tanker. "Bloody hell."

Chad steps in front of the wreck. "How many fingers am I holding up?"

"Three." He's craning to look around.

"Can you squeeze my hand?"

"I'd rather not, actually." He seems to be coming around.

"Who is president of the United States?"

"Fuck off." He presses Chad aside.

"He's fine!" Chad declares.

"Don't mind Aunt Chad." Rangi hands the driver a paper napkin for his lip. "Sorry for your trouble, mate. I'm Rangi."

"Ken." Ken has begun blinking again.

"Semi tow truck with crane," Rongo holds up his cell phone, "is on the way."

After more awkward introductions, they all stand facing the tanker, a great shining curve of polished steel that reflects them, the road and landscape behind, warping everything.

As if reading RayAnne's thoughts, Cassi whispers, "It's like the Bean in Chicago."

Rongo pockets his phone, "Forty-five minutes is the guestimate."

They watch as milk pulses from the broken seam of the tanker to spill across the road.

"Fucksake." Ken knuckles his temple. "That's me then. Carked."

"Could be worse, mate," Rangi offers.

"Yeah?" Ken slumps. "How?"

"Well . . . ," Rangi considers the milk for a moment. "Could be a petrol rig?"

"Point."

Rangi, RayAnne realizes, is the optimist.

Their own predicament dawns: the tanker is completely blocking the road in the direction they are headed.

The local police arrive well before the tow truck and crane. After Officer Dan and Officer Denise determine no one is injured, they circle the wreck and take a few phone pics before Dan returns to the squad, coming back with a cardboard tray of coffee, explaining, "We were at Starbucks when the call came in. Hope long whites are okay."

"Really?" RayAnne asks. "They have Starbucks here?"

"No way," Cassi marvels.

"It's New Zealand, not Oz." Rongo turns to the officers, explaining, "Americans."

Denise pulls out a pad and pen. "I'll need to get your names."

RayAnne looks alarmed. "Because we're Americans?"

"No," Denise smiles. "Because you're witnesses."

"Oh."

Dan fills out an accident report and questions Ken, apologizing in advance for having to administer a Breathalyzer test.

Cassi trudges the ditch, looking for a way to drive around the truck. She reports back.

"We're going to be late."

"You think?" RayAnne sighs.

"Sarcasm isn't going to get us there any faster." Cassi starts thumbing on her phone. "Surely there's a detour we could take?"

Rongo and Denise give her pitying looks.

While they wait for the tow truck the sky lightens, and Rongo has the presence of mind to take video of the scene and gets Ken's email so he can send him the file. Listening for the truck, they watch more milk seep from the cracks. To everyone's credit no spilt-milk jokes are made. They watch it flow across the road and under a fence, pooling in a field where a small dairy herd graze. One by one, the cows approach to investigate, slowly making a circle around the growing puddle of milk. They commence drinking as if at a watering hole. Everyone moves closer to the verge to watch cows drink cow's milk, silently contemplating the weirdness. There is a fair bit of mooing and fetlock shaking, as if the cows are contemplating the same.

Ken paces along farther up the verge, talking on the phone with his dispatcher—the dreaded call. Irate exhortations and expletives are shouted loudly enough on the other end they can all hear. They lob glances at one another. Poor Ken. Poor fucker.

Cassi makes her own dreaded phone call to the fishing boat captain they are due to meet, explaining why they will be delayed.

"Uh-huh. Accident. Yes. A real mess. Just waiting for the tow truck. I'm so sorry. Uh-huh. Quick as we can." Hanging up, she gives RayAnne a look. "Unhappy would be an understatement."

"We have a decent excuse."

"Don't count on it."

Ken, off the phone now, confronts the tanker. He shouts a string of obscenities worthy of any trucker and commences kicking the tires until stubbing his toes, producing a yowl that gets even the cows' attention.

He limps back, crestfallen.

Officer Dan says, "She'll be right, mate."

At that, Ken quietly commences weeping.

Everyone tries their best to cheer Ken. Denise pulls out her phone to show him a replay video of the previous evening's rugby match, when the All Blacks trounced Australia.

They take turns standing in front of the overturned tanker with Ken for pictures, assuring him this will all be a big laugh one day. Cassi climbs up the shiny chrome of the tank and demonstrates the jump splits that Prince had taught her. Cassi informs them that she and Prince Rogers Nelson were exactly the same height, five-foot-two and three-quarters. "He always claimed five-three," she says. "Don't believe it."

They all turn at the sound of a truck, and when it comes into view they cheer. While they've been waiting, several more vehicles have lined up, and a few have turned back. It's an hour before the wreck is cleared enough to maneuver around it. They feel a little bad about abandoning Ken, but what can they do? Work is work.

They pile in the vehicles, drive across the ribbon of milk, and get back on the road. The moment they're out of sight, gas pedals are stomped. Even though Cassi had allotted more than an hour for breakfast and planning, they will still be considerably late.

At the dock they all grab gear cases and sprint up the gangway of the *Virago*. The moment they're aboard ropes are thrown and the engines throttle into reverse.

"About damned time." Captain Ellie Mann is wiry, her acorn-tan face crowned by a thatch of cropped, salt-bleached hair. She hitches an equally salty brow at their rock-solid excuse, saying, "A milk lorry?" in a way that suggests they might have come up with something more plausible.

RayAnne lifts one of her Keds with its crusty tide mark, drying now, but still exuding a milky odor. Chad frowns. "You'll want to hose those down before they start smelling like Stilton."

As if being late wasn't enough, Captain Mann had only expected to accommodate three people because Cassi had neglected to include herself and RayAnne in her initial query, listing “a crew of three.” As fishing trawlers go, the *Virago* is not large, and the five of them take up a fair bit of space.

The seven-man crew greets them with crossed arms and man-spread feet.

“Be bloody careful around the rigging and pulleys.” A short fellow with neck tattoos sticks his chin at Rongo and Rangi. “’Specially you two.” It’s hard to tell if he’s being sizeist or racist.

To Cassi, Captain Mann is blunt: “I’m not keen to lose a single fish for the sake of entertainment.”

“Totally, and we—”

“Pulling skipjack isn’t for nancies.”

Chad leans in, “*Nancies* means—”

“I got it,” RayAnne assures him.

With that welcome, the captain turns on her heel, leaving them to set up. As the trawler gets underway, the guys scope out places to mount GoPros. The deck crew are cursing neon blue streaks wherein every modifier begins with *F,* never great for broadcast television.

Cassi says, “Welcome to *this* bleeping segment.”

“Hey.” Rongo shrugs. “Can’t be any ruddier than *World’s Deadliest Catch.*”

“Yeah, but we’re not cable. On WYOY, every show . . . ,” Cassi begins and RayAnne finishes . . . “is a *family* show.”

RayAnne dares to follow the captain to the pilot house, where the digital clock confronts her with the time, nearly 7 a.m. Ellie takes the wheel from the second mate and navigates the trawler through a busy marina of commercial vessels and pleasure boats of various vintages, states of repair, and disrepair: a squalid rust-bucket ironically dubbed *Shipshape* rocks next to a beautifully restored wooden yacht called *MoneyPenny.* A stealthy-looking black fiberglass number with a sonar sweep looks like the sort of boat Batman might pilot but appears to have no name. A schooner named *Marakihau* sports an intricately carved half-human bowsprit with shell eyes and nasty looking teeth in a red-lipped smile.

"Wow. *Marak . . .*"

"*Marakihau.*" Ellie pronounces the name for RayAnne before she can slaughter it. "It's a mythical sea creature that likes to tip canoes—a bit of mischief that prowls the depths." By deigning to engage in conversation, Captain Mann seems less irate. As someone with a fresh haircut does, she habitually touches the shaved sides of her scalp and rakes fingers through the thick top.

Cassi, who had edged in, hazards a comment. "Nice crop."

The captain scowls at Cassi's own multicolored dye job. "I pilot a trawler. I don't have time to think about hair, even when we do shove off on time."

RayAnne casually leans in. One thing she is realizing out in the real world (away from the sport circuit) is that women need to stick together.

"You gotta admit, Captain, you do have a pretty awesome haircut."

She frowns at them both. "Thanks."

When the *Virago* passes another trawler, RayAnne puzzles over the name.

"*What Hump*?"

"Skipper's a dead ringer for Marty Feldman."

"Oh, is he that . . . ?"

"Bug-eyed bugger played Igor in *Young Frankenstein.*"

"Cool. I haven't actually seen—."

"You're serious?" It's not a question. "You've not seen *Young Frankenstein*?" Captain Mann bestows a less grimacey expression that approaches a grin. "Well, then, something to look forward to."

Young Frankenstein is her brother's all-time favorite film. RayAnne somehow made it into her thirties without ever having seen it, and when Ky learned that, he had insisted she save it to watch with someone special.

"Because?" she'd asked.

"Just save it for a human being."

Human being—childhood vernacular with roots in another movie, *Little Big Man*—is sibling code for a worthy or exceptional person, someone you'd consider lending your toothbrush to or mate for life with.

"You mean a guy-human?"

"Unless you're lesbian or whatever." Kyle shrugged. "Just watch it with *somebody*, and if you laugh at the same jokes and finish each other's quotes, then marry them."

"Jays, you sound like Gran. Next you're gonna tell me that's how you snagged Ingrid."

"It is, actually."

"Seriously."

"I shit you not. We were eating in Vescio's when some guy at the table behind ours complained that his date had barely touched her food. We both dropped our forks and started fingering our linguine, gazing into each other's eyes. You wouldn't think that pasta would give a guy a har—."

"No . . . ," RayAnne held up a hand. ". . . details." She in particular did not want to know what might arouse her brother.

"And that was that—I proposed over the tiramisu."

"So, you married Ingrid because of *Young Frankenstein*."

He sighed. "You wouldn't understand. You're not a complete human being until you've seen the film."

"Right."

"Like three times."

"I. Get. It," she said, poking him right back.

Not that Ky was any influence, but after he'd relayed that story, she hadn't rushed to watch the film because . . . well, because maybe she should save it for a human being.

"God, tell me you didn't, Ky?"

"Didn't what?"

"Propose at Vescio's?"

But now, in her midthirties . . . . "The question is," she says, turning to the captain, "am I ready to watch it?"

Ellie laughs but then clams up as if caught at something. RayAnne looks around to realize half the crew are watching from the lower deck. Perhaps Ellie can't afford to be anything but tough in front of them.

RayAnne knows this all too well from working in male territory. Keep up a front, no matter how you're perceived. The captain lowers her voice so only RayAnne can hear. "Since we're talking movies . . ." Her voice changes to a Boston clip. "'Sometimes you have to be a high-riding bitch to survive.'"

"Thank you, Dolores Claiborne." RayAnne solemnly nods.

Skippering a commercial trawler would be a tough-enough gig, but being the "lady captain" on a tuna boat with an all-male crew . . .

"Mind if we look around?" Cassi asks.

"Knock yourselves out," Captain Mann says.

RayAnne and Cassi wander the decks, looking for places to conduct an interview later, perhaps after the catch is in or after they dock.

"Away from the crew?"

"Definitely," Cassi agrees.

They stick their heads into the galley, but it's cramped. The lounge is bigger but the smell coming from the head is eye-watering. Cassi shakes her head. "Maybe on the wharf?"

"Yeah."

Just as they circle back to the wheelhouse the captain is pressing the PA button to address a crew member loitering near the propane tanks with a cigarette. "Oi, Brian, unless you're planning a Buddhist barbie, you'll wanna keep that fag clear of those tanks."

Ellie's vantage point is that of a raptor as she scans the deck. She crackles on again, "Doug, get the finger out and secure that cabbie winch now before it cracks someone's melon." She lets up on the button, muttering, "Yours, if there's a god."

RayAnne remembers the rest of Dolores's line: *Sometimes, being a bitch is all a woman has to hang on to.*

Cassi, who had sidled close to the fishing crew to eavesdrop, sidles back to ask Chad, "What are *JAFAs*?"

Chad laughs. "Just Another Fucking Aucklander. Plural in this case since there's three of us."

Rongo adds, "Might wanna steer clear of the bogans."

"They may be bogans," Rangi says, "but they're hardworking bogans."

RayAnne nods, turns, and smacks headlong into a crew member who looks a bit like Kyle. He mumbles and maneuvers around her.

She wonders what her brother is up to since she'd stomped out of his house. Hopefully he's behaving. The day before leaving for New Zealand, she'd dropped by to say hi and bye, but truth be told, she wanted to test the waters—having begun to worry, frankly, about her grasp on reality. If anybody could reel her back in it was Ky. And if she told him about Gran's being not quite gone, neither here nor there, not quite as dead as the parrot but existing somewhere in the ether as a flock of pixels that forms and unforms on her sundry personal device screens or her imagination? Ky might understand, having been pretty tight with Gran himself.

She never got the chance to find out. The second she asked how he was doing, coping, Ky waved the question away. "Griefwise? Way ahead of the game."

"Oh, it's a game?"

"I'd say I'm two-thirds of the way through depression."

"C'mon, Ky. You keep a spreadsheet?"

"You don't?"

Ky is a semiretired sports statistician and a full-time dad, or, as he refers to himself, a cul-de-sac foot soldier. He claims the home he shares with Ingrid and their two hyperactive twins is "a fucking war zone."

"I have the scars to prove it, Ray."

He's had a deviated septum from multiple head buttings, healed-over bite marks on "the hand that fucking feeds them," and a pin in his ankle since skidding on stray Legos scattered like land mines on the stairs of their suburban Deephaven McMansion.

"This burn?" He'd pulled up his sleeve. "Spaghetti sauce. They've learned to use their spoons like trebuchets." He pointed to a side table where the glass eyes of two grotesque plastic blobs stare wonkily through fused mats of acrylic hair.

"Therapist suggested I get them each a baby doll. Ten minutes out of the box I find 'em in the kitchen, micro-tasing the heads that they'd ripped off the bodies. Imagine living with Chucky, times two."

"Oh, Ky." Her brother did seem done in. "Are you all right?"

"Montessori has expelled them again. One more strike and they're out. From kindergarten!"

"That's awful!"

RayAnne remembers them as babies, impossible to pick up and hold without their going rigid in their onesies, like launching flying squirrels. As much as she adores her nephews, time with them hasn't exactly triggered her biological clock. She's quite happy to be, as they call her, Auntie RayGun.

Ky claims he's lost count how many nannies have quit on them, and Ingrid simply isn't home, up to her neck as she is in the morass of global economics where she's a policy wonk and consultant. Ingrid is miserable that she can't be more present, but at least her insane salary pays for the perks of therapy, nannies, and Ky's Zoloft, which may or may not be working, if his moods are any indication.

"Grief!" She chuckled. "I dunno, Ky, phase-wise you *might* still be stomping around in Anger."

"Bullshit!"

RayAnne loves her brother, she really does. But Kyle can be his own worst enemy. She has learned to count to five, just as he does with the twins.

"Okay, Ky. But if it's not anger, or even denial, what exact hair is up your ass? Because you do not seem your actual self."

After a pained pause, Ky admitted. "It's Gikka."

"What?"

"Not what. Who."

"Gikka is . . . ?"

"Our new au pair. Ingrid's cousin."

"You got another au pair?"

"With the Brexit mess, Ingrid's on the road like twenty days a month now."

True. These days RayAnne never knows whether her sister-in-law is in Brussels, Buenos Aires, or Blaine. Ingrid was born on the Faroe Islands near the Arctic Circle in a place called Tórshavn, which she claims is warmer than Minneapolis in winter. Her economics professor father brought the family to Minnesota when she was fifteen. Following in his Nobel-nominated footsteps, Ingrid graduated Harvard at twenty, the London School of Economics at twenty-two, and in the dozen years since as a political economist has become a regulatory expert, her name often mentioned alongside some guy named Francis Fukuyama.

Unlike Mr. Fukuyama, Ingrid looks like a Norse goddess, willowy and frost-blond with chlorine-blue eyes. Her blinding presence is only tolerable to RayAnne because Ingrid is also the sweetest, most sincere person she's ever met. It's hard to equate the Ingrid she knows—mom of twins schlepping around in Uggs and sweats making peanut butter sandwiches—with the precise, badass-in-heels talking-head version that shows up on *Face the Nation,* in boardrooms of major financial institutions, and in prime ministers' offices.

"I know she's away a lot, Ky. I saw her on CNN twice this week. You knew she was a dragon slayer when you married her."

"I knew *that*—not that she'd produce a matched set of krakens."

"Oh, like you had nothing to do with—"

Ky ignored her. "So now we've got Gikka."

"But aren't the twins nearly seven?"

"You do realize seven-year-olds are far more dangerous than two-year-olds."

"Dangerous?" RayAnne crossed her arms.

"Guess how I woke up this morning. Guess."

"How?"

"By having the fucking silverware drawer dumped on me."

"Maybe they're just missing Ingrid?"

"There were knives, RayAss."

"Don't call me that. So now you have more help, right? What is the problem with this . . . Gilda?"

"Gikka. Daughter of Uncle Per. Don't ask me why I was expecting some teenager. And maybe even an ugly one, with a name like that . . ."

"And?"

"Looks exactly like Ingrid did when we met—even sounds like her. But here's the thing, Ray: she's trying to jump me."

RayAnne stood. "Get rid of her!"

"No! We need the help."

At that moment, the front door opened. Ky squeezed his eyes shut, whispering, "It's her. It's her!" When he called out, his voice cracked. "Hey, Gikka, c-come meet my sister."

The woman who strode into the kitchen looked freakishly like Ingrid. Tall and fair, Gikka peeled off her stocking cap to a cascade of corn-silk blondness, breathing huskily.

"Oh, hallo! You are the famous RayAnne? Such pleasure to meet you." Her accent was somewhat thicker than Ingrid's. She nearly could be Ingrid, albeit a younger, more voluptuous version.

Gikka's aqua gaze was very direct as she cocked her head to scrutinize RayAnne.

"So much prettier in person than on the television!"

Gikka peeled layers of spandex down to a tank top. A single drop of sweat trickled from her clavicle toward the cleft between a pair of gravity-defying breasts with erect, gumdrop nipples. As RayAnne followed the progress of the bead of perspiration, Gikka swiveled the alabaster shoulders of her perfect torso and slouched alluringly, as if to say, *Oh, these old things?*

She fanned the air with an elegant hand. "Ooof, I must smell like some goat. Nine miles today!"

Gikka did not smell like a goat; she smelled as if spritzed with musky pheromones. It had been years since RayAnne thought about a woman *in that way*. Not since her junior college year of sexual fluidity, when she'd decided to be open to anything—whatever form "any" or "thing" might take. But after two awkward, overthought encounters with girls, she assigned herself as "hitherto hetero." Of course, there'd been no one like Gikka on the tiny St. Olaf College campus in the Minnesota corn belt.

When Gikka leaned over the sink to gulp water straight from the faucet, there was no avoiding the skintight leggings stretched across slopes of buttocks defined with a perfect thong of perspiration. RayAnne swallowed. Was this something she was going to have to tell Hal about?

"See?" Ky's foot pressed hers until she snapped to attention. The twins barreled squealing into the room to attach themselves like a set of polio braces to Gikka's endless legs. She ruffled their blond mops, clearly as enamored of them as they were of her. They barely registered RayAnne other than to show off their newest prize. "Look, RayGun, it's Gikka!"

"Your brother," Gikka smiled at RayAnne, purring, "he makes good children, yes?"

RayAnne dared not make eye contact with Ky until he was walking her out.

"Tell me you are not tempted."

"Right."

"Send her back."

"No! You saw how she is with the boys." Ky looked, for all the world, pained.

"I *saw* a lot. Tell me you're not tempted, Kyle. Because if you are, I'll kill you. After Ingrid kills you, I will kill you again, and you will be double-dead." She punched his arm. "Do you hear me?"

"Ow. Yes, I fucking hear you."

Obviously her brother wasn't in the best place to listen to RayAnne's problems: hallucinations of Gran didn't seem all that distressing in comparison to his state.

"Let's hope so." RayAnne got in the car and rolled down the window.

Once out of punching distance, Ky mused, "But really. Is it cheat-cheating if it's with a clone of your wife?"

"And who do you suppose you are reminding me of right now?"

"You realize I'm kidding."

"You could be in divorce court right alongside Big Rick next. That's coming right up, if I'm not mistaken. Where are you going?"

"Garage. Gotta slam the beer-fridge door on my dick a few times before I can go back in inside."

"Thanks for that image." Shifting into reverse, RayAnne leaned out the window to ask, "When does Ingrid come home?"

"Not soon enough."

RayAnne is blasted into the present when a large trawler they are passing, the *Hummer,* sounds its airhorn. Standing at the door of the wheelhouse, a tanned and wiry guy in short-shorts waves his red bandanna at Captain Mann, shouting, "Oi!"

The look Ellie shoots across the bow of the *Hummer* is as friendly as a torpedo, but the man only hollers louder to be heard above the engine noise.

"Jaysus, El. You only just heading out now?"

Ellie makes as if she cannot hear him.

"'Cuz we're back and packed out." He jabs his thumb toward the wharf where a refrigerated JACKO Fisheries truck is pulling away. Below him, men in yellow waders are hosing down the deck, while others are examining the huge net hanging from the rigging, a purse seine.

The guy blasts the *Hummer*'s horn a second time and Ellie plants a pair of mirrored aviators on her face, making no sign she can hear him.

"Camera crew, aye?" the man shouts. "You gonna put them to work, too?"

Ellie shouts back, "Not exactly skux in those stubbies, are ya, runnerbean?"

RayAnne's best guess at translation is that the guy isn't exactly *hot* in his *hotpants*—and is skinny besides.

RayAnne ventures, "Who . . . ?"

"Purse seiner," she spits the words, adding, "and fucking wanker."

RayAnne hopes Ellie might be less colorful with adjectives during the interview since they'll need footage that can actually air.

"Wanker," Cassi repeats the word, savoring it. They watch as the wanker runs his hand repeatedly through his hair. They both look from the wiry guy to wiry Ellie, also raking her scalp.

Ellie sees RayAnne's look, admits the now obvious. "Yeah, my brother."

"Right." To this RayAnne can relate. "Brothers."

. . .

As usual, Cassi's done her research, but RayAnne already knows the pros and cons of purse seining versus pole fishing. Purse seining, which brings in larger hauls, is lucrative but ultimately not sustainable. Seine fishing can scoop up an entire school of skipjack along with any other species swimming among them: sharks, grouper, squid. Not to mention the unreported legions of dolphins and sea turtles that perish in fishing nets. RayAnne had grown even more interested in fishing ecology upon learning Gran's will left a decent chunk to Seastainable Chef, an organization of restauranteurs sourcing their seafood from best-practice fisheries. Another large sum went to a pollinator support organization called SurvHive.

What was left went to RayAnne and Ky. Gran owned only a few significant possessions: a sweet painting of bottles by the prewar Italian minimalist Giorgio Morandi (now insured and hanging in RayAnne's bedroom) and a pair of sculptural iron bowls always on the front hall tables in Gran's houses, used as catch-alls for car keys and change, heavy enough they were sometimes used as doorstops, often played with by Ky, who was happy enough to inherit them. Until the reading of Gran's will, no one would have ever guessed they'd been made by a dead Japanese sculptor named Noguchi and were worth a fortune.

Gran's generous endowments piqued RayAnne's curiosity. Here was a passionate side of Dot Dahl she knew little of. She's since signed up for memberships with both organizations herself and has pushed to find ways to feature them on the show. Now that it's taking off, now that *Fishing!* has high ratings, it may become something people pay attention to, become a platform for change. It was through Seastainable Chef that they'd been able to track down one of the few pole line fishers in New Zealand, and possibly the only female tuna boat captain in the country. RayAnne looks up to see Ellie steadily giving her brother the finger as they pass the *Hummer,* thinking, *Gran would love her.*

. . .

The *Virago* travels at speed over open sea toward the fishing grounds. Now that they are underway, the crew have set to work repairing equipment, affixing fresh hooks to lines, scooping baitfish from a live well into buckets. They're gearing up, caffeinated, anticipating. As they reach designated waters, the morning sun breaks hotly from behind a cloud as if in ambush. Cassi pulls sunproof gear from her pack and the crew watches with open amusement as she slathers sunscreen and wriggles into her UV coveralls. Thanks to Rangi, Cassi's pith-helmet-sunhat is now mounted with a GoPro, as well as a boingy wire spring with a tiny propeller, which he claims is a wind gauge but looks decidedly like mischief.

The engines throttle down and the *Virago* bucks gracefully forward on its own wake before settling. The crew shift into position, each armed with an eight-foot rod.

"Fun's about to start." Captain Ellie looks up from the sonar where she's been tracking a school of tuna. As they begin to close the distance, she tosses RayAnne a helmet with a clear, flip-down visor.

RayAnne looks at it. "Really?" Then notices everyone is putting them on.

Ellie scans the screen. "Time for the shitshow."

"Shitshow?"

"Chrissake," Ellie gives her a look, "you've never fished skipjack?"

"Well, no . . ." She barely has her chinstrap secured before being handed a bucket wriggling with live baitfish. The crew are braced belly up to the bow rail, poles rigged with short lines and tackled with smooth, barbless hooks. They all watch Ellie watch her sonar screen. Another of the crew, also with a bucket of bait, edges a bit too close for comfort and instructs RayAnne, "When Cappy thumbs up, we bait. Any chance you're a sou-pah?"

When she realizes he's said *southpaw,* she looks at her left hand. "Yes."

"Mean as. I'll toss starboard. You take port."

"*Mean as*? What . . . I'm not sure?"

"Ah, Christ, you're a *Yank*? *Mean as* means great, hunky dory."

"Okay."

Water jets lining the forward gunwales are activated to rough the surface. To her questioning look, the guy explains, "The skipjack think it's food." He shoos RayAnne to the bow. Her cue to start tossing bait.

"Stay clear of those poles!"

There is something about sticking her hand in a tub of live bait—a mosh pit of minnows. She never used to be squeamish about such things; it's just that since Gran, she's become so aware of the frailness of living creatures and thinks too much about skin—such a ridiculously frail membrane between life and death. Lately she finds herself hurrying past the butcher case at the supermarket, unable to square the sight of red meat—of muscle straining against plastic wrap—as food.

Many of the slimy baitfish escape her hand before she can toss them overboard. After they fall to the deck, she watches several skid across into the stomp and shuffle of gumboots worn by the crew. The next handful she hurls overboard with all her might, reckoning that if thrown far enough, surely some might escape. *Go, little fishes!*

At a signal from Ellie, the crew begin whacking the surface with their poles to propel the hooks downward to the teeming school. Crew on each side of the bow smack the water repeatedly. When the skipjack are snagged, the poles are jerked up and back with enough force to dislodge the fish from its hook. The skipjack thuds to the deck where it slips and slides, flopping along to the guttered middeck. There, an open hatch reveals another crew member below, waiting to dispatch and gut the fish before fitting the carcasses into shallow crates of pebbled ice. Once filled, the crates will be pushed into the refrigerated hold. Ellie, out of the wheelhouse now, scrutinizes each fish, scooping up any that look undersized, tossing them overboard.

Fish are flying aloft like so many silvery projectiles, eight-foot poles whacking every which way. They're coming faster now. Everything ramps up a notch, adrenaline kicks in. She winces, ducks.

Rangi is a blur in the periphery, clutching his handheld. Chad is helping steady-cammed Rongo to stay upright, negotiating the slippery deck while dodging flying tuna. RayAnne is barely even tossing bait anymore. She watches one GoPro get repeatedly smacked by fish. If the camera survives it might have some amazing, if slimy shots. The only safe spot on the boat, it seems, is the wheelhouse, where Cassi has retreated. Captain Mann skids along the deck, occasionally stopping long enough to shout something at the crew, or urge RayAnne, "Bait!"

The scene is chaos. The crew haul and whoop. Many of the skipjack flopping around the deck are bleeding; the hooks may be barbless but are hardly benign. RayAnne throws her handfuls of baitfish as if trying to strike out a batter.

In twenty minutes, the deck is ankle-deep in fish. After another ten minutes, the pace slows and RayAnne takes a breath, realizing how noisy it's all been only when the din subsides. It truly has been a fishing frenzy. The crew are now talking instead of shouting. It appears the school is moving into the depths. In their wake, everyone is out of breath, sweaty and slick from salt spray and slime. The crew seem disappointed at the size of the catch. A few more shift to below deck to help gut and stack. Three keep fishing, but hits are fewer and farther apart.

Captain Ellie climbs back into the wheelhouse, checks the sonar, and her voice crackles to on the speaker, "Show's over, boys and girls."

The last rods are lifted. Once the sprayers lining the bow are turned off, Rongo pulls up the underwater camera. The vessel slowly swerves right and aims in the direction they've come from, the green horizon of land. Ellie engages the throttle and the speed creates enough wind to lessen the reek of blood and fish, reviving RayAnne but not quite settling her stomach. The fishing may be over, but the work isn't. Below deck, '80s rock blares where half the crew are jammed in, sorting and gutting. The icemaker rumbles and spews. On deck, the balance of the crew repair equipment, change out lines, replace bent hooks, stow poles, hang helmets, light cigarettes.

Back at the wharf, offloading commences the instant *Virago* is docked. More shouting as pallets of iced fish are winched from the hold and stacked near where Ellie's refrigerated van is backed down to the wharf. The captain is front and center lifting and loading forty-pound trays as if they are empty drawers, making some of the guys look like slackers.

Rangi takes down cameras they've mounted to the mast and wheelhouse, assessing damage. The deck is a holy mess, with sun now heating up the sluice of fish slime, chum, and blood. Just as RayAnne is thinking she should find some shade and a place to sit, one of the crew hands her a power hose and a squeegee.

"Not above a bit of swabbing, are ya?" He speaks without removing the wet Marlboro wedged in his teeth.

She gulps bile. "'Course not."

When he turns his back, she sticks her tongue out at him. Hearing a snort from above, she looks up to see Rangi grinning, his camera trained on her.

"Hey!"

"C'mon, give us a swab then."

"Sure," she says. "How's this?" She sprays back and forth across the deck a few times before raising the hose to spray a neat line across Rangi's knees.

To his credit he does not move or flinch. "That'll do me, thanks."

She finishes the deck with barely time to hose down her shins and shoes and rinse the slime off her arms before the pumps are turned off and the water cuts to a trickle.

"Time to roll!"

The shout is meant for her. Cassi's had the idea that RayAnne and Rangi ride along with Ellie on her rounds in the van. She doesn't just skipper the *Virago*. She delivers its daily catch.

When RayAnne climbs in the front seat, Ellie gives her such a look RayAnne nearly backs out. "Sorry, I thought . . . Cassi said you wouldn't mind the company."

"Did she?"

Rangi, climbing in behind, has to fold himself like origami to fit in the seat next to the compressor.

"You too?" Ellie turns.

"Ignore me. You'll barely know I'm here." It's meant to be a joke, but Ellie is stony-faced. "You want to film me delivering fish?"

Rangi nods enthusiastically, giving her his best, double-dimpled smile.

"Have it your way." The captain shoves the vehicle into gear and roars up the ramp and rocks onto the road, hitting it at speed. Ellie opens her window, cranks the radio to a metal station, and steers with one finger while a thumb taps a nervous beat on the wheel. She takes Rangi literally, ignoring him as she drives on, also barely registering RayAnne.

Ellie passes cars as though the van is an ambulance. They arrive at the loading dock of the fish market just as action is winding down for the morning. The broker she usually sells to is in his truck and about to pull away. "Goddammit." She guns the van and cuts him off.

The man slides out of his cab, red-faced. "Taking your sweet time today, Miss Nibbs."

Ellie is out of the van, helping the man open his hatch. Rather than explain her lateness, she merely nods at the van and RayAnne and Rangi, the culprits.

"Oh, boy, we're in the shit now, aren't we, Rangi?"

"Is that a rhetorical question?"

While they're not entirely responsible for the delay (Ken the milk tanker driver did his part), RayAnne and crew are the reason Ellie is behind schedule.

Rangi unfolds himself and hops out to help, taking the tray straight from Ellie's hands, insisting on doing the rest. "Least I can do, Cappy. It's our cock-up."

He shifts a dozen trays, giving Ellie the chance to soothe her ruffled fishmonger.

The guy thaws a bit, at least seems to, while he and Ellie watch Rangi load. "You might take on a few more like this bloke, Ellie."

When they climb back in the van, Ellie lets out a great sigh of relief before turning on RayAnne.

"You nearly cost me half my catch."

"I *know*, and honestly, I'm so—"

"Don't say it."

"Mea culpa?"

"Great." Ellie snorts. "What are you, Catholic?" She grinds the van into reverse.

Their next stop is the alley entrance of a bayside restaurant, gulls wheeling and screaming above in the slice of sky. Ellie turns to Rangi, "You stay in the van."

She does not wait for a response, just climbs out, and leaving the radio blaring, yanks a tray from the back and hauls it into the entrance.

Once Ellie's out of sight, RayAnne turns the radio down and pivots.

"Maybe this wasn't the best idea."

Rangi's squinting into his handheld. "Meh. You never know what you'll get."

They can see into the kitchen hall now, lined with crates of produce and sacks of potatoes and onions; at a big open cold chest Ellie deposits the fish. Once outside she dumps the excess ice, grabs a second tray, and repeats the process again, this time joined by a tall man wiping hands on his apron and looking over the fish. They exchange a few words, the guy shaking his head, not looking pleased.

Back in the van she turns to address them both. “Not only were we late to market, the load is light because we didn’t get out in time for peak fishing, so I won’t be able to fill out every order. Some disappointed customers today.”

RayAnne shrinks slightly. “Again, we’re really so—”

“Don’t.”

“Right.”

They set out for the next delivery.

RayAnne hasn’t seen Ellie take a drink or bite all day, so reasoning hunger might be exacerbating her mood, she digs in her pack to offer up an energy bar, which is flatly refused. Seemingly, Captain Ellie is fueled by air, like one of those tenacious little plants everyone has on their fridge.

“You sure?”

“Yup.”

“Right.” RayAnne turns. “Rangi?”

He accepts the bar, his eyes practically misting in gratitude.

The next four restaurant stops are replays of the first. Finally, all the fish are delivered. They are now thirty miles from the wharf and it promises to be a long ride back. Rangi, out of battery, puts the camera down, pulls his hat over his eyes, and in minutes is drooping and breathing like a bear. RayAnne cannot judge whether they have gathered enough footage for a decent segment, but considering the day so far, any opportunity for a sit-down interview with Ellie seems slim. She’d be justified in refusing, given their late start and what RayAnne and crew have already cost her.

RayAnne might as well risk getting her head bitten off to ask a few questions, take some mental notes, and maybe record a version of her observations to lay over the morning's B-roll. As well, she could ask someone at Seastainable Chef for commentary about the role suppliers like Ellie Mann play. There's plenty RayAnne is curious about, and since there's nothing to lose, she dives in.

"Why'd you decide to get into commercial fishing?" As far as RayAnne can tell, it's a pretty harsh endeavor, the *Virago*'s ornery crew aside.

"Decide?" Ellie scoffs. "Makes it sound like a choice. Who in their right mind would choose this?"

"Fair enough." RayAnne rephrases the question. "*How'd* you get into it?"

"Our people have been fishing these waters for three generations. Granddad Bert built a good business, had a fleet of six trawlers, a half-interest in a little cannery up the coast, and a primo stall at the Auckland Fish Market."

"So a family business."

"Then our dad ran it, until he fucked off to Australia with a *dancer.*" Ellie makes air quotes. "Our mum took over for a while, but it was too much, so she ended up leasing out the boats. My brother and I took over when I was nineteen, after I just started uni and Jack graduated high school. By then the fleet was arse-deep in debt. All that was left was a pair of trawlers mortgaged to the gills."

"Oh."

"Turned out the old wanker still held all the deeds, sold off three trawlers behind our backs before we even caught on."

"Oh." Ellie's dad makes Big Rick seem like an eagle scout. "You still in touch?"

"Haven't seen him in twenty-five years. Not sure I'd recognize him." Ellie turns and makes eye contact, a first. RayAnne resists the urge to lay a hand on the woman's arm, sensing she is not, as Big Rick would say, the touchy-feely type.

She suddenly feels a prickle of guilt for how she's avoided

her own father, who is, after all, grieving like the rest of them. Albeit in his own special way, which means latching on to the next woman in his path. No real details yet on who this one is, but that's the latest rumor according to Ky.

It's entirely possible that RayAnne has conditioned herself to remember only her father's worst behaviors, conveniently forgetting how he's always generous, and always there, for anyone, whenever things go south. He's even kind to Gran's little rat dog, Trinket, now his.

"What were you going to study?" RayAnne asks. "At uni?"

"Journalism."

"Yeah? That's what I was going for."

"But you were in sport fishing?"

"Sidetracked into it. Long story. I was my dad's driver on the circuit one summer after his license was suspended."

"Drunk driving?"

RayAnne is supposed to be the one asking questions, but fair is fair. "My Gran paid me to keep an eye on him, and since I was there and liked to fish, I entered a few tourneys. Had some beginner's luck, and the prize money was good . . . so, went again the next year."

"But school?"

RayAnne shakes her head. "Barely graduated. Besides, by the end of my senior year, *newspaper reporter* was listed as the second-worst career prospect for new grads. How about you, Ellie?"

"I was going in for broadcast. Investigative reporting—take down the bad guys." Ellie's laugh is bitter. "Talk about naive."

"Oh, I dunno. I can see it." RayAnne can totally picture Ellie grinding somebody up in an interview.

"And look at me now."

"What?" RayAnne takes the comment literally. "So you're a first-class skipper who employs a bunch of people and feeds a bunch more. And probably gives up a lot of income in order to do it sustainably."

"Don't butter me up. I'm unbutteruppable."

"Yeah, I can see that. Listen. My grandmother, who just died, left a good chunk of her savings to Seastainable Chef because she believed in people like you."

"Oh shit. Your grandmother? I'm so sor—"

RayAnne, who doesn't normally interrupt, does. "She'd be so psyched I'm doing this with you right now."

"No . . ."

"Yes. And I can see how you'd have made a great reporter, but c'mon, you're a hell of a tuna boat captain. And to people like my Gran, you're a hero."

"Hero?" A smile cracks Ellie's face. "Get out."

"Plus, you're pretty funny."

"Just not fun."

"I wouldn't say that." RayAnne forgets herself and soft-smacks Ellie's arm.

"Maybe," Ellie shrugs, "when the bitch switch is turned off."

"Well, seems it's off now. Listen, we're not gonna press you on an interview. I see now how busy this operation is. We've taken up enough of your time."

"But if you did . . . what sorts of stuff would you ask? It's not like anyone's ever interviewed me before."

There'd been a list of questions she'd meant to read over breakfast, but breakfast hadn't happened—the milk tanker had. "I guess . . . *I'd* want to know what it was like, you being so young getting into it. How many women were out fishing back then?"

"Here? Thirty years ago? Exactly one, moi, 'lady fisherman.' I still get called that. Among other things. My favorite is 'the hooker.'"

"That's got a ring to it. Has it gotten any better?"

"Some. A few younger gals are out here these days. And lot of the old buggers have carked it by now, so yeah. Half the younger guys are chips off the old block, but better at keeping their mouths shut. And by now it's obvious I'm not going away. It's fair to say a few even respect me, sort of."

"Back then, what was the worst of it?"

"A bloody laundry list," Ellie sighs. "What wears you down though is the small stuff—the power-play nonsense, verbal dick-shaking, like the fisheries inspectors who fined me for my catch being a nano overweight, when they let the guys off all the time, then would offer to let it go in exchange for a gobby—"

"Gobby?"

Ellie makes the international tongue-in-cheek gesture for blow job.

"Eew, gawd!"

"Then tripled my fine when I refused. My boat was very frequently inspected . . . stories from the trenches, right? I imagine you have your own."

"Some. Having my dad on the circuit meant it wasn't as bad as it might've been." There were advantages in having Big Rick around. They'd actually been close in those days—a sort of team. She wasn't harassed too much, but he wasn't always there.

"I started dressing like one of the guys, wore mirrored sunglasses," says RayAnne. "If I had a dime for every time I was told to smile . . . well, you know the drill. Half the time I just kept my face in a book."

"I bet they hated that."

"That's a type for sure—but we're talking about you?"

"Right, fun and games." She ticks things off on her fingers: "Always being assigned the crappiest moorage on a dock; having my gear sabotaged; being harassed daily—that was a given."

"Sounds rough."

"Meh, the actual worst, more than the specific stuff, was just the overall *absurdity*—that by dint of being female I was some sort of threat—*that* was the worst. Actually worse than the attacks."

"Oh, no. Ellie . . ."

Ellie shakes her head, "Well, there were high points—I was

never raped!" She laughs. "It got around that I knew how to use a knife."

"Jesus."

Just as that settles in, RayAnne's phone rings. "It's Cassi, she'll be frantic." She fishes it from her pocket. "Hey, Cassi."

"How's *la capitane*? Her thong still riding?"

RayAnne and Ellie look at each other before cracking up.

"Sorry, Cass, you're on speakerphone."

"Oh shit." After a slice of silence Cassi says, "Where are you?"

They both chime at once, "On our way."

Back at the wharf they wave goodbye to Ellie. When she's out of earshot, RayAnne sighs, "Shame we didn't get an interview."

"Ha," Rangi says. "I'd say you got a stellar one. So busy yammering you didn't notice this?" He holds out a GoPro. "Right there taped to the dash? I got the entire drive to the wharf!"

"But you were asleep."

"Nap tactic works every time. Love it."

"You weren't asleep?"

"I was doing sound, woman. I even teared up at parts, and tough not to laugh by the end there, you had me in bits." He turns his viewfinder. "Here. Have a shufti at this."

Too famished and grubby to sit down in a restaurant among the civilized, they eat takeout in the vehicles. Fish and chips wouldn't have been RayAnne's first choice considering the morning; the smell of wrappers littering the Rover does nothing for the overall air quality. They all need showers.

RayAnne rolls down the window and dog-noses out to the breeze. On the horizon, a few more trawlers are coming in from farther fishing grounds. Nobody is talking. Cassi's dazed from too much sun, and Rangi is intent, his head no doubt full of edits. The hot midday air settles seaward to warp an illusion so the trawlers appear to float just above the water. RayAnne thinks about what Ellie's day-to-day must be like. Other than being physically taxing and dangerous as hell, to make a living fishing depends on the health of the waters, weather in a changing climate, the state of the boat and equipment, and competency of the crew. Kudos to her for sticking it out. In her few hours aboard the *Virago,* RayAnne has learned pole fishing is not for the faint of heart and certainly not for the lazy. She'll remember Ellie Mann each time she opens a can of tuna.

It's more than a year since RayAnne walked away from pro fishing, not that there's any comparison. When people asked why she quit, she never said, "Loneliness," and more often joked, "So I could join a book club" or "I wanted a dog," which are essentially the same answer.

It had been sheer luck to stumble into the show. RayAnne knows in her gut that what she and Cassi are doing is worthwhile, and who knows? *Fishing!* may even turn into something. Gran certainly thought so or she wouldn't have made such a stink, insisting RayAnne promise to give it "a real whack."

RayAnne is whacking, daily: every segment tackled is a test passed; every next guest could be hit or miss; interviews can soar or sour. The best advice RayAnne has gotten has been the simplest: *Forget it's television. Pretend you're having a beer with a friend.* Big Rick can be quite practical sometimes.

At a book event, one of her favorite writers was asked why she wrote the stories she did. The writer confessed being completely selfish, saying, "I'm simply writing the stories I'd like to read." Which is exactly what RayAnne is doing with the show, hoping to make it into something she'd watch herself.

New Zealand is paradise. The rattiest roadside here is practically a postcard compared to Minneapolis, where scabby snowbanks and lip-cracking wind are the harbingers of late February. The road swerves inland into a dense green woods with the sort of plants only ever glimpsed in greenhouses back home, where this time of year people loiter in the houseplant sections at IKEA just for the chlorophyll fix. RayAnne closes her eyes and takes in slow breaths, inhaling the greenness.

After a few minutes, the salt smell returns and she opens her eyes to see they are back paralleling the water, nearing a beach dotted with picnickers. Pods of teens loiter on the sand while families and oldsters shelter in the shade of trees. At the shore a fleet of tiny sailing skiffs are being launched to set off in a regatta. The boats are skippered by little kids in blue windbreakers.

"They're called Sea Scouts," Rangi explains. "Like your . . . whadya call 'em? Club scouts?"

"Cub scouts. You breed tiny sailors here?"

"Yeah. You have your woods and Smokey Bear, we've got pots of ocean. Kids here gotta learn the water."

Needs must, as the Brits say. Lately RayAnne has been reading her way through the books of dead English authors Gran left for her.

Gran loved making lists. Lists she could manage—suicide notes, not so much. Writing did not come easily to Dot Dahl, making RayAnne wonder if her own unease with writing might be genetic. Years ago Gran abandoned written greetings and condolence notes altogether, even Christmas cards, choosing to send edibles instead—some confection befitting the occasion to avoid writing the predictable, canned words. Email horrified her.

"It goes *where*? What cloud?"

Gran sent madeleines to the bereft and grieving; colorful macaroons for celebrations and anniversaries and new babies; ginger merengues for post-ops and get-wells. Major upheavals and tragedies warranted a Pavlova. In no instance would she ever send anything so pedestrian as a casserole or, god forbid, soup.

In addition to preparing and freezing her family's favorite dishes in the days prior to topping herself, Gran had purchased gift cards for a St. Paul bookstore, leaving them with lists of books propped on the dining room table. Perhaps knowing that marzipan and cheddar-chive potatoes alone would not be enough,

Gran, running out of energy and time to impart much of herself, had chosen a few dozen wise authors who might carry on for her.

For Big Rick, Gran chose a number of adventure-adversity stories like *The Perfect Storm, Into the Wild,* Cormac McCarthy's *The Road,* and slyly slipping in women's titles like *Out of Africa* and Beryl Markham's *West with the Night*; a biography of Amelia Earhart and a novel about nurses in the Boer War. *The Handmaid's Tale* was definite commentary. For Ky, Gran offered a mixed bag of Joseph Campbell and lots of Steinbeck and poetry by women. Calvin and Hobbes. RayAnne was surprised to see *Fight Club* on his list, but that was Gran. "Never typecast a type," she'd say. *The Road* was also on Ky's list. Bernadette's books included relatable male characters who weren't bastards: *A Gentleman in Moscow*; the novel version of *Mr. Smith Goes to Washington*. A few titles addressed Bernadette's personal causes in historical context, such as *The Cider House Rules*. Bernadette wondered over the inclusion of *Shackleton's Voyage*. And again, *The Road,* which Dot hadn't even liked herself, claiming it physically pained her to follow along next to a hungry kid. RayAnne's list included a dozen novels by undervalued British women novelists of the twentieth century—and *The Road*. They had to wonder if Dot Dahl imagined her bereaved family would bond over a dystopian trudge into the gray future? Perhaps she was hoping to distract them with a story more grim than their own?

They'll never know.

Gran had directed them to meet sometime before Christmas at the bookstore, to trade lists and have the books wrapped—basically, to do her holiday shopping for her. "Posthumously bossy," said Ky. "I like it."

They found themselves reunited on a snowy Saturday in the bookstore, weaving among stacks, standing in line for the gift-wrapping table with armfuls of books. They went out for coffee afterward to meet Ingrid, the twins, and Hal at Bread and Chocolate, where they seemed like any large family, shedding jackets and parcels into a pile, talking over Christmas music at a long table.

RayAnne suspected that this was Gran's way of showing them what post-Dot might be like for the family. Bernadette and Big Rick, if not friendly, were at least civil; he was sober by then. They all talked about the upcoming holiday. They grilled Hal, the newcomer, giving him a good-natured hazing. *Welcome to the Dahl House.* And for the first time in a long time, they laughed.

In the front seat of the Rover, Cassi, revived, is downright animated. She and Rangi are tossing around ideas for bookending interviews with an intro-to-New-Zealand-slang tutorial for Americans.

"RayAnne? Whadya think?"

"Nice." It is a good idea, but all she can think about is a shower.

She screws in earbuds and pulls up the playlist Hal sent the night before, *Songs for a Homesick Hottie*. Indeed, scanning the list she wonders if the selections are meant to induce homesickness, because Hal has pulled together favorites by Minnesota musicians: the Replacements singing "Skyway"; the Suburbs' "Love Is the Law"; her favorite Owls tune, "Air." He's included songs by Dessa, Har Mar Superstar, Prince, and a Jeremy Messersmith tune in which everybody gets a kitten (silly, but it makes her miss Hal even more). The scenery ticks by in blurs while she listens. Trip Shakespeare's "Snow Days" reminds her that winter is waiting for her, that she should breathe in the warmth and humidity while she's able. Nearing the town where they'll be staying, New Plymouth, she nods along to "Raspberry Beret." Having never heard of the band Ahem, their song "Sunspots" is a sweet surprise.

Once checked in to their rooms, they scatter like roaches for showers.

An hour later they meet in Chad's room to watch the dailies

and see what might work for the segment. They edit down the files to a reasonable size for Cassi to send along with notations to Billy, the only editor at WYOY trusted to weave raw footage into the sort of punchy, fast-paced segments that have become the signature of *Fishing!* Team Tripod are making his work easier, having clearly done their homework by watching some of the previous season's best-of segments. They get it and seem to know exactly what to capture.

They huddle around the monitor and laptop, all business. Cassi has her tablet fired up, furiously typing notes and directions for Billy.

RayAnne cringes at the shots of herself flinging feeder bait.

"We can edit that," Cassi says to Rongo. "She's making a weird face for most of this bit."

"That bucket wasn't exactly aromatic," RayAnne balks.

Chad leans in. "You don't think she looks angry?"

"You're talking about me as if I'm not in the room." RayAnne crosses her arms.

They watch the candid conversation in the van between RayAnne and Ellie. Cassi keeps nodding. "Perfect—just the sort of stuff viewers have been responding best to, when RayAnne relaxes enough to be herself."

"Again, I am right here." RayAnne stands.

Three different camera angles capture the moments before and during the fishing frenzy; the camera inside the wheelhouse is trained on the captain, looking intent while doing a number of things at once—checking readouts, watching the horizon, and listening to the shore report, not to mention keeping track of her crew and the five extra bodies on her boat.

"Would it kill her to smile?" Cassi says.

Chad sniffs. "That boat's not called *Virago* for nothing."

"Why? Does *Virago* mean pissy captain?" Rangi ventures.

"*Harridan* would be the proper definition," Chad adds.

"Hey," RayAnne says, "if Ellie was a guy and was acting

exactly the same way, would you be on him for being intense? What makes you think she's angry? Maybe she's just doing her job?"

They go still, looking at her like an interrupted herd of deer.

After a beat, Rangi agrees. "Point."

"Okaaay . . . ," Chad says carefully.

"Got it," says Rongo. "You all right?"

"Excuse me?"

"Nothing, it's just . . ."

There are over two hours of video to rake through, including the shots harvested from the underwater camera and those affixed to the foremast and the drone footage. "You don't need me to go over all of this," RayAnne says.

"We don't. Take a break." Cassi looks at her watch. "Reservation for dinner is six-thirty. Across the street. Mabel's."

"Don't wait for me," RayAnne says. "I may grab my own dinner."

"Okay. Sure. Whatever."

As she leaves the room, she feels eyes on her. Before the door closes she can hear Chad mumble, "Hangry?"

"Something," answers Cassi.

After helping herself to a map of the highlights of New Plymouth, RayAnne wanders a street of interesting-looking galleries and museums, but by the time she gets to Puke Ariki with its woven metal facade, it's closed. After walking along the waterfront to a park, she stands awhile on the fringes where some sort of festival or market is winding down, volunteers cleaning up. A number of boys watch, looking too young to drink as they pass a bottle. Turning away to leave, she slips, twisting her knee before regaining balance amid a waft of something putrid.

Of course she's stepped in vomit. Of course she has.

Two of the teens crack up, one pointing, "Lookit, she's stomped the chunder!"

RayAnne had packed exactly two pairs of shoes: her trainers, coated this morning with milk and then fish slime (now soaking in the hotel sink); and these, her favorite huaraches, now vomit smeared—or "chunder," as she's been so viscerally enlightened. RayAnne limps furiously down to the surf and steps in to let it rinse across her feet and ankles, coarse sand invading the spaces between her toes. The leather will be ruined by the salt water.

A woman walking her Pomeranian stops to ask, "You all right there, luv?"

"Oh yeah. Peachy." Greasy vomit floats to the surface.

"Goodness." The dog starts barking and the woman moves along.

She can smell barbeque. In spite of the vomit, she's starving. Making her way back to the hotel she passes one café after another where her wet shoes with their unappetizing squish with every step might not be appreciated. There are a few food trucks around, so she makes do with a sausage roll and ice cream cone.

Slammed by a wall of jet lag, she pinballs back to the hotel.

Kicking off her wet sandals she pads to the window and pulls the drapes. Sitting heavily, she weighs calling Hal to thank him for the playlist, but would she be able to string together a coherent sentence? Her phone decides for her, chiming in with its low battery warning. She paws around for her charger, but once it's located she stares stupidly at the wall outlet—its configuration of slots approximating a sad face, as if to say, "Sorry!"

She needs one of the adapters, which are in the electronics cases that are in Cassi's room, which might be number 22, or 23, or possibly 32?

Picking up the hotel phone she calls the front desk.

"Cassi Olson, please."

"One moment." After three moments, the woman is back. "Sorry, that line is busy."

"Okay. Can you just tell me her room number—I'll go knock on her door."

"Sorry, miss, I'm not allowed to give room numbers. I can leave a mess—"

"No, you see, we're traveling together . . ."

"Sorry, I still—"

"We're working together?"

"Again, ma'am, I'm so sorry. Is there anything I can do for you?"

"No. Wait! Do you have any electrical adapters . . . for American plugs?"

"There should be one in your room. One moment."

After four moments the desk clerk chirps back on. "Sorrrry," she says, sounding the opposite. "Any extra adapters are lent to guests at the moment."

"Great. Forget it." RayAnne puts down the receiver. She checks every outlet; none has an adaptor.

She falls back on the pillows, phone in hand. She must have left it on vibrate because not a minute passes and it hums in her hand to tell her again that the battery is low. The icon on the screen disappears and Gran's face frowns back at hers, crackling onto the screen.

She's wearing a visor, dressed for golf.

"No need to be rude."

"What?"

"To that desk clerk, you were curt with her."

"I was not."

"Goodness. Who woke up on the wrong side this morning?"

"How come you don't need battery power to show up on my phone?"

"My electric personality?"

"Ha. So, while you're in there, would you mind charging it with some . . . protoplasm, or whatever?"

"I think you mean *ecto*plasm, but this isn't Ghostbusters, sweetie."

"Wow, such a know-it-all."

"With death comes knowledge," Gran sighs.

"Yeah? How's that working out for you?"

Gran leans close as if to examine RayAnne for smudges. "You're quite the stinker today, young lady. You should never have eaten that sausage roll."

"Gran."

"On top of fish and chips for lunch? You're asking for it."

"So?"

Gran gives her the look she and Ky call "The Gran."

"There's one in the lower drawer."

"What?"

"Adaptor. Bedside table."

"Sure there is." She looks. There isn't.

When she turns to complain, her screen is completely black, Gran gone.

The second slumber she falls into is darker, limbo-esque. RayAnne wakes in roughly the same position she'd fallen asleep in, sunk into the memory foam so that she more or less must pry herself out of bed as from a presentation box. Her phone is dead. On a whim, she opens the bottom drawer, where there is indeed an adaptor.

"Where, again, are we going?" It seems they've been driving for hours.

Cassi looks up from the itinerary notes on her tablet. "Lake Taupō."

Rangi turns from the front seat. "You're gonna love it."

"If we actually get there, Rangi, which is more likely if you keep your eyes on the road. What's the name of this river we keep seeing?"

"Whanganui. The river of tears. Another legend."

"Whose tears?"

"Okay, first thing you gotta know is that mountains here are gods and warriors."

"You mean named for them?"

"More like the physical manifestation of or whatever. There's a lot of legends. This river—"

"The Whanga-what?"

"Whanganui. Was formed after an epic dustup between a couple of warriors."

"That were mountains?"

"You're catching on. Okay, so there were eight mountains, aka gods aka warriors. Pīhanga was the only female and apparently was pretty fit as mountains go. There were seven male mountains, Pūtauaki, Ngauruhoe, Tarawera, Tongariro, Ruapehu, and Taranaki."

"That's six," Cassi says.

"Bollocks—Tauhara! I always forget that one. Anyway, they all grew up together. Tauhara and the others became warriors, and eventually every one of 'em started giving Pīhanga the eye, looking for a wife."

"Because mountains . . ."

"Need sweet lovin' too. So Tongariro, bit of a piker, insisted that Pīhanga choose."

"But she . . . didn't want to choose?"

"Couldn't choose?" Cassi ventured.

"Bingo. So major battle, blah blah, one by one, each mountain got defeated by Tongariro until it was Taranaki's turn, and they were pretty evenly matched."

"Like you and Rongo?"

"Hardly. Anyway, the battle raged on until Pīhanga herself was almost destroyed. To spare her, Taranaki, being the decent bloke, conceded. Tongariro got the girl. Millennia passed with each of the vanquished mountains retreating and moving away: Ruapehu and Ngauruhoe went south. Tarawera, Tauhara, and Pūtauaki fucked off up north. Then there were Pīhanga's children."

"Cuz mountains . . . breed?"

"It's a legend, right? Sometimes mountains even cheat, because one of the kids, Panitahi, looked like the milkman's, which pissed off Tongariro no end. He laid a trap and caught the missus with Taranaki. Tongariro got so mad he shot his top off, as volcanos are known to do, and the crater he made became Lake Taupō. Taranaki nabbed his kid, Panitahi, and took off. All along the journey to the west coast they gouged a deep track." Rangi points to the river. "On the coast, a more hospitable mountain, Pouakai, I think, said, 'Oi, take a load off, mate' and took them in. It's a lot of names to keep straight, right? Anyway, that's where Taranaki beached, with Panitahi at his side."

"But how did the river—"

"I'm getting to that. Tongariro, realizing he'd lost everything, packed a sad and had a massive cry, his tears filling Taranaki's trail. And that, kiddies, is how the Whanganui became the Whanganui."

"Aw," Cassi says, "that's kind of sweet."

"Cried himself a river. But . . . ," Rangi considers Cassi a moment. "Why's it always 'sweet' when a man cries?"

RayAnne leans forward from the back seat. "When was the last time you cried?"

"Sunday." He bows his head and RayAnne is almost afraid he might cry right then. When she pats his arm, he takes a ragged breath. "When Mahoney got traded to Wales."

She pokes him.

"Ow!"

"Is that soccer, rugby, or football?" Cassi invariably needs to know everything.

He answers in a tone reserved for toddlers. "Rugby *is* football."

"Yes." Cassi files that away, as she does everything. "Of course."

. . .

They're on their way to Lake Taupō to interview Rebecca Horton, avid trout fisher, retired history teacher, and author of historical feminist fiction, which RayAnne did not realize was a genre. Her sleuthing protagonist, Melody Howell, is a suffragette fighting for the women's vote. New Zealand women got the vote in 1893, nearly three decades before the United States and Britain. Rebecca's third novel, *Elusive Melody*, is out to great reviews. RayAnne had started reading it the night before and could barely put the book down.

As they come into view of Lake Taupō, Cassi gets a text from Rebecca.

"Uh-oh. Looks like we won't get to fish."

"What?" RayAnne says. "I thought we were going out for lake trout?"

Cassi reads: "The wind's come up, it's too choppy . . . they won't be biting."

"Crud. Do we postpone?"

Cassi reads on. "Wants to cook you a trout lunch instead, promises the fish will be very fresh." Her phone pings a second time with a photo. "Look—the view from her veranda—you can see the boats keeling. We can interview her over lunch."

"Damn." RayAnne isn't all that comfortable with straight interviews.

"It'll be a breeze for the guys to set up, and we could all use an easy day after Captain Bligh."

Ms. Horton ("Becca, please!") turns out to be as bubbly and welcoming as Ellie Mann was not. RayAnne had somehow equated *author* with *frumpy* and *introvert*, but Becca exudes the frenetic energy of a teenager. Her auburn hair has silver wings lacquered into place and her lips gleam with fuchsia gloss. She wears an electric-blue apron over a vivid yellow tracksuit of the type rappers favor. Her trainers are incandescent orange.

When Chad fits her with a mic, she teases, "That tickles a bit, cheeky ranga!"

"What's a ranga?" Cassi asks.

Chad rolls his eyes.

"A ginger!" Becca laughs.

"No way." Cassi cracks up. "So that means Tripod is Rongo, Rangi, and Ranga!"

"Ha," Chad pretends to be good-natured about it. "*Ha.*"

The interior of Becca's modern house is as colorful as she is. The exception being the imagery hanging on the walls: etchings; enlarged black-and-white photos from the suffragettes' movement: women in action, marching, posing, arms linked in solidarity; speaking from pulpits, but also in handcuffs; some on the ground, beaten. A particularly disturbing image shows a hunger striker tied to a chair being force-fed with a rubber tube; another is skeletal, looking at the camera with sunken, haunted eyes, flickering yet with determination.

It's stunning, thinks RayAnne, what these women went through. Crass editorial cartoons depict the suffragettes as ugly spinsters, women abandoning homes and children, beleaguered husbands and crying babies left in their dust. A framed set of cartoons show women with their heads jammed in various contraptions to keep their mouths shut, or gagged. Without exception the women are portrayed as immoral, crazy, wanton, or even criminal.

"Jeez." Examining the wall, RayAnne's scalp prickles.

"Something, wasn't it?" Becca singsongs. "What these women went through. And even after their sacrifices there's women today that can't be bothered to show up at the polls."

In the dining room, Rongo is muttering about the lime green wall behind the table, saying, "It's bloody perfect."

"What is?"

"Green screen. You could totally key in whatever you want in post."

"Is that lingo for something?" Becca asks.

"Basically," Cassi explains, "it means the wall could act like a sort of big movie screen, with you and RayAnne sitting in front of it, and we could add in images later—some of your photographs of the suffragettes." Cassi points to one of three young women who have chained themselves to a pillar outside the House of Commons. "Your muses, the women you based Melody on could appear bigger than life."

"Oh. This is good, right?" Becca asks.

Rongo is chuffed. (RayAnne is pleased to have remembered the phrase.) All agree it's a great idea.

But first, there are fish to fry.

Becca's kitchen is large and flooded with soft light. When Rangi hangs a camera from the pot rack above the island, Becca claps, "Like a real cooking show!"

RayAnne is beginning to fidget. "Becca, you'll give me something to do? When I don't have a fishing pole to hold, I never know what to do with my hands."

"I've the perfect chore for you. Green beans. Washed, ready to snap. Just as soon as we take care of those two out on the deck."

RayAnne follows her out wide sliding doors. *Those two* are a pair of fat trout swimming in a galvanized tub. "Caught 'em this morning. After I heard the forecast, I dashed out early before the wind could pick up. Good thing, too. It's a rough ride out there now."

Rongo is focusing on the fish as Becca lifts it out. "This fella's a beaut, innut he?" She holds the trout to the camera before pinning him to the counter, apologizing, "Sorry, Charlie!" She picks up a steel kitchen mallet and dispatches Charlie with a resounding thwack to the skull. Cassi gasps. Chad goes still and unblinking. Rongo and Rangi, seasoned lensmen, stay glued to their eyepieces.

"Oh dear!" Becca laughs. "The looks on your faces! I should have warned you!"

Cassi backs up. "Okay . . . lemme, just . . . I'm gonna step out of frame here so you can finish . . ."

Becca makes to hand the mallet to RayAnne, who smiles while shaking her head. "Thanks, though."

"Just having you on! No one likes to kill them," Becca muses, "but it *is* much easier if you think about a certain somebody, say, an ex, or some naughty uncle, or the neighbor that chopped down the boxwood hedge . . ."

"I imagine it is kind of cathartic," RayAnne agrees, "but there isn't anyone I'm currently that angry with . . ."

Becca laughs. "Oh, usually any vile politician will do, and you Americans have no shortage of those . . ."

RayAnne watches the second trout taking his final laps, unaware of the fate awaiting him.

"Well, since you put it that way." She doesn't have to think too hard to come up with an office-holding grifter. RayAnne takes the mallet and scoops the second trout from the tub, pinning it to the counter to strike it such a blow that everyone is left open-mouthed. Rangi and Rongo pop up from behind their cameras like twin gophers, looking to each other.

"Goodness," Becca says. Now it's her turn to blink. "He's well carked, isn't he? I suppose you could say, the harder the whack . . ."

They are interrupted by Cassi's sudden, "Eeeow!"

Everyone turns in time to see her swat at her shirtfront, then hop away when something nearly lands on her shoe.

"Jays," she squeals, "is that . . . ?"

RayAnne swoops down and plucks up the offending article, tossing it to the tub but not before Cassi realizes it's a fish eye.

Cassi yelps.

"No biggie." RayAnne wipes her fingers on her jeans as Cassi beelines for the bathroom.

Now even more uncertain over what to do with her hands, RayAnne picks up the fillet knife, then quickly puts it down. "Oh, sorry. I'm just usually the one that dresses them."

"By all means," Becca says.

RayAnne makes quick work of gutting the fish, depositing the entrails into the bucket held by Becca. She turns back to the camera to demonstrate how to make the incisions along the dorsal fin. She butterflies the trout open and deftly removes the spine and pinbones. Becca watches with great interest.

RayAnne folds the fish closed like a book and tips its head back into place so that it looks like an intact fish, sleeping. "Voilà."

"Goodness, where'd you learn that?"

"My grandmother—she called it 'the boneless coup.'"

Once Charlie is filleted, RayAnne reaches for the second, singsonging, "Looks like it's Mitch's turn!"

Once they sit down to lunch, Rongo frames them on the green screen and Rangi works close-ups. For large men, they manage to be unobtrusive enough that RayAnne nearly forgets they're there.

In addition to the blackened trout and garlicky beans, Becca serves a citrus kumara salad. There are two opened bottles of New Zealand wine: a local rosé and a sauvignon blanc from Marlborough. She extols the virtues of the country's viticulture and the boom in wine exports, all while managing to down a full glass.

RayAnne takes a sip. "Tell us about your research. How'd you come up with the character of a sleuthing suffragette?"

"Mostly from old correspondence found in archives—letters sent to and from England where lots of women were in the movement as well, though Britain didn't get the vote for another three decades. Not for lack of trying."

"New Zealand was first? How'd that happen?"

"I think being away from the influences, so far out here in wop-wop, was an advantage."

"But you'd think they'd have been behind in some ways?"

"Oh, far from. You can say a lot about the colonists, but many coming here were forward-thinking. New Zealand settlers were better educated than that lot dumped in Australia."

"So settlers here . . ."

"Tended to land with vocations, trades; most were literate." Becca takes a drink.

"And the women?"

"By dint of being pioneers they'd have been more essential here than they'd have been back in Britain, more needed, if you will. They were scrappy settlers, toiling right alongside the men, so they earned a say in things. Imagine suggesting to some woman who's just sheared a dozen sheep that her opinion doesn't count?"

"Still holding the shears, like your rancher character Louise?" RayAnne laughs.

"Exactly! Some of the old letters and anecdotes suggested that women here had to be given suffrage if only to keep the peace."

"That does makes sense, but for everywhere else . . . ?"

"It literally took the Great War for women to prove they deserved the vote. They worked farms, munitions factories, mills; drove streetcars and trains; operated fishing fleets, hauling nets alongside old men pried out of their rocking chairs. Not to mention the war work, all those nurses shipped nearly to the Front, for heaven's sake, driving ambulances, being mechanics in the WRAF—all of that."

Becca is quite animated now, two distinct spots of high color on her cheeks. "Women kept it going. All the while raising the children." She pours herself another glass, shaking her head as if it must be done. "Yet there's still so much to do. I mean look at

America: here it is, 2020, and men sticking their noses in *birth control,* of all things . . ."

"Tell me," RayAnne steers the conversation back. "Your character Melody is a secret suffragette who exploits men's indiscretions and shady dealings, and in some cases even crimes—to further the cause. Is any of that based on fact?"

Becca waves a dismissive hand. "Fiction, so, you never know . . ."

"Class was a big advantage for your protagonist?"

"Women from all walks fought the good fight, but Melody understands the power of her social standing. She's the wallflower who is all ears at the right dinner parties, sitting on committees with knitting in her lap, looking for all the world like someone's harmless auntie."

"Yet her inner life is so passionate." RayAnne picks up the copy of *Elusive Melody*. "This is from chapter two—I keep coming back to it." She reads: "'Melody concentrated her anger into energy. She knew that if held within, it would burn her up; knew her emotion must be distilled into a flame for good, for progress, for change.'"

"Yes. So she casts a net to gather dirt on men of influence—in government, business, the church. Melody knew then what's true today—that power comes with a license to abuse it." Becca holds up a finger. "She never publicly names these men, never outs them."

"Can't blow her own cover, right?"

"No, and in protecting them gets everything she needs, which in the end, is the necessary influence, and the votes."

"Morality of the time seems to have been her most effective weapon." RayAnne reads on: "'Through a charity for "destitute women," Melody became acquainted with "women of the night" and madams, making generous "donations" to the charities in exchange for the names of their most esteemed and respected clients.'"

"Oh, yes. Melody's digging could put a bandicoot to shame. She knows who sired illegitimate children, who the nancies were, who kept a bit of fluff on the side or has a weakness for opium."

"Right, Melody's sister is married to a doctor, and together they rifle medical records for information on who is being treated for syphilis or suffers mental disorders," says RayAnne.

"Remember, this was during a time when a sound mind mattered. Men in power were held to a standard. Integrity meant something."

"Right, she doesn't keep *all* her discoveries secret—pedophiles and predators are fair game, civilian or clergy."

"No spoilers!"

"I just love this character," RayAnne laughs. She's had a bit of wine herself, because it would be rude to refuse a top-up. "She seems so real, so conflicted."

"I know!" Becca hiccups and fingertips fly to her lips. "Oh my!"

RayAnne laughs. "We can edit that out."

"Thank goodness." Toasting that, wine sloshes out onto Becca's hand.

She licks it.

RayAnne doesn't need Cassi making slashing gestures behind Becca's back to understand it's time to wind the interview to a conclusion.

"Real or fictional, Melody has some great adventures to take readers along on. And the next book in the series comes out in May, is that right?"

"Yes, *Dissonant Melody*."

"In which . . . ?"

"Melody's journey takes her back to London to lend a hand to the cause there. Along with her English comrades, she creates quite a-a shtorm."

RayAnne turns to Rangi's lens as if to address the audience. "And who doesn't love a good storm?" She winks before turning back. “Rebecca Horton, thank you so much for this time, opening your home to our crew, and what an inspiration! I just hope your book tour will bring you to Minnesota!”

“She was fun.” RayAnne stands at the curb outside Becca’s house watching the guys load. Any offers of help are only met with looks, because there is a method to the madness of getting gear into the van. Cassi is still inside, making coffee for Becca.

“We can edit out the swilling,” Rangi offers.

“Pissed as a chook by the end there,” Chad says.

“Did she really kiss you goodbye?” RayAnne asks.

“On the lips.” Chad turns pink.

Once back in Auckland, RayAnne goes shoe shopping, scoring an excellent pair of trainers that smell nothing like sour milk or fish, taking great pleasure in tossing the old ones.

After a solo lunch in the company of an advance reader’s copy of *Dissonant Melody,* RayAnne sits at the pier and watches gulls hang in the drafts, waiting for a human to drop a chip or bit of waffle cone, some greasy crumb. Occasionally two particularly bold gulls will swoop for the same morsel and the ensuing fracases are comical and awkward, the losing bird looking as if it is sulking, reminding her of the sole fight she’d had with Hal, which wasn’t really a fight, more like mutual pouting.

On a visit to his loft, she’d peered through a telescope aimed out the bank of windows toward the Mississippi. It was trained on an eagle’s nest, not far from the heron rookery. The nest resembled a river-snag of baseball bat–sized sticks and detritus, high in a treetop, looking as if it had been deposited by some biblical flood. Hal told her how the eagles terrorized the rookery, preying on the heron chicks. It seemed to RayAnne that an eagle might pick on something its own size but she supposed that’s not how survival works.

Watching, she thought of how every time she sees the news or Facebook it seems humans are acting more territorial, hackles up, as if their baser instincts are kicking in—survival mode. It wasn't just her—it's been in the air. Most everyone she knows seems to be finding it increasingly difficult to relax and just be when the future feels so uncertain.

She'd taken another look through the telescope. The nest wasn't neat, but she supposed curb appeal wasn't a priority either. The nest contained a bunch of coniferous greenery, the kind you place on graves at Christmastime with fake berries and ribbons printed with messages like *Missing you at this special time*. The eagle had incorporated this funeral spray into the nest's structure, along with garland, bits of yellow upholstery foam, and a filthy plaid shirt wound among the sticks, the whole shirt, sleeves and all. She had to laugh because it seemed as if the eagle was going for homey. Despite being decorated by a raptor, the nest did have a certain boho vibe.

When she pointed it out to Hal, he shrugged. "Killer bird need a crib too, babe." But he didn't look, just headed back to the kitchen.

He served dinner and watched her eat it while picking at his own. Afterward he cleared the table, then banged around the kitchen cleaning up. Was he usually that loud? As if she should be annoyed, considering she had a boyfriend who cooked *and* cleaned?

Once finished, he commenced making his own sort of nest on the couch, but on the far end, as if claiming territory. He seemed to be . . . not quite sulking but something.

"Heya." She sidled over a bit. He didn't sidle back. "Something I said?"

"Meh, more like something you didn't say."

RayAnne is not good at confrontation. She's awkward in conflict, has two modes: she lashes or turtles. Because disagreements upset her, probably for having grown up watching her parents gnaw and snarl at each other like understudies for *Who's Afraid of Virginia Woolf?*

"What didn't I say?!"

Both Hal's hands went up as if she'd pointed a knife. "Whoa. No need to go Lieutenant Ripley on me."

"Who?"

"Oh, my God. Did you not see *Alien*? Is that even possible?" Hal's hands fell to his sides.

RayAnne sputtered, "Well, no, so . . . wait, hang on. You were about to tell me what it was I did not say."

"More like what you keep not saying."

"Such as?" Her arms folded across her chest like crossing gates.

"Such as . . . 'Hey, big fella, need some help there in the kitchen?' Or, 'Hey, boyfriend, wanna make this . . . hotdish together?'" Hal, it seems, is also an awkward arguer, though his style is dopey humor while hers is high offense.

"You haven't noticed yet that I have zero kitchen skills?"

"No. Sort of." Hal shrugged. "But it seems intentional."

"Damn straight it's intentional. I'm personally hoping to make it to ninety without chaining myself to a stove."

"Isn't that a bit dramatic?"

She didn't answer.

"Oh . . . I see, it's a statement. Okay, that I can live with, knowing the score—that you're not going to help out in the kitchen. Good to know."

"Wait, now you're being . . ."

"What?" Hal turns, clearly unaware that he's being anything, not least of all passive aggressive or condescending. "I'm being what?"

They both sulked and for the next half-hour pretended to be checking phone messages, scrolling headlines, looking at Instagram. The cold slice of time of their first falling out (it hadn't quite qualified as an argument since it was actually the avoidance of one) became intolerable. RayAnne considered putting on her coat and seeing how that might go over. In the end, she caved, realizing she'd been a cow about not offering to help in the kitchen, yet not knowing how to explain.

Thing is, she would be up for playing along in the kitchen and participating in whatever Hal and his inner foodie get up to. Going to the farmers' market and chopping things side by side actually sounds kind of romantic. It's just that Gran was always trying to lure her into the kitchen life—that she might at least learn some basic skills, like peeling an apple. Who peels apples? But relenting and putting on an apron would seem like caving to Gran, and frankly RayAnne was still good and mad at her grandmother. She was, she knew, being wholly, utterly irrational. Even mean.

Rather than fess up, RayAnne simply edged closer to Hal on the couch ever so slowly, her fingers walking the last few inches toward him. Just when she was about to yank contritely on the hairs of his forearm, Hal spun toward her. He'd somehow fit the entire Roku remote sideways in his mouth, lips stretched around it in a maniacal grin.

She screamed. Then laughed until she fell off the couch, then had to bolt for the bathroom, having peed just a little.

When she came back he grabbed her. "Girl," he looked deeply into her eyes, "did you soil yourself?"

Once she recovered from that, she said, "I'm sorry if you're sorry."

"I'm sorry. I think."

She nudged close. "Wanna go marinate something?"

A half-hour later, nothing had gotten marinated, but they'd managed to stir the sheets on Hal's bed into a froth. They were heaped on the mattress like marionettes, Hal still wearing his sexy leather wrist brace and nothing else. They'd been in that sort of hurry.

She was staring at the ceiling, the back of her hand smoothing

Hal's chest hair. "So silky," she said languidly, "like a sable halter top . . ."

"Halter top? Thanks, Dahl—so much for my mojo. You can kiss this erection goodbye."

"I certainly will. You have another?"

"Not anymore."

And there they lay, heaving long, postcoital breaths. As happy as she'd ever been, RayAnne rolled, poised to say it, then changed her mind and the three small words dissolved in her still-opened mouth. What if he didn't feel a hundred percent exactly the same? She couldn't risk that. Could she? Instead, she said the next thing that needed saying.

"We have to learn how to be with each other. Especially when arguing."

"You got that right, Dahl."

The next morning she'd discovered why Hal didn't need an alarm clock—it was the first time she'd stayed over on a weeknight. In the predawn (7 a.m. on a Minnesota December morning) she found herself standing next to the bed, having leapt up at what sounded like the steel girders of Hal's building being wrung like some metal rag. Hal was stretching and smacking his lips as if to taste the day while RayAnne whimpered and spun, looking for something to shield herself with. "What is that?!"

"Hmm, that?" One of Hal's eyes fluttered open. "Crushers." The clash and clang and mechanical yowls from the scrap yard on the opposite bank of the Mississippi, amplified across the water. Hal squinted at the bedside clock. "Yup, right on time." He rolled and patted the bed for her to come back, then he saw RayAnne clutching a pair of snow boots to her naked body and snort-laughed.

Preferred mornings at Hal's were Sundays—his day off-off, meaning he unplugged from everything but his stereo. She would wake to the smell of coffee and pastry from the Czech bakery, the paper strewn as he winnowed it down to the essential sections of outdoor, travel, entertainment, and book review. They had breakfast in bed on Sundays and invariably ended up making love a second time, sometimes falling back to sleep amid crumbs and sections of the paper. RayAnne usually woke alone, to quiet, Hal having risen to take Rory for a run along the river or to walk to the co-op for ingredients for Sunday dinner.

He's that sort of domestic, the sort of guy people fall all over themselves to point out what a great father he would make. She's terrified the topic of children will come up at some stage—because it will. The inevitable conversation is like a distant cloud making its way like weather into their perfectly sunny relationship. No wonder she can't spit out the words *I love you*. Because how do you then tell the man you love that you don't want his—or anyone else's—baby?

Gran weighed in with a posthumous opinion while RayAnne dozed, interrupting her dream of Hal.

"He'd make a fine father," Gran said. "What is it young folks say now, a baby-daddy?"

"No one actually says that, Gran."

They'd had a version of this conversation regarding every previous boyfriend since college—the men Gran referred to as RayAnne's "Come and Gones."

"Gran, not all women feel compelled to produce some mini-me or mini-he."

"Maybe you don't. Yet. But he will. Let's not forget the size of men's egos." Gran looked wistful. "Speaking of size, is Hal?"

RayAnne exhaled. "Really? Are there no filters there in limbo or purgatory or wherever it is you're parked?"

Gran tisked. "Well, he's obviously able-bodied."

Able-bodied?

Gran was chewing the cuticle of her misshapen finger, indicating deep thought. "Perpetuation of the species, RayBean. Your generation can't just raise dogs."

3. BARGAINING

RayAnne's never seen anything like this valley, but since arriving in New Zealand she could say "I never . . ." a dozen times a day. Never has she encountered, as they had at the Asian grocery, the eye-watering reek of the durian fruit, smelling like a linebacker's socks. Finally, the inclusion of a clothespin in Dot's ingredient list for Durian Mooncake makes sense. Every new corner turned here is a potential thwack to the senses—some Technicolor/Surround Sound/Smell-O-Vision threatening to overload her capacity for awe.

As RayAnne takes video on her phone, she imagines the voice of Sir David Attenborough narrating the scenes. Until yesterday, she'd never seen kiwifruit hanging in bunches from woody vines like some testicle festival. Nor had she heard the insane sounds of a tui bird, not even in a zoo. The one perched near their window that morning sounded so much like a jammed cash register that RayAnne dreamt of being caught in the middle of a convenience store robbery (wherein she jumped on the diversion to stuff her pockets with chocolate bars—the good kind). When the gun-toting robber swung his loaded barrel from the hands-up clerk to RayAnne, shouting "Gotcha!" her eyes flew open, and there was the tui on the other side of the glass. It stopped making its cash register clang and began meowing like a kitten. Was it teasing her? It looked straight at RayAnne and rounded out its medley with the sound of a tin hammer bashing the keys of Schroeder's piano.

There was movement from the other bed and the pillow over Cassi's head lifted like a clamshell long enough for her to blearily offer, "You duct-tape that bugger's beak shut, you can have the entire day off." Knowing the offer to be hollow, RayAnne sighed and cranked open the window so that the bugger might be better heard.

It is *so* not a day off. She can only wish she was back in bed, being annoyed by some tropical bird, because sometime in the next five hours RayAnne is going to hang glide. For the show. Not because she dreams of soaring, but because one of the executive producers does, and has pounced on the notion of living vicariously through RayAnne as if she's some thrill puppet. The suggestion being that since RayAnne was being sent to the literal end of the Earth at great cost to the affiliate, she probably wouldn't mind flying off the top of a cliff. Since, you know, she was there.

Before agreeing, RayAnne had wanted to know—since hang gliding is neither in her job description nor her idea of leisure—what, besides hazard pay, was in it for her? She taps Cassi to double-check. "You told them I want to choose the next Location?"

"Yes!"

"And they've agreed it can be Norway?"

"Arctic Circle if you want. Sure, Norway—but to fish for what, herring?"

She has no idea what sort of fish are to be caught in Norway but wants to go because it's a chance to scatter more of Gran's ashes. For Gran, going back to visit her birthplace had been on her unfinished bucket list—the list RayAnne is now steward of, along with Gran's ashes. It may not be a proper paper list, but

RayAnne knows better than anyone what Dot Dahl's dreams were because the two of them talked every day, either by phone or on Skype, Gran going on pretty much nonstop about everything. It's possible RayAnne knew Dot's desires better than she knows her own.

Should it be any surprise to RayAnne that Gran's preferred venues for haunting are the screens of personal devices?

Well, not like flying off to Norway is going to happen anytime soon, but maybe sometime next season she'll be able sprinkle a handful of Dot around some fjord in her homeland. RayAnne idly wonders, once Gran's ashes are gone, will her visits stop as well? Will her pixels disperse for good? The notion gives her pause; then, that she's even entertaining the notion gives her pause. Jet lag. Right?

She shakes back into the moment. "What's wrong with fishing herring?"

"Not exactly exciting." Cassi shrugs.

"Well," RayAnne points up to the sky where hang gliders hang, defying gravity, "not like every segment should require signing wrongful death waivers."

"*Insurance* waivers."

"You know what I mean."

They are drinking coffee near the beach where the incoming kites land, Rangi explaining how, once RayAnne is airborne, the drones will follow along above and behind her, while Rongo shoots from below. The hang glider frame is already rigged with two GoPros. With a third attached to her helmet, they'll get all the footage they need.

Rangi rubs his hands together. "This'll be a blast."

For you. RayAnne looks to the distant peak where a number of people move like ants around the takeoff site. From here the kites resemble something you might decorate a cocktail with.

The pilot-passenger duo that has just landed nearby are

strapped together like conjoined twins. The passenger is unbuckling as if it's a competition. Once freed, she stumbles into nearby bushes and proceeds to quietly retch.

RayAnne turns to Rangi. "A blast?"

The puking woman continues puking but holds up a finger to indicate she'll only be a sec.

"See?" Chad ventures. "Tickety-boo."

"Why," RayAnne shakes her head, "is everyone so freakishly polite here?"

"Small island?" Chad says.

"And we're all stuck on it together?" Rongo ventures, eyeing Chad.

Rongo reminds RayAnne of Kyle. Her brother has always been the egger-onner, the inciter. The one that dares one to actions that result in consequences, while he himself seems always able to dodge them. Rongo may pose as the more mature twin, but RayAnne isn't so sure.

Another glider has launched.

"That looks so fun!" Cassi, clearly eager to hang glide herself, claps. "Doesn't it look amazing, Ray?"

RayAnne considers her. "How about this? How about *you* go—in the helmet and goggles no one would know you aren't me." RayAnne plucks at her T-shirt. "We just swap outfits and—"

"No can do, Ray." Cassi shakes her head. "Can't dupe viewers like that. Imagine if some troll caught the switch and posted about it. Besides, sponsors are counting on it."

"I can think of one sponsor that might not want to see me crash."

"But Hal would appreciate you perished for the program!"

"Very funny."

RayAnne had promised she'd give the show her all—promised Gran as much. And a promise is a promise, so there's that.

Rangi's nearly hopping with excitement. He turns to Rongo

and Chad. "You'll need to mic that chin strap to get any . . . um . . . of her—"

"Shrieks? Last words?" RayAnne's arms are crossed.

"You're a stitch. Ready set?"

She's barely nodded before they are all jammed in the van, bumping up the steep road to the takeoff point. As the van climbs, Cassi has the great idea that reading aloud the statistics on the rarity of hang gliding deaths might calm RayAnne, the numbers being, "*Really* low, in comparison to say, drownings, car accidents, or mass shootings."

They all look at RayAnne before swinging their gazes back to Cassi.

"Seriously. You have more chance of being struck by lightning than crashing."

RayAnne doesn't remember ever specifically promising Gran that she would do things that scare the crap out of her, but it does seem to have become a theme. And now she's among people who don't know her well enough to actually love her and who seem comfortable tossing her to the winds from the top of a mountain.

But then, if she does crash, how awful for them, because this crew of people she's found herself among are really all very nice, and, as she's discovering, nicely odd.

"Whoa!" Rangi is watching a video on his phone and is whispering to Chad.

"This dude? Took off in Switzerland with no harness at all! Oh my God, pilot has to hang onto him. Lookit, lookit, poor fucker hanging from the bar."

Cassi elbows Chad, whispering, "Geez, don't let her see that!"

"Don't worry, I don't want to see it."

Chad holds the phone out to RayAnne. "See, *this* muppet made it and he wasn't even strapped in! They forgot to clip his harness!"

"If it makes you feel better," Rangi reassures, "even if you do bust a bone or split your head open, we fix it for free!"

"We?"

"Us! New Zealand."

"Oh, that's very . . ."

"Socialized medicine, we call it."

Cassi and Chad embark on a conversation comparing health care systems. Chad launches, "The U.S. of bloody A.—most powerful country in the free world—can't suss out how to patch up a kid or dole out meds without bankrupting the family piggy?"

RayAnne tunes out by screwing in her earbuds. She used to engage in such conversations, but these days sees little point in flogging the issues with like-minded people—nothing gets accomplished besides everyone getting frothed up. RayAnne watches lips move but is decidedly elsewhere. It does seem lately that she feels less present. It's been noticed. On their last trip, there'd been a moment when Cassi had pulled her aside during a taping, looking her in the eye, asking, "Hello, you with us?"

"What do you mean?"

"You sort of disappear, as if you've gone somewhere else and we're left with just your . . . face."

Grief is its own country, the therapist had said.

And RayAnne is nothing if not a tourist these days.

She watches the scenery out the van window—strange foliage, ferns the size of men—glad for the music muffling the conversation.

They are at the top of the hill, out of the van. Beyond the parking lot is the broad platform, which had seemed so tiny from below but from here is clearly a ramp to infinity tipping into nothingness. Cassi, filling out and signing more waivers, elbows her.

"Who is your I.C.E.?"

"My what?"

Cassi sighs. "In Case of Emergency contact?"

Until recently it had been Gran; Big Rick had always been

too unreliable; Bernadette is too frequently out of the country with her mavens; and Kyle, in addition to being too Kyle, is too harried and beleaguered by the twins to be relied on. Listing Hal at this point seems presumptuous; becoming someone's emergency go-to is the sort of thing discussed up front. And of course, shouldn't it be someone with whom you've formally cemented a relationship somehow? Perhaps by declaring your love for them. Out loud?

Or the person you spend the most time with, which is what RayAnne settles on, turning to Cassi. "Well, considering we're halfway across the globe? During this trip, I'd say you're it."

In minutes RayAnne will be airborne. She's trying to listen in as a nearby pilot coaches his next passenger on safety. Her own pilot steps forward and offers a hand.

"Hiya, I'm Christopher."

She wipes her sweaty palm on her shirt before shaking his. "As in Robin?" He does look awfully young. "You're old enough to fly this thing, right?"

Christopher smiles as if he's not heard this tired joke a thousand times.

He has very nice hair. She would hate to throw up on it; perhaps she should apologize in advance in the event she does.

Christopher describes how they will be strapped together and shows her the ramp they will launch from, by running off of it. Once she is clipped into the funny apron-thingy, they make a few practice runs on the flat area near the cars. This she can do—start off on the same foot as he does and run together like tag-teaming in a two-legged race. "It's important," he says, "that you do not stop once we start running." He repeats this. Since Christopher Robin isn't much taller, their strides are well matched: they complete three ten-yard dashes. Thumbs-up. Easy peasy.

Piece of cake.

"Between the wind and helmets, it can be hard to hear," he

tells her, demonstrating shoulder taps—one for yes, two for no. "Three quick ones like this, for *emergency.*"

"What sort of emergency?" RayAnne laughs nervously, "A bathroom emergency?"

In a parental tone, Christopher says, "You'll be grand." He actually seems convinced. Chad checks her earpiece and clips a tiny mic to the chinstrap of her helmet. The kite is made of a thin, nearly translucent fabric no thicker than her high-tech rain jacket—a garment that folds to the size of a brownie—and this is what will keep their three hundred pounds of combined weight aloft? Even with a knotted stomach, food analogies abound.

Straps are checked and double-checked. And then she and Christopher Robin are at the starting mark at the back of the platform, ready to run and tip over into the sky.

It will be just like running off a dock and into a lake. Something she's done hundreds of times. RayAnne takes a deep breath. There would be some trick to not freaking out—some life hack Bernadette always has loads of, but her mother isn't here. If she was, she'd insist it has to do with breath and breathing or becoming one with the kite or the sky. *Be the kite.*

She grips the flimsy aluminum frame of the rig. Or maybe it's titanium? A girl can hope. RayAnne is not going to be the kite. She only wants that the kite be the kite—be its best kite. Straps are checked a second and third time. In front of them is the ramp they will run down, and beyond that the far distance and vast ocean and the far-far distance of Tahiti and beyond that the far-far-far shores of South America. RayAnne no sooner squidges her eyes shut and covers them with damp palms than she realizes, *That's it!* The trick for this particular situation isn't breathing or psyching herself up for the thrill, but simply keeping her eyes closed! She will go along, albeit blindly, sparing herself the vertigo. Simple! She can feel the rig tipping forward as Christopher Robin takes the first step, saying, "Go!"

Funny, but it's almost easier to run with eyes closed, plant one foot in front of the other. They pound across the boards and run down the slope, plant and launch, plant and launch, Ray-Anne's feet finding purchase until they don't, when her sneakers make a few airborne revolutions.

They are flying.

Light shifts across her closed eyelids. There is sun, brightness. She can feel the air whooshing along her sides. The cocoon of the apron-thing strapped to the kite frame rocks her minutely side to side while somehow feeling quite secure.

Once they are soaring, she listens to what she's not seeing. The dome of the kite traps small noises: the nylon-against-nylon sounds of their cocoon, little aluminum dings of a carabiner tapping the frame, the many tension wires occasionally strumming a note as if the kite is a stringed instrument. There is wind rushing past, and on the other side of the wind, the other side of the kite—is silence.

Fifteen minutes is the advertised length of the trip. RayAnne knows firsthand that one can do anything for that length of time. When she was thirteen and fourteen, her father used to take her to the orthodontist after school once a month to get her braces tightened—the outings would be blocked out in increments—the fifteen-minute bounce to the clinic in his white Lincoln with bad shock absorbers. The drunken swerves at each corner, the hood ornament nose-diving each time her father hit the brakes. In those instances Big Rick sometimes *was* the car. Then there was the fifteen-minute interval of torture in the dentist's chair. Followed by the trip home that was at least halved with a stop at Bridgeman's, where she got all the ice cream she wanted.

After two airborne minutes—just thirteen to go—the kite doesn't seem to be descending but rising. Christopher Robin whoops once and shouts out something that sounds like, "Wonder kid!" Is he shouting at himself? Sounds happy, though, which is enough for her.

As they fly farther she can feel the air grow more humid,

imagines they are above the ocean now. Three minutes. Twelve to go.

Crackling into the headset Gran's voice urges, "Oh, for godsakes, RayAnne, open your eyes."

"Nuh-uh," she mumbles.

"Open your eyes, girl."

"No way."

"Fine."

Suddenly the static is gone, Gran has decamped, and Christopher Robin is shouting a word RayAnne cannot make out. Without thinking, she opens her eyes.

They are soaring. He is pointing ahead to an airborne scatter of color—a flock of parrots in toy-aisle hues of gaudy red, yellow, blue, and acid green.

Escapees from some zoo, surely. This trip gets weirder by the minute.

"Rosellas!" he shouts again. The glider is gaining on the birds.

RayAnne has never seen wild parrots. Who knew they flew in flocks? It all looks so fake it could be VR: the sky, the clouds, the turquoise water beyond neon birds flying like a squadron of plush toys. Too fake to be frightening: reality looks nothing like reality. They are above the birds now.

When a luft of air hoists the birds higher and closer she can make out the ruffling feathers, sunlight frilling along them, they are that close. Next to her, Christopher Robin gives a thumbs-up and repeats the phrase she'd barely made out earlier, "Wonder-wind." His face splits with a wide grin.

Wonder-wind seems an apt description for the air pressing them upward. As she looks around, taking in the panorama, wind lashes strands of hair into her gaping mouth.

Everything comes together at once: RayAnne, an insignificant creature in the grand scheme, a mortal speck, feels suddenly expanded, as if breathing not only oxygen but all she sees and hears: the wind in her ears; the taste of the humid air; the color of the parrots; the creaks of the frame under her palms; the laundry-line sound of the kite material snapping like a wet sheet. Their own shadow skims over the surface of the water at speed like a cursor across a screen. As for the sea stretching to infinity below, its unfathomable fathoms seem somehow, for the moment, fathomable. And all of this is happening against the cinematic diorama of blue sky over green Pacific paradise. It's all a bit much. Overkill, really. Sir David's voice declares, in summation, "Magnificent!"

Gran's voice crackles into her headset as if just back from a commercial break.

"You see, RayAnne?"

Upon opening her mouth, nothing comes out; she is dumbstruck. Struck dumb. So that's what that means. Yes, she sees.

I see.

When she does find her voice, her barest whisper echoes as if in a cathedral.

"Is this what the afterlife is like?"

"No, mitten, this is what *life* is like—or can be, when you open yourself up to it."

RayAnne considers, nods. "So what is the afterlife like?"

Gran sighs. "Breathers can't understand."

"Breathers?"

"It's what we call you. The living."

"What do you mean, we?"

"Us, the dead."

"Wait. You're with other dead people?" It never occurred to RayAnne that there might actually be anyone on the other side, but here's Gran talking like she's at a bridge tournament or sorority reunion. She suddenly feels a stab of jealousy—Gran is with others?

"Let me get this straight. You're dead, but you're among people, so you're *somewhere?*"

"Well, nowhere interesting . . . and you don't exactly get to choose whoever else dies the same day as you."

"That's who you're with?" A jumble of questions crowd into RayAnne's head; she feels the makings of an interview coming on. "How many?"

"Well, I can see a few hundred from here."

"Here. Where is here?"

"Limbo, goose." Gran says it so matter-of-factly, as if it's really a place, like Bloomington.

"Oh, c'mon, Dorothy Dahl, I don't believe you." She says this whenever Gran makes any outrageous claim. It's an ancient joke between them originating from when RayAnne was learning to read.

One afternoon at Gran's, where the kindergarten bus dropped RayAnne every day so that Bernadette could take afternoon appointments for her life coaching clients, she was met at the bus by Gran as usual. Once they reached the gate, she would hand over the front door key, RayAnne's cue to run ahead and perform her two favorite tasks: unlocking the door (not as easy as Gran made it look) and collecting mail from the little wire basket under the brass slot on the inside of the door. She had recently advanced to sorting the mail into separate piles—circulars and junk mail in one, the more important-seeming envelopes and letters in a second stack.

But that afternoon, just as Dot entered the vestibule, RayAnne was already sorting and plucked up a piece of mail to show off her new reading skills.

"Res . . . ee . . . dent?"

"Resident. Very good, Bean! Now, which pile?"

"Junk!" She slapped it down and picked up an envelope, hesitating, "M-Mers?"

"Mrs." Gran repeated it more slowly.

"D-ort-he-ah . . ." RayAnne already knew how to pronounce Dahl, its being her name as well, but stumbled some over *Dor-*

thea. Until then, she thought she knew all Gran's names, first and foremost being Gran, then there was Mom, which is what Big Rick called her. (It's worth mentioning that as a child Ray-Anne called her father Big Rick, and for whatever reason, no one discouraged this. Somehow, *Daddy* just didn't fit him.)

And finally, there was Dot, which was what everyone else called Gran.

"Who is Dorthea?"

"That's me." Gran made a curtsy, pinching the hem of her raincoat with dainty fingers. "Ta-da, Dorthea Dahl."

"That's your name?"

"'Fraid so."

"Dorthea Dahl?!" Until that moment RayAnne believed Gran existed pretty much for her and her alone: her entertainment, her needs, her after-school snacks, story time, their big-girl naps. That Gran had a whole other identity in the adult world was a rude awakening and all a bit much, RayAnne being tired from a tough day at kindergarten, where boys yanked on braids and would sometimes snatch the snickerdoodle right from your lunch bag when you weren't looking. She was hungry, still smarting over the lost cookie, and needing to pee (but had held it because the little soaps in Gran's bathroom are just so adorable, but she's only allowed to use them after actually "going"). Little RayAnne slumped where she stood in the foyer, dramatically flinging the offending envelope to the floor, stomping a foot and jutting her chin in its puckered, pretears stage, and planting both hands on her hips. She shouted, "Dorthea Dahl, I don't believe you!"

When Gran laughed, RayAnne upped the game by yelling while stomping, "Dorthea Dahl! I don't believe you!" RayAnne could tell Gran was trying not to laugh because her shoulders shook like they did, and when Gran folded softly to the carpet like a stork, RayAnne knew, because when Gran laughed that hard she usually had to hang on to something or someone.

Thirty years later it still makes them both laugh.

"So, Gran, what's this . . . limbo like?"

"Meh. Rather like the Minneapolis airport."

"Really?"

"The waiting area of one of the gates."

"And you've been there since . . . ?"

"Ever since. I'm just in line here to get up to the desk."

"What does that even mean?"

"Once I get there, it'll mean I can finally board the plane."

"A plane to . . . ?"

"I've no clue!" Gran laughed, and in a teasing voice added, "But I have a feeling it's a dead end!"

It takes RayAnne a second, but then they both bust out.

"RayAnne?" Christopher Robin is shouting. "You all right?"

"I'm fiiiiinne." She's still laughing, breathless but able to gather enough air, ready to ask, "How about you?"

No sooner does she than the bottom falls out of the sky.

They stall. More surprised than alarmed, RayAnne laughs again. She looks at Christopher and is about to say, *Nice trick!* but when she sees the look on his face the laugh cracks off. He is wide-eyed, frantically checking the altimeter on the crossbar. They seem to have entered a pocket of dead air or have been dumped by the previous loft. The kite is rapidly descending at a steep angle.

RayAnne's stomach relocates itself somewhere under her ribs—she swallows but her throat won't have it. Looking down to the ocean surface, she feels fear grating at her. Hitting the water will be no cushier than hitting a cement wall. *Oh shit.* Are they about to crash?

Are they? *Are they*?!

As if to confirm, Christopher Robin says, "Fuck. Fuck. Fucking hell!"

The kite angles hard.

RayAnne squeezes her eyes shut, expecting her life to flash in the classic cliché ending. But it's not scenes of her life dancing like GIFs across her lids: it's the faces of those who will be left behind—her mother, Hal, Kyle. Rory. Her father.

Interesting, the order: it says something that her dog comes before Big Rick, and admittedly, there is work to be done on the father-daughter front, but given her current circumstances, it might be too late for that.

They are still plummeting. She is clutching Christopher, who is clutching the bar.

If I get out of this alive . . . She opens her eyes. As the ocean looms, she commences bargaining with the universe while at the same time wondering why she isn't more panicked than she is, because by all rights . . .

"Perhaps you're not panicked because there's not a damn thing to be done," Gran sniffs.

"What if I promise to be a better human being?" RayAnne haggles with the speed of a voice-over recitation of the disclaimer for a drug commercial. "What if I swear to absolutely rock this existence and be my best, my *very* best, like that Mary Oliver poem and live my 'wild and precious life' 110 percent, 200 percent? Dedicate my life to good works? Join the Peace Corps? Give blood more often?"

"Afraid it doesn't work that way, RayBean."

"Oh, shit." The glinting surface of the water is coming at them, crystal clear and clearly shallow, mined with the same jagged, volcanic rock as the headlands jutting from either end of the sandy beach. RayAnne sees it's going to hurt, this dying business, yet she is more sad than scared. For whatever reason, in spite of the turmoil there is at her core a nugget of remarkable calm—for lack of a better term, a *centeredness*.

It's not her body that she's concerned for so much, but where will the rest of her go? The essence of her?

"Oh, for fuck's sake, Gran."

"Language, RayAnne. I'll give you a pass this time, considering . . ."

"Gee, thanks." She closes her eyes again.

"Oh dear, you're not quite getting it, are you?" Gran's voice is tight with impatience.

"Getting what?" RayAnne moans.

"The bit about facing your fears. About living life."

"Which? Facing fears, or living life?"

"They're the same, sweetheart. Everything's a choice."

RayAnne pauses. "Like how you chose to die?"

"Oh, for crying out loud, who chooses to die? The choice I had to make was how to die. And I chose my own way."

"You see how that worked out."

"What can I say? Maybe it was selfish, wanting to die outside, under the stars. If I'd stayed in, Trinket would never have barked like that. No ambulance would've been called, and I'd have been sleeping with the angels instead of carted off to a hospital and trussed up to those machines, and you would've been spared all that."

"Trinket." RayAnne had been at once grateful to the little dog for giving her a chance to see Gran alive—and pissed, knowing it put a crimp in Dot's plan, leaving her hanging somewhere between life and death while a pump did her breathing and kept her heart beating its phony tempo.

"I never said my plan was perfect."

It was a decent effort, though, RayAnne had to give her that. Gran had injected a massive overdose of insulin, which, along with the cache of narcotics she'd ingested, should've done the job nicely.

"Trinket was just doing what dogs are supposed to do."

"Still."

And now it's RayAnne's turn. She looks straight at the water and the jagged rocks, and her heart flips into her throat. A burst of adrenaline and an urgent conviction snap her firmly into the moment. *I don't want to die.*

Then, as abruptly as the sky dumped them, it takes them in its palm and in a gentle updraft lifts the tip of the kite to slow their trajectory. They are gliding again, not diving, aiming for the sandy beach at a leisurely descent.

Miraculously not dead, RayAnne lets out an unworldly laugh-sob that startles even her. Christopher Robin's own laugh has a good deal of choke in it. They come in low over the water paralleling the beach, not far above the heads of swimmers. Either some twist of fate has decided it's not their day, or Christopher Robin has employed some crazy good piloting. Or both, but whatever the case, they touch down on the sand as lightly as a moth.

Once she's unstrapped and walking on stick legs like a baby deer, it is RayAnne's turn to quietly barf into the bushes.

Cassi is running toward her, whiter than usual, which apparently is possible. "God, RayAnne, that was . . ."

"Awesome?" Remarkably, RayAnne is able to feign nonchalance and sits down in the sand as if she means to. "Where are the guys?"

"Just coming down now, figured they better keep filming . . . you know, in case."

"In case."

"In case you crashed and were hurt."

"Hurt?" She wipes her mouth. "Try *killed*."

"You all right?" She digs in her pack for gum and hands it over.

"Might have wet my pants a little bit."

Cassi peers into her pack. "I can't help you there."

Christopher Robin, fussing with cables and the kite, is watching them. She gives him a thumbs-up.

He gives one back.

The men come roaring up the beach. Rongo with the camera on his shoulder, Chad jogging behind with the big fuzzy mike on its pole. When Rangi sees RayAnne, he sprints ahead despite Rongo shouting, "Yo, you're in frame!"

He drops to his knees where she sits. "Keerist, RayAnne. You okay?" He's looking her over to see if she's in one piece.

"I'm fine."

"Clearly not, you're shaking."

There is such concern in his voice that RayAnne nearly tears up. "We almost crashed."

"We saw." Rangi looks to Cassi, who shrugs helplessly. Christopher Robin is waiting in the wings to approach. When Rangi wraps RayAnne in his big arms, she does leak a few tears.

Actually? The notion of death hadn't seemed all that terrible. Knowing it was coming, she could see the necessity of giving into it—when it seemed an absolute and immediate inevitability.

Rangi suddenly lets her go. "Oops, hope that was okay."

"That was very okay." As nice as each twin is, it seems Rangi is the one with the gooey center.

She pats his big-bear chest.

"I wish you were my brother."

"Don't you have a brother?"

"Yeah, but who can't use more brothers? My own is being a bit of an idiot at the moment."

"Trust me," Rangi pulls her to standing and steers her to the picnic table where she sits. "All brothers can be idiots."

At his approach, RayAnne looks up at Rongo. "Are you filming me *now*?"

"No. Well, camera's running, but . . . you okay? Crikey, you must have been terrified?"

"Yes and no. It was weird."

Chad checks her with a critical eye and hands over a handkerchief.

Christopher Robin steps up to speak.

"Jays. Sorry 'bout that. Pucker factor pretty high just then. We'll refund you, of course."

Cassi laughs. "Pucker factor."

RayAnne takes his hand. "You're a very good pilot."

"Meh, maybe your prayers helped."

"Oh, I wasn't . . . did you think I was praying? I was just arguing with my grandmother." She looks around. "My *dead* grandmother."

A few glances are traded. "Hey, whatever works." Christopher Robin nods cautiously. "Right?"

He looks a bit pale himself. It occurs to RayAnne that he'd have been scared as well. "So, what are the odds—of what just happened to us?"

"Sink out like that? So fast? 'Bout one in a million."

"What about the odds of it happening a second time?"

"Mm. Maybe one in ten million?"

"Good. I want to do it again."

After the second run—during which RayAnne flings her arms wide like the corny scene in *Titanic* where Kate Winslet goes all bowsprit—she's still buzzing with the thrill of it on the drive back to the motel, can sense her companions stealing furtive glances at her then each other, as if concerned what she might do next.

In the motel she sits curled next to the open window, chronicling the entire day in an epic text to Hal, closing with "I LOVE YOU." Her thumb hovers over the send button a moment before backspacing over LOVE and replacing it with MISS. "I MISS YOU." Hitting the send button, she thinks, *Coward*.

They have an early flight in the morning, heading to the South Island to film their next segment, but RayAnne cannot fall asleep and finally manages only a few hours before the alarm crows. Her first thought upon opening her eyes and looking at her phone comes back like an echo. *Coward*.

It's a full day of travel, beginning with a hasty breakfast on the road to the airport, where all of Tripod's gear is stuffed into the hold of a commuter plane the size and diameter of a culvert.

"Sure you're all right? To fly?" Cassi gives her an assessing look.

"In fine fettle."

She has no idea where that sprung from. Perhaps it was something Dead Ted used to say. Dead Ted was Gran's Ted, not to be confused with Alive Ted, Bernadette's estranged father. And now that she thinks of it, how insensitive of her and Ky all these years, referring to him like that, even in front of Gran. He'd died when RayAnne was just five, and she remembers him mostly as a jovial echo—either laughing over something Gran said or repeating it, as if his bride of nearly fifty years was the most hilarious and surprising woman on Earth.

Their maternal grandfather, Alive Ted, aka Grandpa Mills, lives in a care home in Oregon and is a "complete bastard," according to Bernadette. RayAnne wonders sometimes if Alive Ted is the reason their mother seems so mad at men in general. RayAnne has met him only twice. On birthdays he still sends gift cards to her and Ky, for suburban chain restaurants like Olive Grove or Famous Amos—places they would never go. When he does send a useful card—to, say, Target—it invariably has odd amounts of credit, as if used. Or maybe he just felt like giving $12.87 one year, and $93.50 the next.

Still. There are so many more wonderful men in the world than mediocre ones. Hal lands solidly in the good-guy column. He's honest and kind; she's seen how he is with employees, knowing so much about them, their kids. Recently, he'd been offered a buyout by a big company, which he's turned down, too worried that they would reduce employee benefits.

"It's a lot of money." RayAnne might have been testing him when she brought it up.

"It is." He'd shaken his head. "But then what? Retire at forty? Besides, there'd be no guarantee they'd keep sponsoring *Fishing!*"

"You talk like we're going to be on the air for years . . ."

Hal stopped her. "Faith, girl, and you will."

Never mind he's the sort of guy she can get wobbly over ("a knicker-dampener," Gran would joke in her best *Downton Abbey* whinny). RayAnne has been exactly who she is with him, and he hasn't run screaming yet.

Not that landing in the good column automatically gets a guy out of the dickhead doghouse. Her brother is a good guy, and she is truly worried about him: would Kyle do something so stupid as sleep with Ingrid's cousin? RayAnne can only hope he does not take actual aim with the woody he currently harbors for . . . what is her name? Gikka? She shudders, having just considered an erection and her brother in the same thought.

Yes, Hal is a great guy. She wishes the barrier of distance between them would vanish—one of those watch-what-you-wish-for wishes that if granted literally would result in something comical, like, say, the Earth would disappear, leaving them suddenly reunited by the soles of their feet and adrift in space. Lack of sleep has her thinking stoned thoughts.

Cassi laughs nervously, commenting that their ten-seater prop plane is just the type you most often see in aerial footage of wreckage strewn over the sort of mountainous terrain they will be flying over.

Mimicking Hal, RayAnne tuts, "Faith, girl."

As she straps into the window seat, RayAnne feels quite calm. It goes to reason that since she'd nearly hang glided to her death the day before, there is no way this flight will go anything but perfectly. And while unsure just how such things get negotiated in the cosmos, she is certain just the same.

Up until the approach to landing, the flight does go perfectly smoothly. Conditions are ideal. They soar off into a cobalt-blue summer sky over undulating pastureland. Below, random tight clusters of sheep are scattered like so many nubby wool rugs.

After leaving the pasturelands, Rongo leans over to point out the Tararua Forest of dense hills.

From the air Wellington vaguely reminds RayAnne of the city of Duluth—if Duluth were on steroids and its hills were steeper, and if Lake Superior was a frothy ocean. When they hit a band of turbulence upon approach, Rongo asks, "Did anyone mention this is the windiest airport in the world?"

Cassi says, "*Anyone* did not."

When the plane hitches and bucks, Cassi makes distressed-kitten noises.

This is not your garden-variety turbulence—it's as though the plane is on strings being controlled by a maniacal puppeteer. Out the window RayAnne can see the wing juddering as though it might disengage from the plane. As they hitch and sway toward the runway there is palpable tension among the other passengers. Rangi is now gingerly rubbing Cassi's back as she hunches over an air-sickness bag.

RayAnne isn't worried in the least. The opposite—she looks out the tiny window thinking, *Do your worst,* even as the pilot aborts his first attempt to land, when everyone but RayAnne moans. She's certain the second attempt will be just peachy because, not to beat a dead horse here, but she had cinched that deal surviving yesterday's potential crash. There's no way she's dying anytime soon, and certainly not in the air. They eventually make a very bouncy landing.

Cassi seems shaken to the point her eyes seem loose in their sockets.

They immediately board a somewhat larger plane bound for Queenstown and cross a choppy Cook Strait to the South Island, where RayAnne can make out miles and miles of Queen Charlotte Track snaking along green spines of terrain.

"Not your grandmother's hike," Rongo offers.

"No," RayAnne says, "it certainly isn't."

When they fly over the neat quilts of vineyards, Rongo informs her they are above the Nelson wine region. Their vantage point is like that of an Imax film. Rongo points over ridges at things they can barely see: the Franz Josef and Fox glaciers. He tells her the range of southern alps are called Kā Tiritiri o te Moana. There are also British-sounding place names like Marlborough and Canterbury. Rongo lists the native names of these places as he cranes toward the window to identify the peaks, valleys, and rivers. Matakitaki, Rotoroa, Kaikoura. Rongo can't exactly help his size, and while a bit squished between the window and his girth, RayAnne doesn't want to mention the manspread and interrupt his musical recitation of magical-sounding places.

It's only a ninety-minute flight, but the time literally flies as she gazes out the window, unaware that Rongo's nodded off until a blaze-orange jet flies below and she elbows him, saying, "D'ja see that?"

Startled, he mutters, "What?" sitting up to smack his head on the overhead compartment.

"Sorry."

They are deeper into the mountain range now, where solid clouds have settled evenly below them like a great sea of foam, with mountain peaks poking up here and there like islands. Somewhere up ahead under the cloud is their destination, Queenstown.

As they near, the plane banks and drops gently, angling toward the mountain range as if intending to slam into it. Behind her, Cassi whimpers.

"Oi. No worries," Rangi assures her. "You'll see, in a minute."

They sink into the cloudbed to submerge in depths of white, completely blind. A moment later the cloud thins and the plane begins to clear, parting the white like a curtain. Indeed, they break through over a view of a long, narrow jewel of a lake.

Rongo points. "That's Lake Wakatipu."

And at its far end, Queenstown. Neighborhoods are set into the green slopes along the shoreline between wrinkles of hills, looking more like a string of small communities than a city. At first there doesn't appear to be any central area of Queenstown.

"There she is."

"Gorgeous!"

At the far end of the lake they descend, swooping so close to houses that roof shingles are distinct. They scrape the air over a narrow industrial area to the single airstrip in the middle of the valley, the runway seemingly the only straight line in a country of wild hills.

Landing is smooth. *I could have told you that,* RayAnne thinks, turning to see Cassi's wild look. While Queenstown had seemed intriguing from the air, there's no time to linger on the ground.

"For the best," Chad suggests. "Wall-to-wall Americans. We're heading north."

They load into a large rental van. Their next stop is several hours away. The landscape is much more dramatic than the North Island. They travel steeper roads, between more green hills and foothills, distant mountains that Chad points out, describing how in winter they are draped in snow and are full of skiers and snowboarders. High above them are a number of ski resorts.

They settle in for the drive, aiming for a place called Dingle Burn, which RayAnne can only hope does not live up to its name. Their destination is Kirehe Farm, a former sheep station set near the edge of another glacial lake, Hāwea.

Lake Hāwea is sidled by steep slopes of lush green reflected across the surface, producing the effect of an emerald bowl—a sight that makes RayAnne wonder if there isn't some point at which the mind can't process any more amazing sights. Might the synapses, having overgorged on beauty, simply overload and tumble all these jaw-dropping visuals together like some kaleidoscope?

They first see Kirehe from afar as evening sun glazes the

landscape. The buildings are washed tangerine, every window reflecting a hot slab of light. At the farm they will join a dozen dog owners who have spent a year or more on the waiting list to attend a program run by dog-training guru Petra Koslov.

"*Kirehe,*" Rangi informs them, "means animal."

"So basically, the place is called Animal Farm?"

"More or less."

People pay outrageous sums to stay at Kirehe, where supposedly they will learn to think like their dogs—or at least live like them for a while. Cassi reads aloud from the brochure: "'In addition to committing two weeks to the intensive program, participants must meet the rigorous physical criteria of being able to spend extended periods outdoors as well as on the ground.'"

"On the ground. Why . . . ?" RayAnne is flummoxed.

"The idea being, 'They experience the physical world as their canine does, to commune more effectively with them.'"

Rangi shrugs, "So this Petra—"

"Koslov," Cassi says.

Chad laughs. "Seen her on the telly. Complete nutter."

Making a whirling-finger gesture at his temple, Rongo agrees. "Batshit. You've not heard of her?"

RayAnne looks at Cassi. "Only what I'm told."

Rangi asks, "What does this place have to do with fishing, again?"

"Apparently," Cassi explains, "Koslov has taught her own dog . . ." She flips through her notes. "A Hungarian vizsla named Uma, to fish."

"Right."

RayAnne budges in to read: "'Ms. Koslov is just back from an international book tour for the paperback release of her bestselling book, *Who Is Training Whom?*'"

"Woof." Chad sighs.

As they near the cluster of buildings they can hear the din of barking.

From the brochure it's clear that the farm is serious business. "Humans of Kirehe," Cassi reads, "will live as their dogs do, adjusting their habits to experience an existence as near as that of their canines as is humanly possible."

RayAnne chews on the sentence, which surely qualifies as an oxymoron. She's about to ask when the van rolls to a stop.

There is no one in the small building marked "office." A note has been left, directing them to their rooms, and informing them they'd missed dinner—there are no room keys. While the lodging building looks exactly like a motel, it isn't quite. RayAnne opens what she thinks is their door to find a room with no beds, just two tartan-upholstered futons on the floor, like large dog beds. The room divider separating the two sleeping areas is a chain-link fence. The floor is covered in raked pea gravel, which at first glance looks like low-pile carpet. The room smells very much like dog.

"Wait . . ."

"Wrong room." Cassi points to the number. "My mistake, we're up a level. I'd say this isn't even a room."

"Let's hope. Wait, maybe not." RayAnne reads the notice on the wall near the door: "'Each human guest will be assigned a toileting area for themselves and their animal. Please refrain from using others' potty places so as not to disrupt territorial order. You are responsible for burying (and in some cases reburying) your own feces as well as your dog's. Your toileting area number coincides with your room number.'"

RayAnne backs out, pulling the door shut. "Jeez, how serious is this training business?"

Up a flight of exterior stairs, their own rooms are the traditional motel model. Thankfully they do not smell too bad, and behind the bathroom doors there are indeed toilets.

"Huzza," Cassi says. "We get to poop inside."

On the wall is a framed list of Nonparticipant Guest Rules.

"That's us. *Nonparticipants.*"

No interaction or speaking with the handlers or their animals.

No photography or video of animals and handlers without written consent.

"Huh," Cassi puzzles. "How d'you s'pose we get consent when we can't interact or speak with them?"

"Right." They read on.

Keep canine hours! Lights out after dark.

Breakfast served at dawn.

Both squeal, "Dawn!?"

While we endeavor to make meals as pleasant as possible, handlers will consume what their canines do.

RayAnne muses. "My neighbor has a dog that eats poop right out of the cat box, coated in litter like Salted Nut Rolls. S'pose there're any cats around here?"

"Stop." Cassi pulls a face. "Dawn?"

They step out onto their balcony and Cassi squints across the field where grassy areas are marked with numbered posts near little "privacy" areas surrounded by waist-high stacks of baled hay. The numbers coincide with the first-level rooms. "Remind me to stay upwind of that."

"Who besides dog owners would come here?" RayAnne wonders.

"Us? Voyeurs come to watch the show?"

Hearing a bark, RayAnne turns to the source and points. "You mean that?"

Beyond the fence on a mowed field, a number of humans are scattered about, all in the act of mimicking the dog nearest to them, or in some cases the dog they are tethered to with a harness. One man wriggles on his back, grinding his scalp into the turf as the German pointer at his side does the same. A woman on all fours wearing carpel tunnel braces on her wrists leans forward and growls at something unseen in the same posture as her snarling blue heeler. All of the handlers wear kneepads. Some just lounge or nap or pant alongside their animals. A fit woman in muddy clothing is going head to head with her Shih Tzu, both tugging a length of filthy rope in their teeth. Another man appears to be gnawing the same sort of rawhide treat as his Labrador.

Chad and Rongo come out to join them on the balcony. Chad's mouth drops at the antics on display. Rongo holds a small camera with a long lens of the sort paparazzi and bird watchers use. Looking through the viewfinder he grins. "You cannot make this shit up."

"Where's Rangi?" asks Cassi.

"Toilet?" Chad ventures.

"He is not," Rangi says, coming up from behind, referring to himself.

"Huh, in third person. Just like the American president," Chad sighs.

"Or your queen," Rongo quips.

"By the way, Chad, hope you brought your inhaler."

Elbows on the railing, they all watch the dogs and their owners. After Chad starts sneezing violently, he retreats to his room to take his allergy meds. A moment later, a yellow-sheeted mattress wedges out the door and collapses to the deck like a drunken SpongeBob, ejected. His door then slams as well as a sliding door can.

Cassi and RayAnne have lost track of time. Their chairs are tipped back, ankles hooked on the balcony railing, each nursing a bottle of beer. From the trio of sonorous exhalations coming from the rooms sidling their own, it's evident that the twins and Chad are hard asleep. The full moon has risen, no doubt fueling the distant and not-so-distant baying of a dozen dogs, most balefully from the room below, where earlier they'd seen a basset hound drag its bejowled, look-alike owner through the door.

For somewhere so remote, Kirehe is loud. From the nearby pond and surrounding grasses comes a cacophony of toads, tree frogs, bullfrogs, crickets, cicadas, night birds, and whatever else is out there ribbiting their fat necks or rubbing insect knees together to make night music.

"Otherwise it's totally quiet," RayAnne observes before going silent herself.

After a moment the night chorus is broken by a lonesome howl.

Cassi asks, "You miss Rory?"

"Sure. Among others."

"Hal?"

It's occurred to RayAnne that not constantly thinking about Hal is a positive sign, since for the first time ever she is neither fretting nor obsessing about the man in her life. Even from halfway across the planet, he feels rock-solid—and though he is out of cell phone range, Hal somehow registers as five bars.

"Actually, I've been thinking a lot about my grandmother."

"Huh, so was I. Mine, I mean." The moon reflects in Cassi's already lunar-blue eyes and her smile flickers. She looks at RayAnne in the way Rory sometimes does when waiting to see what she might do or say next.

"Oh geez." The front legs of RayAnne's chair hit the deck. "I'm such a dope—of course you're missing your grandmother!"

"Great-gran, actually. Nan Ursa—who was pretty great if you could get past the resting bitch face."

Nan Ursa had died just as Cassi started working on the pilot of *Fishin' Chicks*. A surreal environment in which to be grieving, RayAnne thought at the time. Both had just landed their jobs and were barely settling in when they realized just what a train wreck the show was—that it wouldn't likely survive past filming the pilot.

"Best to keep busy," Cassi had insisted back then. And they were busy indeed, scrambling for ways to keep the literal boat afloat. Both were certain the pilot would be canceled after Mandy Cox stormed off set. Given the whack concepts the producers and program director tossed about in attempts to appeal to a broader audience, it was a marvel the show ever made it to production stage. With their own ears Cassi and RayAnne heard, "*Oprah* in a boat" bandied over the conference room table; "*Duck Dynasty* for liberals"; and the kicker criteria one producer listed when the search for a new host commenced: "If Garrison Keillor were forty years younger, a woman, didn't look like a frog, and fished."

RayAnne was recruited as temporary host—apparently having met at least two of the criteria, most important, that she did not resemble a frog. That's how low the bar was. *Well, that's that,* she'd thought at the time. At that point there was little to lose. Producers couldn't think straight, so she and Cassi began to, wondering aloud how the two of them might save the show as if it were theirs to save.

Cassi began plotting. The plan involved a few of the crew who were cajoled into shooting several interview segments behind the director's back. Cassi handled bribes, an influx of samples from a cousin in Colorado who'd recently opened a cannabis dispensary, gummies being the camera operator's weakness. The grip and sound guys were partial to lollipops. They cherry-picked a few fringe guests from the list and managed to produce five interview segments on a budget of edibles. Cassi was able to coach RayAnne into a reasonable facsimile of a host, all while keeping producers at bay—not too difficult since they mostly just huddled offside, gnashing their dental-plan teeth. One assistant producer who had pretty much given up could be found in the catering tent, stress-eating and slumped over her iPad, scrolling job postings with a buttery thumb.

RayAnne, faking her way through interviews, couldn't have known how cleverly Cassi was wielding subliminal influence, both at the fore and behind the scenes, somehow able to inject a better vision into producers' heads as subtly as a mosquito wheedles virus into a vein.

"Amazing, really, what you were able to accomplish. When Dot died, there were mornings I couldn't get dressed, let alone comb my hair. But you saved the show."

"I had to stay busy." Cassi shrugs. "I couldn't bring Nan back to life, but I could make sure the show didn't drive into its own bridge."

Could that have only been a year ago? And yet, all this time—even now, knowing what it feels like facing each day with a grandmother-shaped hole in it—RayAnne has barely checked in on Cassi's loss. Initially, it felt too awkward to inquire, and now it simply hits too close to home. The notion, that someone who has loved you since before you could pair the word to its little floods of happiness, could blithely step out of your life (and their own) as casually as if heading off to bowling league, or to watch the sunset from a favorite deck chair . . .

"Did she really do it on purpose, you think? Are you sure it was . . . ?" RayAnne still stumbles around the word.

"Suicide?" Cassi chews her lip. "My family refuses to believe it. My dad still insists it was a venison score gone wrong."

"A what?"

"Nan lived through the Depression. A total opportunist when it came to putting meat on the table—my uncle swears he'd seen her chase wolves from a moose kill. For sure she wasn't above intentionally bouncing a yearling off the grill of her Pontiac."

"Whoa."

"It was suicide all right." She holds a finger up. "(A) It happened the day before she was scheduled to move from her cabin—her messy, fit-her-like-a-glove cabin that she lived in for sixty years."

"She didn't want to move?"

"Dreaded it," Cassi says. "Leaving the lake and twenty acres where she'd named every white pine, to live in Senior Cedars? Nan doesn't like people in general." Cassi corrects her tense: "Didn't like people—except me, but she really didn't like old people—forget that she was ninety-three herself. And (B) . . ."

Cassi often ticks things off alphabetically, as if possibilities are not infinite but top out at twenty-six. "She had the reflexes of a NASCAR veteran and knew that road like it was programmed into her. It was daylight, the road was dry. There were no tire marks, which meant she'd never even tried to brake. And, she'd been . . ." Cassi pauses.

RayAnne waits for her to go on. For Cassi, an unnaturally long time is a few seconds rather than a half-second.

"She'd been what?"

Cassi shakes herself back to her alphabet. "(C) She'd begun to forget things, was losing moments. Even forgot a few times who I was. That was the only time I ever saw her really scared. Of anything. Then she began to forget bigger chunks, then to forget about forgetting. She reacted to my mom as though she didn't recognize her—though that might have been intentional. Other times, she was completely herself. It happened a week after Nan told me that if she disappeared on the ice some night, I should wait a day before looking in the fishing shacks. I knew exactly what she meant at the time but pretended I didn't, so that she would have to explain."

"What did she say?"

Cassi meets her eye. "That she'd just go off and freeze to death like the Inuit do."

"But why in an ice house?"

"I suppose so coyotes wouldn't get to her. Or wolves."

"Oh, jeez." RayAnne gives Cassi a pat.

As if the mention of wolves conjures it, the moon breaks through a cloud. "But it wasn't winter, and there were no ice houses, or ice, so she had to go plow into a tree at the bottom of a ravine."

As moonlight casts across Cassi, her eyes gloss with tears.

RayAnne edges closer.

What a grandmother might choose to do with her own life is something both have thought hard about. Cassi knuckles away a tear before it can roll.

RayAnne inhales. “Can we blame them?”

“Maybe the real question is, Can we forgive them?” Cassi’s words are left to hang and flicker like the fireflies in the distant bush.

For a while they gaze into the void of night. RayAnne’s almost relieved for the darkness—a shade pulled over whatever stunning landscape is out there. It’s getting a little exhausting, the beauty. Of course the only person she could complain to about such a thing was Gran.

“Who would you trade?” Cassi asks.

“Who would I trade . . . ?”

“To get your grandmother back?”

“You mean like a sports team?” There are parameters, apparently.

“Yeah,” Cassi says, “like who in your family?”

RayAnne barely hesitates. “My dad. I’d trade Big Rick to get Gran back.”

There is a WORLD’S GREATEST DAD mug in her father’s cupboard, yet she has never given him one, and neither has Ky. Only lately has RayAnne had the revelation that while one can care about a parent—worry about them, love them, be the dutiful daughter—one is under no obligation to like them.

“Who would you trade?”

“Either.”

“Either what?”

“Parent. My mom. My dad. Both.” To sweeten the deal, she adds, “I’d throw in the twins.”

“Wait. You’d cash in your whole family . . . ?”

“For one cranky, dues-paying member of the NRA who wore

hockey socks for hand warmers and never had anything nice to say about anybody? Yeah."

Before Cassi joined the show, she'd lived with her great-grandmother on the same lake as Location. In fact, it had been Cassi who'd scouted the very spot they now lease, a portion of a long-defunct resort with its weird name, Naledi.

"What was she like? I mean besides . . . ?"

"Curmudgeonly? Nan was the only person in my family who didn't obsess about my tattoos, my hair, my looks. She never once told me to smile more and couldn't have cared less that I refuse to 'identify' as gay, straight, or bi, and was really amused that it drove my parents apeshit. She understood what should matter and what shouldn't."

If only they *could* trade people.

Cassi sounds wistful. "But we don't get to make such deals, do we?"

"Nope." RayAnne picks up her now-warm beer to clink her bottle to Cassi's.

"To grandmothers."

As if approving, a half-dozen dogs begin howling at once. As the baying dies down, they sit a moment in silence. When they get up to head inside, Cassi pauses at the door to hold up a finger. "And (D) Nan was wearing her best underwear that night. I mean, c'mon—for bowling league?!"

Breakfast is eaten at a long table in the mess tent. It's true that they eat what the dogs do, albeit prepared and served somewhat differently. The dogs get raw lamb with oats, chopped apple cores and egg mixed in. For humans there is a buffet of poached eggs, tepid oatmeal, lamb sausage, and apple fritters. An exception is made for coffee, which is excellent, hot, and served in china cups on saucers, incongruous civility on the grimy slab tables under coils of fly tape fuzzy with insect carcasses.

A German shepherd walks by dragging its low-slung rear

end, looking like one of those low-rider cars set down on its chassis. Or two halves of different dogs.

"Is he crippled?" Cassi asks.

"Overbred." Chad explains how they are purposely bred to achieve dog-show standards.

"But it's like a birth defect!" RayAnne frowns.

Cassi asks, "Why? Who does that?"

"The people that brought you the dog shows like Westminster, American Kennel Club—*dog* people, who are anything but, when you get down to it." Chad ticks off examples of overbreeding: "King Charles spaniels with such tiny skulls they get constant headaches; dachshunds with bodies too long for their legs to support; Boston terriers with eyes that can literally pop out."

"God." RayAnne considers the poached egg wobbling on her plate.

When a diminutive, curly-haired woman approaches their table, Chad elbows RayAnne and whispers, "That's her."

They stand.

"Sit!" Petra Koslov's voice belies her size. She speaks with such authority all their bottoms hit the bench in unison.

When RayAnne reaches out to offer a hand, Ms. Koslov shakes her head, saying, "No. We eschew human social refinements here."

"We do?" Cassi asks.

Rangi's dimple twitches. "Do we sniff each oth—"

Cassi elbows him.

Petra Koslov gives Rangi a withering look before instructing them as to exactly where they can and cannot go around Kirehe Ranch. Basically, they are grounded.

"Unfortunately, there will be no meeting Uma" (the chinook-fishing vizsla) "until tomorrow. She is still in estrus."

RayAnne, assuming estrus is a place, asks, "When will she be back?"

"She is . . . *on heat.*" Ms. Koslov considers RayAnne as if she might be the stupidest woman alive.

"Ah."

"So . . . not until tomorrow?"

"Uma has been mated daily for the past week. Safe to say she has took by now. Should be fine by tomorrow, if a bit randy." Ms. Koslov offers nothing else.

So they have another day to kill.

After breakfast they attend Petra's first lecture of the day. RayAnne and crew sit on chairs behind the group of dogs and their people—all down on the hard dirt floor of the tent. Petra Koslov bobs her head of standard-poodle hair.

"You can read all you want about incentive," she says, "but when you and your dog are going head to head, it's really a matter of what you have to offer, and how you offer it—that's the communication part."

When a dog owner raises her hand, Petra ignores her.

"What does your animal want to do, versus what you want your animal to do, versus what bargaining power you have."

Petra walks among them. "What kind of deal can you negotiate? Is your animal food-motivated? Is simple praise enough? Is pleasing you his motivation . . . ?"

The tone of her words have a hypnotic quality to them.

"Believe it or not, your animal wants to behave, wants to belong, be part of the pack, have a leader, have a purpose . . ."

RayAnne finds herself lulled as she listens. Just as Petra has them relaxed and hanging on her next word, she emits an ear-piercing whistle and all heads snap to attention.

"See? Your voice is a most effective tool. You want your animal's attention? Set the tone—one voice to calm them, another for when you seriously want their attention. Along with your clicks and whistles, you should employ a menacing tone, one that means business, one used only when praising. Dogs have language—it just doesn't have words." Petra scans the faces. "Your dog has dozens of ways to communicate. Learn them."

She claps her hands. People sit up straight. "You can either choose to understand them." She looks around and pauses for emphasis. "Or you can expect them to understand you."

There'd been howling in the night that triggered a barking jag, when RayAnne had crammed in a pair of earplugs. If dogs do have language, she has no interest in what they might have to say at 3 a.m.

"Your dog is communicating to you. Respond in return—even if that response is no response. If your animal is whining for no acceptable reason, don't respond. Don't yell or cajole or explain why Fido cannot go howl at the squirrels. Sending no message at all can be the message in itself."

Another long pause for effect. From behind her Chad whispers, "I'm totally trying that with Molly."

RayAnne turns. "I didn't know you had a dog."

"Molly's my girlfriend."

RayAnne's snort elicits the stink eye from Ms. Koslov.

She assesses her group glumly: a week ago they were upright suburbanites and city dwellers and now register as a motley lot of disheveled, sleep-deprived schmoes who have barely scratched the surface of serious dog training. The humans have all been in residence for ten days. As per instruction, they do not bathe while at Kirehe. As per that, RayAnne and crew keep their distance.

One of the requisites to get into Kirehe is that participating dogs have level-two obedience certificates—Canine Good Citizen status—which basically means your pet isn't a menace to polite society. RayAnne has to wonder if there is any requirement for the humans, other than paying the stupendous cost.

More instructions are given: owners and dogs are lined up to go off on their various assignments.

"Dismissed!"

. . .

There is an hour break between one lecture and the next. While the humans follow their dogs to the toileting areas and the waist-high privacy huts made of hay bales, the guys go off to gather footage in the few places they are allowed. Cassi finds a knoll to sit and read on her tablet.

If RayAnne has learned anything about communication in the past hour, she might as well try putting it to use. Seeing her phone has four bars, she presses speed dial. She'd pinky-promised Ky to check in on Big Rick in return for Ky promising to behave himself around Gikka. A deal is a deal.

It's barely 7 a.m. back home, but her father will be up and raring to go, now that he's sober and no longer communing into the wee hours with his besties, John Jameson and Jim Beam. His new routine includes getting up early to walk Trinket, Gran's gunky-eyed Pomeranian, now adopted as his own. He's also on a program of ninety AA meetings in ninety days. Big Rick is very busy, nearly manic, if his Tweets are any indication. There are now more hours in a day than he can fill—those previously taken up finagling opportunities to procure drink, then find places to sneak away to drink, then make it appear as if he'd not been drinking. So much time freed means Big Rick now has loads of leisure. Never good. The rumor RayAnne is hoping to debunk is that her father has taken up with a new woman.

Before she has time to blink, he is heartily bellowing into the phone.

"Hey, RayBee. I was just talking about you!"

"No need to shout, Dad. Talking about me to who?"

Or is it *whom*? She may never get that one right.

"Sally!"

So it is true. Kyle had texted: EXPECT AN ANNOUNCEMENT. HE'S SNAGGED ANOTHER—AT LEAST THIS ONE'S RICH.

"Who is Sally?"

"My gal, Sal."

"Ky mentioned. What, ah . . ." She remembers *tone* and edits midsentence, switching to chipper. "What does Sal do, Dad?"

"More like, What *doesn't* she do?"

For a panicky moment RayAnne imagines Big Rick is going to launch into some description of their sexual relations.

"Can't wait to hear about her."

A lie. She can wait. Her father is a serial monogamist—cannot just have a girlfriend. He is forever marrying them. Early on, RayAnne and Ky developed a code of initials for each wife: first was their mother, of course. Bernadette is NU for Numero Uno. In descending order, next is Anne, known as PS for Possibly Psychotic (Ky wasn't the best speller at age ten). Then Delia, the backup country western singer was BG for Bronco Girl. For the duration of his marriage to BG, Big Rick wore a Stetson and pointy boots and walked around with a piece of straw between his teeth. RayAnne had to give her father credit: when he took a woman on, he went all out, which seems both romantic and pathetic at the same time. Poor Gloria was next—SS for Sad Sack, who had actually been sweet and tolerable until she drifted away on a sea of tears.

RayAnne may not have liked them all, but she would root for these unions and hope for the best, because for as long as Big Rick had some romance or marriage on the front burner, he drank less, behaved more. Some were trouble from the very start, like Ellen, aka TV for The Viper, who'd left the biggest mess in her wake after having bilked their father of a good chunk of his savings. Last and least, Rita had been the shortest-lived, realizing her mistake so early in the game she'd been assigned her initials after the fact, HR for Hasty Retreat. Ink on that divorce decree is barely dry. Of course, the wives are impossible to remember in order, even for Big Rick, who'd come up with the acronym of their initials, BADGER.

Here we go. Sally. RayAnne might as well sit back and take notes in the event BADGER becomes plural.

As her father begins extolling the wonders of Sally, RayAnne looks across the field to where trainees are out, being pulled along by their dogs that lift their legs here and there and curl into *C* formations to crap. Her father burbles along about how he'd met Sally in AA (she's been sober for eight years) and boasts of her consistent golf score of below ninety. He regales Sally's traits as if she is a real estate listing.

"Very active . . ."

Oh god, was he going to mention sex after all?

". . . for an older gal."

RayAnne sits up. Older? This is new. With the exception of Bernadette, all subsequent wives averaged twenty years Big Rick's junior—for whom *active* could mean anything from figure skating to mechanical bull riding. "Oh. Is she retired, then?"

"Semi. Still runs the family business. They do exhibition services for large trade shows."

"Yeah? Like the Rod and Gun Expo?"

"Exactly like that."

"Wait. Dad, you don't mean Sally Leighton?"

"Bingo! Sally said she'd visited your booth in Chicago when you and your little albino were there."

RayAnne and Cassi had been roped into hosting a booth at the Rod and Gun Expo in hopes of recruiting members for National Public Television—at a gun show. Because so few women visited the booth, RayAnne remembers them. One, familiar looking, wore an open-carry holster slung from the hip of her Chanel suit. She was also wearing a diamond-crusted crucifix. RayAnne remembers that she made the lowest possible donation in order to get the membership perk of a T-shirt saying, *I'm a woman, I fish. Deal with it.*

"Dad. First of all, Cassi's not an albino, and even if she was, it's not . . ."

"Sally watches your show!"

On the other end of the line she hears the tell-tale rattle of Big Rick's Cadillac.

"W-wait," RayAnne stutters. "Where are you?" It's early to be out on a Sunday.

"Just driving in to pick her up at her whatchacallit—pied-à-terre." He pronounces it *peed-a-terry*. "You know her building, the Stevedore?"

Nobody doesn't know the Stevedore—a glass spear jutting from the banks of the Mississippi. When her father says "her" building, he doesn't just mean the building where Sally lives. The Stevedore is one of several Leighton-owned edifices along the Minneapolis riverfront—certainly the most incongruously named, considering it was built by the notoriously anti-union Leightons, with money made off the backs of nonunion laborers.

A story Gran told her springs to mind.

"Dad, did you know stevedores ate river-rat stew? And not just during the Depression?" Gran had a recipe for it, fallen out of some old cookbook found in a thrift shop.

"I did not know that." His voice takes on a gloss of ire.

"I bet Hal would whip up a batch for this Sally."

"*This* Sally?" He's clearly annoyed now.

She shouldn't bait him. "Where are you two off to so early on a Sunday?" None of the usual brunch spots would even be open yet.

"Church."

She nearly fumbles the phone. "Church?"

"Yup. A building with a steeple? Cross on top?"

"You are going to chu—"

"Gotta go, Ray. Here she comes!"

As the phone goes dead, her mouth hangs. She stares at the screen, waiting to see if Gran might chime in. Gran does not.

Her father lands on his feet every time. The Leightons of the mansion on Summit Avenue next to the governor's; the two-hundred-acre island on Lake Vermilion; the chain of home improvement stores; the exhibition services company; the golf course in Orono with its gated community that made Gran's expensive condo in Dune Cottage Village look like Section 8 housing.

A tick at the corner of RayAnne's eye revs. Sally Leighton isn't just the matriarch of the Leighton clan: she's also elderly, albeit a surgically smoothed, golf-fit elderly.

My father, the gigolo?

The afternoon lecture is on desensitization. RayAnne isn't sure what that might entail; the description reads "quelling your animal instinct to react to distractions or provocations." Had it meant to say "your animal's," meaning your dog's? Or your own "inner animal"?

Perhaps she could desensitize herself to her father.

Attending the lecture are a dozen dogs in a cornucopia of breeds and sizes, from chow to mastiff, tired handlers in tow. Petra does not call participants by their name, but by the breed of their animal, as if they are one.

"Mastiff!" She points to a spot. "Spaniel!" This goes on until all are settled in a formation that satisfies her. Petra Koslov seems a bottomless font of discipline and control. When she goes still and quiet, so do all attendees. She need only nod and all turn their attention to the front of the tent where today's guest is patiently awaiting his cue.

A lean, caramel-colored pointer stands frozen in the classic hunter pose atop the very table they ate breakfast on. He is shaking with anticipation, accessorized with a jaunty pair of matching testicles quivering between taut haunches.

"Gunther," Petra deliberately walks a half-circle behind the animal to assure she has all eyes, "is my vizsla stud."

Rongo whispers, "With the cojones to prove it." He is rewarded with a withering look from Petra, who apparently possesses dog hearing.

Ah, so this is the mate of Uma, currently sequestered in estrus, RayAnne realizes.

Petra calls their attention back with tongue clicks that bring to mind sonar blips. They all wait, as does Gunther, paramour to Uma, and Dog knows how many other bitches panting in the wings. The room goes quiet as they await the next move of their trainer extraordinaire.

Gunther remains frozen in his valiant duck-stamp posture. One has to admit that Petra, stern and focused as she is, seems a bit valiant herself, like one of those determined comrades in Soviet propaganda posters.

RayAnne looks around the room: the shivering woman with both knees slimed in gray mud the color of her Weimaraner; the fellow who's been walking around with a pair of eyeglasses duct-taped to his forehead since his lab chewed the stems off; the Yorkshire terrier matron with four fingers wrapped in oozy little bandages. The lengths to which people will go for their pets. Some might argue that the cons of dog ownership outweigh the pros—dogs don't exactly contribute: there's the cost, the bother, the mess, the fact that they are essentially four-legged turd machines. Not to mention the energy and resources, the carbon footprint of dogs.

But then, consider a world without them.

Until getting her own dog, RayAnne hadn't thought much about the canine-human connection. Rory has certainly made her life better. He's forced her out into the world, budges into her self-absorption with his demands—taking attention that otherwise might roll over to moods, to grief. Sometimes, just having Rory at her feet is enough to force her into the moment.

Gunther is like the dog in an eighteenth-century oil painting. RayAnne tries assessing him as if she were a dog. In that light, Gunther is admittedly a very handsome beast. All is in the right places—his dog penis is behaving, remaining in its sheath and thankfully not doing that thing that's enough to ruin lipstick for a prude. At the moment only Gunther's manners are on display: he is the embodiment of "good dog"—calm, dignified, pointedly ignoring the asthmatic pug in the front row.

Yes. *If I were Uma,* RayAnne admits, *I'd be climbing that. All that.*

"Your dog should not give in to distraction. Desensitizing an animal is not for the faint of heart, believe me; control is not an easy behavior to train into your animal."

She's glad Rory isn't here. He wouldn't like Petra's methods. He's hunkered down in subzero Ontario with Hal, likely under the worktable in his crate lined with old sweaters and a fine coating of fur from Hal's late-great mutt, Ditch, a husky-shepherd named for the location where he and his litter mates had been found, shivering and starved. Ditch's rugged puppyhood had been followed by fifteen happy years as Hal's best buddy. Gone now.

She looks around the tent. Still, nothing is happening—they've all been lulled, just watching Gunther. Petra still poses next to him. Without warning, she reaches out to yank on Gunther's penis. Hard.

Everyone gasps, including a yelp from Rangi. Petra now has their attention. She certainly has Gunther's. Amazingly, while he is obviously concerned, Gunther does not react. Without looking, RayAnne knows instinctively that all three guys queued next to her have either crossed their legs or are doing the athletic cup thing with their hands, perhaps considering backing away and out of the tent. But they would be seen, of course, and so stay put.

Without letting up or letting go of Gunther's very personal appendage, Petra addresses all.

"Children you'll meet on the street will think this is a handle . . ." She gives another vigorous yank, ". . . a toy."

RayAnne wonders what sorts of children Petra might have known back in Ukraine. Are they the reason she lives with a pack of dogs in the remote bush half a world away?

Gunther somehow remains still. His eyes, however, are running relay races.

"Welcome to *Desensitization!*" Petra barks. Finally letting go her vice grip, she takes a step away. Gunther, while not shifting his posture, visibly relaxes.

"Omg," RayAnne exhales. Not keen to see what Gunther might be in for next, she takes advantage of the smattering of applause to back away and out.

"We're here on beautiful Lake Hāwea on New Zealand's stunning South Island." RayAnne nods to her left and the camera swings to view the lake and snowcapped mountains beyond. When focus lingers on the mountain and doesn't pan back, she budges into frame and snaps her fingers. "Hello? You can see how easily the scenery can steal the show here, but today we're featuring a guest you won't want to miss, Uma Koslov, who fishes using no lures, no poles, no special gear, no spears, no nets. Uma has taken trophy fish with nothing more than . . . wait for it . . . her teeth!"

RayAnne turns to the second camera, shaking her head as if she can't believe it herself. "I know, right? Well, today we're going to go fishing with Uma and see what we catch. We'll meet up with her after a quick word from our sponsor, Lefty's Bait."

Focus pulls out to show RayAnne sitting on the edge of the long fishing pier, shoulder to shoulder with Uma, a sultry, toffee-hued Hungarian vizsla—the canine equivalent of those rarified humans let in to exclusive clubs while all the other schmoes watch from behind the velvet ropes. Uma's svelte frame would be the envy of a bulimic.

"Hey girl." RayAnne turns from Uma to address the camera. "Lots of creatures fish, and it turns out dogs are no exception."

Uma's snout nuzzles to RayAnne's ear. RayAnne responds by pretending to listen. Then answers, "Except that dogs don't usually fish, but you're special. Right, Uma?"

It had been Cassi's idea to dab peanut butter behind Ray-Anne's ear so that every time she posed a question and cocked her head, the dog would nose in as if whispering an answer, which RayAnne would pretend to understand. She looks up. "Uma says, 'Enough small talk. Let's go fishing.'"

Uma looks directly toward the camera, stretching her long body forward.

Rangi pulls back just before the dog can lick the lens. Second camera pans from the left as Cassi holds up a finger so RayAnne knows where to aim her words. "This lake is amazing. I'm told there are brown and rainbow trout and Quinnat salmon here in Hāwea. And believe it or not, just under this pier is decent trout habitat."

Uma begins pacing the very edge of the pier, stepping neatly across RayAnne's knees on lanky, naturally high-heeled legs. Once the dog detects movement underwater, she goes stock-still, zeroing in.

"Wow," RayAnne says. "I wish I'd possessed that kind of concentration in college." Half to herself she mutters, "But then, I'd have graduated and would probably have some desk job right now." The mic of course has picked up her comment. A tinny voice urges into the earpeice, "Quick, say more." Cassi seems to have a knack for encouraging RayAnne's better tangents.

"Sooo, instead, here I am interviewing a dog that fishes . . . in paradise. And how awesome is that?" RayAnne looks to the camera as if unable to believe her own good luck. "Maybe not all failings or flaws are actually flaws, you know? My grandmother used to say they're just *unique-queties.*"

Suddenly, three feet to RayAnne's right, Uma drops into downward-facing dog and goes still, eyes darting around the clear water beneath. From high in the dog's sinuses emits a medium-frequency whine.

RayAnne's voice drops to golf-announcer tone. "And, safe to

say, I'm in unique company now. It looks like Uma is about to do her thing. Oh look, we can see the fish . . ."

There are trout swimming below, unaware. The guys have dropped underwater cameras. Rangi, having donned scuba gear and wetsuit, is anchored under the surface trying to stay still while pulling focus. His air bubbles burble to surface where he's been under for ten minutes.

RayAnne is impressed anew with Team Tripod. As their reference had suggested, they are up for anything, and apparently the more bonkers the better.

Everyone is a little anxious. If Uma doesn't dive, all the day's preparation and work will have been for nothing. This is their second attempt. Hours earlier, they'd had a rough start when Uma—bird dog to her core—went quietly insane the moment they'd launched the drone. For a while RayAnne was afraid the dog might actually shake herself into some sort of seizure, poised to spring skyward as if to bite the drone out of the air. After the drone was put away, it still took awhile for Uma to calm down. Now, finally, she's focused, intent on the fish.

Petra had been offered a spot in the boat with Chad but had demurred, preferring to stay on the pier just out of camera range. "When it comes to water," she'd said, "I'm like a husky—loathe the stuff."

Uma is statue-still, waiting with a focus and patience few humans could muster.

All eyes toggle between dog, handler, and various viewfinders. Cassi is clearly tiring of holding up the fuzzy mic-on-a-stick that looks like a squirrel on a branch. Just as the dog's whine pitches to a higher register, Petra gives the signal, and Uma launches from the dock like a missile.

One camera angle catches Uma in super slow motion. Later, watching dailies, they will marvel at how her already elongated body seemed to stretch even longer just before piercing the surface. Not feet-first as you might expect, but nose-first, like a seal.

The underwater POV is an explosion of bubbles, with Uma's snout zooming for the bottom as if launched. The underside of the pier is old wooden timbers with flags of waving moss. Plenty of places for fish to float undercover. A number of tails scatter. Uma's jaws open to a flash of white teeth, a fishtail flashes, and then, the chomp—caught!

RayAnne can hardly believe it.

Bursting up to the surface, Uma dog-paddles a furious circle while looking quite panicked—as one would if their jaws were suddenly inhabited by a thrashing brown trout. Petra gives a whistle and Uma paddles pier-ward where RayAnne is ready with a net, practically squealing, "Good dog, good girl!"

Uma ignores the net and struggles up the slimy pier steps and gently drops the fish at RayAnne's feet before proceeding to shake water, ears flapping violently, spraying RayAnne and all the nearest camera lenses.

The fish is a beauty, and no worse for wear—barely a tooth dent on it. Uma's long line has been bred for "soft mouth"—to not bite down on whatever game they are tasked with retrieving, usually grouse or ducks, but Uma's instinct has deftly evolved to include delivering trout.

The fish is held toward the camera, RayAnne making a fuss over it and soundly praising Uma. When RayAnne hugs the dog, Petra lobs her look. Pedigree aside, she's just a dog, RayAnne reasons, and dogs love love.

Uma catches four more fish. By the time they call it quits, RayAnne is soaked from Uma's coat shakings. Her own jaw aches for how often she'd dropped it in the course of the hour, because Uma stalking and diving—this elegant creature fishing—is a sight to behold.

"I honestly cannot tell," RayAnne shakes her head at the camera, "if Uma is hunting or playing. If this is work or fun?"

The fish are taken from the live well, measured and then released back into the lake, at which point Uma loses it. RayAnne can barely be heard above the sharp barking as the dog frantically paces the dock's edge watching as all her efforts are dumped. RayAnne faces the camera straight on, practically yelling to be heard over the yips. "And there you have it, a great day of fishing here on Lake Hāwea with my new pal, Uma the vizsla." RayAnne brushes damp hair from her temple and digs in her pocket before turning to shout, "Who wants a treat?!"

An hour later, after their somewhat less exciting interview with Petra (Uma is a hard act to follow), the crew pack up and wave goodbye to Kirehe.

The drive back to Queenstown seems to take forever. Fog forces Chad to drive at a grandpa pace. Any views are occluded, the weather effectively sealing them in the van. It's just them and the road. They resort to corny car games. The current one being, *Would you rather wake up in bed with* blank *or* blank?

"Squid or spider?"

"Squid." RayAnne doesn't hesitate.

"Why?" Rongo asks.

"It would be out of its element and probably weak, right?"

"Point."

"Voldemort or Frankenstein?"

Rangi considers. "Frankenstein. He was just misunderstood. Probably a really nice bloke."

Since Rangi answered, it's his turn to ask. "Genghis Khan or Mr. Burns?"

Chad, bobbing his head behind the wheel answers in song, a '70s tune, singing, "Genghis is just all right with me, Genghis is just all right, oh yeah . . ."

RayAnne laughs. Chad's not half-bad. Cassi gives them her puzzled grin. "I get the Mr. Burns reference, but that song . . . ?"

"Too old for you to know . . . the Doobie Brothers." RayAnne is surprised someone Chad's age knows this band. She's only familiar with them from car trips suffered with her mother.

"The *what* Brothers?"

"I know, it was their actual name."

The game continues. "Lizzie Borden or Charles Manson?"

"My turn already?" Rongo taps his chin. "Remind me, was Lizzie Borden hot?"

"She was an ax murderer." Cassi frowns.

"Sure . . ." Rongo shrugs, "but *he* was crazy. Lizzie, final answer."

"Raggedy Anne or Andy?" Rongo asks.

"What? That's just . . . no." Cassi crosses her arms.

"Oh, brother." Rongo sighs. "Okay, since we're on dolls, this one's for Cassi. Ken or GI Joe?"

"Ken."

"That was fast."

"I've never cared for camo?"

The fog out the window is a little claustrophobic—they could be anywhere.

"RayAnne?"

The others play the game across her now, three more rounds as she blinks at her own reflection in the window blinking back, until her image is overlaid with Gran's image, distinctly mouthing, *Pissant.*

"C'mon, Ray. One more?"

She sits up, but imagination fails and the notion of playing a game feels flat. She sniffs. "Cancer or a heart attack?"

After a nano of silence, Chad mutters, "Bit of a mood killer, that."

Cassi turns in her seat and says, "Just say *pass* if you don't want to play."

Rangi softly elbows RayAnne. "Cass mentioned you'd lost your granny. So sorry. Did she die of cancer?"

"More or less . . ."

"Well, at least with cancer you've got time to say your goodbyes. So that's it for me. Cancer. Final answer."

RayAnne looks up. "Can we stop?"

Looks are shuffled. Cassi says, "Sure, RayAnne, whatever you want."

"No, I don't mean the game. I mean can we *stop* soon? I need a pee."

They spend the next two days in Queenstown. RayAnne mostly wanders on her own, finding a homey café around the block from their hotel. Maudes has comfy, futsy chairs and the most amazing cookies. At first, she'd thought the café sign was missing an apostrophe, but on her second day learned both partners are named Maude. What are the odds? The scones at Maudes are the best she's ever eaten.

There are stacks of British tabloids to thumb through while RayAnne idly listens to the Maudes gossip and talk about their grown children and grandkids; the weather; their physical woes, which include bursitis, polyps (is there a grosser word in the English language?), and varicose veins. They are on their feet all hours, and both also volunteer at the hospice shop next door. The only time they sit is when working over handfuls of string with crochet hooks tatting the doilies for the arms and backs of the flowery upholstered chairs. They call these knotted creations "antimacassars." Since RayAnne's laptop is clammed open to suggest she is somehow occupied and not simply in a sugar stupor, she occasionally looks something up: *antimacassar* is derived from the wide floppy collars worn by sailors of old to protect their uniforms from the Macassar oil, which is hair oil, which explains the "anti" but begs the question, why'd they wear so much of it in the first place?

Cassi heads off with the guys to film B-roll in places with names like Devil's Staircase or Double Cone, which sadly has nothing to do with ice cream. They leave her to the café, which has the atmosphere of some old neighbor's kitchen where the door is left open so that anyone might come and go. Like Gran's kitchen.

Her phone occasionally dings with some text from her father, which he signs off with GOD BLESS. According to Ky, the bible-thumping AA group Big Rick has joined with Sally is practically a cult. He even has his own handle now, @drytweetjesus, as if being born again and getting sober at once is a thing. Ky reports that their father had brought Sally to the house for dinner, where she gave the twins creationist coloring books, which Ingrid tossed before Sally's Mercedes was out of the driveway.

RayAnne wants to know yet doesn't, and asks anyway. HIYA DAD, HOW'S IT GOING WITH SALLY?

Big Rick responds: GANGBUSTERS. HOUSE ON FIRE. IF PEOPLE KNEW WHAT WAS GOOD FOR THEM, THEY'D EMBRACE THE LORD AND A GOOD WOMAN.

RayAnne is not going to touch this.

"Good grief," she mutters, wiping crumbs from her screen.

By the way, *good grief*? Since when is grief good? Her phone dings as if in answer, and when she glances down, Gran's smile lights up the screen. "Grief is good, RayBean, when you allow it."

Since when is she not allowing it? "I'll tell you what's good, Gran." She holds up a confection that is a crispy rolled cookie filled with vanilla-scented whipped cream. "This. It's called a brandy snap. And it's possibly the best thing I've ever tasted. These Kiwis know their way around a pastry slab."

"Oh, for heaven's sake." Gran rolls her eyes and the screen goes dark.

Pissant, indeed. Why are we meanest to those we love most?

The Maudes of the brandy snaps look over at RayAnne and then to each other and shrug.

That girl again. Talking to the black screen on her phone.

4. DEPRESSION

They eat breakfast on the terrace of the Masonic Hotel. RayAnne and Cassi have the day off, and next to Cassi's plate of eggs is a stack of brochures with possibilities, compliments of the concierge. Choices include a reptile farm, sheep shearing, a vineyard tour, a former prison, or a cliffside hike.

RayAnne pushes away the reptile farm brochure without discussion.

"The prison?"

"Nuh-uh."

"This looks pretty?" RayAnne opens a page to sweeping views of ocean cliffs from a high vantage point. "Some place called Cape Kidnappers . . . sounds fun."

"Vertigo." Cassi shakes her head. "Sorry. Besides, I'm still half-blind from yesterday."

The term *blinding beauty* could have been coined in New Zealand. The day before they'd spent two hours on a white sand beach at high noon, surf fishing, which was totally fun for RayAnne and miserable for Cassi. Even under an umbrella and wearing prescription sunglasses, it took hours for Cassi's eyes to recover. This morning she is milk pale, wearing a T-shirt that reads Got Melanin? Her condition is labeled "achromasia," and she is the only person RayAnne knows who celebrates Minnesota Novembers.

"Just curious, Cass, given your allergy to the sun, why'd you choose New Zealand?"

"Well, it was this or Location. We could have stayed home, gambling on guests who might want to travel to a frozen lake, then sit for an interview in an eight-by-six-foot ice shack that smells like bait and PBR."

"Couldn't we have just taken the show south, like snowbirds?"

"Maybe, but . . ." Cassi hesitates. "I didn't think you'd want to go back to Florida so soon—after, you know. And the Alabama boycott is still on, and Texas is *Texas* . . ."

"Point." RayAnne nods. "You choose where to go today. I don't care."

"Since when do you not care?"

"Since today."

Chad arrives at the table, having stayed overnight at the home of nearby relatives. He's carrying a Tupperware container of cookies. "Aunties, you know?"

"Sweet." RayAnne, who had reluctantly passed on the breakfast muffin, looks at the container and feigning nonchalance, inquires, "What kind?"

"Kind?" Chad sets them down on the empty chair. "You mean flavor?"

"Yeah, like snickerdoodles, or peanut butter . . . ?"

"Um, cookie flavored, I reckon."

Her hint has fallen flat.

Cassi blinks and stands. "Crap. Forgot my eyedrops. Back in a flash."

Just as she leaves, Chad's phone rings. He fishes it out, frowns, and gets up. "I should take this." He walks down the terrace, leaving RayAnne alone with the cookies.

. . .

Ten minutes later, they all descend on the table at once. RayAnne straightens, giving her lips a furtive dust-off. Rangi and Rongo fall into their chairs and open a map. The crew will be spending the day scouting a trout stream where they will film the next day's guest, an eightysomething flytying legend, famously reclusive.

As for Cassi and RayAnne, the day is theirs.

"So guys," Cassi fans out the brochures. "If you were us, and had one day to waste here, what would you do?"

Chad chuckles as he shuffles the brochures. "Sheep shearing? Great if you're in the mood for a broiling barn and a bunch of ewes pissing themselves."

"But not laughing?"

Chad looks over imaginary glasses. "Not everything is a euphemism."

"Vineyard Experience: Sauvignon Stomp?"

"Classic," says Chad. "They *charge* tourists to help them harvest grapes, then corral them in a trough to stomp it all down to a pulp. I'd pay to watch that."

RayAnne is absorbed in systematically peeling the membrane from the last orange sections on her plate.

Cassi picks up the last brochure, which looks as though it was put together by someone's cousin. It's for a theme park less than an hour away. "A Rings park!" Her pale eyes light up despite Chad shaking his head. "That dump? It's just a rip-off of the real place, Hobbitcon. Whatever you do, do not go to the Shyre."

RayAnne scrutinizes the sod roof of Bayg End. "Shyre, my arse. That grass looks fake. For ninety bucks, you'd expect the real deal."

"I wouldn't, actually." Cassi taps her chin, looking disappointed. "I mean, we were warned."

They are eighteen minutes into the Shyreville's two-hour tour. When RayAnne bends to tie her shoelace, bracing herself against what looks like a boulder, it shifts to separate from the Astroturf, exposing a seam of concrete beneath. Caught off-balance, she falls in slow-mo to thump on her backside.

Both she and Cassi bark out little laughs, then immediately clam up when a straggler on the tour turns to give them the eye. Thankfully, they are the tail end of the group—most others have barged ahead to the grog house. The tour is scheduled to conclude with a lunch of pork pie, mead, and something called Cram. RayAnne and Cassi opted out of the later tour, which included a banquet with some kind of creature roasted on a spit, with guaranteed Hobbit sightings between courses, doubling the ticket price.

RayAnne raps knuckles on the *rock*. "Some composite or whatever."

"I think the point is to pretend."

RayAnne shrugs, pushing the section back into place. "Whole place is fake."

"You know it could be fun, if you let yourself ima—" Cassi is cut short when the hinges on a round window of Bayg End squeal, the casement yawns open, and one of the actors, in full-on pointy ears, huffs indignantly. "Admittedly, there are a few bits of artifice here and there. But I assure you, lovely ladies, the Shyre is real!"

To their blinking stares, the hobbit blinks back, his eyes locking on Cassi's hair. Then, as if remembering his manners, stutters, "It *is* r-r-eal. As real as me." He hands over a card to Cassi as if to offer proof.

"*Bylbo Baggyns*? I don't remember so many y's . . ."

Bylbo sighs. "Copyright issues." He sticks a smallish hand out the window for them to shake.

"Ah. I'm Cassi. And this is RayAnne." As an afterthought, she offers, "We're real, too."

Bylbo certainly does look the part.

Cassi smiles, which is rare. "I didn't know this was a reenactment dealie. Ray . . ." Cassi elbows her, a bit vigorously, "did you know that?" Cassi has a habit, when she needs your full attention, of grabbing forearms or stilling your foot with hers, even employing the little punch to the arm. Cassi fights this habit but had grown up with a pair of twin sisters three years younger, both wildly ADHD—the perfect storm.

RayAnne steps out of range. "Nope."

At the sound of a shout, Bylbo holds a finger to his lips. "Shh." He cranes out the window down the path of the retreating group. "They'll hear you."

"Who?"

But when they turn back, he's disappeared from the window. The door handle is turning and a rusty squeal accompanies the opening of the front door.

RayAnne whispers, "He looks just like that actor, Morgan Freeman."

"*Martin* Freeman, Ray—Morgan was tall, very dark, and handsome. Drove Miss Daisy?"

"Right. Whatever. But he does look like that guy, doesn't he?"

Cassi nods. "Cuter, actually."

The door swings open. Expecting a full-sized actor to greet them, both are surprised to find Bylbo is actually half a head shorter than Cassi, who makes RayAnne feel tall. He's wearing a wine-red coat and short pants, just like in the films. When he steps fully out onto the path, RayAnne's gaze stalls at his bare feet, hairy and broad. "Wow. Those look really real."

"What do you mean?" Bylbo talks around the pipe clenched in his teeth. He looks at his feet.

"It's okay, you don't need to stay in character."

"Beg pardon?" He nods toward the door. "Are you coming in or not? The kettle's on and I've just taken a seedcake out of the oven."

"Oh?" RayAnne looks warily into the dim hall. Despite feeling ravenous, she says, "We're not really hungry."

Cassi gives her a look and turns to Bylbo. "I am quite hungry, now that you mention it."

Before RayAnne can reach for her, Cassi's popped in after the little reenactor-actor. Sighing, RayAnne ducks in and closes the door, which does seem solid and weighty on its wrought-iron hinges. Inside is larger than she would have imagined. Curious now as to how true to the story the place is, she follows as Bylbo slaps his big bare feet across the wooden floor and down the arched hallway.

Cassi sticks close to Bylbo while RayAnne hangs back, running her hand along the oak paneling, which for all the world looks real and feels solid. Reaching up to touch the curved ceiling she sees the plaster is crackled like the plaster on her own hundred-year-old ceilings back home—ceilings the realtor had insisted added "character," which cost RayAnne an arm and a leg to fix.

Even the floor of Bayg End creaks authentically, making her wonder if there aren't little hidden devices to add ambience. The place somehow exudes a genuine, fusty aura of hobbity bachelorhood. Drawn by the scent of pipe tobacco, she stops at the entrance to a dim side room. Roughly drawn plans are strewn across a workbench; neatly hung are old awls and chisels with handles black from use. In progress is a scale model of a whatchamacallit, to hurl things—a trebuchet—held together with teeny wooden pegs. RayAnne picks up a dainty hammer and sets it down, sniffs the faint smell of oil and sawdust. A literal man cave, the room's quaint aura of industry is very much like her grandparents' basement, where Dead Ted pounded and sanded to the drone of baseball games broadcast on the transistor radio, cobbling together woodcraft projects.

So few people make anything these days. Hal is an exception, crafting prototypes for lures he has designed. He could more easily employ a CAD program and 3D printer but prefers the tactile appeal of chisels, the smell of balsawood. Also, he's just so glad to be able to use his hand. He paints his lures as well, and the sight of him bent with his tiny brushes, wearing the dweeby magnifying headgear, is oddly moving. He says each lure carved feels like an exercise in gratitude. He'd staked a hand on medicine, and medicine came through for him. RayAnne only learned about Hal's generosity after he took her to a fancy gala for big donors to organizations funding research for vascular surgery and veterans' services for prosthetics.

And, well, Hal in a tuxedo . . .

There is rather a lot to love about the guy. Of certain things, RayAnne has no doubt.

She's nudged from her reverie by her name being trilled from somewhere deeper in Bayg End.

Cassi, *trilling*?

They are in the tidy kitchen with walls that begin to curve to the ceiling just at shoulder height. RayAnne gives up on posture and slumps to accommodate, feeling Amazonian. Bylbo motions them to sit on daycare-sized chairs while he bustles, boiling water, making tea. Everything—plates, wooden spoons, and goblets—are scaled to size. After much clanging at the burners of an old-timey woodstove, Bylbo, now wearing a rough linen apron, turns with a tray laden with a teapot, wee jug of milk, mugs, and slices of cake.

"I'll be mother," Bylbo pours. "Do tell. Your journey. Was it long?"

"Long-ish? You mean from LA?"

"LA? Is that near . . . ?"

"Enedwaith," Cassi offers.

"Ah!" Bylbo seems pleased.

Apparently, Cassi is up on her Middle Earth geography and has decided to play along. RayAnne wonders how long she'll be able to keep it up. For herself, staying in the moment is enough of a challenge. She's distracted, drawn to the view out a porthole-shaped window. In the distance, other houses pock the hillside, their chimneys huffing realistic smoke. Bylbo and Cassi make ridiculous small talk, mostly in reference to characters from the stories. Bylbo imparts news regarding them as if they are real. In the reflection, she can see Cassi with chin planted on palms, leaning coquettishly toward their diminutive host as they drone on about some trip he'd taken to Mordor, as if it actually happened.

Really, RayAnne thinks, Kiwis must get so bored of this *Lord of the Rings* business in the way people in Minnesota are so over Lake Wobegon, where all the children are *not* above average and—guess what?—not all the men are good looking.

Bylbo cannot peel his eyes off Cassi. The feeling appears mutual, as if some chemistry is brewing between her and this man-boy with fake hairy feet.

Bylbo Baggyns reluctantly excuses himself from the table to replenish water in the kettle, using a wooden ladle to retrieve it from a barrel. *Jeez,* thinks RayAnne, *they've thought of everything.* Somewhere there will be cracks and they will soon see the wires holding everything together.

Cassi chews her seedcake slowly, her eyes practically rolling in pleasure. "Ray, you gotta try this."

"Nah." She mutters her confession. "I had a cookie earlier."

Cassi smiles. "Not one of Chad's, I hope?"

"Why not Chad's?"

Cassi snorts. "The weed cookies? I could smell them through the Tupperware."

RayAnne swallows. "No, not one of Chad's." Then bites her lip. It is true she hadn't eaten *one* of Chad's cookies—she'd had three. She stiffens and takes stock of herself, looking to her reflection in the window. Bit of a mistake since it's old, bubbled glass. She doesn't seem stoned, just warped, fun-house fashion. She can smell the seedcake Cassi is eating—the caraway, which reminds her of licorice, which reminds her of fishermen on the circuit and their horehound drops, considered candy only by old men.

Cassi daintily takes a second bite of cake while looking into Bylbo's eyes, chewing. "Mmmm."

Cassi Olson, Senior Location Producer, is so blatantly flirting RayAnne must stifle a snort.

Bylbo blushes hotly to the tips of his fake ears.

RayAnne sits up, smacking her temple on the arch—his *fake* ears? Right. How is it they are red? Nah, not possible. Just the glow from the red glass shade of the paraffin lamp, obviously.

Paraffin?

The moment she thinks it, she can smell it.

She is. Stoned. Totally. It's all suddenly too much. Fresh air is what she needs. Focusing on the dregs in her cup, she practices an excuse—a sentence to begin with, but only one word of it comes out.

"Cassi."

"Hmm?" Cassi, limpet-eyed and charged with pale sensuality, reluctantly peels her attention away from Bylbo. RayAnne has to admit the little man has his charms, were one into dwarves of old. She's forgotten what she was going to say.

"We should go, actually." She almost hates to rain on Bylbo's strange little tea party, but perhaps if she doesn't act soon, Alice herself might pop into this scenario with a bottle of Drink Me.

Bylbo slumps. "Oh? I was just going to offer you mead—and from my best batch yet." A faint furrow has formed betwixt his furry brows.

Betwixt? RayAnne checks her reflection in the window as if to confirm, *Did I just think in Old English?* "Yeah, no. No mead for *moi*."

"We don't *have* to go." Cassi shoots her a look. "I mean, not like we have to be anywhere."

Bylbo politely backs into the pantry to pretend-busy himself with a crate of bottles, humming hopefully as he bashes around.

RayAnne leans. "Cassi? What the . . . ?"

"I like him," she whispers back.

"But you don't even know who he is—I mean, he *is* somebody else when he's not . . . not this."

Cassi looks solidly unkeen to go.

"Right. Well, maybe *I* should go then."

Cassi has the keys out of her bag in an instant. "Great. I'll be back to the motel . . . when I'm back."

"Me? Drive the Rover?"

"It's a straight shot back the way we came, Ray. You can manage." It's a rebuke, not an encouragement. Cassi looks to Bylbo, who is back with a bottle clutched in each fist, a hopeful look on his face.

"My friend needs to go," Cassi says sweetly, "but I'm happy to stay."

"Yes?" Bylbo gulps nervously as if he cannot believe his luck. "Oh my." Turning to RayAnne, he lies, "Terribly sorry you can't stay," his ears growing even redder. "But at least take something for the journey. Do you have far to go?"

"I dunno, twenty-some miles, er, kilometers."

"Kilom . . ." Bylbo turns to Cassi. "How far is that in gyrds?"

Cassi's fingers ruffle an invisible calculator. "However many gyrds there are in seventy-five furlongs."

"Goodness. And no horse?" Bylbo presses a seedcake wrapped in waxed linen and a corked bottle of grog into RayAnne's hands. "For the journey."

He's not once fallen out of character, she'll give him that. "Right. Thank you."

RayAnne makes her way out, marveling again at how real everything looks. She peeks into the alcove with the juvenile-sized bed, the wool blanket folded neatly over authentically wrinkled linen sheets, the pillow dented as if by a Bylbo-sized head. She's in either the most exacting theme park on the planet or reality has slipped a gear.

Or maybe she's just that stoned.

The door shuts behind her with oaken solidity. Making her

way along the path she might as well be journeying Middle Earth for as long as it takes. How authentic everything seems. Not until nearly to the parking lot does she notice any references to the present—an electrical utilities box planted in the ground—and she hears the distant drone of traffic. Looking behind her down the path (in hopes Cassi has come to her senses) she sees it's empty.

In no hurry to get behind the wheel, RayAnne hangs in the parking lot a while, giving Cassi more time. While sitting on the hood of the Rover, the beat-up Shyreville bus rocks into the parking lot and comes to a dusty halt. Another tour has arrived. Out tumble two dozen tourists, all wearing neon-green caps emblazoned with the name of the company SOMETIME FUN TOURS. Their tour guide carries a bright but torn flag that reads SOMETIME FU.

Many in the group have wizard wands and selfie sticks. Several wear fake hobbit ears. They laugh uproariously as they bonk each other with the wands or tug each other's latex ears. Countless pictures are taken. As they set off on foot, the driver watches them go with a sigh and, the moment they are out of sight, sits on the bus bumper and takes a fat spliff from his shirt pocket. He lights the spliff, takes an epic toke before holding it up in offering.

She shakes her head, hoping he doesn't come over. Even from across the parking lot, the smell is pungent and skunky.

Both watch as the group ascends the steep curve of the hill, then appears and disappears along the Shyre's paths, a neon-hued gaggle, bobbing and weaving.

So much for having Bylbo to yourself, thinks RayAnne. The tourists will arrive at Bayg End soon, laughing and yowling their vowels at volume, whacking their wizard wands and being otherwise obnoxious. They are bound to be a disruption, at worst an interruptus . . .

She turns back to see the bus driver has crossed the parking lot, again with his offer.

"Thanks, no."

After he has a second toke, he reluctantly grinds the embers across a flat stone and slips the cold spliff into his shirt pocket. "Third tour of the day. I'm knackered."

"Right."

"You're American."

"Yeee-up."

They both continue watching as the line of tourists reach the farther hill, several with their umbrellas open against the sun so that they now move like a colorful dragon.

"Well," she sighs, "so much for the peace at Bayg End."

The driver looks at his watch. "Oh, no worries, they won't be stopping there—they'll hoof it straight to the banquet for their roast beast. They'll be back here, sleepy and munted, by sunset."

"Munted?"

"Rat-arsed." He yawns. "None of 'em can hold their mead." He turns toward the bus. "Nearly time for my nap, I reckon." He happily takes the offer of seedcake and grog before shuffling off.

Perhaps she should be getting back. Perhaps have a nap herself. Cassi never would have entrusted RayAnne with the keys had she known the actual number of cookies snarfed . . .

The phone in her pocket dings with a text. She squints warily at the screen, half-expecting Gran, perhaps with some commentary on her behavior.

It's from Cassi. I'M STAYING.

A sleepover with her hobbit?

Fine, then.

RayAnne checks herself. Touches her toes, vigorously shakes her head, and deciding she is fit to drive, climbs into the vehicle. Realizing she's in the passenger seat, she huffs and clambers over the console to settle behind the wheel.

Really, why shouldn't hardworking Cassi enjoy herself? Would it kill RayAnne to root for her colleague and her wee Romeo?

. . .

Frankly, RayAnne is still in a state of mortification over the previous day's Skype debacle with Hal—Hal's mother, to be more precise. At least she can say she's met Mrs. Bergen now—albeit in the most embarrassing manner in which anyone has met a boyfriend's mother in the history of all time.

After dinner Cassi had gone out with the guys to a local bar and RayAnne retreated to her room, glad for the chance to catch up with Hal. There was a decent enough connection, and he'd answered immediately. The delay was less annoying than usual.

Hal looked over her shoulder at the wide-open window. "Nice. You've got sun—soak some of that up for me."

"I wish you were here."

"*I* wish I was there."

It all started out well enough. Hal looked particularly handsome, dressed as he was for the weather in layers: cable-knit sweater, plaid shirt jacket, down vest, and scarf looped seductively around his neck. He was also wearing the fingerless gloves.

"You headed outside?"

"Hell no." He shook his head. "Just trying to stay warm. Look." He panned to where Rory was curled on the couch, burrowed under an afghan, snoring. Hal turned the camera to the cabin windows and walked closer so she could see the frost built up around the frames like icy upholstery, each glass pane crazed with geometric ice patterns—one of those sights that could sell a person on winter.

"My spring project will be storm windows."

RayAnne felt a sudden stab of guilt for being warm. She was barelegged, wearing a cargo skirt and a little tank top. "Yikes. How cold is it?"

"Minus sixteen. Maybe thirty below tomorrow. Schools in town are already closing. What's it like there?"

"Oh, you know. Hot." To mitigate any vacationesque perceptions, she frowned. "Too sunny, actually, which is no good for Cassi, or for filming."

"Right."

"There's no ozone layer here, you know."

"Yeah? You should ask for hazard pay."

"Wait until you see the hang gliding footage!" She could see behind Hal and into the kitchen where wisps of steam rose from a skillet on the stove. "Are you cooking?"

"Spaghetti sauce. Hang on, I gotta turn it down."

Hal disappeared for seven seconds then was back, vaulting over the back of the couch to land in frame. "It's stirred, and simmering . . ." In his best Barry White voice he added, "like me." Hal suggestively unwound the scarf from around his neck while hefting an eyebrow. "Show me your tan line, Dahl."

"My what?"

"Your tan line."

"I don't really . . ." She pulled the strap of her tank top aside. "Cassi makes me slather up with SPF 50 every morning."

"Then show me your un-tan line. We've got a much better connection this time."

"Ahhh. Well, we do, don't we?"

"How much data you got, girl? Cuz this could take awhile."

"Oh, I got data." RayAnne leaned back on the chaise and positioned the iPad on the side table so Hal could see more of her. "I got data . . ."

"Bring it."

So she did, rolling up the tank top seductively, inch by inch, all while he told her exactly where and how he would touch her, what he'd be doing with his hands, his mouth.

He pointed to her bare midriff. "Show more."

"You show me more."

Hal divested himself of layers, shrugging out of his shirt

jacket. Since there is no sexy way to take off a heavy sweater, he simply yanked it over his head and tossed it behind him. He was down to his unbuttoned Henley.

"Your fly," she said. "Unzip it."

He did, then tugged the waistband of his jeans low over hips to expose plaid boxers. If Hal's hair weren't standing on end from sweater static, he'd be a northwoods Calvin Klein ad. Even with dork-hair he's the sexiest man she's ever seen. She told him as much by the time she was topless and nearly bottomless, having wriggled out of her skirt, wishing she'd worn something lacy instead of the beige quick-dry underpants.

Hal's boxers were doing a poor job of constraining his eagerness.

"All right, lumberjack, let's see that ax of yours . . ."

Just as Hal was running his thumb under the elastic of his boxers, the light over his shoulder was interrupted, a shadow passing across it. A shape came into focus like a slow-moving football.

What the . . . ? RayAnne stiffened. "Ah, Hal . . ."

"You see how much I'm missing you, babe?"

"Hal . . . wait." RayAnne leaned forward, shifting focus—nearly yelping as she reached out as if to stop the next thing, because there was someone in Hal's cabin.

"Someone's there!"

Suddenly, Hal's eyes were covered with a set of hands. Lady's hands, with rings and a bracelet. Some woman had broken into Hal's remote Ontario cabin on an oppressively cold winter's day to . . . what? Rob, *murder. . .* ?!

"Surprise!"

Hal yelled.

RayAnne yelled.

"Goodness, Pookie." The woman's voice went singsong before breaking into laughter. "I surprised you, didn't I!"

Pookie?

"Surprised? You scared the fu . . . crap out of me."

The face looming over his shoulder belonged to a handsome woman in her sixties. She went to wrap her arms around Hal's neck but he twisted free. "Mom!" He yanked an afghan over his lap and opened fly. "You might have knocked!"

"What are you watching there, hon?" Eyes behind stylish but fogged glasses squinted at RayAnne.

Mrs. Bergen looked like one of those capable types who chair every local arts or civic committees from Toronto to Topeka. The sort of woman who can walk into any gathering and immediately organize it.

"Goodness, aren't you cold, Halvorson?"

Halvorson? RayAnne squealed.

"Good Chri—"

"Sorry, Pookie! I really didn't mean to frighten you!" She laughed.

"Yes, you did!"

"I could tell you were watching *something* in here." Her glasses were crystal-clear then as she leaned over Hal to peer directly at the screen—to half-naked RayAnne.

"Good lord!"

Hal reached out to cover the screen but too late. RayAnne, having cast her tank top aside, clapped a hand over each bare breast.

"Oh, I seeee!" The woman's expression was a cocktail of mirth. The resemblance is clear: Mrs. Bergen has the same aqua-blue eyes as her son. Hal also has his mother to thank for the widow's peak RayAnne finds so endearing.

"Oh, honey." Mrs. Bergen smacked a hand to her cheek. "I'm sooo sorry. If I'd known you were watching porn . . ." Spinning away to face the wall, Mrs. Bergen's shoulders shake in silent laughter.

"Mom. It's not porn . . ."

"Whatever, honey. No worries, I'll just . . ." RayAnne could hear the woman clearing her throat before saying, "Take your time there. I'll be in the kitchen."

"Mom, it's not . . ."

"At least you've chosen a normal porn girl. Glad to see that's an option now."

"What?"

She'd turned back and pointed to RayAnne. "Women with small breasts. They should have their day, too, and it's about darned time if you ask me."

RayAnne looks down at her neatly cupped breasts.

Hal turns. "Seriously unbelievable, Mother. This isn't a *porn girl*." Having finally gathered himself after the shock of clammy mother hands he says, evenly, "It's RayAnne. My girlfriend."

Hal's mother took a slight stumble toward the screen. "No!"

Hal leaned back, resigned. "RayAnne, meet my mom."

"Um, I . . ."

"Mom, this is RayAnne."

"No. For real?" Mrs. Bergen pressed hands to heart. "*The* RayAnne!? Well, hello to you, dear!"

Ever polite, RayAnne gives a little wave, momentarily setting one breast free before clapping her hand back. "Ah. Nice to meet you, Mrs. Bergen."

Hal makes a sort of bark as Mrs. Bergen sits, butting in next to her son, dislodging Rory from his perch. "Oh, heavens, call me Binnie! Please!"

So this is Mrs. Bergen—Binnie—who in spite of colossally poor timing, seems very sweet.

"I hope I've not embarrassed you."

"Well, um . . ." RayAnne hunches down in frame so she's only visible from the shoulders up.

"Oh dear, of course I have!"

"Well, actually . . ."

Hal and his mother are now vying for space in frame. "Mom. Justine. Please. Can you just . . . go stir the sauce?"

She bogarts the frame. "Halvorson knows I hate it when he uses my real name. I prefer Binnie."

From offscreen, Hal replied, "And, I hate when you waltz in without knocking, Justine."

Hal's mother leaned in as if she and RayAnne were co-conspirators, saying, "Well, maybe I deserved that." She has the full, throaty laugh of a dedicated smoker. "No worries, dear. We'll meet properly. Soon, I hope! I'll um, let you get back to . . . it?"

And then she was gone, footsteps ticking away before pot and pan noises commenced from the kitchen. RayAnne could only shake her head at Hal, who could only shake his head back.

"I should go. I . . . pah . . ." She was fresh out of words.

Hal held up both hands. "Dahl, I promise you—we will laugh our asses off over this someday."

"Oh, I'm already laughing. *Halvorson*?"

After the screen went dark, RayAnne sat staring at it, then laughed until her back ached.

Hal had said "someday" so casually, as if there is a someday down the road in the future. So there's that.

She looks out the Rover's window and frowns as a fast little tear of homesickness salts her upper lip. She hadn't even had time last night to ask about Rory—what sort of man-and-dog capers they might have been getting up to—or to fish for hints as to how much Hal might be missing her.

Flipping the visor down, she's faced with a mirror. She knuckles away a second tear and chides herself. It's only a few weeks! Anybody can do anything for a few weeks, and shouldn't she be thrilled to be here, when Ontario is seized in a vortex and Minneapolis has entered the blackened-snowbank phase of late winter, everyone maxed out on Netflix, sick to death of their parkas, and gnarly with cabin fever, while here in paradise all RayAnne has to do is go fishing with interesting people in tropical blue waters?

She really does need to call off the pity party. It's only another week or two of work, and in the meantime, there's all that New Zealand has to offer—even such weirdness as the Shyre.

Pulling her phone from her backpack she sees Hal has left a message. It is a joke-line of kitten emojis, along with a link to a phrase list of Māori words. She scrolls down the page of tongue twisters, attempting to read them aloud.

Whakamāhanahana 1. (verb) (-tia) to animate, enthuse, stimulate.

Many words beginning with *wh* kick off with an *f* sound. *Fahka-ma-hana hana*. Upon repeating it, a person nearly could become animated and enthused. Simply attempting to pronounce the word lessens the leadenness in her chest. She closes her eyes and leans back.

RayAnne could use some whakamāhanahana about now. Just as she's thinking it, Gran's visage pixilates into form.

RayAnne frowns.

Gran frowns right back. "Good lord. You haven't been this mopey since the summer you were sixteen and had to go out guiding with your father."

"Yeah, well, that was the summer Robbie Bukowski moved in next door. But hey, what sixteen-year-old wouldn't want to spend the summer watching Robbie in his Speedo at the pool when they could sweat it out in a bass boat with Big Rick and his cronies—who pinched my bottom, by the way, Gran. And how do you suppose Dad responded? Told me to stop wearing shorts, like it was my fault."

"Yes," Dot says, sincerely this time, "your father can be an ass. He's never known how to just *be* around females. I wonder sometimes . . ." Even on the grainy screen, Dot's pensiveness comes through. "If Betsy's death messed him up around girls . . ."

Betsy. Not a name often evoked in the Dahl family. RayAnne is never sure if it's all right to bring her up. "Your father was only five, and oh, did he look up to her—adored her. Perhaps, after

Betsy, Ricky never trusted that other girls, or women, wouldn't disappear, too?"

"Hmm." RayAnne nods. Of course. As usual, Gran, in her meandering, tentative brand of wisdom, is able to unearth what you wouldn't think to dig for. "You might have something there, Dot Dahl."

Gran went on, seemingly more to herself than RayAnne. "I failed him when Betsy died—in a way he lost me, too. After the accident I didn't talk for a month, not a word—your poor grandfather thought I might die of a broken heart. Those were black days."

"Oh, Gran."

"I only came around because I had to—to raise your father; otherwise I might have thrown myself into that horrible swimming pool."

Gran's grief, old as it is, eclipses RayAnne's, making her feel suddenly like a pouting, spoiled brat. Losing a child? She is silent a full minute before asking, in all seriousness, "Gran, do you keep coming back to make this easier for me? Or maybe to teach me something? Is there some lesson in these visits?"

"Well, for starters, you keep reeling me back. If there's a lesson in that, RayBean . . ."

Does she keep reeling Gran back from the depths, like some pike? In keeping her on the line is she denying Gran the eternal rest she'd sought, the relief she'd so painstakingly plotted out?

Gran's voice is faint, distorted as she faintly tuts, "RayBean. It's a choice, you know."

"What . . . what is a choice?"

"Moving on."

RayAnne opens her eyes. Has she been dreaming? After sitting perfectly still for what seems like ages, breathing (mindfully, mind you—even Bernadette would be impressed), she sets herself back into the reality that is the dusty Shyre parking lot, sits straight, and turns the key in the ignition. Let Cassi carry on with what's-his-ears down in Bayg End: *she* is moving on, at least with this afternoon.

When the navigation screen flickers on, she turns it off before Gran has any chance to fizzle forth with any of her driving advice. Though she's only traveling a country road—it is on the back-assward side—she'll need all her powers of concentration.

She doesn't feel at all stoned. Really.

At least the brake and gas pedal aren't reversed. Putting the Rover in gear she remembers Chad's advice: *the driver is always closest to the center line.*

Navigating out of the parking lot she thinks, *Easy peasy,* in spite of the vehicle being larger than she's used to, not to mention the road being narrower. Once turned onto the somewhat wider main road, she is relieved at the lack of oncoming traffic. A mile into the journey she successfully negotiates her first roundabout. Really, the wrong side of the road isn't that hard to manage. Indeed, it is the little things. She celebrates her achievement with the audacious multitaskment of turning on the radio.

The announcer has one of those sleepy-sounding voices of public radio announcers everywhere. RayAnne knows nothing about classical music or opera—wouldn't know a concerto from a sonata or a tenor from an alto. The flutey song matches her driving pace and in a way, even the landscape. What's that word for a word that sounds like what it is, like *murmur* or *belch*—something impossible to spell . . . *onomatopoeia*? The music playing is the perfect soundtrack for the low, sloping green hills and curves she is negotiating. Coming to a T as the music works up to a crescendo, she turns naturally toward the hillier land as if led by some piper. For the moment, RayAnne has mastered driving in another country, staying on the proper side of the road. Plus, New Zealand is really pretty.

The announcer informs her the next song is an adagio for

voice, and what comes next is about the saddest music in the world.

The Rover roves on. Now that she thinks of it, she doesn't remember a T in the road on the way to the Shyre, but then she hadn't been driving. The voices of the choir match the patterns the breeze ripples across a field of some soft, grassy crop on either side of the road. This music is exactly the sort that should have been played at Gran's funeral. But Dot had planned her own memorial in advance and set the tone, turning the event into an extravagant dinner party, leaving behind two CD mixtapes of favorites: old show tunes, jazz, and downright sappy songs like "You Are My Sunshine," or that perennial funeral favorite, "Mambo Italiano," piped in to coincide with the pasta course as a hearty red was poured.

Hey mambo, mambo Italiano, hey mambo mambo Italiano
Go go go, you mixed up Siciliano
All you Calabrese do the mambo like-a crazy with the
Hey mambo don't wanna tarantella, hey mambo no more mozzarella

There was exactly one appropriate piece of music at the funeral, when a navy cadet picked up his trumpet as everyone tucked into their second glass of Chianti. The young man played a flawless version of "Taps," which began somberly enough, precipitating a flash flood of tears among mourners. But even "Taps" got Dahled up as it went on, with jazzy notes and an ending that transitioned directly into "St. James Infirmary," when even the creakiest mourners got up out of their seats to shimmy-conga around the party tent, hands on each other's sagging waistlines and sloped shoulders.

Gran would have loved her own funeral.

Despite free-rolling tears, RayAnne realizes she's smiling. An oncoming driver gives the universal country-road one finger off the wheel greeting as they pass each other.

She drives over half an hour, so caught up in the music that it takes rather a while to realize she should have reached the motel by now and, since she hasn't, has likely been traveling in the wrong direction. The Rover's navigation screen says, "No signal." Assessing the landscape, she sees it's more remote and rugged than any she's encountered.

Well, she'll just drive on to the next turnaround.

This will be remembered as her second mistake (the first will be thinking it was a good idea to drive off alone into the wilds of New Zealand). As the pavement narrows, the road descends sharply into a valley, not promising as cell reception goes. Just when trees encroach closer to the road, the blacktop stops and the road transitions to gravel. And now she would turn around except there is nowhere to do so—no driveways, not so much as a sheep crossing. She watches for wide spots in the road, anything.

A mile or three later she passes through a set of gates, where the road suddenly stops. She's dead-ended in a . . . place.

"Hurray. I think."

Just a place to park a few cars.

Back beyond the trees are a few small clearings that might be campsites, a large fire ring with log benches around it. She's apparently stumbled onto some gathering spot. Not exactly a prime destination—more the sort of place one reaches after running out of road. There is barely room to turn around.

She relies on the rearview mirror, avoiding the dashcam because this is precisely the sort of opportunity Gran would pounce on to pipe up with the advice she's so generous with. Once in reverse, RayAnne feels a slight resistance behind the rear tires. She slowly gives a bit more gas. The tires resist again and lift minutely as if trying to clear some obstruction, but then the Rover appears to give up.

RayAnne slaps the steering wheel. "You're a *Range Rover*!" By rights it should be able to climb stairs. She gives the pedal a stomp and the vehicle roars back over the hump. A log? *Now we're getting somewhere.*

Having spoken too soon (not for the first time), RayAnne yelps as the Rover tilts high and commences a sickening backward slide. A glance at the dashcam reveals nothing but dark foliage. She jams the gearshift into forward and guns it, but the tires only spin. Braking results in nothing. Both the front and rear end seem to be off the ground; the angle of the tilt shifts from concerning to alarming when the vehicle settles back to an abrupt *thunk* in the posture of a jetliner taking off. The front wheels are a good two feet off the ground. RayAnne rocks forward as if her own weight might totter the vehicle out of its teeter.

"No no no no. *No.*"

Ramming the gearshift into all-wheel drive, she steps on the gas but the rear tires have no purchase. She takes a breath. "This isn't happening."

After cutting the engine, she struggles to keep the door open while climbing out, wedging it with an elbow so it cannot slam until her limbs are cleared. She hops to the ground.

Yes, it had been a log. But behind the log—on which the chassis of the Rover now rests like a fulcrum—is nothing, just space, a narrow drainage ditch several feet deep, with a trickle of water running through its pebbly bottom. The rear bumper is wedged solidly and muddily on the opposite bank.

Channeling her father, RayAnne flings hands and words skyward. "Oh, for crying out fucking loud!"

She has landed herself in the sort of place high school kids go to get drunk and high or fool around. There's a ring of blackened stones around a shallow scorched crater, the site of countless fires. The log benches around the firepit are smooth from wear.

"Great," she says. "Kumba-fricking-ya."

Digging for her phone she chants a little chant while hoping for reception. Of course there isn't any. She spies a picnic table and clambers to standing on it, holding her phone toward the heavens—where, if indeed there is a God, she'll surely provide a few bars of cell coverage.

One bar. With some difficulty, she climbs back into the Rover and lays on the horn. Maybe someone camping or living within earshot might be annoyed or curious enough to come check out . . . what? Maybe there are hikers. Opening the sunroof, she climbs out, slides down the windshield on her backside to the hood. From there, she carefully turns around and steps down to the Rover's narrow bumper—when did bumpers become so measly?—grabbing the bug-crusted grill and bracing heels against the fog lights, she squats, putting her hundred-thirty-pound frame to work. Nothing. In the off chance motion might do it, she swings her hips side to side like some primate, then up and down, but even twerking, there is no way she can counter the imbalance. It then occurs that she's got no plan in the event the Rover's front end does yield to her wishes—she could be sent flying, or be crushed. She clamber-crawls back up the windshield and drops in the sunroof to screw herself back into the driver's seat, now positioned so that the view is through a canopy of unfamiliar leaves of species of trees she cannot name.

She restarts the engine and attempts to pull up the GPS, only to see the gas light has now come on—perfect. She wants to think it's the tilt affecting the tank. Fiddling with the radio reveals there is zero reception.

When had the music stopped?

She climbs back out. Daylight is draining. Given that it's about to get dark, walking back to the main road—miles—probably isn't a good option.

Breathe is what Bernadette would say if she were here. Freaking out does no good, ever. Since attacking an inanimate object is an option, she kicks at the log the Rover is so maddeningly hung up on, hoping to dislodge it. This proves somewhat satisfying until she kicks too hard and jams a toe. Howling, she hops away in a circle.

The most rational thing to do would be to find wood and light a fire before it gets too dark for anyone to see the smoke. After limping around gathering sticks and dumping them in the firepit, she wrestles back into the Rover to look for matches or a lighter, emptying the glove box and console between the front seats. There is no cigarette lighter, only charging ports for phones and tablets—all the modern conveniences and none of the archaic ones.

What would MacGyver do? Make a fire by rigging up something with spark plugs and kindling? Axle grease?

Then, another doh moment occurs: why would anyone come to check out smoke from a known fire ring?

Taking inventory of what food and drink she has—in case she truly is stuck—she counts a cold takeout coffee (flat white—one sugar); half a bottle of warm water; two pieces of gum; a mashed energy bar; and three loose gummy bears found in the bottom of her backpack, which she brushes off and eats. What had she been thinking giving Bylbo's seedcake and grog to the stoner bus driver?

She sits in the driver's seat as the sky dims, gazing out at the run-down campsite that evokes memories of teen indiscretions and keggers, a scenario RayAnne cannot help relate with poor choices and tempting fate.

Settling in as well as she can, she tilts the seat to full recline, which is actually comfortable despite feeling like a dentist's chair. Her view out the sunroof is a canopy of treetops; the smallest opening of sky is an ivied porthole, beyond which a few dim stars begin to glitter. Pulling the beach towel over her face, she tries not to hear the underlayment of noises surfacing since the sky has blackened: crickets, night birds, and who-knows-what sort of nocturnal, red-eyed creatures have commenced punching in for the night shift. Reptiles, probably; things with fangs, maybe. At least she's in a vehicle and not a tent, and not in Australia, where so many poisonous creatures are. Preparing for this trip, she'd

Googled “most dangerous creatures in New Zealand”—one site had glibly listed “Americans behind the wheel.”

Of course the moment she becomes comfortable, she has to pee. After briefly considering opening the door and squatting on the running board, she remembers Chad telling them that tourists comprise the lion’s share of emergency room visits here: tourists pose more dangers to themselves than any natural hazards on offer. She climbs out and down and sets a speed record for peeing before clambering in. Back under her beach towel, the sorts of thoughts that will keep her awake descend. People do just disappear—there one minute, gone the next. Those women near Piha, for example. As a practical matter, shouldn’t people just be chipped, like dogs?

The last time she was in such a place as this was back in high school.

Kevin Carlson had been a sweet semi-dweeb with a crush on RayAnne, one of the few good-looking boys who didn’t understand he was good looking—just a nice, hot kid, if maybe not the brightest. They were still “just friends.” By the time his seventeenth birthday rolled around, RayAnne had grown uncomfortable about the amount of time, gifts, and unrequited attention Kevin lavished on her. Having forgotten to get him so much as a card for his birthday, she rashly decided to surprise him with what was at hand—her virginity (which, truth be told, she was tired of dragging around anyway). So under a waxing moon atop a damp sleeping bag . . .

The condom broke.

RayAnne convinced herself that since it was her first time, the odds of getting pregnant would be miniscule at best, and proceeded to not worry about it. But biology trumped optimism and that wily, sperm-meets-egg thing happened after all. One of those million little wigglers as eager and tenacious as Kevin himself had triumphed.

In case anyone wonders, or is cocked and ready to judge, RayAnne does not regret the abortion she had during her senior year of high school. Nor does she regret telling Gran, who took her to the clinic and rubbed her back all the way home in the taxi and never uttered a word of lecture—for once having zero to say.

Such are the ties that bind.

RayAnne manages a smile. They'd both been rattled by the anti-choice protesters harassing them on the way into the clinic, accosting them with hymns and placards. RayAnne had never seen Gran stare daggers at anyone until one woman kept trying to get in front of them with a poster showing something graphic and bloody, clearly looking to confront them. When she got too close, Gran pressed the poster aside and stepped into the woman's personal space, saying something RayAnne could not hear, then pushing forward as if ready to walk *through* the woman. Once inside, Gran stopped short, as if she might head back out and throw down the gloves. RayAnne got her into the elevator, where Gran breathed like a boiling kettle for seventeen floors.

Of course, she could've spared Gran all that and gone straight to Bernadette, knowing her mother would have been all business and common sense and empowerment—she'd marched in Washington for *Roe v. Wade,* for heaven's sake. Bernadette would have insisted Kevin Carlson man up, acknowledge his part, and foot the bill, meaning RayAnne would have to tell him, and that was not about to happen.

With Gran, it was safe to just be distraught and sad. At the clinic counter after paying the invoice, Dot turned to RayAnne, still clearly ruffled, and said, "You will never insult me by trying to pay this back. This is not a transaction or a favor—it's your future."

They sat on a slippery vinyl couch waiting for her name to be called. "Do you know," Dot asked, "that trope 'Blood is thicker than water' doesn't apply to families at all?"

"Really?"

"No. It's about soldiers. It's about being in battle together."

The nurse at the doorway looked very kind and competent. When RayAnne's name was called, Gran began to get up.

She shook her head. "No, Gran. This is just me, I think."

It was in that next step, walking off on her own at seventeen and a half, that RayAnne faced her first adult moment, doing what needed to be done.

It is dark out there.

Should she be frightened? This campground would be a convenient place to dump a body. New Zealand has relatively few murders. Of course there's crime here—it's not Disneyland. Cassi, appreciative of all things tattooed, had shown her photos of New Zealand motorcycle gangs with full-on face tattoos, a nasty twist on the traditional moko: inked symbols on foreheads; swastikas and bulldogs on cheeks; gang names etched across noses. Imagine waking up to a mug like that every morning? Which could totally happen should she be kidnapped and sold by sex-trafficking bikers. She locks the Rover's doors against the remoteness so perfect for nefarious activity. On the other hand, there'd been a news story about a gang that had stepped up after the horrible mosque massacre in Christchurch, standing guard and escorting Muslims to and from Friday prayers. RayAnne supposes there are two sides to every coin. Or tattooed face. She curls in the driver's seat under the beach towel, fervently hoping for teenaged drinkers to happen along.

Gran, beam of optimism that she was, would often counsel RayAnne to *think of the worst thing that can possibly happen*—then weigh the mathematical probability of it actually happening (miniscule!) and then let it go, which really only allows room for the second-worst thing—the odds of getting mauled by a wild hyena or stabbed by a roving lunatic. Moving on to more realistic third-worst-case scenarios, she realizes those merely involve tomorrow, the show, and Cassi.

They have an interview scheduled first thing in the morning.

RayAnne sleepily wonders if Cassi is in the little bed in Bylbo's bedroom. Is she having some hot, Middle Earth interlude, engaging in some game of hairy footsie with her theme-park reenactor?

"Why so judgey?"

"Jeez!" RayAnne sits up. "Gran!" The dashcam is so brightly lit it seems her grandmother has pixelated in rays of Florida light, wearing her terrycloth rainbow muumuu.

"So what if the girl is getting her ashes hauled by that darling man?"

"Let's think about that, Gran. If Cassi is getting her *ashes hauled,* it's a distinct possibility she won't make it back to the motel: she might sleep at Bayg End in Bylbo's wee bed."

"And?"

"Then she won't realize I'm missing, and I might spend the night here."

"Might? Oh, honey, odds are you will be spending the night here. Let's not get foolishly optimistic."

"You're saying I'm not going to get rescued?"

"Where did you last see Cassi?"

"In Bayg End. Bylbo had just handed her another flagon of mead."

"Flagon?"

"I know. This trip, right?"

Gran cocks her head. "Those nice boys working with you won't notice you're gone?"

RayAnne thinks on that. "Maybe Chad, he's a bit of a hen, and the interview is an important one."

At the thought, RayAnne groans. It had been a coup for Cassi to score the interview they'll likely have to bail on. The subject, Marion Meke, is a flytying legend famous for her salmon lures. Several of her creations are patented. The Meke Nymph and Marion Jiggly—prized possessions to anyone lucky enough to own one, are considered trophies in their own right. Many of her flies are never fished with—more often are framed and displayed. There's even a black market in Marion forgeries circulating through sites like *Trout Fanatic, Fly Paper,* and *Fishnet.* Her flies are commissioned by diplomats and royals and are coveted. Many of Marion's most famous customers have made pilgrimages to New Zealand to collect their orders in person and to watch her work. But in semiretirement she's made herself scarce. A documentary had been made about her, one RayAnne had in fact planned to be watching just about now, tucked up in the comfort of her motel room with a sandwich and glass of milk. Her stomach growls at the thought.

"An interview? Anyone interesting?" Gran asks.

"A known crank, and really old. She's, like, eighty."

Gran tsks, not taking the bait.

She can only hope Cassi has a backup plan for filling any gaps of all they're expected to come up with. Executive producers and sponsors are expecting successful fishing forays, scintillating interviews, and enough travelogue-quality B-roll for five half-hour episodes—half the entire season! Producers have a big investment in this trip beyond the cost (Tripod's day rate is breathtaking—thank goodness they are as good as their reputation), because . . . really, a women's fishing show on public television?

No pressure.

RayAnne tosses, hunger nudging her awake now and again, having had nothing to eat since morning besides a bite of cake at Bayg End. She hopes Bus Driver is enjoying his bounty. When was the last time she'd gone to bed hungry? RayAnne taps the dashcam screen, where Gran appears to have fallen asleep. "I don't suppose you know where I can get a burger around here?"

"Don't be silly, goose. Keep your eyes closed. Stop trying to wake up."

It's now completely, moonlessly dark, and she's utterly, completely alone.

Happy place. Happy place. She imagines being curled and asleep between her adorable man-man (Hal rolls his eyes every time she calls him that) and, Rory, her oh-so-soft companion. Now that she's away from them again, RayAnne wonders why she has such a hard time letting herself completely enjoy Hal and Rory in the moment—does not dare embrace them completely, all-in. Hook, line, and sinker.

Because . . .

Perhaps because Gran's suicide still hangs offside in the periphery, like weather. Of course, RayAnne's holding back has not gone unnoticed by Hal, who says as much when he half-jokes out the side of his mouth, in a gangster voice, "Don't worry, Dahl. I'll be here for you when you break out."

Things will get better, she knows—or the many platitudes and clichés suggesting so wouldn't exist: that "Times heals all wounds"; that "This too shall pass"; and that "What doesn't kill you will make you stronger." Surely that one is rubbish, because what doesn't kill you surely dents you some.

One day she may shake the bottomless feeling, those awful memories of Dot trussed to so many monitors in the hospital, watching so desperately for spikes and blips on the screens. During those endless days in Florida, her family had been grounded back in Minnesota by Snowpocalypse, a storm that shut down MSP for forty hours, so that RayAnne was alone at Dot's bedside. Sitting and waiting, waiting and sitting, as doctors and nurses came and went so grimly because they knew. Then the visit from the kind woman representing the organ donation program, to whom RayAnne had not been particularly kind in return. Sign away pieces of Gran? Parse her out like parts from a junked car? Having gone two days with no sleep, her manners weren't what they could have been.

Then the moment when it had all gone weird. Less than a

minute after the organ donation woman left the room, Gran piped up for the first time—at least her voice had. Not from her pale, inert little body with the tube doing her breathing for her, but one of the monitors.

"Good lord," Gran had sighed.

In her onscreen debut, Dot stood at her kitchen island as if on some cooking show, wielding a boning knife. "So they've come for my liver, have they?"

Gran loved Monty Python.

RayAnne knew hallucinations were part and parcel of sleep deprivation. She was suddenly costarring in some comedy alongside Dot, so decided to play along.

"But you're so ill, Gran. Who would even want your liver?"

"Research, goose!"

The voice got serious then. "C'mon, Petal, let them have me."

She consulted the family via a surreal conference call. Big Rick blubbered, Ky stuttered like he hadn't since grade school, and Bernadette, patched in from somewhere off the Scottish coast, seemed as remote as her location. The family had left it up to her. She'd called for advice and they told her to trust her gut.

RayAnne had stood in the hall while nurses spruced Dot up before the admin doc unplugged the machines. Because it was dawn and no one was around, they indulged RayAnne and allowed the bed to be wheeled out to the rooftop terrace. The least RayAnne could do was to see that Gran got her preferred seating—if not a sunset, at least a sunrise.

Gran died. Then her family descended, followed by the funeral, followed by Hal, who just showed up, having driven twenty-four hours because he imagined that RayAnne, having lost her grandmother, might take solace in the company of her dog and, hopefully, maybe, him.

It's been more than ninety days now but who's counting. Denial. Anger. Bargaining. Depression. Acceptance. She knows them by heart now but has news for this Kübler-Ross person: this notion that phases of grief happen in some order is crap. Grief can't be compartmentalized or defined. To RayAnne, grief is a cement truck that ceaselessly unloads formless piles of gray where your loved one used to be.

"We all grieve differently," the counselor told her.

Indeed. After the funeral, her mother wandered off on retreat, feeling her feelings, burning herbs, keening. Bernadette had tried to convince RayAnne to go with her to a shaman for a peyote séance, which, even if it didn't rouse Dot, would at least blow RayAnne's mind.

If her mother knew she was more or less engaged in an ongoing electronic séance with Dot, her own mind might be blown.

Gran is now tapping the other side of the dashcam like it's a window, looking annoyed.

"You don't know the first thing about that book."

"*On Death and Dying*? Two stars."

"Really, Bean." Gran only calls her Bean when she is being as dumb as one.

"So now I've read the wrong book."

"You didn't even read it."

"Skimmed deeply?"

"That's an oxymoron. You memorized five words. Go back, read it from the point of view of someone in my shoes."

"Your shoes?"

"Knowing I might live four months, six tops, and that most of them were going to be extremely unpleasant for everyone."

RayAnne blinks at the dashcam.

"Did I go through all those stages? I decided that first doctor was wrong because he didn't look intelligent enough somehow. That's how one rolls in denial—deciding a doctor is a card short of a deck because he has a weak chin. So, I went to another, and hearing the same thing, I decided, *Well, she's too pessimistic.* And besides, neither of them knew me well enough to know I could easily beat their silly diagnosis. Turns out this pesky cancer doesn't give a whit who you are. Or who you think you are. And you can bet I felt like a dope finally realizing that."

"Gran."

"Anger wasn't far behind that . . ."

Gran leans closer, her image warping like someone on the other side of a peephole.

RayAnne places a finger on the dashcam screen and traces the line of Gran's cheek.

"Gran?"

"Stop trying to wake up, dear. The night will go faster than you think. We'll be out of this crappy campground before you know it."

"We?"

What she misses most is her grandmother's physicality: her smell (butter, Emeraude, and cardamom), the clap of her floury hands, the warmth of her, the way her goofy laugh shook her entire body.

Leaves rustle, breezes blow in a swirl above the rabbit hole of her dream. Another noise, distant and familiar, nearly wakes her. A car? A truck?

When she does finally, fully wake, she is curled sideways, drooling, head still covered by the beach towel, which she's now sweating under. A *pthlip, pthlip* of something ticking across the roof of the Rover as she wipes her cheek and slowly pulls the towel away to see a pair of small creatures standing directly above her on the sunroof—the undersides of squat brown somethings that from the bottom look like tiny beavers with worm-colored bird feet. Just as she's thinking what an odd perspective she has, one lifts a foot and squirts a helping of poop onto the glass just above Ray-Anne's eye—a swirl of brown and white like a mini soft-serve. Yes, definitely birds.

For a moment her hunger pangs lessen.

When underbrush snaps nearby, RayAnne realizes with a joyous jolt she is no longer alone, crapping birds aside. Somewhere in the brush near the Rover she can hear a human. A woman, singing the sort of timeless tune women everywhere sing or hum while working. Nothing she can make out, but the cadence is somehow familiar. There is a sense of purpose in the song.

Her visitor has brought smells, faint woodsmoke, and could it be . . . coffee? It smells too good to be real. RayAnne cautiously lifts her head to peer out.

The woman sits at the fire ring, calmly poking smoking embers with a stick. RayAnne lets out the breath she hadn't realized she'd been holding. She's saved.

RayAnne works her limbs into action and manages to open the door and tumble to the dewy ground, collapsing like a marionette on her sleeping leg. Struggling to her feet she waves awkwardly, grinning like an idiot. The woman rises, blinking twinkly eyes behind old-style cat-wing bifocals that magnify her eyes to a comical effect.

The woman has a *moko kauae*—a chin tattoo, which RayAnne actually knows the term for because Cassi had sent a lengthy article on the practice, and RayAnne remembers enough of it to understand a Māori woman's tattoo is considered the physical manifestation of her true self. It's believed every Māori woman wears a moko on the inside, close to their heart, and when they are ready, the Tā moko tattoo artist simply brings it to the surface. The designs are chiseled into the skin using a tool called an *uhi*. The ink is then smudged into the carved lines—which sounds rather more painful than needles—but it is believed that during the act of receiving the moko, the woman visits another realm where she encounters ancestors, the pain being that transformative, and then, upon returning from the abyss of agony, she is a person in full, marked by the essence of herself for all to see.

All of which makes RayAnne's own tattoo seem more meaningless and silly than it already is. A regrettable misstep as a sophomore on spring break in New Orleans, the slender green gecko wrapping her left ankle is at least tastefully done, and she's thankful to have been sober enough not to have chosen some tramp stamp.

Bernadette, armchair anthropologist, knew all about the moko tattoos and had asked RayAnne, "If you see any women with them, please get pictures, and maybe their stories?"

"No, Mom. That's what the Internet is for."

"Just if you happen to run into any?"

"Not gonna happen."

"Why not?"

"Because I can just see you and your mavens doodling on each other's faces with Sharpies or henna or whatever." For someone so PC, her mother lags somewhat behind on what constitutes cultural theft (Bernadette calls it *honoring*) and has been known to drag her mavens through all manner of borrowed, appropriated rites during their Blood-Tide Quests. Her mother has good intentions, but sometimes is one of those people who can do or say the right and wrong thing in the same breath.

Bernadette had always been a free spirit, save the dozen years she'd been sidelined by her unlikely union with Big Rick, which she still appears to be making up for. She travels the globe with her menopausal clients to sacred hot spots, where they ritualistically bid adieu to their menses and journal through their transitions from madonna to maven—or, as Big Rick puts it, from "hottie to hag." Wherever she roams, Bernadette "borrows," collecting and hoarding meaning from other cultures, perhaps because her own consumption-driven, middle-class Midwest is so bereft of any.

Clothes are central: her global-village wardrobe ranges from Andean capes to Zambian chitenge and everything between: elvish Sami boots, embroidered Guatemalan huipiles, gold-threaded saris, billowing caftans, pretty hijabs, mantillas, itchy dirndl skirts. You name it. RayAnne used to try on the most beautiful of the clothes: a silk kimono, the wearing of which felt like she imagined sex might be like; a flamenco dress from Andalusia that fit her like paint and compelled her to twirl and stomp. You are what you wear!

RayAnne's own stint of cultural appropriation was brief, back in grade school. After watching *Little Big Man* about eighty times, it seemed essential that she emulate Jack Crabb's native wife Sunshine by wearing a suede fringe dress, braids, and beaded moccasins.

Most of her mother's wardrobe celebrated the female form. Once, when Bernadette was unpacking from a trip to Kabul, she pulled out a voluminous garment of dull blue fabric that she insisted RayAnne try on. It covered her completely, yards flowing from a tight headpiece with a sort of embroidered screened window to look out of. The weight of the garment cascaded directly from the crown of her head. Once encased in it, RayAnne had no peripheral vision. Besides making her feel utterly claustrophobic, it was too cumbersome to move in with ease; there was no way a person could run in such a thing. It certainly ruled out driving or riding a bike, roasting a marshmallow, *fishing*.

Bernadette had marched her to the full-length mirror where her image was eerily formless. She could be anybody, anything, for that matter—a covered post. Suddenly she couldn't breathe.

"Get me out of this."

"Give it a minute." Her mother's tone was such that RayAnne knew they weren't just trying on clothes but were in the midst of a teaching moment. "Let that feeling sink in. Seriously. Remember this."

"Thanks, Mom, no."

Bernadette tugged the headpiece tighter. "Where I've just come from, this is life for most young women. They will never go to college, or play tennis; drink a glass of wine, go sailing. Do much of anything outside the home, for that matter. This is what they have to look forward to, this, obeying their husbands, and babies."

It took minutes to extricate herself from all the folds, to find the opening at the bottom to escape. Her mother didn't help, only said, "Careful not to rip it."

Once freed, RayAnne rubbed her forehead where the itchy headpiece had left sweaty marks. Bernadette again turned her toward the mirror, and together they looked at their reflections, RayAnne red-faced, wearing a cropped tank and cutoffs, having kicked away the heap of blue cloth.

"Remember this, too," Bernadette said. "This is freedom." She retrieved the burqa from the carpet and shook it out to fold it. "Oppression is oppression. I don't care what dogma it's wrapped in or what sacred texts in which it is written. *By men,* by the way."

Having a radical feminist for a mother could be trying, but the important lessons had sunk in. Now, so many years later when encountering women in burqas, RayAnne can only shudder.

Ironically, these days her mother is eschewing clothing of any kind, ensconced as she is at a nudist colony, "researching" postmenopausal body image. Since she scored a six-figure book advance for *Mavenhood,* the pressure is on for Bernadette to finish her manuscript, overdue to the publisher. She's "feeling every breeze" and is wrestling with her final chapter, "When I Am Old, I Shall Wear Nothing." Much to Bernadette's amusement, the nude ranch is called Imagine—"Where nothing much is left to!"

RayAnne misses her mother.

The woman approaching the Rover could be anywhere between seventy and a hundred. She wears a colorful housedress that seems the typical fashion for a woman of a certain age in these parts. She also wears supremely muddy rubber boots. Heavy gray braids coiled atop her head. As well, she wears a number of birds. From a bamboo yoke balanced across her shoulders, a half-dozen little woven cages hang, each housing a songbird; a few uncaged birds perch untethered on the pole.

She nods to RayAnne.

"Ata mārie!"

RayAnne hopes it is a greeting and does not refer to trespassing.

"Ata mārie to you too!"

The woman nods toward the Rover's sunroof. "You saw them."

RayAnne looks behind her and back. "Them?"

"That kiwi pair."

"Those were kiwis on the roof? Kiwi birds? I thought they were extinct."

"Endangered. Rare, for sure. We have some in zoos, mostly. Some still in the wild. You got a rare sighting. I'd say not everyone gets a kiwi-shit hello."

RayAnne relaxes. "Somehow I'm not surprised."

"They're home by now, maybe safe from the possums and rats—all off to bed now the sun is up." The woman's own birds chirp and trill as she feeds them from the deep pockets of her dress, holding out a palmful of seeds. The woman takes off her yoke of birds and hangs it between the forked branches of a nearby tree. "Good thing that pair led me to you, I'd say?"

"Were you tracking them? To catch?"

"Oh no. Just making sure they get home all right. And maybe see if they leave me any prizes." To demonstrate, the woman walks to the Rover. More nimble than she looks, climbs up the running board and peers across the roof before reaching for something. For a moment RayAnne thinks she's going for the kiwi crap. The woman grins widely, holding up a long wispy something that looks like fuzzy string. "Bingo!"

"Yeah?"

"Kiwi feather!" She carefully winds it around her finger before hopping down, then nods at the tilted Rover and states the obvious. "You have some trouble here."

“I do. And am I ever glad to see you.” She holds out a hand to shake. “I’m RayAnne.”

“RayAnne.” She tilts her head far back to peer through her thick glasses. “You’ve been here all night?”

“Yup.” RayAnne’s croak is dry.

The woman takes a bottle of water out of one of her voluminous pockets and hands it over.

“Drink some.”

“Thank you. *Thank you.*” RayAnne cranks the cap open, takes a too-big gulp, and commences coughing.

The woman openly examines RayAnne as she recovers, thumping her several times on the back. The moment she lets up, RayAnne nods at the birds, asking, “Are these . . . your pets?”

The woman laughs. “My suppliers.”

“Oh?”

Whatever that means. Perhaps the woman is the local lunatic? RayAnne wonders when she might bring up the topic of rescue, whether the woman has a phone, or can somehow conjure a tow truck or a Lyft to ferry her back to the motel. She’s going to be late for the interview in any case. Digging in pockets again, the woman takes a greasy brown bag from her pocket—it smells as good as anything Gran ever pulled from her oven.

Thoughts of a tow truck dissipate under the aroma of actual food. The woman presses the parcel into RayAnne’s hand. “Breakfast?”

“For me?” She nearly drools while saying, “Really?”

“Eat up.”

Not knowing the woman’s name, she cannot thank her properly. “I really am . . . so hungry.”

The woman nods. *Eat already.*

“Thank you.” Unwrapping the paper, she’s thrilled to find a sort of savory turnover. The pastry is flaky, and the filling is some gravy-kissed meat, maybe lamb, but she cannot stop eating long enough to ask. It could be rattlesnake for all she cares, because it's hands-down the most delicious thing she's ever eaten.

The woman clearly enjoys the spectacle of RayAnne wolfing down her offering. "Mwmph," RayAnne says a few times, nodding and chewing.

"Almost forgot!" The woman opens one of the birdcages and pulls out a to-go coffee. "Hope a long white is alright?" A beautiful paper cup of warm coffee. RayAnne is just able to put down the pie long enough to bow and make prayer hands.

"You'd think I'd given you the moon, girl. You could have got one yourself—the petrol station opened at five."

"Petrol station?"

The woman nods in the direction of the far end of the clearing, beyond a thicket of trees where a square gray cinderblock wall takes shape as the woman speaks of it.

"Right there."

The back wall of an entire building that she'd not seen? Granted, when she'd arrived at the campsite it had been dusk, but . . .

"Right there?"

RayAnne had thought she'd heard a familiar sound while drifting off but had chalked it up to tui birds, thinking how annoying that they could mimic the *ding* of the sort of bell cars trigger when pulling into a gas station.

"The PetroPump, just there. Where I got that pie and coffee."

"The PetroPump?"

"You repeat things, don't you?"

"So all night while I was here . . ." RayAnne's jaw drops.

The woman nods, waiting for her to braid it all together.

She straightens. "Forgive me, I'm a little punchy—let's start over here. My name is RayAnne Dahl."

"And I'm Marion." A ginger-root hand is offered. "Marion Meke."

Should anything about this trip surprise her? RayAnne dissolves in a fit of giggles. After finally catching a breath she says, "Of course you are."

"I saw your vehicle there in its predicament and wondered, even as I saw it, if it might hold the Americans coming to document me."

RayAnne opens her mouth then closes it.

The woman steps closer. "Now that we are introduced, a proper greeting." Marion leans forward on the balls of her feet to press her forehead and nose to RayAnne's.

"There," she says. "We call it *hongi*."

As they peel away, RayAnne knows she'll not soon forget the little buzz of joy that sparked when Marion Meke's forehead fused with her own.

The PetroPump, which in addition to having petrol, hosts the holy trinity of WiFi, cell service, and pay phone, from which Marion calls her son, Roger, who promises to be "down in a tick." RayAnne's phone dings with ten notifications, which she ignores while taking great pleasure in texting to Cassi: *Meet me at the Location—at Marion Meke's.*

Roger arrives within minutes with his truck and pulls the Rover back to rights. After determining there's no apparent damage under all the crusted mud, she fills the tank at the PetroPump and follows Roger's truck. Marion stands in its open bed grasping a handle on the cab roof—her pole of birds still slung. RayAnne knows from all the articles and her bio that Marion is in her eighties. The truck climbs for a mile up into a narrow, winding canyon. The road crisscrosses a stream on several wooden bridges, dead-ending at the Meke mailbox.

Marion jumps down and opens the gate. Home is a modest Victorian bungalow with a curved metal roof, freshly painted lattice work, vast gardens, and a distant view of the sea. Inside, Marion hands over a clean towel. "I imagine you'd like a shower?"

"Please."

After her most excellent shower, RayAnne is given a tour of the gardens. Marion points past the fence to a lower field with a flock of sheep in tight formation, a trio of tricolor border collies pinning their coordinates. "Those are Roger's merinos."

They wind back nearly to the porch and Marion makes for the door, saying, "I'll just put the kettle on."

A horn toots as Cassi and crew show up. Roger waves them to a parking place and insists on helping them unload.

Cassi rushes over to RayAnne. "How the heck did you find this place without GPS? We haven't had it for miles?"

RayAnne shrugs.

"Chad said you didn't come out of your room this morning."

"Aha!" RayAnne holds up a finger. "Which I would deduce to mean *you* didn't come out of your room either?"

Cassi blushing is a sight: pink travels jawline to scalp like a goblet being filled with Pepto Bismol. "I was back by seven! But you were already up and out? Where were you?"

"Having breakfast with Marion." RayAnne laughs because it is the ridiculous truth.

She expects more of a grilling, but Cassi, famously undistractible, seems distracted. In addition to the blush, she sports a calm, satisfied smile, looking for all the world, happy as she hands over the wardrobe bag, casting an eye over RayAnne's gravy-stained shirt, her wet hair, and wrinkled cargo pants, cheerfully accusing, "You slept in those clothes."

"I did." She's about to hazard some excuse when they are interrupted by Marion, calling them to come in for coffee.

Her kitchen is homey and cluttered. The toaster, coffee maker, blender, and teapot all wear colorful crocheted cozies.

"This is lovely. Thank you, Mrs. Meke."

RayAnne narrows an eye. Cassi, smiling *and* polite?

Marion laughs. "Mrs.!? You see any mister 'round here?"

"Oh." Cassi pretends to look under the table. "I guess not."

RayAnne takes the wardrobe bag to the bathroom and changes into fresh cargo pants, clean button-up (with sleeves pre-rolled), and her fishing vest. She skeins her damp hair back into a decent ponytail.

Cassi knocks, wedging her grinning face through the crack in the door like Jack Nicholson, saying "Heeeere's makeup!"

RayAnne leans to the mirror. "Got anything for these?" She points to a few bug bites on her temple.

Cassi pulls out a cover stick and dabs at RayAnne, using her thumb to blend the makeup.

"Sooo," RayAnne meets her eye, "how was Bylbo?"

The blush creeps again. "Just fine, thank you."

"How'd you get back to the motel? Did he carry you on his hairy back?"

"He has a horse."

"A *horse?*"

"Don't arch: you're creasing the lines."

"Aw. You like him."

"Maybe."

"Clearly."

Over coffee and scones Roger has pulled from the oven, Marion, supposed curmudgeon and recluse, keeps them in stitches. Rangi and Rongo are good-natured as Marion mines them for information regarding what regions their families hail from and who they might possibly have in common. In a six-degrees-of-Kevin-Bacon moment, they land on a car dealership in Kapiti, where the twins' cousin is a manager and Marion's nephew is a panel beater. They explain to RayAnne that a panel beater is a person who does body work.

As they move to yet another connection, RayAnne only half-listens. Humans, she thinks, are pretty much the same everywhere, in every culture, so often casting around for some link, some connection.

They are on to a third person in common when Roger, clearing plates, suggests, "Mum, maybe time to . . . ?"

"Right! Two shakes." She slaps the table, suddenly all business. "Shall we get to it?"

Marion's "shack" is bright and airy, a low wooden building with double side doors that open to face the stream bank. Chad and Rongo set up a tripod; light readings are taken. On the wall opposite Marion's tying table is a bulletin board with handwritten notes and letters from clients. Notable ones are featured front and center. RayAnne and Cassi scan the board, raising eyebrows at each other: Jimmy Kimmel, Harrison Ford, David Beckham, Emma Watson. When pitching to the executive producer, Cassi had claimed Marion was rather a celebrity herself—at least in the flytying world. When RayAnne sees the letterhead and the "Barry Obama" signature, she makes a small noise, elbowing Cassi.

Cassi doesn't often look impressed. "Whoa."

Rongo straps into his steady-cam. They are ready to roll.

Marion comes from a very long line of fishermen. "Here, you can see what my ancestors fished with." She shows them a case holding old fishing hooks, *hei matau,* carved from bone. Some are made of wood and shell; most are twined together with finely woven cords of waxed flax, *harakeke.*

"And this one?" RayAnne points to one partially wrapped with ancient, corroded wire.

"A string from a violin that my great-great-grandfather took in trade from a *Pākehā* settler. First stringed instrument seen by my people—they imagined it was magic—a metal string that makes music. It was considered a treasure."

"What did the settler get in the trade?"

"A fishing cove."

"Oh."

"A common-enough story."

RayAnne has a list of questions Cassi has written, but since meeting Marion, her own questions have been piling up. Once they are both sitting and the camera rolls, she asks, "Tell us about your *suppliers.*"

"My boys. Let's go see them!"

To Rongo's alarm, Marion jumps up to lead them out the door and to a second shed. They scramble to follow. Rongo tries to keep focus on the moving target, trotting backwards in front of Marion.

The shed is stocked like a tropical bird store, lined with woven cages, most left open, leaving the birds free to come and go.

"Most folks get their feathers from catalogs—but they're sold in whole-wing or whole-skin, so the bird gets killed. No reason for that."

Marion reaches into a cage and pulls a downy bit of bright red fluff along with a tiny green-and-black feather from the straw lining. From the floor of another cage she lifts an orange-and-ivory-spotted tail feather. "See, I don't need much. These days I only tie as many flies as I have feathers for—what these fellas decide to give me."

Rongo's steady-cam seems to intrigue the birds. A few circle him. He ducks.

Marion points from bird to bird, naming the species as they land on the various bits of the steady-cam: the shoulder yoke, *Hihi*; the viewfinder: *Kea*. "All the best plumes are from the male, of course." Marion belly laughs. "They need all the help they can get."

The birds land or swoop as quickly as she can identify them. *Tauhou, Kererū, Pīwakawaka*. They are tame and some are quite bold. A little parakeet lands on Rongo's lens hood and tries to peck at the glass. When another lands briefly atop his head, everyone cracks up.

"Right." Rongo attempts to shake them off. "It's all good fun till equipment gets crapped on."

"They like you." Marion pokes his arm. "*Tamaiti manu.*"

Rangi leans to RayAnne, saying, "Means bird boy, more or less."

"That's right, missus," Rongo grins. "Cuz all the birds want a bit of this boy."

Marion shakes her head and turns to RayAnne. "Never good for a man to know he is handsome." She claps twice and the birds disperse, hopping to their cages and roosts. The humans file out to return to the shack. Back to work. Once everyone is seated they start again.

Marion slaps the surface of her tying table: a repurposed door set atop old card catalogs. "Salvaged after our library shut down."

"Oh?" RayAnne frowns. "No more library?"

"It's a fish-and-chip shop now," Marion frowns, "and not a good one."

The dozens of drawers that once held library cards now house Marion's supplies: feathers, fur, down, all manner of beads meant to approximate the heads of insects, tiny double beads for eyes. She opens other drawers to show them spools of waxed and colored threads and cording. Hook drawers are labeled, sized 4 to 24, BARBED, BARBLESS, BRASS, STEEL, BRONZE, along with fine decorative wrapping wire in various metallics.

RayAnne squints. "What do *you* fish with?"

"Oh, I don't fish." She pulls out a square of sheepskin burred with flies. "But if I did . . ."

RayAnne knows there are flytiers who don't fish, but she's never met one. Marion holds out the flies for RayAnne's perusal. "Here's some favorites."

Salmon and trout flies comingle like princes and paupers. Attached to each of Marion's flies is a typewritten ribbon of paper similar to the lines pasted onto old telegrams. Each is a recipe of ingredients and colors Marion has employed in each creation.

RayAnne reads the instruction for a Wooly Bugger aloud: "*Hook*: Dai-Riki #700 Size 10. *Bead*: Cyclops Wapsi 5/32 Gold

Bead. *Thread*: UTC Brown Olive 140. *Body*: Lead wire 0.02 wt / Chenille (olive). *Hackle*: Whiting Bugger. *Tail*: Marabou Olive Blood quill."

"It's beautiful."

Marion nods. "Not a fancy fly, but useful."

How much showier in comparison the salmon flies are, dressed as if for courtship.

"Over the top, aren't they?" Marion shrugs. "Salmon aren't even fussy eaters. They'll strike most anything that moves—don't give a toss how it's served up."

"Then why so . . . ?" RayAnne touches a complex, colorful salmon fly with no less than six different tropical feathers.

"Tarted up?"

"Yes." So much color and flash reminds RayAnne of her high school friend Monica, always on Facebook with perfectly foiled hair and acrylic nails, fluorescent-white teeth, and way too much makeup, dressed in low-cut, short-short everything, teetering along in impossible heels.

"It does seem a little desperate."

Marion nods. "It's all show for the fishermen, of course—the salmon could care less. Most of what I tie now never even gets to meet a fish."

RayAnne's attention is drawn back to the trout flies. Still thinking of Monica, who would definitely be a salmon fly, she muses aloud, "If I were a fly, I'd probably be a Wooly Bugger."

"One of my favorites," Marion says, looking pleased. "The ones that appear simple are always hardest to tie. Every flaw shows."

"That sounds about right," RayAnne says.

"So," says Marion, "ready for your lesson?"

RayAnne looks uncertainly from Marion to Cassi and mouths, *Lesson?* "I hope this is a beginner's class, because I've never actually tied a fly . . ."

"Perfect. Nothing to unlearn!" Marion slips an apron over her head, dislodging her mic so that Chad must step in to reattach it. The half-apron/half-tool belt has loops and compartments that hold delicate clippers, tiny scissors, wire snips, an old-fashioned Zippo lighter, tweezers, and a bottle of super glue. On the table are more tools: bobbin holders, hackle pliers, slender crochet hooks. When Chad finishes with the mic, Marion, as if unable to resist, pats his ginger hair before he backs away.

A human being, RayAnne thinks, looking at Marion's open, kindly face.

Marion presses RayAnne onto a stool in front of a tying vise jerry-rigged to the table with a C-clamp and duct tape. Her own vise looks like a praying mantis of worn brass, pitted in places from sea air and oxidized green at its base, with several weld marks where it's been repaired.

"I know, she's seen better days." Marion nods to a shelf where two unopened boxes collect dust, both stamped with the logos of British purveyors of outrageously expensive fishing gear. "Companies keep sending me newfangled ones. Very kind of them. Not sure why they bother."

RayAnne knows why they bother—sponsorship.

"Work with a new vise at my age when I have a perfectly good one that I know?" Marion pats her vise like a cat. "We understand one another, Millie and me."

RayAnne can relate. Sometimes a thing is more than a thing. Take her boat. Currently parked in her garage back home, *Penelope* has become RayAnne's bolt-hole over the past months—a place to curl up on the bench seat with a book or pint of Häagen-Dazs, sometimes just with a wad of tissues. Her mother believes RayAnne has fixated on *Penelope* in an unhealthy attachment. "A boat is no substitute for sisterhood."

Ky seems to get it, nearly—he'd at least agreed to go check in on *Penelope* while she's away. He'd offered to start RayAnne's car as well, as if it might be an equal concern. Her hybrid hatchback had been relegated to the driveway like a red-headed stepchild, now sleeping under a cairn of snow, likely with a dead battery.

"Today we won't tie any pattern—just learn to use the tools, tie what we want." Marion pulls out trays of feathers, colored spools, and scraps of fur from the many drawers, handing over a small snips and a spool holder.

RayAnne leans in, fully aware that an opportunity to sit down with a master of anything does not happen every day.

Marion indicates the trays. "Imagine this is a buffet. Imagine you are the fish, and you're hungry. What looks good to you?"

RayAnne hesitantly scans the feathers, then looks to the display of salmon flies, but Marion says, "Ignore those. We'll just make it up as we go. Today we only play."

Well, in that case . . . She chooses cream-colored emu; a peachy-toned dyed guinea feather with black spots; soft gray for the hackles; and for the body a bit of silver possum fur and a muted sea-green cord for the wrap. More peach shows up in the beads. She chooses a wrap wire of charcoal gray.

Marion is a natural teacher and keeps the conversation fluid between what questions RayAnne has the presence of mind to ask, concentrating as she is on keeping the tension on her spool tight while miming Marion's movements.

"Wind that bit a little tighter, dear."

Their heads are close as RayAnne watches Marion's fingers, swift despite obvious arthritis. She's occasionally jarred by a quiet prompt from her earpiece, Cassi directing her: *lean right; modulate; ask about Emma Watson.* She's making it difficult to concentrate, so RayAnne pretends to scratch at her earlobe while prying out the earbud and slipping it into her pocket. She'll say it fell out.

When Marion wraps her knuckley fingers around hers to redirect the winding of filament, a lump forms in RayAnne's throat. Marion's hands are warm and soft. *Granny hands.* She exudes the well-being of someone settled onto her old bones and in full possession of her ability. Women like her and Gran make old age seem almost reassuring—until you consider what might be lurking and poised to strike: diabetes, brittle bones, and everything else.

Cancer.

They talk on, rambling. RayAnne dodges a few looks from Cassi but gets the message and brings the conversation around to Marion's career over the years. She's able to incite a few choice comments from Marion regarding her famous clients. When President Obama's name comes up, Marion taps her cheekbone, saying, "She kissed me goodbye. Here."

"She?"

"The wife. First Lady Michelle."

Marion points to a wall of framed photos. Rangi follows and pulls focus on a shot of Marion flanked by Michelle and Barack, both in baseball caps and fishing khaki, looking like any other tourists save their unmistakable smiles. Dwarfed between them, Marion wears the same stained and mended apron she now has on. The picture was taken in this very room.

"They came here?"

"Indeed. But I didn't have to rescue them."

Both laugh at their private joke as the others exchange looks.

"He sat in the chair you're in."

"*Did* he?" RayAnne wriggles minutely. "What was he like?"

"Lovely manners. A good healthy laugh on him." Marion smiles wistfully. "They both smelled good."

"Did they?"

"Quite, yeah. Snip the end there."

Somehow, over the previous three-quarters of an hour under Marion's tutelage, RayAnne has produced a decent fly.

"Well done." Marion loosens RayAnne's vise and lifts out the hook, turning it. "There you have a sort of damsel nymph, I'd say."

"I do?"

"What shall we name her?"

"She?" RayAnne squints.

"Of course. Lookit her."

Marion holds "her" close to the camera, turning the fly slowly so Rongo can zoom. "That's a well-put-together nymph for a novice."

Now that it's complete, RayAnne realizes the feathers and trimmings she's chosen are all Gran's colors—the ivory of her hair, peach of her cheeks, all the charcoals and soft greens and salmon colors that comprised her grandmother's wardrobe. The fishing lure is inspired by nostalgic synesthesia.

"How about *Dorthea*?"

"Lovely name for a fly." Marion smiles. "I'm guessing Dorthea was someone special?"

That word again, *was*—the resounding past-tenseness of it, said aloud in reference to Dot's was-ness. RayAnne nods. "She was my grandmother."

Marion lays a hand on RayAnne's arm. "Well, shall we take your grandmother fishing?"

RayAnne climbs into a pair of waders while the guys set up on the riverbank and Rongo wades in. Cassi is knee-deep, holding the fuzzy mic on its pole over her head. RayAnne has put on her fishing vest, which now has several Marions hooked to its sheepskin badge, along with her jewel-like Dorthea Damsel.

Marion kicks off her jandals and ties the front and back hems of her housedress into a knot between her knees, transforming the garment into a sort of onesie that won't tangle in the current. She wades in barefoot ahead of RayAnne, pointing.

"There's excellent overhang ahead by that bank."

RayAnne, feeling overequipped and very much the amateur, doesn't really want to wet her Dot Damsel because . . . as the word suggests, *wet*. She sets her rod on a flat stone and reluctantly hands over the lure so that Marion can attach it to the line with a clinch knot, pinching off the excess filament with her teeth.

She makes a few tentative casts into the dark pool near the bank while Marion observes silently. She's barely reaching the underhang.

"Try a soft back-cast and lay her down."

"Like this?" Her second try is better, but she snags the hook on something static and unseen—a log, maybe. She reels and drags the line in and sees to her relief that the nymph is no worse for it.

"Step out here where you've got some room."

RayAnne follows farther into the stream until thigh-deep.

"Divine the seam," Marion encourages. The *seam* is where currents and pools converge. On big rivers, whitewater rafters know to avoid the seam and reckless kayakers aim for it to ride its attendant eddies. Large game fish dine at its edge where leeches, shiners, and crawfish trundle along like conveyor-belt sushi. The seam is the holy grail of fly fishers—the nerve of the river, the *soul,* to be Bernadette about it.

RayAnne wedges her heels against larger stones for stability. To find the seam she must scrub extraneous thought, concentrate on a singular exploration of the surface. Shadows thrown by tall trees and dappled sunlight pose challenges, the breeze another. She sweeps her gaze back and forth across the water until the patterns form: current, calm, churn.

Finding the seam requires patience, but there, finally, it is. Once she identifies it, RayAnne follows its length to the flat pool she'll aim for. In a fluid motion she raises her reel high and slightly behind before casting, as if her rod is a wand she might tap a cloud with. The whir of the reel's vibration travels from RayAnne's wrist up the length of her arm and to her shoulder.

"That's it," Marion encourages. "Now let your damsel kiss the water."

The nymph is sent forth in a long, drawn-out purr, the filament soaring above the canopy of shade to catch sun, making its undulating curve glow. RayAnne's arm feels nearly like an extension of the pole, her fingertips as sensitive as the line. She's fishing now.

In the twinkling between casting her damsel nymph forth and its alighting on the water, the world falls away. *Go, Dot, go.* The extraneous noise of the present recedes for the moment—all that's been weighing her down—not just the pressure of her every move being filmed, but all the rest of it: the undulating grief; the shift work of worry over her family; Rory, the dog she's supposed to be providing a forever home to, regardless of rarely being in it; the anxiety over the daily news cycle; the uncertainty of hosting the show, a task she is uniquely unqualified for. She often feels the weight of it all at once, but as her line soars, RayAnne falls headlong into the moment, any worry unspooling as the filament flies from her reel.

The water flows around her thighs, effectively braiding her into the stream; her toes feel indistinguishable from the pebbles underneath. For the moment all is in harmony, in confluence. Instinct tells her to pounce on this moment, clear as the beads of water strung across her filament—clear as the drops splashed up from the river to pirouette and tumble, each capturing everything in range of its reflection, however briefly, including RayAnne and all that's reflected in her own eye.

Forgetting the little microphone clamped to her collar, she mutters, "Let the record show that I, RayAnne Dahl, am present. In the moment."

Memories are what she has of Gran now. From the worst: watching the already faint pulse of one blue vein on Gran's wrist grow faint, then fainter, then stop altogether. To the best: several yellowed frames of a summer afternoon on a family trip to the Oregon coast. She was riding on Dead Ted's shoulders, in caboose position in the family train snaking through scrubby pines on a sandy path. Their shepherd mutt, Bruno, doubled back and behind to herd the family along. Her father was in the lead, one arm balancing a cooler on his shoulder, the other weighted with a heavy beach tote. Next in line was Bernadette, laughing and struggling between carting the beach umbrella and holding Kyle on one hip.

Bobbing along just in front was Gran, at least the top of her head, the appearance of which RayAnne was puzzling over: why was the hair closest to Gran's scalp silver like a dime, while the rest of her hair was brown?

The pines thinned and the path widened. The family clambered up a sandy ridge to pause at the crest of a dune, taking in a view of beach and headlands, a sky the color of beach glass, sea smells delivered on a warm breeze.

"Oh look." Dot set down the picnic basket and reached up to grasp RayAnne's small hand, sheer happiness flooding her next words. "Look, little RayBeam, the ocean!"

The damsel nymph arcs high above the river to begin its descending trajectory toward the glassy pool next to the seam. Just as it's about to splash, RayAnne takes a deep, fulsome breath, as if to swallow the moment, just as some fish below may be poised to do the same.

A moment.

5. ACCEPTANCE

"It's an obsession," Fiona Parata says. "Practically an addiction."

"Addiction . . . ?" RayAnne asks.

"To consuming, shopping . . . acquiring. Gagging for the next season's togs in order to stay neckline and neckline with what influencers are trending in their feeds."

RayAnne blinks, nodding. Fiona's a lively one.

They sit squarely in Rangi's viewfinder, feet dangling off the edge of the concrete pier at Lyall Bay near Wellington, not far from where Fiona's clothing line, Kākahu, is designed and produced. They're not catching much: just a small snapper and a kingfish so far, both returned to the sea. Today RayAnne is more interested in her guest than fishing.

"Fair enough, but you are a fashion designer," RayAnne points out.

"*Anti*–fashion designer," Fiona reminds her. "Thing people don't get is that wearing something that's all the rage doesn't make you look great: wearing something that suits you and fits you does. Tripping over ourselves to buy the latest fashion just makes us nobs—what do you say in America?"

"Easy marks?" RayAnne ventures. "Chumps?"

"No fault of your own, most consumers are frankly clueless as to how clothes get made—the human cost, not to mention the industry dragging the environment down the toilet."

"Right." Until days ago, RayAnne herself was clueless. In preparation for their interview she's been reading all manner of hideous things about the fast fashion industry: its carbon cost to manufacture and export, the tsunami of waste. Fiona isn't simply a clothing designer: she's an advocate and an activist. Media savvy, she steers the interview to her talking points, making direct contact with the camera.

Whenever Rangi looks up from his viewfinder, he grins lopsidedly at Fiona, bringing to mind one of Gran's antique words—*beguiled.*

As if inured to such attention, Fiona remains so focused that not even a rakish man-boy instinctively flexing his impressive biceps and dimples in her direction can distract. For a moment RayAnne is so engrossed watching him watching Fiona, she misses what her guest is saying, tuning in midsentence.

". . . it's practically criminal. All so we can wear twenty-dollar Bangladeshi-made yoga pants? It's not just the cheap clothes either, but the upscale seasonals all the Karens simply must have to show up piss-elegant at the next vineyard brunch or fundraiser, never to be worn again."

RayAnne nods, realizing she'll barely be getting a word in.

Fiona addresses the lens as if reluctantly relaying bad news to a friend. "We all own heaps of clothing, and most of it really is crap. We have to face ourselves on this one and do the right thing."

"Which is?"

"Just stop. Stop the excess. Buy less and much *better* clothing. The only way to change the industry is to change our demands."

"But how?"

"Research manufacturers, investigate your brands and labels. Use social media for good—boycotts can be very effective . . ."

RayAnne's earbud crackles with Cassi's voice. "Maybe reel her in some, Ray."

Cassi knows as well as RayAnne that more than one of their sponsors source their outdoor clothing lines and activewear from third world countries. She'll try to avoid any such mentions.

But RayAnne will not reel Fiona in. They'd known Fiona was a rouser since she hit the radar for her in-your-face marketing. Some retailers find her clothing tags too "frank": photos of marginalized workers in sweatshop conditions; girls sandblasting denim with paper masks when a respirator would be the minimum safety requirement; two older women awaiting first aid, one clearly ill, breathing portable oxygen; workers stacked like sardines in floor-to-ceiling bunks in factory-provided dormitories, complete with shots of the disgusting communal showers and filthy toilets. The tag that most disturbed RayAnne was a close-up of a doe-eyed teenager feeding shoe leather around a blade, his thumbs and fingertips shiny and dented with scars.

Such Dickensian images are not easily unseen. Fiona's inspiration had come from the graphic pictures of diseased lungs on her father's cigarette packs. She intends to make consumers uncomfortable—to confront them with the human cost of *chic*.

The text sides of the tags list the fabric contents as well as facts and statistics for the number of gallons of water required to grow cotton versus bamboo, hemp, or linen; the toxicity of a chemical dye compared to natural; percentages of garment workers suffering from silicosis. *Reel her in?* If anything, she'll give Fiona more line, because the world needs to hear what this woman has to say.

"And c'mon, fashion season?" Fiona pitches a tone, voice booming and her fist hitting the tackle box. "*This* is what you're going to be wearing, in these colors and this style—whether it suits you or not. Next season you shall stop wearing *this* and commence wearing *that*! Think about it—'Slave to fashion' isn't a saying for nothing."

Fiona's indignation is a thing to behold. Her tone lightens, but not her intensity, reminding RayAnne of her mother. Bernadette maintains there are two kinds of people: handwringers quick to broadcast their precious opinions; and those who actually do something. Fiona is clearly a doer—having created a sustainable alternative to fast fashion with her capsule wardrobes made with renewable textiles and woolens sourced in New Zealand. Her garments are gaspingly expensive but beautifully made to last. Both Oprah's Favorite Things and Gwyneth's GOOP have taken note of Fiona and her mission. When RayAnne mentions them, Fiona sighs in relief, crossing her fingers.

"We're making it, finally. Nearly in the black now."

The more RayAnne learns about fast fashion, the more guilt stings for her own mindless consumption. She's not yet forty, statistically not yet halfway along her buying journey, though surely has burned through her allotted carbon footprint, perhaps a few times over. But guilt rolls in on swells, and what swells ebbs, as it had that morning when she'd hastily popped into a store to buy a pair of jelly jandals in which to wade their stony hotel beach. In the store she'd requested "thongs," which had been met with a sudden blush from the teenaged clerk. She tried again. "Flip-flops?"

"Ah ho!" he chortled. "I didn't think you really wanted bum flossies."

"Bum flossies?"

"Thongs!"

RayAnne is beginning to suspect that simply being American makes her a source of entertainment here in the Southern Hemisphere.

The jandals are clear plastic shot through with glitter, probably made by schoolgirls. Did she ask herself, *What would Bernadette do?* No, but she has begun to regard her mother in full these days. Certain seeds of parental wisdom sown in her path have recently germinated. Until Cassi pointed out the numbers of women the show reaches with its ever-growing audience, RayAnne hadn't thought much about what possible difference she might make. What they have, in influencer parlance, is a platform.

Bernadette's own hard-earned platform was decades in the making. Before her big book deal, her Blood-Tides blog fans and podcast followers might fill a bowling alley, and much of what she'd shouted echoed into a void. And now she's an influencer to half a million postmenopausal mavens. Growing up, RayAnne watched her mother toil in poor-paying, often thankless jobs (hippie gigs, Big Rick called them), canvassing house to house in conservative suburbs for human rights organizations and environmental nonprofits, in all weather, giving a new definition to *cold shoulder.* Conversely, Bernadette couldn't fathom RayAnne's foray into sport fishing—wondering aloud if RayAnne had been brainwashed into it as if into a cult.

"There *is* the occasional check that pays my rent. And sponsorships," RayAnne would defend her choice. "I get paid to fish."

"Well, I like to get through my days knowing I haven't killed a living creature while willingly rubbing shoulders with conservative yahoos." Bernadette's tone was one reserved for fascists.

"It's catch and release, Mom. And most of the old yahoos are just that."

Men on the circuit weren't exactly woke, but not all were the deplorables Bernadette imagined. Few were actually bold enough to wear their politics on their sleeves or MAGA hats on their knuckleheads; most knew to keep their opinions and confederate flags to themselves rather than offend sponsors. "And I can assure you, Mother, no shoulders—or anything else—are getting rubbed."

Had Bernadette worried RayAnne might suffer her own fate, wind up with a pro fisherman?

After Bernadette's marijuana-farmer fiancé was incarcerated for possession (three years!), she had self-solaced by scything through a quick succession of lovers. Unlikely as Big Rick was, he had been knee-weakeningly handsome, attentive, and intensely virile in a way her stoner boyfriends were not. She'd regarded him as a possible conversion project but had been sidelined by lust (as if RayAnne might care to dwell on such details) for a man of questionable politics, but with an animal masculinity that was intoxicating.

Until it was simply toxic.

After discovering Bernadette was pregnant, Big Rick went full caveman over the prospect of fatherhood. Hormonally induced lapse of judgment and sheer exhaustion prompted her to accept his fifth proposal. Otherwise, RayAnne likely would have been aborted—information her mother casually offered up before hastily reassuring her. "But then I wouldn't have you, would I, sweetheart?"

Bernadette Mills married Big Rick and water-birthed RayAnne in a kiddie pool in the rec room of the four-bedroom faux-Tudor he called Ground Zero and Bernadette half-jokingly dubbed Manderley. Braided and Birkenstocked and out of her element in their WASPish neighborhood, Bernadette slung baby RayAnne across her back with a batik shawl, hoisted a rainbow flag, tore up Big Rick's putting green (the beginning of the discord) to plant a bee garden. She grew corn on the front lawn for the hens, which neighbors heartily petitioned against at zoning meetings. She was that neighbor.

RayAnne's toddlerhood was a warm blur of vegetable gardens, moonbaths, squash patches, and the yeasty-smelling kitchen where yogurt cultured in vats and dust bunnies abounded. Bernadette believed in fresh air, trundling RayAnne outdoors in all weather to play in the sandbox frequented by stray cats, in a yard dotted with compost bins and rusty found-metal sculpture. In summer she splashed in the same kiddie pool she was born in, and in autumn sought warmth under heat lamps in the chicken coop. Bernadette credits RayAnne's freakish healthiness to her early exposure to filth and fowl, unaware to this day that Gran took both grandchildren to her own doctor for all the vaccinations her daughter-in-law eschewed.

RayAnne's early years were calm enough. And when marital battles flared, there were plenty of outdoor diversions, including a tree fort perfect for a little loner. Her friends included sleepy beetles, garden snakes and caterpillars, stray cats and a rooster named Mick for his strut. Mick hated everyone but little RayAnne, who fed him buds from Bernadette's "special plants" in a bright corner of the grow-house she was never, ever supposed to play in.

After colicky Kyle was born too early, Big Rick was pressed into parental service, and RayAnne became his fishing buddy. Suddengly she was on the circuit, and, being the only child, she naturally became its unofficial mascot.

Back home, whenever puny Kyle took one of his rare naps, Bernadette got stoned in order to make the brief slivers of quiet seem longer. Even at age five, RayAnne suspected other mothers did not mumble at the radio, scribble in journals into the wee hours, or sit in the hall closet biting one of Ky's teething rings.

When RayAnne was twelve, Big Rick had an affair with a sponsor's wife. After it became public, he was booted off the Bass Channel. Bernadette kicked him out of Manderley, then enrolled herself in grad school to pursue a master's in feminist literature. Gran, having finally closed the doors on Dorthea's, stepped in, cleared the clutter from Bernadette's kitchen, and tied on an apron to take part in raising her grandchildren.

When not in class, Bernadette was pinned to her desk with stacks of novels by dead writers and pints of Ben & Jerry's, committing passages of *The Human Woman* to memory like scripture. Having broken from the chrysalis of wedlock, Bernadette emerged a winged feminist. Her journal rants took on digital form as a blog, which became the thesis for her dissertation.

After graduation, she began taking women on the weekend retreats that evolved into her famed Blood-Tide Quests. Bernadette's radical-fem boots were made for walking *and* marching.

RayAnne is well aware such boots are hard to fill.

As were Gran's white Keds. Dot Dahl's footwear of choice not only matched her crisp chef's togs but allowed her to be nimble on her feet, essential for any woman navigating the whack-a-mole workplace misogyny of the '50s and '60s. After her years in postwar Naples in cooking school, Dot assumed a suburban supper club would be tame and reasonably safe.

"Hardly!" Gran would tell of having to dodge sommeliers and fishmongers, sous chefs, even patrons. "While their wives were in the powder room!"

"Ew."

"A bigshot lawyer, the kind with those terrible commercials? Followed me out back to the grease drum—hopeful, as he put it, for a bit of sugar."

"Grease drum?" RayAnne shuddered. "Sugar?"

"He was Southern."

"Did he get any?"

"He got a gallon of hot fryer oil on his wingtips."

"Gran!"

"The burns were barely second-degree. He was back chasing skirts and ambulances inside a month." Gran tsked. "Good lord, we women were naive. Men dished it out and we just took it. You expected the worst, because everywhere you turned there were fingers coming at you. If you were lucky, it was just some mouthy fella and a pinch. The good old days were anything but, I can tell you."

Both her grandmother and mother worked twice as hard, RayAnne knew, had to be twice as good to get half as far as a man, twice as vocal to be heard. She understands this since working the circuit. Bernadette is quick to remind her that every generation since Eve has slogged through the predicament of patriarchy. Since old enough to sit in a booster chair, RayAnne had been hearing about inequality.

"Yet she persisted," RayAnne yawned.

Bernadette flashed one of her looks of ultimate patience. "Don't be sarcastic, sweetie. It doesn't suit you."

When her mother disappeared on election night of 2016, RayAnne half-expected her to do something dramatic and illegal. As it turned out, she'd only gotten in her VW van to flee west for a silent retreat of forest bathing on a gulf island in British Columbia, taking raingear and a single book, *The Art of War.*

Upon her return, RayAnne was shocked to see her mother's auburn dreadlocks shot through mostly white. She listened open-mouthed through her explanation: Bernadette had stopped to watch election results in an all-night diner in North Dakota. Not since the passing of Citizens United (three days fasting in the backyard yurt) had Bernadette been so despondent. She walked out of the diner that November predawn into a changed world. When she caught her alarming reflection in the rearview, she'd realized that, while watching electoral maps being filled in with red, the color had drained from her own follicles. She accepted her shock-white hair as a badge. Returning to Minnesota, Bernadette was uncharacteristically calm and steely, no longer angry, simply determined. "I'm prepared to die on this hill."

RayAnne might normally chalk up such comments to her mother's penchant for drama. Not this time. Hair aside, she seemed fundamentally changed—posture straighter, gaze fiercer. There was something of a Valkyrie about her.

"And if *he*" (having vowed to never utter the president-elect's name) "makes a second term," Bernadette stated, "I will train as a ninja assassin."

What would Bernadette do? RayAnne imagines her mother's voice when asking herself such questions as, "Do I buy these jelly shoes or not?" Bernadette would have first considered her desire against the consequence of her purchase.

Where did these jelly jandals come from? How far did they travel to reach this store shelf? Who made them, and from what? Will they one day ensnare and drown a baby sea turtle?

Necessity doesn't enter the equation, since no one in the history of ever has needed jelly shoes, so if the question is to buy or not to buy, the answer is a resounding, "No!"

It's going to take a lot more women like Bernadette Mills and Dot Dahl to effect real change—women aware that the mess is wide and deep, and that as with all epic messes throughout history, they are going to be the ones to clean it up. Women like Fiona Parata, fierce and fearless.

"The other irony is that 'fashion,'" Fiona finger-quotes the word, "professes to encourage individuality, yet banks on us to follow the pack. How often do you see women walking together dressed almost exactly alike?"

"So you're encouraging women—"

"To be ferociously themselves," Fiona says, "and dare to drop out of the popularity contest and buying spree of fashion."

"So if plaid is in next season . . . ?" RayAnne ventures.

"*Screw* plaid. Wear what you love and ignore what you're being pressured to buy."

RayAnne need only open her closet to be reminded of her own bad choices: the suede gauchos; a mossy velvet maxi dress with crazy sleeves that could only ever be carried off at a Renaissance Fair; the olive-green hemp coveralls she'd paid a week's wages for and adored until seeing a picture of herself in them, unaware how they creased at the crotch—not so much a camel toe as a camel foot.

Her favorite clothes reveal her practical side: cargo skirts and pants in forest-ranger shades of khaki, greens, and the UPS brown that evokes chocolate. The more pockets the better, her wardrobe a fusion of Rough Riders meets Girl Guides on safari.

Fiona's own outfit perfectly suits her, a belted flax tunic in rust red over a light-gray cotton T. Gray woven rope jandals dangle from her feet. She's wearing a sea-green pendant the size of a spatula that perfectly matches her eyes. The floppy straw hat is the circumference of a small umbrella, shading her broad shoulders. Fiona dresses to enhance her full height and hourglass build, claiming her stature is inherited from her father, who'd been a rugby legend. When Cassi mentioned his name at breakfast, reading Fiona's bio aloud, Rangi's jaw dropped. "The Pulverizer? I had his posters above my bed as a kid!"

Fiona is the smoothest-looking person RayAnne has ever seen, as if boneless or carved from teak. As if reading her mind, Fiona plants her hands on her hips and challenges, "Here's one. Can you classify your own body type?"

"Type?" One of her self-effacing blurts bubbles forth. "I reckon I'm probably a typo!" She really should check that spigot of self-deprecating remarks.

Fiona smiles. "I meant classification. You know—ectomorph, mesomorph, or endomorph?"

"Riiight." Her mother ascribes to the ayurvedic versions—pitta, vata, and kapha. "I used to know this. I think I'm a vata, which makes me . . . a *meso*-something?"

"Mesomorph. Average. And we all know clothing isn't designed for average or above-average women." Fiona slaps her meaty thigh. "Like me."

In the echo, Rangi can be heard swallowing.

"Most clothing is designed with the ectomorph in mind—literally, the smallest portion of the population."

"Now you're changing that."

"Sure, but I'm just one designer. It's gonna take an army."

"You hear that?" RayAnne looks at the camera, winding up the fishing segment of the interview. "Any young designers out there interested in enlisting? Check Fiona's website and Instagram for info on organizations and resources."

Fiona laughs. "So, that's the future of fashion, sorted!"

"But in the meantime, what can we do?"

"Shop responsibly. Resist cheap clothes and curate your wardrobe for *you*."

Both grab their hats before a gust of wind can nab them.

"Welcome to Welly McWindface!"

Laughing, RayAnne turns to the camera and points inland. "And when we come back, we'll visit Fiona's workshop and boutique just over there in windy Wellington."

The crew packs up and they move on to Fiona's workshop. In the alley they all watch wind sending a paper cup skittering along the street followed by a broken, half-open umbrella.

The workshop is a renovated boatbuilder's shed. The production area has been refitted with rubber flooring. A dozen slick, kidney-shaped sewing tables are positioned under wide skylights, cutting tables in the middle. A clear plexi garage door opens onto a loading dock that doubles as a patio. Beyond the rooftops, Wellington Bay froths, the whitecaps adding a salt tinge to the breeze.

Each worker has a sea view. A few wear headphones, but most bob along to pop tunes playing on the sound system, drowning out the low hum of machines. Fiona employs ten stitchers and a cutter. There are two supervisors moving among them, delivering cut pieces and supplies, checking machines, stopping to change threads on the sergers, gathering completed garments for the inspection table. Fiona motions RayAnne up the open stairs. As the crew begin to follow, a Lizzo song comes on and Fiona turns around just above them to squeal, "Mean *as*! This one mentions your state! Turn it up, would you, Nia?"

As music cranks, Fiona commences dancing. Rangi cannot hit record fast enough, the barrel of his long lens following her.

Fiona begins lip-synching to Lizzo—hip-synching as well—and pointing a finger at each of them along with the beat, pointedly stopping at Rangi. "Why men great 'til they gotta *be* great?" Everyone joins to belt out the lyrics. The stitchers know every word. When they get to "New man on the Minnesota Vikings," Fiona fist-bumps RayAnne before turning, to pied-pipe them up the stairs with the sway of her backside.

Rangi is blinking, flummoxed as he watches Fiona move. Step sway, step sway.

"Bom bom bi bom bi dum bum bay!"

RayAnne believes she can now claim to have witnessed a grown man falling in love in real time.

The boutique across the street is a Victorian bungalow that's been refitted for retail by essentially ripping off the entire front and replacing it with slabs of glass. They pause under the wrought-iron sign creaking in the wind, a stylized outline of a shirt, with the small letters of KĀKAHU welded onto the pocket.

Fiona pushes open the door and calls out to the sales clerk. "Kia ora."

Kākahu is one of those shops where everything is coordinated and spare, every sight line and light source weighed and considered. The clothes are curated to a degree that RayAnne can imagine burning every item of her own clothing and stocking her wardrobe afresh. Fiona has made very clever use of the house as a house, with its still-recognizable rooms. Plus-size and average-size mannequins are posed in domestic vignettes: one near the door is reaching for a set of car keys on a hook, her coat half-shouldered, ready to rush out; in the living room, another wearing an elegant sheath dress is frozen in the act of rising from a chair in front of the fireplace. Three additional empty chairs surround the coffee table, where fabric swatch books and style books lie open for the next customers to browse.

RayAnne looks over a rack of merino tweed coats—sculptural, funky versions of the classic trench, swing, and peacoat.

Fashioned from rustic yarns in exaggerated weaves, they have handsewn top-stitching in vibrantly hued colors. The wildly patterned linings coordinate with the stitched-thread accents.

RayAnne hefts a sleeve, surprised at how light it is. "These are winter coats?"

"Our winter, yeah. Doesn't Minnesota have some crazy-low temperature thing—is it called ice snap?"

"Cold snap. Aka polar vortex."

What RayAnne would give to have a winter coat not based on its R-value or the number of hours one can expect to survive in subzero temps while wearing it. Fiona's coats won't protect RayAnne from the death claw of a Minneapolis winter. She reluctantly drops the sleeve, unable to even consider it as a shoulder-season garment, because it's not waterproof.

Moving along the hallway of the very homey Kākahu, RayAnne laughs out loud at the open bathroom door. The mannequin perched on the toilet wears silk pajamas from Fiona's new line—bottoms pooled to the tile and ankles askance, she is absorbed in the pages of a fashion magazine balanced on knees, hand reaching blindly for the toilet paper that has a paltry single sheet clinging to the roll.

In the former kitchen, Fiona has flipped the marketing stereotype. A buff male mannequin wearing only a barbeque apron and oven mitts proffers two trays arranged with simple accessories by local designers: wallets, keychains, phone cases. A second mannequin lurks near the back door, a porkpie hat pushed back from his forehead, trench coat flapped open to reveal a number of similar accessories, as if he's peddling knockoffs.

In one of the bedrooms, a RayAnne-sized mannequin wears an unbuttoned shirt and pink underpants embroidered *Unday*. The mannequin is in the throes of deciding between two garments. RayAnne touches the oatmeal-gray blazer. From the mannequin's other thumb dangles a vest in a complementary olive hue of the same fabric. She eases it from the hanger and slips it on. It settles neatly across her shoulders. The multiple pockets include a phone-sized slot in the perfect spot, and a pair of invisible rib-hugging slit pockets to warm hands. Slightly flared at the waist, it could have been tailored for her exact contours.

She's looking in the mirror when Fiona and Cassi find her, Rangi wasting no time coming up the rear. As RayAnne admires the handsome bronze carabiner just above the breast pocket, Fiona sees her questioning look.

"For glasses."

"Ah!" RayAnne takes the sunglasses from atop her head and slips them through the ring. She lifts the price tag and blinks, letting it drop.

"Expensive, isn't it?" Fiona is unapologetic. "So much tailoring goes into a piece like that. People have been buying cheap clothes for so long they've forgotten what real, bespoke clothing can cost. *Should* cost, if we're honest. Come take a look from here."

RayAnne steps up onto a riser in front of a bank of mirrors. Fiona half-circles her, tapping her lip. Tugging the sleeve of RayAnne's sun-proof cantaloupe-colored button-down, she is frank. "Is this something you would normally wear?"

"Oh no. This is sponsor's clothing. I just wear whatever they send."

"You don't get to choose?"

"Nope." RayAnne turns to Rangi. "Hey, can you . . . maybe back up enough to get both of us in frame?"

"Sorry."

Even with the unflattering shirt, the vest looks amazing, moves as RayAnne moves. The front pockets happen to land exactly where her hands dangle. She pets the fabric where it meets her hip. "Feels like my grandmother's dress coat—is this cashmere?"

"Woven possum and merino."

"No kidding. Where does the possum come from?"

"A pair of trappers that live in the hills. Sisters. They're a story in themselves."

"I love this vest."

A second bronze detail is a retractable key chain that extends from a hip pocket so the keys can either be stowed or dangle. RayAnne unbuttons the vest to admire the lining. Discovering the inner hidden pocket is lined with silk printed with the faces of the Super Mario Brothers, she nearly yips. Looking up, she sees Fiona glance at her watch.

"Oh, geez, we've taken up so much of your day!" RayAnne scrambles to wrap up the segment, but with Rangi so close she has to step in front of Fiona to face the lens. At a nod from Cassi, she employs the tone the voice coach has been helping her with.

"Fast fashion," RayAnne says. "Well, I'm feeling enlightened. Fiona Parata has been our very inspiring guest. You can find out all about the mission behind Kākahu on the website of the same name, and see some behind-the-scenes pictures of her workshop and read what her workers have to say about the day-to-day in this employee-owned enterprise. You can also find links at *Fishing!*-dot-org."

RayAnne turns. "Fiona, any final words to share with viewers?"

"You've heard the term *fashion dictates*?"

"Of course."

"My final word," Fiona says, facing the camera, a woman to be reckoned with, "is *resist*!"

After a beat Chad declares, "Wrap!" and claps everyone to attention like a kindergarten teacher.

On the way out, RayAnne buys the vest, flatly refusing when Fiona tries making a gift of it.

"I want viewers to see me wear something amazing from a small label." She faces Cassi, ready for an argument. "I'm wearing this on the show." She adores the vest in the way she adored her lucky pants, a pair of Hepburn-style nubby raw-silk trousers in a dark tomato red—pants she's worn to every successful job interview and every promising third date since graduating college.

The van is packed and RayAnne is halfway to the Rover with her beautiful garment when she remembers the note in Cassi's cramped handwriting in the markup margin of Fiona's bio.

She turns on her heel, calling over her shoulder to Chad, "Don't wait for me. I'll walk back to the hotel."

RayAnne has no specific words for Fiona, or any idea what she'll say, but grief isn't always the thing that needs acknowledging—when the elephant in the room is the person not in it.

Just as she's reaching for the door, Fiona flings it open. "Oi, I was just coming to catch you!"

"Yeah?"

"Close your eyes."

Fiona takes RayAnne's hand and folds something smooth and warm into it, some manner of stone. Her instinct is to squeeze, as if it might hold something essential. Unfurling her fingers reveals a jade pendant about two inches long, smooth, shaped like a rudimentary tool, notched at the thick edge and tightly noosed with a waxed woven cord.

"A *toki,*" Fiona explains. "Carved from *pounamu.* We wear them in remembrance of ancestors. Some believe they contain the mana of the dead."

"Pou . . . ?"

"*Pounamu.* This toki is made from Tangiwai pounamu, which translates to 'tears that come from great sorrow.'"

"Well, that seems . . . about right." Her voice catches. "D-did Cassi tell you about my grandmother?"

"No. But . . ." Fiona pauses to straighten RayAnne's collar. "Some say grief is its own tribe, so maybe we recognized each other?"

"Huh." RayAnne grins. "A month ago I was told grief is its own country."

"Sure." Fiona smiles. "That, too."

"I'm so sorry about your father."

"Thanks."

RayAnne and Fiona lean into a hug. As lovely as it would be to just sway in this embrace with a kindred spirit, RayAnne breaks away to point at the boutique. "You're doing something here that really matters."

"I am, yeah. Just like *you* are."

They stand in the silence of that, both turning their faces to the sun and a wind that delivers, no great surprise, Rangi. Strolling up with hands deep in his pockets, he poorly feigns surprise at seeing them.

"Just sauntering by?" RayAnne asks. "Remind me to play poker with you."

"Well," Rangi shrugs, "the others have taken off, so . . ."

"No worries, dude. I'm leaving too." She and Fiona exchange a glance over his shoulder. RayAnne gives a slight bow, prayer hands caging the toki. "Wow . . . this." The toki is sublime in its simplicity. "Thank you."

Fiona turns to Rangi and exhales, her voice husky. "Took you long enough."

He takes the steps two at a time. The door bumps shut behind them, muffling laughter. As RayAnne walks away, she turns the toki over in her palm, pauses to hold it up to the sun to see compressed layers, strata of light and dark stone. Slipping the cord over her head, the pendant settles at the dip where her collar bones rendezvous—the soft depression Hal calls *base camp* because his thumb, lips, or fingertips so often return to it during his excursions and explorations of her. Lost in thoughts of Hal, she pauses at a restaurant window. As suspected, a slow burn of blush has crept up her face. Seeing how the pounamu reflects light she turns this way and that before suddenly noticing an old man just on the other side of the glass, staring right at her.

"Ooh!" She gasps, then laughs when he offers a broad smile.

His face is kindly and ancient; the swirls of his moko tattoo are faded and interrupted by deep wrinkles. Whenever Gran described someone very old, she'd say they were "old as stone." The man's eyes have the skim-milk cast of cataracts. She instinctively reaches for the glass. His fingers meet the pane where hers have alighted. Intentional? How much can he see? He presses his entire hand to the glass and nods as if encouraging her to do the same.

Sun dips behind a cloud and the reflection between them evaporates.

Times slows. Simply, he and RayAnne seem to have been stilled in the same ray of benevolent light. There is no hesitation. RayAnne presses her palm to the cool glass, holds her hand flat, and looks directly at the man's eyes. Maybe he can see her silhouette or shadow; she might be a blob but is certainly a stranger. For the moment they are merely fellow passengers acknowledging one another on their loops around the sun.

You never know, RayAnne muses, when you might encounter a human being. As films go, *Little Big Man* got a lot right, but perhaps that is what it got most right.

She's grinning now, and so is her new friend, his eyes practically disappearing in the squint of crinkled flesh. Then, as abruptly as he'd appeared at the glass, the man steps away, distracted by some voice she cannot make out. Someone has addressed him—either his table is ready or his takeout order is up. As he shambles away, the fogged outline of his hand on the glass evaporates at the same speed he recedes into shadow.

Thinking of *Little Big Man* makes RayAnne consider calling her brother. She's avoided Ky, particularly angry over his potential idiocy around the temptations of Ingrid's doppelgänger cousin, au pair with a pair. Not sure she can trust herself to not sound angry, she settles on texting him instead.

NZ HAS MANY HUMAN BEINGS.

It's less than a minute before her notification pings.

WRLD CN'T HAVE ENOUGH HB'S. YOU HEARD FROM INGRID?

Has she heard from Ingrid? RayAnne swallows. Has her brother done something stupid? Her fingers fly as she texts back. NO! WHY?

COUSIN HAS FKD OFF TO FAROE IS.

RayAnne can only hope it's not because anything has happened between Ky and Gikka. Before she has time to cringe, he's texted again.

AFTER TELLING ING ABT HVING HOTS FOR ME.

RayAnne snorts, typing. OMFG, NO ONE SAYS "HOTS."

SHE CONFESSED TO IMPURE THOUGHTS!

ROFLMFAO! She adds a laugh-crying emoji.

TLD U I WAZN'T CRZY!—SHE WANTED MY ASS!!!!

RayAnne sends the donkey emoji with her next question. NEW NANNY?

He answers with an eye-roll emoji. RUTH: ANTABUSE FOR VIAGRA. MIND LIKE STEELWOOL—SNSE OF HUMR PFCTLY MTCHED WITH TWNS. 4'9" WITH ASTHMA. NEVER SLEEPS. IMAGINE SNEEZY UNDERFOOT ALL HOURS.

She laughs. Perhaps the first time in months she's laughed at her brother. He sounds like himself, like he hasn't since the funeral. Half of RayAnne's anger with her brother had been about his jeopardizing what little faith she has left in marriage. She idealizes what Ky and Ingrid have as her gold standard. If their rock-solid marriage could fail, any marriage could.

GUESS WHO IS GOING TO PARIS CONFERENCE W. ING NEXT WEEK?

U? WHT. AS HER ASST?

PARAMOUR/STUD.

After sending a vomit emoji, she waits. She's about to pocket her phone when it pings.

DODGED A BULLET THERE, RAY. NEARLY FORGOT THE PLOT. ALSO, LOSING GRAN MAY BE BGGER DEAL THAN THOUGHT.

May be? His response gives her pause, but since he cannot see her face, she only text-scoffs: U THINK?

Has he finally stopped managing his grief like a spreadsheet and given in to it? Gran is indeed gone, and nothing—no book or neat set of phases—will bring her back. What's the grail they are supposed to be striving for? Acceptance?

WHAT PHASE U IN NOW????

It takes a full minute for his next ping. GRATITUDE.

It's not like Ky to be serious or real with her.

I LIKE IT. Her fingers fly. LT'S GET STONED WHEN I GT HME.

She waits for the ping. I'LL MAKE SNICKERDOODLES. Her brother has taken an interest in baking. Sweet.

RayAnne gravitates to the waterfront to walk idly among the tourists more intent on recording the proof of their visit than experiencing it. The wind drives her farther into the city. In no hurry to get back to the hotel, she roams Wellington, content to follow where streets lead.

The Friday afternoon crowd of downtowners filter from buildings and shops to settle on café patios; others move with intent on errands, carrying groceries, aromatic brown bags of takeout, flowers, six-packs, wine bottles twisted into newsprint. The millennials are sealed in clunky headphones, trained on their phones and safe from eye contact. Some things are universal.

It's a bit early for dinner, but on an out-of-the-way street, the aromas coming from a tiny corner restaurant beckon. The bald waiter seems to be the real thing, greeting, "Benvenuta, bella signora . . ."

He seats her at a tiny table with a checkered tablecloth.

The menu is a single page, very reasonably priced. The place feels a bit worn around the edges; faded black-and-white photographs of the canals of Venice and hilltop villages are the only decor. She orders the house red and a plate of gnocchi with chive pesto and prawns. The bread is crusty and warm, the olive oil is the color of an olive.

The entrée arrives sizzling and garlicky with a sprinkling of asiago broiled golden on top.

Gran loved a hole-in-the-wall restaurant with no pretense, where food is the focus. She would approve.

RayAnne's dinner companion is a candle dripping like crazy down the sides of a Chianti bottle. She takes a picture of the table and the scene beyond, the old waiter leaning at the open door in the distance, the fat Chianti bottle front and center. She sends the picture to Hal, texting MY DATE, WAXING PROLIFIC.

The only other patrons are a couple in their sixties. Few words pass between them, but they exchange forkfuls, tasting each other's entrées. They trade nods and gestures, sipping, sighing satisfied sighs—the communication of seasoned companions. Furtively watching them, RayAnne muses that perhaps what they have is enough—that after the passion ebbs, a lucky couple might settle into mutual contentment, happy with the smalls in life, like a nice meal. Perhaps the best, lasting relationships age into something palatable, like cheese.

The next day dawns bright and, no surprise, windy. Rangi shows up late for breakfast with a sheepish grin wearing the clothes he was last seen in. No one comments on his tardiness. There's no time: the crew have a boat hired to spend the day in Wellington Harbor, gathering B-roll of the city. No time to waste.

Cassi and RayAnne sit on the hotel terrace with laptops until noon, answering emails from the mothership in Minneapolis, mostly regarding editing of the interviews they've already completed and uploaded. Cassi leans into the work, actually interested in such minutia as the legalese of permissions and releases and insurance waivers. A lover of precision, she's happy to look up the exact GPS locations, the spelling of place names, making sure all transcripts have the proper diacritical marks on any Māori words.

After lunch they learn that the next day's guest must cancel. The Seastainable Chef they were going to interview has had her kitchen closed due to a gas leak after road workers nearby hit a main. It will be days before it's fixed. RayAnne is crestfallen, but Cassi kicks into gear to find a replacement. None on their alternate list is near enough to work anything out. By evening, she's found two contenders, courtesy of Fiona Parata, who had mentioned a pair of sisters who trap possums and supply a mill that sources woolen goods for Kākahu. They also operate a small fishing charter.

Since they know nearly nothing about them, RayAnne is hesitant. "What's the hook?" RayAnne catches herself using producer lingo.

"A success story: they're both in recovery and making a go of it. Meth is a big problem in rural New Zealand." Cassi looks at her. "It'll be fine."

The Rover bumps and grinds up the rutted, pothole-pocked road. They pull into the muddy parking area just as a four-wheeler with two riders comes into view high on a sheep track in the distance.

"Oh boy."

"S'pose that's them?" Cassi looks worried.

As if in answer, the four-wheeler veers in their direction to judder and bounce down to the base of the hill. The riders whoop as they skid and spin a donut in the mud, splattering the windshield of the Rover. Cassi nods at the brace of possums slung across the shoulder of the driver. "S'pose the dead possums are a dead giveaway?"

"Ya think?" RayAnne sighs, then puts on her best chipper intro-voice. "Today's guests are the Cousins sisters! A pair of possum-trappin' Fishin' Chicks!" A nod to the show's lamentable original title.

They climb from the Rover to meet Kate and Angie Cousins.

They are forty and forty-one but look seventy and seventy-one. Between them they do not possess a full set of teeth—a side effect of meth. Kate, the elder, has very green eyes.

After a round of handshakes, the Cousins sisters lead them through a gate where twin caravans are parked. RayAnne and Cassi exchange looks behind their cornrowed heads and the jouncing bandolier of dead possum. The steep yard overlooks a neighboring field where a dozen cannibalized vehicles rust in the weeds, some with trees growing from open or missing hoods. Close to the fenced garden an old school bus—the Fuck Bus, according to the graffiti—has been converted to a chicken coop, complete with rooster strutting atop, cockadoodling toward the buzz of a distant chainsaw as if in call and response.

The Cousins' yard is bald from dogs and chickens. The roofs of both trailers are topped with loops of razor wire. A pair of penned mastiffs bark continuously until the possums are whisked away and strung up out of sight in a rusting Quonset hut. The dogs shift gear to focus on Cassi. When Angie opens their pen, they blare forth like megaphones of teeth.

RayAnne grabs Cassi, who feels remarkably light, and flings her like a waltz partner up and out of range onto the picnic table, realizing too late that it's scattered with fishing gear and possum traps in various states of repair, some with blood on them. Cassi, fleet-footed, is just able to avoid them, like a caber-dancer hopping her swords. Her eyes bug at RayAnne. At a shrill whistle from Kate, the dogs skid to a halt, close enough that RayAnne can smell their breath.

Angie sweeps the traps and reels off the picnic table and into a box. Once Cassi is breathing again and the dogs are still, save foamy streamers of saliva teasing the breeze, Angie wipes the table with her sleeve. From somewhere a pot of coffee and cups are produced.

"Pothums are a fact of life," Kate says, idly cleaning dried blood from under her nails with the blade of a boning knife, wiping it on her jeans. "They've changed New Thealand, and not for the better."

"But they're here," says Angie, whose eyes are unnaturally dark as if still dilated. "Though we gotta make the betht of it."

"They make dethent barbie."

"You eat them?" RayAnne swallows.

"Exthellent protein."

RayAnne wonders how they can chew with the nubbins of meth teeth.

"Hey, wherth your camera crew?"

Kate's question is answered by the distant roar, the van laboring up the Cousins' steep drive.

"That should be them now."

"Rongo, Rangi, and Chad," RayAnne says.

"Men?" Angie brightens.

"Crickey!" Kate slaps a hand over her mouth. "Totally forgot!" She pulls a plastic case from deep in her pocket. Angie follows suit and both turn away. When they turn back, both are smiling with white teeth far too large for their mouths.

"Brilliant." RayAnne smiles, her voice unnaturally high.

With dentures installed, the sisters' sunken cheeks puff out, and they suddenly look a lot like Chip and Dale, the polite cartoon chipmunks. Kate checks her reflection in the blade of the knife before giving it a twirl and stabbing it deep into the wood of the table. RayAnne watches it twang and vibrate, mesmerized.

From somewhere above, a tui bird mimics the alarm on RayAnne's iPhone.

The van's engine rattles to stillness and the guys spill from within. After introductions, Rongo and Rangi must work to extricate themselves from the sisters' handshakes.

The Cousins ply them with coffee and offer possum jerky, warm and unwrapped straight from their hip pockets.

"Wanna go up to thee our trap line?" Kate nudges Rongo. Her tone suggests more than traps might be seen.

"Film us thkinning the varmints?" Angie entices.

Rongo looks to RayAnne with panic in his eyes.

A staccato tapping commences from the underside of the picnic table. At first everyone laughs, but when RayAnne looks underneath to see which of the pranksters is doing it, no one seems to be responsible. The tapping suddenly grows in volume to pounding, seemingly coming from the wood itself. When she looks up, everyone has vaporized and the pounding has grown to a sinister din as the table begins to buck. She exchanges a horrified look with herself, now seated across the table, both of her two selves frozen in fear.

"WAKEY-wakey!" Cassi is pounding the hotel room door.

RayAnne bolts up to sitting, tangled in bedcovers, sweating. "What the . . . ?"

Cassi's voice is muffled. "You awake, Ray? Is your phone even on? We're gonna be late for the Cousins sisters!"

"Oh, crap!" She pedals out of the sheets and hits the carpet at speed, addressing the door as she trips past it. "Ten minutes!"

"Five! We're out front, ready to go."

Speed-brushing her teeth, RayAnne shakes her head. As with most dreams, she is left wondering from what murky corners of her psyche such weirdness springs, shuddering to think that her trailer-trash depiction of the sisters is the fruit of her imagination. Before even meeting them, has she painted them with the brush of judgment her father would wield regarding drug addicts—the same man who once declared that whiskey baron Jack Daniel should be canonized as a saint. RayAnne blanches at her reflection in the mirror.

What if prejudices are inherited?

Were that the case, she'd be one conflicted girl.

Woman, she corrects her reflection, remembering she is also Bernadette's daughter.

. . .

In her parents' phenomenally mismatched marriage, clashing values pitted Bernadette and Big Rick against each other in such battles that young Kyle was inspired to furtively record them on his My First Sony. For a period of months before their divorce, their parents unknowingly starred in *The Rick and Bernie Show.* Broken dishes and noise complaints from neighbors provided material for the very best episodes. The production was a thoroughly juvenile take on family dysfunction delivered with words normally forbidden to Ky. His audience of one, Gran, pretended to be shocked, scolding him even while she giggled through his promos and teasers: "Next week on *R and B,* did Bernadette cut the buttons from Big Rick's goddamned shirts? Who destroyed the herb garden with the fucking riding mower? In our how-to segment, sugar in your mower's gas tank? Try this unsuccessful fix!"

Yes, Bernadette had snipped Big Rick's buttons so that his shirts flayed open Elvis-style to his navel. RayAnne remembers him red-faced, fumbling with double-faced tape at the mirror. By the end of it everyone was relieved when the marriage—and show—were both canceled.

The Rick and Bernie Show whetted her brother's appetite for broadcasting. He'd developed a gift for impersonations. Like Big Rick, he had a voice and was recruited by the vice principal to lend his talents to the school's PA announcements. Throughout her final year of high school RayAnne strolled corridors serenaded by the voice of her little brother, as if she didn't get enough of him at home. Years later, after Ky blew out his shoulder during his single season in the NHL, he auditioned for a sidekick announcer gig on CNN and covered two seasons of playoffs. When offered a contract, he turned it down to follow Ingrid to Berlin for four years, where he put his own degree to use and freelanced as a statistician and sportswriter.

There is showmanship in the Dahl genes. Gran's great regret was turning down an offer to host a cable cooking show.

Bernadette's passion makes her a natural on her Blood-Tides podcasts. And with mister showbiz himself, *Big Rick's Bass Bonanza* was just becoming a hit, destined to eclipse Babe Winkelman's *Good Fishing,* when he embarked on his affair with Mrs. Lunkerville. The rest is history they would all rather forget.

There are days RayAnne has the sense that her family is living vicariously through her. No pressure.

Now they are going to be late meeting the real Cousins sisters because of her.

Climbing in the Rover, she volleys a breathless round of apologies. "Sorry, sorry, sorry!" Buckling up as Cassi pulls into traffic behind the van, she watches out the window a moment before turning with a sigh. "I hate work dreams, don't you?"

Cassi shrugs. "They're the only kind I have."

At least they can laugh. RayAnne has noticed Cassi's mood is much elevated since her interlude with Bylbo, though she doesn't dare ask about him in the event she's regretting her little fling.

They meet the Cousins sisters at the marina. Hardly the rough characters of her dream, they do seem aged, as RayAnne supposes one would be after years of addiction. But neither is meth-poster-ravaged, and they have their own teeth; they are well spoken, and neither gives Rangi or Rongo any deranged looks. They could be members of a book club.

To make ends meet, Angie and Kate work several gigs. They process possum pelts and supply the mill where Fiona Parata sources her woven blends; their extensive garden stocks a farmers' market booth with organic herbs, carrots, kale, and duck eggs. In season they take small groups out fishing in their Chesapeake Bay fishing boat, *Serenity.*

Serenity bobs next to the much larger charter boat the crew will film from.

Stupid dream. She shouldn't have dreaded the interview, but while the sisters seem perfectly lovely, RayAnne is a little twitchy interviewing anyone about their recovery while still on pins and needles waiting to see how spectacularly her own father will fall off the wagon. Because up until now, he always has. Odds-wise, Big Rick will likely drink because his entire history suggests it. Granted, this time there are differences. For one, he's attached to his AA group like a barnacle; he'd promised on his mother's grave to quit for good; he has even Tweeted about getting his ninety-day medallion. Until now Big Rick has never been "openly" sober. In the past he seemed to resent every moment of not drinking, so it never came as a surprise when he'd start again. This time, for the first time, her father seems thankful to be sober.

Aside from being conflicted, is she really the best person to give the sisters the interview they deserve? Will she ask the wrong thing? Or somehow leak her own skepticism or judgy vibe?

"What's up, Ray?" Cassi asks.

"Nothing."

She simply decides to not be the one to bring up the topic of recovery. She will stick to questions about fishing and New Zealand and simply spend time talking with two hardworking Kiwi women. If the Cousins sisters bring it up themselves, fine. She looks to Cassi and repeats, "Nothing."

It's a two-boat shoot by necessity. The crew and Cassi will loom alongside in a fifty-foot charter with a radar sweep, flashy chrome, a captain, and a deckhand. It's overkill, but with the last-minute booking, Chad couldn't find a smaller boat, or, to Cassi's dismay, anything cheaper.

Stepping aboard the *Serenity*, RayAnne thinks, *God, grant me some.* Because it would take no small amount to accept the twenty-seven-thousand things that she—or anyone else—cannot change.

After testing her mic, getting a thumbs-up from Chad and a hand signal from Cassi, both boats get underway and begin to chug slowly from the dock.

RayAnne rolls her shoulders, puts on her "voice," and smiles broadly toward the camera mounted on the stern. "Hey, everybody. Here we are on New Zealand's stunning east coast aboard the *Serenity,* where we'll be fishing with the Cousins sisters, Kate and Angie."

Both women wave for the camera. Kate steers the boat as Angie hauls in the dock bumpers.

As they head toward open water RayAnne makes her signature gesture, as if inviting the world to go along. "C'mon aboard," she calls out above the sound of the engines. "Let's go fishing!"

They are angling for something called John Dory.

"*Kuparu* in Māori," Angie says.

Kate finishes outfitting a line for RayAnne, handing over the pole.

John Dory is possibly the ugliest fish RayAnne has ever landed. The three now swimming in the live tank are plate-shaped and mud gray with large, jelly-lipped sucker mouths and spine sets like punk rockers' hair. They feature a weird false eye on their flank to fool predators into thinking they are much larger.

"Best eating fish, if you ask me," Kate says.

"Better than snapper?" RayAnne asks.

"Captain Cook thought so," Angie offers. "He ate them on his first voyage here in 1769. Liked them so much he had a load pickled in barrels to take home."

Kate pipes up. "I'd wager the eejit wished he'd stayed here."

"Right." RayAnne has a vague memory from a history class. "Wasn't he murdered in Hawaii?"

"Murdered? That's what the history books would say. Was caught attempting to kidnap a Hawaiian king, more like. I'd say he was asking for it."

"That was when, Ange?"

"1779, thereabouts. February."

"Ah." RayAnne pauses. Angie sounds a little like a teacher. "What were you before . . . ?"

"I was a meth addict? I managed a school library." A grin threatens the corner of her mouth. "Did you expect we'd be total bogans?"

To RayAnne's great relief, Angie's hearty laugh is joined by Kate's.

"And I," Kate offers, "was a partner in a cleaning service. Up north. Devonport, Takapuna. Did posh houses by the beaches. It was decent, could actually get a swim in between jobs most days."

Both are silent a moment as if remembering their old lives. "We lost three years to meth," Angie says.

"But we're still here," Kate says, "which is pretty much—"

"A bloody miracle!"

Both laugh, shaking their heads as if they cannot believe their luck.

The ensuing conversation is not the one RayAnne dreaded. The sisters know exactly how to relay their story since they do it weekly in a program they volunteer for—a secondary school drug-awareness campaign. They tell RayAnne all about the program and the kids; they answer her questions with candor and are as approachable and familiar as every other woman RayAnne knows: the neighbor, the cleaner, the library lady.

After they catch several more of the ugly fish, the sisters show RayAnne how to fillet them while avoiding any bones.

By the time they get back to the dock RayAnne knows that finding the sisters had been a stroke of luck. She'll thank Fiona Parata for the suggestion.

People do recover, she's reminded. She's nearly tempted to call her father.

Later that evening she tries. When Big Rick doesn't answer, it occurs that he's either in his daily AA meeting or romancing the

Holy Roller, Sal. Because that's how he operates, his keen attention focused on whatever woman lands in his crosshairs (as Ky puts it). This one, though, is keeping him sober, so already has more going for her in the pros column, despite being a wacko evangelical.

To quote Bernadette, "Sometimes you gotta give a pass."

The drive to Auckland takes seven hours. RayAnne spends what's left of the afternoon shopping for proper gifts to bring home, leaving her phone in the hotel on purpose, because a person should just be able to be phone-free once in a while. (Or would that be *phree*? She does sometimes amuse herself.)

The stuffed-sheep chew toy she buys for Rory likely won't last a day before it's reduced to stuffing under her couch. In another store she buys stupidly expensive honey for the Location crew back home. A woven backpack with a Māori design would be perfect for Bernadette, but her mother is downsizing these days, and besides, will it spark joy? Trying it on for herself the strap tangles with her new pendant, which inspires her to simply buy a toki for everyone. She's made a list that includes Hal's mother. Up until now she's been able to avoid venturing too far into boyfriend-family territory. But it's hard to apply the term *boyfriend* to Hal: it's too lightweight a title, since he's possibly *the* guy. She's always equated *boyfriend* with *audition*. It connotes a phase they've moved beyond.

And really, Hal's mother has already seen her topless, so there's that.

The store she finds is more like a gallery, where the clerk shows her gorgeous tokis in various shapes: adzes, spirals, tiny truncheons, symbols and shapes now recognizable to RayAnne as quintessentially Māori. The spiral *koru*; the humanish *tiki*. Thanks to Marion Meke, RayAnne knows the proper name for the stylized, carved fishhook, *matau*.

After choosing a variety of toki—from nearly black jade to

forest to mossy to apple-Jolly-Rancher green, she emerges from the cool gallery into the evening warmth much poorer, but now with ten small gift pouches.

She's even bought one for Sally Leighton. Who knows? The woman may consider it pagan and be somehow offended. But RayAnne reasons that if someone is offended by a gift from another culture, maybe they deserve to be.

Intending to find dinner she is waylaid by touristy shops with revolving racks of postcards. She's tentative, standing awhile before reaching out to rotate the rack. It had been their thing—she and Gran were always sending each other the worst possible postcards from trips. She'd find something truly terrible for Gran, and in turn, Gran, who rarely traveled after moving to Florida, would dig into her own vintage trove—fifty years' worth of kitsch—for such gems as a 3D winking deer, a cartoon wiener dog that barks when squeezed, a lineup of ladies in real cloth bikinis on Palm Beach.

Nothing says she can't pick out a card for Gran. It doesn't have to be sent.

She thumbs through the jokey ones and zeroes in on a possum postcard made of actual possum, because how often do you run across that? It even has a tiny rubber tail. She buys it, because Gran would find it silly.

At four in the morning they are up and yawning their way to the Auckland fish market, arriving just in time to catch early shift workers unloading and prepping. This backdoor tour of the market is something Tripod set up on their own with a vendor they know. When Cassi sees the loading dock activity—the ballet of forklifts, the great ice machines spewing pebbled ice over fish-laden trays, the continuous hosing down of everything, the rubber aprons and gumboots—she claps, "Brilliant!"

It is. A brilliant chaos of bustle and color, set against a perfect storm of noise.

The guys gather shots, then follow RayAnne for nearly an hour as she strolls the opening market. Early customers filter in: chefs, cooks from the fish-and-chips shops, caterers.

A variety of fish and shellfish are on offer, from gorgeous to frightful—many creatures are unfamiliar—all artfully displayed on ice. The fishmongers are happy to answer her questions and chitchat: the older men are terrible flirts and try to either impress RayAnne with their offerings or gross her out. The women working the stalls are droll or hilarious, gesturing at the men with their cleavers and knives. RayAnne submits to submerging her arm in a tank and having a live baby octopus engulf her wrist and hand; the sensation of tentacles testing out her palm is at once awesome and stomach-flipping—certain to become fodder for some future nightmare.

She laughs, turning toward the camera. "Imagine being stoned right now?"

Afterward, so pleased with all the great footage and sound bites from vendors, Chad convinces them to take a ferry to Waiheke Island, standing out on the top deck to blow the stink off themselves. After disembarking, they jump a bus to a vineyard with a view, overlooking a vast, seaward-sloping lawn.

Lunch is lamb burger with beetroot and mint aioli—delicious. After coffee they disperse with a plan to meet later at the bus stop. The guys all head for the giant beanbags on the vineyard lawn, intent on naps after so few hours of sleep.

RayAnne aimlessly follows Cassi to a table in deep shade and sits to watch her pull out a set of pens, a pot of ink, and what look like sheets of parchment; one is half-filled with tiny calligraphy. It turns out she and Bylbo have been writing. His letters come sealed with wax and plastered with stamps that seem too old to be valid but must be, because by some postal miracle his letters manage to arrive at whatever hotel they've just checked into.

Tilting her head, trying to make out an upside-down line, RayAnne is caught by Cassi, giving her a look.

"Sorry," RayAnne shrugs. "It's just . . . the writing is so pretty."

"Yup." Clearly, Cassi wants to get to it.

"What do you two . . . uh?"

"Write about?" Cassi looks up. "Would I ask what you and Hal write about?"

"Ah, jeez." RayAnne gets to her feet. "'Course not. Sorry. Hey, I'll just take a walk." She's already backing away.

"A walk . . . ," Cassi nods but doesn't look up, dipping her nib into the pot, "would be good."

RayAnne strolls the vineyard paths from one stunning view to the next until finding herself among the vines where heavy grapes are ripe to bursting. The sunlit quality of them stills her. The bunches are the palest green, achingly ripe and nearly incandescent, as if the fruit itself is the source of light. When she fishes for her phone to take a picture, it occurs to her that it's been days since Gran has popped up. Just that morning RayAnne had confused a picture of Gran *for* Gran and began talking to her, waiting for a response before recognizing the photo and remembering taking the picture. Gran had been having a good laugh while RayAnne tried out a fisheye-lens app. In it, Gran holds out a snickerdoodle as if it's bait, her broad smile warped, looking like some crazy lady on the other side of the peephole.

When *had* she last "seen" Gran?

Seems not only Gran is abandoning her. Back in Auckland at breakfast the next morning, she's the only one in the dining room. After bolting a yogurt and coffee, she finds everyone out in the parking lot, loading the van and the Rover, not with gear but with coolers, a volleyball net, bags of groceries. Rangi is securing two surfboards to the roof. To her look, he grins.

"Holiday!"

"What do you mean?"

Rangi tosses a rope. "Can you pull that?"

"No. What do you mean? You're leaving?"

"Yup. Just grab it?"

"How long will you be gone?" She reluctantly catches the rope.

Cassi walks over, wearing something weird that could only be called a getup.

"It's in their contract, Ray. Did you see my text? They've been working fourteen-hour days for eighteen days without any real break—we all have."

"We have?"

"Yes." Cassi's eyes narrow. "You read the attachments? About Waitangi Day."

"Right." She hadn't. RayAnne looks up to Rangi and pulls the rope tight. "Tell me again about this, uh, Waitangi Day?"

"Well . . ." Rangi stands to his full height atop the van. "A hundred-seventy-some years ago—"

"Seventy-eight," Chad interjects.

"Right. Leave it to the pale bloke. Anyway, a good long time ago, a treaty was signed up north—basically like every other, in that it handed too much over to the guys in the funny hats. Your typical culture-rape and land-grab brought to you by—guess who?—colonists."

"But you celebrate it?"

"We celebrate the time off," says Rongo.

"Massive barbie," offers Rangi.

Rongo rolls his eyes. "Mostly, we hang with our cousins, paddle a waka race, visit our mum and sister. Tell you all about it on Sunday."

"Fi-o-na's coming," Rangi bobs as if to music.

"Is she? Wait, did you say Sunday?"

"Yuh," Rongo says.

"But that's like . . ." RayAnne looks from one brother to the other. "That's almost five days!"

"Some mean maths skills, there, boss."

Rongo turns. “Don’t worry, the bach where we’re parking you is magical.”

“Bach?”

“Beach house. Whadya call ’em in Minnesota—a cabin?”

“Wait. *Parking* me?” She looks to Cassi, who is nodding enthusiastically.

“This bach is where, exactly?”

“Coromandel Peninsula. Old place owned by a teacher from film school,” Rango says. “Sweet as.”

Rongo agrees. “You’ll love it.”

“Will we?” She turns to Cassi, who is dressed for a different century in a dirndl skirt and blousy linen thing.

“*You* will. I’m off to the Shyre.” Cassi has lavender in her hair.

“Seriously?”

Her getup must have been the package Cassi had been so keen to pick up from the front desk the day before, delivered by courier. She’d suppressed squeals when dashing to her room with it. Cassi eases a wee scroll from her cleavage and unrolls it to show RayAnne. Inked in Old English is a formally worded invitation to spend the holiday at the Shyre. After rolling it back up and stowing it, Cassi turns her back to RayAnne, asking, “Would you mind?”

Her leather bodice with the lace-up back has yet to be tightened or tied.

“You know,” RayAnne frowns as she tugs the laces, “once you get this on, you’ll be at Bylbo’s mercy to get out of it.”

“That’s the plan!” Cassi does not sound at all like herself.

“So, Bylbo—. Sorry, what’s his actual name?”

“That is it. He had it legally changed when he was eighteen.”

“Do you know what his real name is?”

“Why would that matter? It’s who he is now. He identifies as Halfling. Why such a killjoy?”

RayAnne ties off the lacing with an unnecessarily tight double knot. “Can’t he come to where we’re going?”

"Where you're going. No. This is a huge weekend for the Shyre. It's not like he could take time off over a holiday even if he wanted."

As it turns out, Bylbo built, owns, and operates the Shyre and does not in fact spend all his time waylaying young women into his lair to ply them with mead and seedcake and antiquated manners. Had RayAnne, wary being her default mode, been quick to judge?

"Fine. Enjoy. Watch your head." RayAnne turns, faced with the loaded Rover and the loaded van. To Rongo she says, "Wait, I won't have a car?"

"Oh, we'll drive you to the ferry." Rongo hoists her pack into the van. "But where you're going, you won't need a car."

"I won't? Ferry?"

The guys drive her to the terminal where Chad hands over a ticket and points her to the proper gangplank and dock, where her ferry is idling, scheduled to leave in four minutes. Once aboard she rushes up the steps to the top and waves wildly at them, but they are all heading off.

It takes two hours to sail from Auckland to the Coromandel Peninsula. She spends the time watching other passengers: families, couples, friends all in holiday mode. Selfie-taking clusters of travelers share picnics of fish and chips and thermoses of tea, cans of beer. RayAnne finds their revelry vaguely irritating—they are all on holiday, while she is being sent somewhere. Several passengers frown into their devices and newspapers, pointing out things to each other, shaking their heads in the way she has noticed people tend to do upon hearing the news, especially news from America. She'd rather not know what's happened now.

Hannaford's Wharf is a long wooden dock barely wide enough for two passengers. After disembarking, most people get on a bus. Others head to cars. RayAnne has been instructed to wait for a blue pickup. Sitting on her backpack, she watches the road. The ten-minute wait seems like thirty, so that by the time her contact arrives, she's had too much sun and has to pee. Max is a college senior, cousin to Rongo and Rangi. He looks a bit like them both. Unlike them, he seems shy.

"You're an American?"

"Don't worry." RayAnne flings her pack into the open back of the pickup. "You can't catch it."

"Okaaay."

"Sorry. I need a bathroom."

He finds her one in Coromandel Town.

"You're going to need some grub, where you're going."

They stop at a grocery store. Halfway down the aisle she stops and turns in place, arms akimbo. Regretting her earlier rudeness, she tries to explain. "I don't even *know* where I'm going."

Max takes pity, pushing the cart, tossing in crisps and chocolate bars, milk and cereal. What a college kid might buy for himself. "There's a grill." He leads her to the meat counter, trying to be helpful.

She shakes her head and veers for the produce section to choose apples, celery, carrots, and bananas. A person can live on such things if they have enough peanut butter. She grabs a large jar, a loaf of bread, cheese, and a dozen eggs.

"Ah, see? You're golden," Max encourages. When he flashes a smile, she sees the resemblance to his cousins, most evident in his dimples.

At the cash register she is golden to the tune of more than two hundred New Zealand dollars for a bag and a half of groceries and two bottles of Left Field wine, chosen because she likes the labels.

After another half-hour on winding roads they reach Whangapoua. On the way, she learns Max is studying marine biology and is here visiting his fiancée, Tabitha, whose family manages a number of bach rentals, including the professor's. They pass neat little yards and close-set cottages near the beach and head north from town, crossing over an estuary to a secondary road, and then to a dirt track ascending into the trees. At a dent in the foliage, they park. Max flings her pack across his back, hoists a propane tank on his shoulder, dangles another from his hand, and sets off down a path, loaded like a mule. RayAnne lags behind, lugging the groceries and wine. After a few hundred yards the path opens onto a clearing and the cottage.

It was built in the sixties by the film professor's father, Max explains. It has its charms—avocado green countertops in the kitchen and a domed metal fireplace in the living room in the same hue. There are rush mats on the floor, a vintage tweed couch. The place is spartan, but cared for. Above the kitchen is a loft reached by a ship's ladder, where a double bed has a partial view over the trees to blue water in the distance. There is no television or microwave.

Max makes a second trip back to his pickup and returns with two large containers of drinking water. As he grunts them onto the counter, RayAnne asks, "I assume you're getting paid for this?"

He laughs, giving her his cell number. "Just text if you need anything." After he leaves, she unpacks, puts away her groceries, and pokes around. The A-frame is an airy cone of space, the high skylights letting in soft beams to animate the dust motes, making the bach feel nearly like a tiny cathedral.

A bookcase separates the toy kitchen from the living room, where there's a reading lamp and comfy easy chair. Most shelves are stocked with crime novels; one is devoted to magazines like *Yachting,* while another has adventure books about sailing and boats. The bottom shelf holds stacks of yellow-spined *National Geographic* magazines and a mishmash of paperbacks. One is a title RayAnne recognizes, *Gift from the Sea,* a book both her mother and grandmother own. *Owned,* in Gran's case. RayAnne has never cracked it, always assuming it was nature poetry. Not that she doesn't like poetry, but she does love the sea and can't imagine its being improved upon with words. She reads the flap. Not poetry at all, but the sort of title shelved under Inspirational—a genre RayAnne would normally cross a street to avoid. The author is the mother of that Lindbergh baby, kidnapped and murdered around the time Gran was born. The book is a journal, recounting Anne Morrow Lindbergh's sojourn at a remote beach, alone, spending her time looking at shells. Since it is compact enough to slip into the hip pocket of her cargo shorts, she borrows it. Not like she won't have time to sit on a beach and read!

Three solar panels run the place, though there are little notes everywhere suggesting what sort and how many electronics might be powered at once.

Toaster + One Light + One Charger.

Two Chargers + One Light.

Four Lights!

RayAnne vows to not make toast after dark and will only charge her phone and tablet during daylight hours. At the mirror there is a graphic of a hair dryer with a red circle-slash and the warning, *Don't Blow It!* She won't.

She lies on the couch looking up at the many vintage film posters tacked onto the canted walls, most from the 1950s onward. *Roman Holiday, My Fair Lady, The Manchurian Candidate. The Exorcist, Annie Hall, Purple Rain.* She takes a picture of the *Purple Rain* poster for Cassi, but when she hits send, the transmission struggles to launch itself from its measly single bar, then fails. She looks for the WiFi code in the Otto's Bach information binder loaded with hiking maps and menus from the restaurants in town (there are two). She checks crannies where a router might be and discovers there is none. An outdoor check of the roof for any antenna garners the same result. There cannot not be WiFi.

There is no WiFi. She sits quietly with that for a moment, then commences pacing the small space. Twelve steps from the front window to the kitchen door. Eight paces side to side before the walls slope to meet her forehead. What had Cassi—who always plans just the right thing—been thinking? What's she going to do here for five entire days?

She scans for nearby WiFi, but all are secured. Most have clever names: SilenceoftheLANs, RatArsedNet, MoFoWiFi, GILF, and WopWop69. RayAnne will have to make a game of seeing if she can match up neighbors' faces with their networks, keep an eye out for some fine granny.

There is an outdoor shower behind a bamboo screen, and, as she suspected, an outhouse—in its own tiny A-frame, freshly painted and thankfully not smelly. It has a real sink with working taps, an electric light, and little heater.

Otto's decor is masculine down to its pine walls and plaid pillows. The dining table is a wooden cable spool; the chairs are cut from old whiskey barrels, cushions upholstered in burlap from old coffee sacking. Sitting, RayAnne imagines she smells coffee and Jameson in one snort. A neat pyramid of spent, festively colored propane tanks are stacked against the fence like man art, making her wonder if *bach* is short for bachelor pad. That would be a thing to look up, if one only could.

Besides the shaded yard, the property includes a small field, a good deal of scrub, and a steep hillside. One area has a shed with a blackened depression that might have been a barbeque pit. Over the fence, a small flock of sheep graze, the lambs so fluffy and gamboling they might have been sent by central casting. Their tails are mesmerizing, wagging so fast as to nearly vibrate. Thus the saying, she supposes—*two shakes*. She's reminded of the woodpecker they'd seen at Hal's cabin, going nuts on a poplar. Actually, the entirety of Otto's Bach has a vibe very like that of Hal's Nysa; the two could be featured in a glossy spread for Man Camps of Opposing Hemispheres.

She follows a path along a fence, which hooks up with yet another path crossing a hill (more hilarious lambs) before descending into scrub and a forest of fern trees like something out of Jurassic Park. Out of sight, the surf seems to be whispering an enticement, growing louder as she gets closer. At a sandy juncture a sign reads, *Wainuiototo* and New Chum Beach, making her wonder if there's an Old Chum Beach.

After climbing a rougher path she finds herself atop a headland separating two beaches. From the rock where she sits is a vista to the south, the town of Whangapoua and its grid of civilization: holiday homes laid out in perfectly straight lanes. She can almost imagine Rongo's wry commentary, *Laid out with a British ruler.* It's heartening to not see many McMansions like those dominating most American waterfronts. Rural New Zealand seems spared of the bigger-is-better mindset. Here the beaches are for everyone, no warnings to trespassers in sight. Turning north, she faces New Chum, Wainuiototo. If such a place existed back home, it would be monetized—Malibued.

RayAnne sits until realizing she's not simply sitting but waiting. For what, she has no idea. Warm wind lifts and parts her hair one way, then the other; gulls wheel; below, an oystercatcher jackhammers at a clam with its blaze-orange beak. *Torea-pango.* Incredibly, she remembers the Māori name Rongo taught her the week before. Here she is in what anyone would consider paradise, surrounded by all things opposite and foreign to the frozen stillness of late Minnesota winter: the benevolence of humidity; colorful birds with melodious native names; each path a botanical feast. Yet despite the place being beyond beautiful, she remains unstirred by sights that should rouse all the feels. Because there is no one to share such wonders with? Lately, a curtain of unease seems to have been drawn between her and the rest of the world—nothing so straightforward as grief, just something gauzy between her and joy.

Waves pound the headland. Surf foams and recedes along the beach. Beyond is ocean and more ocean. The world could end here. As the sun begins to lower, she stands and brushes off. Now she'll have to hurry to beat the coming darkness. Sunsets are much less dramatic on the east coast—here the light simply dims as if controlled by a switch. Relieved to spot the bach through the trees, she's inside before true darkness falls. The old-fashioned alarm clock in the kitchen indicates she's been gone three hours, making her wonder if windup clocks even keep accurate time.

It turns out *Four Lights!* aren't all that many in making a dent against a moonless night in the bush. At least there is a decent headlamp for dashes to the outhouse and plenty of batteries. Like a caver, she spelunks into cupboards and opens every drawer in the little house, looks over the books again. Plenty to read. Plenty of paths to walk, endless water to wade, even a few blank notebooks to scribble in.

Bernadette would encourage her to journal, but writing does not come naturally to RayAnne, rendering her choice of a journalism degree nearly a punch line. Long assignments had been torture; her first job out of college was for an alternative weekly where every story handed in was too wordy, too self-consciously written—"verbose unease," a kindly editor once put it. She'd been relieved to be laid off, though she will never forget how her boss broke it to her, brow furrowed in concern: "RayAnne, you are so good at so many things . . ."

Just not that really important thing.

Her confidence crumbling, she asked Big Rick to hook her up with a summer job just so she wouldn't have to think about finding something "real." She ended up driving trailered boats from one fishing tournament to the next and lazily stayed on the circuit, eventually entering tournaments and miraculously winning. No one, least of all her, could have imagined she'd spend ten years in the alternate reality of pro fishing. It took that long for her to realize that journalism hadn't been her misstep, the medium had. Instead of concentrating on print, she should have gone straight to broadcasting. Somehow, she'd had it in her mind, either misled or convinced by some professor, that one had to excel as a writer before working their way up to broadcast.

Interviewing is her strength because she is able to get out of her own way and let the subjects tell their own stories, knowing from experience that even camera-shy people can be articulate about the things they love.

So, no, she won't be journaling. Writing about herself has the appeal of a pelvic exam.

Crawling into bed she imagines a perfect world in which Hal would materialize about now. The bach is perfect for two. Seems everyone has hooked up for the holiday: Cassi and Bylbo, Rangi and Fiona. Chad, whose girlfriend is back in Auckland, and even Rongo is lined up for a few Tinder dates. Back in Minnesota, Big Rick will be cozied up to Sally Leighton (or PS, now that Ky has applied a *nom de swoon* to their father's latest conquest, Pious Sal). Ky is off to Paris to inject some life into his marriage and possibly Ingrid, as they are both now convinced the twins might do better with a little sister or brother around.

It's just as well there's no Internet at the bach, since Skype sex may be forever ruined for RayAnne. Besides, by her calculation it's late afternoon at the Minnesota–Ontario border, around the time Hal would be taking Rory out for their postlunch adventure. They could be hiking, ice fishing, watching hockey practice, or yammering with codgers at the local diner. She loves how Hal will talk to anyone—even without the prop of a dog. Just walk up to a knot of strangers and address questions to the least likely person in the group.

Curling around a pillow, she closes her eyes to the image of Hal emerging from the bathroom after a shower. How the towel hangs low on his hips, the perfect amount of seal-sleek chest hair in just the right places. Little beads of water on his broad, freckled shoulders, his neck . . .

. . .

Sleep of the dead. Silence save the distant surf setting the deepest of rhythms, the ocean sounding for all the world like it's breathing. After almost ten hours—ten!—she wakes with more thoughts of Hal, recalling how he'd loved the twenty-second video she had sent of her very first day in New Zealand at the black sand beach at Piha. He'd asked for more, but there honestly hadn't been any free time since, and when there was, they'd invariably be somewhere boring. Since she can't be with Hal, she can at least share the sights with him. She turns the camera on herself and yawns hugely, a regular tonsil airing, then films her toes wriggling under the quilt and pans to the sliding glass door and a break in the green canopy to the distant line of two blues converging—sea and sky.

After making coffee she climbs back up the ship's ladder and onto the tiny deck where she puts her feet up on the railing. Leaf-shaped shade waltzes across her bare shins. Noticing that her skin is no longer dry or terribly white, and that her pedicure has held up remarkably well, she picks up the camera to wriggle her toes again.

She films parts of the path to the field, locates the lambs who oblige her by turning their backs and vibrating their tails for the camera. The path to the ocean is dappled and dark, opening onto the expanse of beach with the drama of a BBC nature special.

The great curve of sand is too vast to capture, so she documents details, taking video of a small tidal pool occupied by a tiny crab, and another that has baby leeches or eels that turn out to be translucent minnows with dark stripes like wild rice. Following a shallow rivulet in the sand to its source, she finds a cool rock face that seemingly oozes fresh water and sprouts tiny ferns. When her battery icon flashes, she pockets her phone and sits staring at the sea.

Her stomach grumbles to announce lunchtime, and she reluctantly heads back to the bach to have a sandwich and wait while her phone charges. The plan is to go to town and send Hal the morning's video and check messages. Maybe get an ice cream. Swaying in the hammock, she reads passages of *Gift from the Sea* until Mrs. Lindbergh lulls her to sleep with her seashells and observations.

After waking (and cursing at the clock as if it is pranking her), she sets off groggily to town. How can she be so tired after so much sleep the night before?

The wooded path to the road is shaded, but once she's in the open on the dirt road, dust roils. At the main road, the heat of black tarmac shimmers up through the thin soles of her horrible jelly shoes. The air is heavy, the afternoon so blindingly bright it hurts to look at the sea, the shiny-side-up of foil reflecting every charged particle between it and the sun.

She regrets not having her water bottle—can picture it on the counter, exactly where she forgot it. Thirsty and feeling puny, she stops and inhales hugely. Whenever energy or resolve begins to wane, her chosen mantra is *Sally forth*. Her mother would urge her to get *in the yin* (she would also say *Cunt up*, particularly if anyone prim was within earshot).

Suddenly and fiercely, she misses Bernadette, vowing to call the minute she has a signal. At the thought of something cold and sweet, her pace picks up. Town is there in the distance—she just cannot tell how far.

At the store—emphasis on *the*—she buys and chugs an entire quart of water, barely feeling guilt about the plastic waste. After wiping her chin, she walks the aisles, furtively filming with her iPhone and providing running commentary under her breath, like a crazy lady. There's motor oil next to tampons next to birthday cards. Sundries on offer include jandals, ping-pong balls and kites, thread and cutlery. The end of one aisle has a lending library; around the corner at the fish case one can also buy lotto tickets.

The service counter offers the essentials: pastry, lager, meat pies, and thankfully, ice cream, and the WiFi code: KIAORA, one word.

At the rear corner of the store lures and bait are on offer, and out the open back door is a bike rental and an air pump. Turning the lens on herself, balancing her iPhone on a planter, she says, as if to Hal, "It's not called the one-stop for nothing. I'm pretty sure you can get a tooth capped over by the revolving jerky rack."

Discovering her phone has a robust signal, she sends her brief videos to Hal, then polishes off a mint-chocolate cone while considering the magazine aisle—glossies on home decor and entertainment rags with celeb gossip. Fitness magazines that might inspire only rouse regret over the ice cream. She'd buy a newspaper but the only two on offer seem a bit tabloid-y with their dire headlines about the end being nigh, some warning of an approaching plague. A new strain of bird flu or something going around. But *pandemic*?

Sending Hal the videos proved to be a vampire drain on her battery, meaning RayAnne must choose between retrieving messages or calling her mother.

Bernadette has been at Imagine Ranch for as long as RayAnne has been away.

Naked retirees on horseback aren't anything RayAnne would pay to see, but her mother had the genius idea to set the ending of her *Mavenhood* trilogy at a nudist colony; her final manuscript is overdue to her publisher by six months. She answers on the first ring.

"RayBee!"

"Hiya, Mom. How's every little thing at Imagine Ranch?"

"It's cold here today, so *all* the things are little, as it happens." Bernadette cracks herself up. "I got your text. You're where, again?"

"Coromandel. Gorgeous, but there's no WiFi."

"Good! And you're staying in a whatcha call it?"

"A bach."

"And you have running water and solar?"

"Yeah, it's okay. There's an outhouse, though. Wanna guess why they call it a *long drop*?"

"Oh, that rolls imagination's camera. Don't the Brits say *loo* for toilet? So much jollier. Listen, Ray, are you staying safe?"

"Um, yeah . . . New Zealand is a pretty safe country, as it happens." Her battery icon flashes. "Quiet for sure. There are hardly any people here, actually. It's like one of your silent retreats."

"Well, give it a chance. You might be surprised."

"Did you finish the book?"

"Nope. Just packing up."

"You're going home early?"

"Seems the prudent thing to do. Now tell me—"

"Wait . . ." *Prudent* is not a word one associates with Bernadette Mills. A question begins to form when the phone dies in her hand, battery icon flashing red.

The next day (Friday?) dawns to reveal itself a near copy of the previous day. She discovers a few more paths on the steep hike inland. The rest of the morning is spent roaming the beach, wading, taking more video—mostly of terns, gulls, sandpipers—their footprints (birdprints?) mingling with her own before being washed clear where sand meets the water. She pulls focus between the shifting water and rippled sand bottom.

This time she's brought lunch, extra water, the Lindbergh book, a net bag for shell collecting, and her beach towel. Not much more a person needs except maybe another person. She's fine with her own company, just not quite so much of it. She has to admit, though, the solitude has allowed moments of not-entirely-unpleasant silence, reflective echoes.

Not a blip from Gran, making her wonder if she ever really did hear her voice.

She's somehow able to think of Gran without her chest constricting or her breath shifting. Not many people around besides small clusters of beachgoers. She says hello. Friendly enough, *just*—everyone seems to be keeping their distance. Greetings feel tentative; she chalks it up to her accent.

Sitting on the sand and examining a gnat bite next to a scar on her knee, RayAnne is zoomed back to the beginning with Hal—an afternoon during the wonders-of-me phase when every mole is a delight, and they engaged in that rite of romantic passage, the show-me-yours-and-I'll-show-you-mine, the Scars Edition. Offering up her palm with the twin dimple-like indentations on the plush heel of her hand, she told of being snagged by a rap-tail treble hook Ky had been casting with. To his eight-year-old credit, her brother had yowled as loudly as she did at the sight of the hook sunk into her swelling hand. Nearly connecting those divots is a fresh scar obtained recently in a DIY catastrophe. Dot. Dash. Dot. "See? I've got an engraved SOS right here. All I have to do is raise my hand!"

Hal sighed. "'Fraid I'm gonna outdo you on this one, Dahl."

Of course his story is a touch more dramatic, having made national news. In the chaos after his accident at the sawmill, a lanky husky mix (mistaken for a wolf) picked up his hand and trotted it home through the blizzard to its master, an artist who then put it on ice and drew the hand while waiting for the cavalry to arrive. It so happens the dog's home is Naledi, the fishing resort WYOY leases shoreline where *Fishing!* is filmed. As a sponsor, Hal occasionally visits Location, each time walking over to the lodge to visit with the artist. He has petted the dog with the very hand it once stole. He owns one of the artist's charcoal drawings, titled *Separation.*

RayAnne looked up the news story during the first blush of their relationship, when Hal said very little about his hand. Later he'd confessed that he'd gotten weird vibes and some disturbing overtures from women.

"One—I'll call her *Eve*—seemed totally normal, except for being morbidly interested in the hours after my accident, like down to the minute, wanting to know how it felt to be free of my hand. That's how she put it, 'free' of it. As if I'd be anything besides freaked out and drugged to my eyeballs. After two dates she fessed up to having stalked me and admitted to having some bizarre syndrome that made her want to have her own hand cut off."

"Shut the front door!"

"Look it up: it's called *xenomelia.*"

She did, shaking her head over every line describing the syndrome. What a peculiar machine the mind is.

The existence of Eve explained Hal's initial reticence to mention his scar other than to make the occasional joke about Frankenhand. Hardly the sort who'd nickname his own body parts (RayAnne once dated a guy who called his penis Mr. Majestic—it wasn't), but the hand deserves a name because for a time, however briefly, it was independent of Hal, having had a rather epic adventure all its own. Frank sometimes cramps unexpectedly, and on cold days the juncture at which bone mended to bone registers every degree of below-freezing temps more accurately than any thermometer.

But the glass Hal holds in his reattached hand is half-full. It's nothing short of a medical miracle that his fingertips have regained enough sensation that he is again able to tie flies or carve lures. "And best of all," he slid his hand into her shirt, uncharacteristically boastful, "they can definitely feel this."

Somehow, two more days and nights on the Coromandel Peninsula pass in a similarly languid fashion, RayAnne roaming the paths, the woods, and the beach, enjoying the little house she's come to love waking up in—even if alone. Stretching catlike while listening to the birds, she watches the first flickers of sun flex through the canopy of leaves.

She knows the local landmarks now: the notable trees, jogs

in the trail, lookouts, the best places to pee undetected. Knows north from south (rather a no-brainer on an east-facing coast) and can crisscross the trails without referring to the signposts. The sound of the place—what one might consider silence—is anything but. First, there's what's missing: traffic of any kind; no voices besides her own as she narrates her videos; not another human in earshot beyond the occasional distant shout or laugh. Scraps of song sometimes drift over at dusk as if carried on the smoke of her neighbor's fire. A woman with an acoustic guitar, stopping and starting as if practicing, repeating entire choruses—all in Māori. RayAnne wonders if she occupies the bach two sections over, just visible from a path up the hill—a tidy place built of cedar with a corrugated metal roof and a veranda with bamboo screens. The woman's song sounds a little like the place looks. When the notes fade in the wind, RayAnne finds herself wishing for the northerly breeze that delivers the music as clear as a radio signal. The air is heady with a briny, floral scent she'd like to bottle and take home. From the promontory she can see town and the long public beach fronting the little houses. For a holiday weekend, the place looks to be oddly quiet. RayAnne doesn't bother walking into town again, not even for ice cream.

With no watch or phone, she's come to rely on her own clock to determine the hour: light, the passing of time, hunger. Able to navigate the little property well enough in the dark now, she sometimes lingers outside in the dusk before going in to flick on the lights. Though she cannot see any shoreline from the upper balcony, RayAnne swears she can nearly feel the pull of the tide as it recedes. Though of course she cannot.

Can she?

Gran sometimes called people who traveled a lot "chronic tourists"—those who keep traveling to check off the boxes of having been but rarely staying anywhere long enough to really be in it. Staying here at the bach feels like . . . She casts for the word—*immersion.*

The videos she's making for Hal are narrated with observations of small sights she'd like to show him in person one day, like the highest point of the trail with its breezy view where she has her coffee. Speaking to the camera as if to him, she marvels that a place this nice is not besieged by mosquitoes, shows him the best shady spots, the little stony cove where she retreats during the afternoon heat. Records the plethora of tui bird sounds. She is not pining for Hal so much anymore as shifting to consider the whole of him from afar, finding it easier to focus on Hal the person at this greatest possible distance—half a planet away.

She falls asleep early, often while reading. The nights are so dark and the bach interior so den-like it always seems later than it is, imbuing a sense of hibernation.

Brushing sand from the pages of the Lindbergh book she reads a passage, rolling onto her back, using the pages as a shield against the sun. After reading, she has a swim. The burning question being, *What might afternoon bring*? Perhaps a nap. Certainly a sandwich. Probably both. When her stomach grumbles she closes the book and sets off for home.

RayAnne is in the hammock, half-asleep when she hears voices drifting up the path. Her first reaction is annoyance. Hikers. That she's become protective of her solitude is almost amusing, considering that only days before, her spell at the bach felt like banishment. She's come to relish the peace and quiet. She sinks a level lower into her reverie, descending steps of slumber.

Dreaming she hears Cassi's distant trill calling. *Ray. Hey, Ray?*

"Yoo-hoo?"

Her eyelids flutter and shut.

"Kia ora." A male voice singsongs, "*Ray-Anne-ah.*"

Cassi? Rangi? No. RayAnne opens her eyes to a number of dark silhouettes just above the hammock—a baby's view from the bassinet when relatives descend. She yelps. When they rear back into the light, she sees it's Chad, Rangi, Rongo, and

Cassi, still wearing her hobbity getup. All heads are cocked in concern.

Chad leans. "Are you all right?"

RayAnne fights a yawn, confused. "It's not Monday already? Is it?"

"No. You okay, Ray?" She's not sure who has asked.

"I'm hot." They all step back at once as RayAnne struggles to sitting, never a graceful move in a hammock.

"What do you mean *hot*?" Alarm sharpens Cassi's tone. "Do you have a fever?"

"No. I'm . . . jeez. Just waking up here, guys. So wait, if it's not Monday . . . ?"

They move closer, cautiously. There are two more players in the mix than RayAnne had first noticed: Max and Bylbo. The scene is practically a reenactment in which Dorothy wakes up after the tornado with Auntie Em and the uncles exchanging looks over her head. They seem relieved. Had they not expected her to be exactly where they'd stashed her?

"You sure you feel all right?" Chad asks.

"As rain." The voice of Gran's specter may have diminished in recent days, but her sayings seem to have settled in the rafters of RayAnne's vocabulary. Looking from face to face she realizes something is off. "What is it? What's happened?"

"We're going home."

"What?" RayAnne barks out a laugh. "What do you mean? We're not finished!" She struggles out of the hammock to standing.

"When? Not today?"

"Tonight, actually."

She looks to Cassi to explain. It's eight days before they are scheduled to fly home, with two more segments planned: one back on the South Island, a pilot who herds sheep in hill country using a helicopter outfitted with loudspeakers and recordings of border collies. RayAnne has been looking forward to that one. And the final interview, in Piha with a ten-year-old surfing champion raising money for climate action.

"Leaving? But why?"

"Program director wants us to head back while we can."

"What do you mean, *while we can*?"

"Before flights get canceled," Rongo adds.

"Why would flights be canceled?"

"Or restrictions are put in place . . . ," Cassi says.

"Restrictions? What the hell are you all talking about?"

"The virus."

"Virus? That newspaper epidemic? That's really a thing?" She'd shrugged off the headline as tabloid fodder.

Cassi's head bobs as it does only when she is emphatic about something. "Enough of a thing we're being called back." She pulls two surgical masks from her bag, as if dangling evidence, saying, "For the plane."

"Seriously?"

Chad looks at his watch, taking charge. "We've gotta get you packed."

"But what about this place? Kitchen's a mess, there's food . . ."

"Max is already starting in the kitchen." Cassi points.

Max sticks his head out the door and calls, "No worries. I'll sort it. Mind if I take this bottle of white?"

Cassi pulls RayAnne's drying sarong and swimsuit from the line and scoops up jandals and stuffs the lot into RayAnne's arms. "Sorry. We've gotta move."

"Okay, okay." She climbs to the loft to pack. Cassi follows but doesn't come all the way up, standing on the ship's ladder to talk, getting her up to speed. "It's not a flu, but it might be from China, like the avian thing was."

"And we have to leave because . . . ?"

"It's the thing to do." Cassi sighs. "You think *I* want to go?"

Cassi, wistful, does not seem herself. RayAnne turns to look squarely at her. "You're in love!"

Before she can answer, Chad calls from the living room, all business. "Three hours to the airport from here. You're on the eight o'clock to LA."

As she looks around, everything seems to take on a Polaroid tint, as if memory is already committing this place to the past. She has loved staying in this odd little house, like living inside the letter *A*. She'll miss the long tromp down to the sea, the climb through the woods and pasture up to the lookout. There's no time for a goodbye to the beach. For as much as she misses home, and Hal and Rory and everyone, she's not ready to leave.

They walk the path single file, Max staying behind to clean. The van's fold-down seats have been flipped up so that they can fit in the three rows.

"Wait," RayAnne says. "Why are you all here, if it's only to get us to the airport?"

"Because . . ." Rongo seems to search for words but trails off. "Just seems . . ."

"Maybe we want to, yeah?" Rangi adds.

Chad shrugs. "It'd be rude not to, right?"

On the long drive everyone is quiet, either sucked into the tractor beams of their phones or pretending to be. In all cases they are mostly mute, as if unsure how to wrap up the journey with words. Bylbo looks slightly stricken, clutching Cassi's hand as if she's wearing the One Ring.

Reading snippets, RayAnne catches up on the headlines, her brow furrowing over reports from major news outlets as she states the obvious, "Whoa. A lot can happen in five days."

Chad, reading some dense article, looks up from his screen. "Should we be worried about our grandparents?"

"Oh jeez." RayAnne suddenly remembers Dot's ashes in the Mary Kay compact and commences rifling her backpack. She'd had it all planned out for tomorrow morning—which was supposed to be her final morning in Coromandel, when she would climb the headland and release Gran's bit of ash to the spirals of wind that huff along the cliff. Perhaps read a line or two of poetry. *Have a moment.*

Her hand closes around the compact and she transfers it to the hip pocket of her cargo shorts. "We have to stop."

Cassi turns around. "Why?"

"I need to stop." She can hardly explain now, but there is no way she's going to jettison Gran's ashes at the Auckland Airport. "For the bathroom."

Cassi eyes her. "You okay?"

"Yeah. Yeah. I just . . . you know."

The next reasonable place to stop is a public beach with a park building and facilities. Luckily, it also has an ice cream truck, which cuts down on grousing over the delay.

"Five minutes." Chad is firm.

Bylbo offers to go buy cones while the guys get out to stretch. RayAnne bolts for the toilet building.

Leaning against the door of the stall, she holds the pink compact between her palms, considering. *Where?* Dump her grandmother unceremoniously on the sand? There's no time for poetry or pretty words, let alone finding any nice place to say them. RayAnne settles with the idea of just heading to the surf and pouring Gran out to mix with sand and sea.

Emerging from the building she's confronted with the most unlikely, perfect spot for Gran. Their first day in New Zealand they'd stopped at an identical truck, when Gran's phantom had hounded RayAnne to enjoy an ice cream cone. She's facing the back side of the truck. Out front, the line of kids has broken up with the arrival of Bylbo, and they've formed a semicircle around him. He takes turns having his picture taken with each, while Cassi buys ice cream. The kids make a great fuss over his ears.

Gran loved nothing more than feeding people—and what makes anyone happier than ice cream? RayAnne sidles around the back of the truck and dispatches Gran furtively and quickly, unceremoniously sprinkling her into the treads of the tires, along the shelf of freezer vents that smell like ozone, around the trailer hitch. There's no time for words or tears, which is exactly how Gran would prefer it. Looking under the truck, she sees ankles and a dozen pairs of kids' feet crowding Bylbo's flat, hairy ones. As she wedges the MaryKay compact with Gran's remaining ashes high into the chassis, she grins. *Perfect.*

Back in the van she eats her Hokey Pokey slowly, savoring each lick.

What was it Gran had said? *We all get our moment in time, fleeting and sweet as it is. It's up to us to make it last.*

As they come into view of the first sign for the Auckland Airport, Cassi stares straight ahead, Bylbo firmly hugging her shoulder.

"This isn't how it's supposed to end." Her voice is small and girlish.

No, thinks RayAnne, swallowing the final bite of waffle cone. This isn't at all how it's supposed to end.

There was something Gran would say to her when she was little. Maybe when she was distraught; she relates it with the salty taste of tears. She cannot recall the exact words, but it was sort of an encouragement, a reassurance, the kind a grandmother would dole out.

It's not the end of the world, Bean. You think you've come to the end, but all you need to do is turn the corner, and there, waiting, is the next perfect thing.

Waiting.

Just for you.

ACKNOWLEDGMENTS

Thanks to the entire staff of the University of Minnesota Press for their patience and support. Despite challenges like a global pandemic, they just got on with it.

Much New Zealand inspiration was sparked by family there: thanks to intrepid guide Mickey Smith for sharing the wonders of her adopted country, and to every single Pollock for their tireless hospitality and humor. To Maire Vieth for sharing her air. The Michael King Writers' Centre of Auckland was kindly welcoming to this Minnesota stray, as was the staff at the Devonport Library. Thanks to Rose Evans for the leads, and Vicki-Anne Heikill, who cast a discerning eye across the Maori characters and details of this story. To them and my Kiwi readers: *Ko koe mīharo katoa.*

Various individuals and organizations provided time and space and funds to work. Thanks to the Minnesota State Arts Board for two Creative Support for Individuals grants: this activity is made possible by the voters of Minnesota through a grant from the MSAB, thanks to a legislative appropriation from the Arts and Cultural Heritage Fund, which protects and funds the two essential resources that make our state sparkle: clean water and the arts.

Special appreciation for the small but mighty pod of artists who helped me weather the plague and so much more: Theresa Angelo and Nancy Randall. *Gu fada.*

Sarah Stonich is a Minnesota native. Her novels include *The Ice Chorus* and *These Granite Islands* (Minnesota, 2013). *Vacationland* is the first book in her Northern Trilogy, published by the University of Minnesota Press, followed by *Laurentian Divide,* winner of a Minnesota Book Award and a Northeastern Minnesota Book Award. She has also written a memoir, *Shelter: Off the Grid in the Mostly Magnetic North* (Minnesota, 2017). She lives on the Mississippi River in a repurposed flour mill.